THE DISCLOSURE PARADOX

THE DISCLOSURE PARADOX SERIES

Book 1: *The Disclosure Paradox*

Book 2: *Disclosure Paradox: Salvation*

Book 3: *What Doesn't Kill Her*

"Though presented in fictional form, anyone familiar with various anomalous phenomena will recognize the fact-based narratives depicted in *The Disclosure Paradox*. Thought-provoking, even those with deep involvement in those fields will find themselves questioning where reality stops, and fantasy begins. Or does it? Many of the names are recognizable and the narrative extremely well interwoven. The physical and spiritual are merged into Louis Silvani's life mission to understand a complex and rewarding destiny."

—John B. Alexander, PhD

"I loved this book! It starts out with Louis on his tedious UFO lecture circuit, easing you into ET culture slowly like getting into a nice warm bath. But before you know it, our unexpected hero is on a cross-country mind-expanding adventure of a lifetime. It is a wild ride! The characters are rich and believable. The ET subject matter is accurately portrayed. In the end Louis finds his roots, and I am left wondering what I can do to improve humanity!"

—Steve Jacobson, BSEE, retired aerospace engineer for NASA, Boeing, Northrop Grumman, and the US Navy

"A fascinating tale about a secret world that we only glimpse dimly through the eyes of a dedicated and obsessive group who give up everything to find the truth and stop a hideous plot to control our destiny. A beguiling blend of horror, science fiction, and riveting action, with realistic characters and plot twists that will leave you breathless. Highly recommended."

—Frank E. Lee, WXRT-FM, Chicago

"Paul wrote in 1 Corinthians 13:11, 'When I was a child, I talked like a child, I thought like a child, I reasoned like a child. When I became a man, I put the ways of childhood behind me.' If we grow beyond childhood, we have to start dealing with more complicated matters than the mostly-carefree times of youth. During adulthood, we have to start discerning questions such as 'Why am I here?' 'What is my purpose in life?' 'What are the limits to my powers?' 'Is there a God and/or spiritual forces?' 'Does God answer our prayers?' 'Is there only one true religion?' 'Is there other life in the Universe?' 'What happens to my essence after I die? 'What is truth?' *The Disclosure Paradox* provocatively tackles some of these heavy questions, especially regarding other life forms in the Universe. It was not long ago that flying saucers/unidentified flying object/unidentified anomalous phenomena were considered tin-foil-hat subjects. However, numerous government whistleblowers have come forward to admit that the phenomena really exist and are a threat to our national security. Vecchiet does a marvelous job in his novel of tying together many of the aforementioned deep questions of life."

—Joseph Marino, President, Shroud of Turin Education and Research Association
Editor, shroud.com

"*The Disclosure Paradox* unfolds to reveal an intriguing story that blurs the edges of reality. Dancing skillfully between science, religion, and the spiritual world, there is a sense of a different existence that is shown to us, where many truths and absolutes are turned on their head with a series 'what ifs' that coalesce toward a dramatic conclusion.

"As a self-professed agnostic and skeptic by nature, this story really tested my sensibilities. To others, the book may reveal something else about their belief system, but for me it is the questioning quality of the narrative that works on so many different levels.

"Outside the profound nature of the book, it is a jolly good read, and as the excitement builds, and we get to know and care about the well-drawn characters, it is hard to put down, raising so many questions. How can this unlikely alliance of slightly damaged people, with unusually heightened senses, overcome seemingly overwhelming odds? Have the players been thrown together by serendipity, or by some divine intervention? Which humans can they trust, and the biggest question of all, what exterritorial dimension will they find?

"Paul G. Vecchiet creates an extraordinary alternative backdrop to our world with *The Disclosure Paradox* clearly influenced by his military background, in parallel with his understanding of human nature and its many facets that make us question … 'What is real, what is normal … and is this all there is?'"

—Laurence Orsini, MCSD, Interior Architect

THE DISCLOSURE PARADOX

Book 1

PAUL G. VECCHIET

WRITE AWAY BOOKS
Carlsbad, California

Published by Write Away Books, USA

writeawaybooks.com

PO Box 1681
Carlsbad, CA 92018

Print ISBN: 979-8-989643-12-7
ebook ISBN: 979-8-989643-13-4
Library of Congress Control Number: 2024950758

Front cover design concept: C. J. Hungerman, artist, and Paul G. Vecchiet

Front cover images:

Tarantula Nebula by NASA, ESA, CSA, STScI, Webb ERO Production Team
Helix Nebula by NASA, JPL-Caltech, University of Arizona

*To Mrs. V. for her moral support, long before
I ever thought to write this novel.*

PREFACE

When considering destiny, we typically recognize four belief systems. On one hand, people think their own actions determine the direction of their lives. On the other end of the spectrum are people who rely on a higher power for guidance. Borrowing from both beliefs, are people who behave as if they have the greatest impact on their own lives while dipping into the well of faith on occasions of personal difficulty. Some meet their fate through a life-altering event that could not have been predicted or avoided. Most people rely on the premise that destiny is determined through a sequence of key decisions.

Then there are the atypical: A very select number of individuals have been granted a life mission, or perhaps a divine assignment, that has put them on a predetermined path. Those that have been designated a specific role in life do not realize it until that role has been revealed, usually in the form of a personal epiphany. Only after they realize the path taken, the critical forks in the road that led them to where they stand, do they begin to understand destiny itself. Until that moment of realization, they are like most people; they think they are in control.

It takes a certain amount of courage and trust to accept that each of us has a role. It takes more trust and courage to follow others as they are in the process of learning their role themselves.

1

HIS GREATEST ENEMY

Man is incurably curious. —Fulton Sheen

UFO research was not only Louis Silvani's hobby, but it had become an obsession that had alienated him from his ex-wife, as obsessions can do. His worn faded office chair creaked as he shifted. It looked like he felt, both approaching retirement. The digital clock radio blazed 1:30 a.m. from its shared space on an undersized nightstand with a simple table lamp. The room was lit just enough for Louis to work on his slide presentation for the upcoming UFO enthusiasts' event in Pennsylvania.

He often looked back at his divorce with remorse, the guilt of knowing he could have given more time to his wife and kids. He was especially sad about having to live away from his two children. Driven by a quest for truth, fueled by an energy beyond his control, he felt his life was on some sort of pre-determined course going into a direction he did not anticipate.

Louis's curiosity in the extraterrestrial phenomenon began one late Sunday night during his sophomore year in high school as he listened to a favorite radio station in bed. The music program phased into a syndicated talk show. Instead of turning the stereo off and going to sleep, his attention was drawn to the mention of a book in the Old Testament with respect to UFOs. According to the person being interviewed, a researcher with a thick Germanic accent, the book of Ezekiel was the clearest documented account of an encounter with extraterrestrials in the Bible. Louis barely noticed the researcher's name, Erich von Daniken, but he intensely followed what von Daniken was telling his interviewer. Von Daniken revealed how right from the beginning, in Chapter 1 starting with verse 4, the prophet detailed the appearance of the phenomenon. The Bible describes a windstorm, an immense cloud flashing lighting, brilliant light, glowing metal, fire, wheels within wheels, the sound of wings like rushing waters, and much more. Louis was riveted in amazement. Why hadn't he learned about this amazing part of the Bible? he wondered. Why hadn't he heard of Erich von Daniken, the researcher?

Von Daniken continued to point out how this event and many other similar events in the Bible and other ancient scripts were misinterpretations by unsophisticated people that witnessed high technology. The researcher went on to claim that Ezekiel did not witness God. He witnessed an extraterrestrial craft. It made a lot of sense and was in line with Louis's suspicions about religion itself. There was more banter, but Louis turned off the radio.

At school the next day, he paid a visit to the library where he found a Bible. Louis flipped pages of the Bible to find the book of Ezekiel and immediately realized that von Daniken appeared to be right. He read the passage:

...an immense cloud with flashing lightning and surrounded by brilliant light. The center of the fire looked like glowing metal.

He was astounded. The entire page was a description by the prophet, using objects and animals to help explain something unlike anything he could have imagined. Louis believed that these passages describing supernatural phenomena may have been actually documenting early encounters with advanced life forms not of this earth.

Louis enjoyed the high school library, which held a rich selection of books and included an audio-visual office where he was able to sign out albums to enjoy during study period. One recording he often selected was the historic recording of H. G. Wells's *War of the Worlds*, narrated by Orson Welles and broadcast in 1938. The recording was based on science fiction, but Louis was interested in the historic significance and what it determined about society. Enough people in 1938 believed that Martians existed and were invading Earth, no doubt further moved by Welles's convincing voice, that it caused a panic in the New York City area. Louis's skeptical views on religion, and his fascination with science fiction and outer space, came together and formed a basis for what eventually became a quest for truth in his adult life.

2

INTO THE RABBIT HOLE

...and you may ask yourself, "Well ... how did I get here?" —Christopher Franz and Brian Eno

Louis continued to work on his presentation, which was not his primary job. As a second career, his UFO and ET research began by visiting groups via social media and following celebrities from UFO-related TV shows. Eventually, he became active in groups organized around UFO stories and built a network of followers, co-researchers, and supporters. His participation in UFO-related organizations and conferences combined with presentation skills allowed him to offer his theories on "interterrestrials"—advanced beings that share the planet with the human race.

His unique, eye-opening experience occurred at Wright–Patterson Air Force Base in Dayton, Ohio, his third duty station as an Air Force officer. There, he was assigned to the Aeronautical Systems Division as a construction manager. One of his duties involved overseeing work by contractors at the Foreign Technology Division (FTD) building, then located in Area A.

FTD's mission was to research weapons systems from other countries, evaluate threats and weaknesses, and then relay that information to Aeronautical Systems Division in Area B. Area B was across the main highway, where existing programs were either improved upon, or new programs were devised to counter those threats or take advantage of the weaknesses of foreign weapon systems. FTD was housed in a large warehouse-type two-story metal building surrounded by motion detectors on its lawn. Access, regardless of the visitor's security clearance, was through a manned entry control point. The need-to-know concept was the prime system of operational security in this building.

One day while carrying out inspections, Captain Louis Silvani went to the second floor in FTD's building. He entered a vestibule that opened into a small utilitarian ante-lobby, devoid of aesthetics and comfort, where he reported to a junior NCO manning the security desk. Louis stated his reason for the visit, signed his name on the visitors' roster, and received a badge indicating in bold red uppercase lettering, "ESCORT REQUIRED." His escort, a young senior airman assigned to the security police squadron, led Louis through the electrically operated double doors into an extra-wide corridor.

"So, this is FTD. It looks like a scene from a James Bond movie," Louis remarked.

Maintaining discipline and only offering necessary information, the airman gave no response.

Louis noticed the floors, walls, ceiling, doors, and door frames were all clean and white or off-white. He saw no directory for the huge, windowless, warehouse-sized facility. Doors were marked by a cypher lock. There were neither numbers nor room names. The offices and their occupants were compartmentalized. The occupants of one office did not have access to the office next door. The escort stopped at a door to an enclosed stairway and entered the code to unlock it. Louis followed up the wide, austere, and faintly lit stairway. The muffled tapping sound of their footsteps on the bare concrete treads echoed in the stair well.

Opening the heavy-duty steel door, they entered an area stripped of all ceiling tiles, floor finishes, fluorescent lights, partitions, doors, and frames. The entire floor was eerily vacant. Lighting was provided only by single utility incandescent bare light bulbs that were temporarily hung and wired. Except for the occasional chatter on the escort's two-way radio, the vast interior space was silent. Louis was there to evaluate the existing conditions, compare them to the as-built drawings, and then check the design drawings for potential conflicts. The space was to serve as a computer room, according to the title on the drawings. There wasn't much to look at; everything was bare, down to the metal building skeleton. While walking around the perimeter, Louis noticed his escort, standing near the exit, reading a book while monitoring the radio traffic. The escort rarely acknowledged what Louis was doing; he was obviously not there to supervise the senior captain.

After inspecting the physical space, Louis spotted a set of drawings rolled up on a contractor's cart. He went to unravel the roll and realized the set was the as-built record drawings. As-builts represented the condition of the building after the most recent project. In this case, there appeared to be no renovation since the initial construction, so these drawings represented the building in its original condition.

Louis flipped through the sheets and made his comparisons. BASEMENT, one read. He questioned its accuracy because he knew this particular building was a pre-engineered warehouse building, and warehouses normally did not have basements. He inspected the drawing more closely, looking at the footprint or the outline of the building to confirm that the basement floor plan matched with the first-floor plan. The captain realized it was not a misprint, and the sheet was authentic. This building, being a renovated warehouse, was not supposed to have a basement. Looking closer at the basement plan, there was no indication of stairs.

He cautiously looked to see if the security escort noticed his reactions. The senior airman's attention remained on the radio and his book, so Louis continued to thumb through the drawings. He flipped to the next page and, to his amazement, noticed a portion of the basement dedicated to a very large facility labelled CRYOGENIC CHAMBER. As if discovering a hidden basement was not enough, he found that it housed a facility designed for preservation of biological specimens at low temperatures.

His face blushed, his heart rate increased, and his breath shortened. The palms of his hands grew clammy with the sobering realization that these drawings appeared to include classified information, and the set had not been labelled correctly. This was more than an oversight; it was a gross error in operational security measures or *OPSEC*. If Louis reported his finding, there would be an extensive investigation that, depending upon the severity of the potential damage to national security, could cause him extreme stress, being targeted for having information he was not supposed to possess.

According to the National Institute of Standards and Technology, cryogenics involves temperatures below -180 degrees C, the boiling point of most gases. The designated volume for this chamber was huge; Louis scaled it to be approximately seventy by ninety. Louis's mind raced with thoughts. *Why have a huge cryogenic chamber at FTD? Why a hidden basement? What, related to foreign technology, requires* frozen *suspension?* Suddenly, it was clear to him what this represented. The cryogenic chamber was large, likely designed to keep large biological specimens in suspension. And since this was in Foreign Technology Division's building, it had to be foreign.

Louis's breath caught. Was the facility designed to store *exotic* cadavers—beings originating, possibly, from other worlds? *Had to be.*

A calmness surrounded him and quieted his previous inner excitement. His composure allowed him to use logic in a disciplined fashion, in this case, to analyze extremely sensitive information— higher than top secret. He glanced back at the escort. The airman's attention was still on his book.

Louis looked down at what he'd discovered one last time just to make certain he did not misinterpret the plans, then rolled up the set and placed it on the cart in the same condition he'd found it. He paused and looked around the room.

"Airman?" he called out. "I completed my work here. Pretty basic stuff, actually. I am ready to leave," Louis exhaled.

The airman put his book down, walked to the locked stair door and opened it without a word. Louis walked away from FTD with the same calm demeanor he felt when he deduced the cryogenic chamber's purpose.

* * *

Years later, Louis left the military service without ever divulging this information to anyone, and he kept it that way for years. Now, in the Chicago area near his parents, siblings, and longtime friends, he had built a new life as a civil servant with the United States Army Corps of Engineers, thanks to his experience as a military officer and to his technical degree. As he settled into the Chicago area, he met his wife, who was 13 years younger. Together, they built a life and had two children.

"Louis," his wife called from upstairs, "have you seen my keys? Alex and Elsa are going to be late for school!"

Louis activated the electronic finder tag he'd hooked to the car keys. His wife was 13 years younger and more forgetful than Louis, so he often found ways to shortcut the inevitable misplacements.

"They're in the kitchen, Laura," he shouted back. "I just heard the beep."

With the usual fussing and chaos of weekday departure, his family rumbled out of the house. As Louis scanned through the television channels for something to watch while he finished his breakfast, he found a show on the History Channel that presented the ancient astronaut theory.

He put down the remote and sat at the edge of the couch to watch an episode about the Bible. To his astonishment, one of the expert interviewees was Erich von Daniken, again explaining the book of Ezekiel, as he had done when Louis tuned into the radio show as an adolescent. The memory of that night was abruptly followed by the vivid memory of his discovery at Foreign Technology Division as a US Air Force officer. He could feel the moment of clarity and purpose return, the interest in space travel, and now, UFOs and ETs.

The UFO field was notorious for attracting people deemed unstable, causing outsiders to ridicule those who claimed to have encounters otherwise inexplicable in conventional dialogue. It was also a field replete with opportunists who hawked books or spewed apocalyptic forecasts through web pages for profit. The victims of these scams were often those who either had a real encounter or those who already harbored a distrust of authority and the government.

Unfortunately, there were more opportunists spreading lies and disinformation than those with sincere intentions. The overabundance of articles and videos on the subject matter, most of them false and fabricated, worked in favor of those who wished to suppress the truth. When false information or hoaxes were presented in the same manner as authentic videos, debunkers pointed to both types of videos as false, burying the truth in lies.

Louis Silvani braced himself for another journey, a Quixotic journey he believed was his destiny, driven by a strong moral need to reveal the truth. As if being nudged awake for a second momentous time in his life, Louis felt a strong need to research. He devoted time to watching more episodes of shows based on the ancient astronaut theory and similar programs. He started a journal and wrote down names of the researchers and associated websites. He spent hours chatting with like-minded people on the computer, learning about UFO events that should have been given much more publicity and attention.

I see them around my property, texted a woman.
Where do you live?
British Columbia.

What do they look like?

They appear as glowing orange orbs, but I normally channel greys and Nordics.

Nordics—I have heard them described as tall whites.

Yes. With blond hair.

Why do you suppose you see them so often?

I think I am a star seed.

A star seed? I have read about that. It means you originate from another race and you are here to help in a sort of spiritual evolution.

That's right.

He discovered websites about "disclosure"—the term used by experiencers and researchers to describe the act by governments to release information related to Unidentified Flying Objects (UFO) and Extraterrestrial (ET) activity in the world. The amount of information, the number of new people he met online, the number of web sites and blogs related to the field were staggering. In a systematic manner, he signed on to social media sites and began visiting pages related to the UFO/ET field. Learning about one researcher led him to another, which resulted in more events to research. There were so many seemingly legitimate encounters throughout history all around the world that Louis found it difficult to understand how the topic was ever viewed as paranormal.

He found evidence that the UFO/ET phenomena's incidents were more than the general public was led to believe. He devoted so much of his time to this fixation, his growing obsession, that he left little for his family. He became withdrawn, chatting primarily with people in ufology groups on social media. Louis would stay up late at night after the family went to bed.

"Are you working on the laptop late again?" Laura groaned. "When are we going to go to bed together? I can't remember the last time you came to bed while I was still awake. I feel as if we're drifting apart, Louis."

Louis looked up from his desktop with a blank expression. He had no words as he fidgeted.

"Aren't you going to say anything? Doesn't your family matter to you?"

Louis remained frozen. Something blocked him from being responsive, from showing an emotion. Laura waited, surrounded by the silence that Louis seemed to refuse to break. It would be one of

Laura's last offerings for Louis to redeem himself and show her that she was more important to him than his time on the laptop.

Eventually, the sad and predictable happened; his withdrawn behavior became too much for his marriage to bear and his wife filed for divorce. The breakup was swift and without disputes but very painful for all involved: Louis, his wife, Laura, and his children Alex and Elsa. The divorce made him feel like a failure. It damaged him, injuring his already fragile self-esteem, making him feel less of a man. What better reason to shrink further from personal relationships and immerse himself, wholly, into his research?

Using social media, he followed groups who discussed the phenomena. He was able to quickly connect with many like-minded people. Almost nightly, he befriended someone that experienced a sighting or had been involved in an alien abduction. There was something special about how he was able to contact so many experiencers in such a compressed amount of time. He asked deep questions about their experiences, their backgrounds, and where they were when they had the encounters.

Reading sworn testimony on alternative websites, listening to podcasts for hours, and chatting with experiencers allowed Louis to gain an understanding of how they dealt with the experiences. Most described them as traumatic, while some felt a comfort and sense of loving beyond what they could imagine. He maintained notes and would return to ask more questions, putting together a database. He would group by location, time of day, type of beings, feelings, and other qualities. His database represented a considerable amount of knowledge. He started to feel confident with his contacts and would get compliments on his approach and his empathy. Many first-time experiencers were desperate for answers, at times, pleading for help in any way. He grew to have a deep feeling for the people who would open up. His focus on the research changed from seeking knowledge to understanding and healing.

So, you say you were an extraterrestrial in your previous life?

Yes. By the way, I was taken.

Taken, you mean abducted? By whom?

They seemed like tall whites. It was painful to look at them. I was about to fall asleep when I saw an amber light shine in my room.

Did you try to communicate?

Well, I'm trying to remember. They put me out, but I remember being on a ship and the gravity was light. I remember being on a table. When

I was returned home, I had to readjust to the stronger gravity. My body felt very heavy. It was hard to walk at first, and I was unusually thirsty and hungry. I think I was gone for a couple days. I had at least two days of growth on my face.

I feel that the ones that abducted you are not a threat. Perhaps they are protecting you based on your past life experiences. You may have been tagged.

Many of the people that claimed to be abducted were timid about discussing their experiences with a complete stranger, but Louis's sincerity and compassion had a way of soothing people's anxieties. He began to realize many of these people felt alone. Being open and social put them at risk of being targeted by the government. As more trusted him, it motivated him to continue to reach out to more people who would hint about their experiences. They shared with him that they had been ostracized by friends and family members, characterized as unstable and weird for their beliefs and personal accounts. After being hurt for trying to disclose the truth about the phenomena based on personal experience, many decided to isolate themselves to avoid any more embarrassment or ridicule.

You say you are a being that is hybrid? asked Louis through an interview.

Yes, and I ask you not to be skeptical or I will stop communicating with you. Just because I have Asperger's syndrome people ridicule me. It has made me depressed.

I was compelled to contact you by an article you wrote ranking the extraterrestrial races in technology.

Thanks for sharing. Yes. First are the Pleiadeans, then the Zeta, then the Reptilians.

Louis realized they needed a support group where they could meet others with similar experiences and problems. He established a group on social media and called it "Unbounded Encounters," inviting as many of his new experiencer friends to join and participate in discussions as he could. The secret group allowed people to be more open and share their experiences with others that had had similar occurrences. Many people in the group, who had been isolated, befriended others who also felt alone. New friendships flourished into genuine relationships, and people began to reach out to others in turn.

I have no fear of aliens, in fact I welcome them, offered someone who was a complete stranger.

I probably would welcome them too.

I have been getting communications.

What sort of communications?

I trust you. I am convinced there are significant changes ahead. I don't trust the men who portray themselves as prophets—for a price.

I understand. So, you say I shouldn't take what I read in those blogs seriously?

Correct.

As Louis met more people who volunteered their accounts with nonhuman sentient beings, he observed similarities in the backgrounds of the individuals. The people that were abducted appeared to have one of the following traits or relationships: some were from military families and experienced abduction at an early age, some just lived near a military installation, some served in the military in some capacity, some either experienced psychic abilities before or after the abduction, and some had a near death experience (NDE) followed by psychic abilities that allowed ETs to communicate telepathically.

In addition, there was physical evidence on their bodies and extremities, such as strange geometric marks on a finger or a hand. A few claimed to have metallic implants. Louis filed all this information away with the intent that someday it would serve him to put together the puzzle, the UFO/ET phenomenon.

Deep into the rabbit hole, Louis was presented with a burden that would radically change his perception of reality. With every new realization exposing a lie to cover up some sort of corporate or organizational treachery, he felt like he was approaching insanity. To make matters worse, friends and extended family members compounded his fears, regarding him in the same manner as they would paranoid and unstable individuals.

Presenting evidence or bringing up discussions for debate was fruitless and only added strain to his few remaining relationships with cousins and longtime friends. Some people merely patronized or ignored him, where some responded with ridicule; they could not entertain the possibility of anything beyond the mainstream conventions. In just a few months, through rigorous research and discussions with scores of fascinating and intriguing people, Louis had been exposed to numerous topics supporting the existence of an alternate reality suppressed jointly by the media, government, and certain corporations.

A key realization was the suppression of energy-related inventions and the perpetuation of dependence on oil, gas, coal, and uranium by a collusion between the energy companies, auto makers, and government agencies. Louis found documentation from researchers who determined that five alternate energy inventors had been killed or imprisoned, a dozen additional families were harassed or paid off, and hundreds of energy-saving patents had been confiscated in the name of national security.

Through the months, his frustration grew with the lack of a public outcry on such matters and the persistent complicity in media. He discovered other evidence of industries without morals: the healthcare industry, in particular its role in the suppression of natural cures and treatments for cancer in favor of "Big Pharma"; prisons for profit and mass incarceration statistics; and a conservative think tank, the American Legislative Executive Commission or ALEC, which enabled big business to have direct contact with members of Congress, providing them with generic legislation to promote a corporate agenda at the expense of common citizens.

Louis considered himself an intellectual, a critical thinker. To his dismay, every one of those conspiracy theories felt more than plausible. In a deep and personal way, this forbidden knowledge pulled him into a dark mental abyss. He realized he had to live with the specter of a controlling and well-organized cartel motivated by power and wealth. He had to accept that he lived in a corpocracy that continued to lessen the personal wealth of citizens, erode civil rights, and weaken laws to protect the environment and natural resources. All of it was happening systematically with the implied support of a naïve and apathetic public.

This pessimism, this fatalistic inevitability, lay heavily on his mind, draining his personal energy. He needed help, and he knew it. He did not seek conventional help; a mainstream doctor of psychology would dismiss Louis's strongly held theories and label him paranoid and unstable. Instead, Louis decided to consult a prominent psychic with whom he was able to communicate via social media. Paris Nance hosted a syndicated show on a major radio network, and she offered readings over the phone for a modest fee.

Paris was familiar with Louis through social media and was able to arrange a call. He had never spoken to her before; the call was their first virtual meeting. Her tone of voice was just as warm as the gentle smile that was her signature look on her website. With a confident understanding of what was bothering Louis, she allowed him to reveal his concerns.

"Hello, Louis, I'm so glad to have this talk with you!"

"Hello, Paris, I'm honored you are taking the time to talk to me. I'm being bombarded by the darkness from many directions. I . . . I can't . . . I don't have the . . . It's taken so much from me. I . . ."

"Slow down. Take a deep breath, then just break down what you feel. Don't try to solve all the problems at once."

"I don't have the time to solve all the problems at once."

"Then don't. You should focus on what is most important to you and most importantly, where you could apply yourself best."

"You're right."

"After this call, you will set yourself a direction and you will stay with it, and you will make a huge impact on what you will work on. I am getting positive feelings on this."

"I trust your intuition."

"That's what is good about you, Louis; you trust people to be their best."

When Louis was done venting his frustrations about being out-numbered and overmatched by the powers-that-be, Paris's simple advice would become his compass to keep him from getting lost in the darkness. She also told him that he needed to let go of most of the matters that caused him to feel the angst; carrying a burden like that would eventually ruin him and his frustrations would grow to a self-destructive intensity.

Louis took her recommendation to heart. As a result of the call, he began to reason that there were three significant truths that, if revealed, would lead to a domino effect of a national awakening, resulting in dramatic and positive social change. Those truths were the truth behind the suppressions of natural cures, the truth about energy related inventions and the conspiracy to suppress those inventions, and finally, disclosure. If just one of those schemes was exposed, he reasoned, it would cause a bloodless revolution—a new renaissance. He already had amassed so much information on disclosure topics and had contact with so many unique people related to the phenomena, Louis realized he would be effective as an activist for disclosure.

Following that phone call to the psychic, Louis again turned his focus on research related to UFOs and ETs—and never wavered.

3

FACTS AND DECEPTION

Only a small number of people were able to climb up from their secret hiding places and emerge into the Fourth World. Legends reveal the Grand Canyon is where these people emerged. —Hopi Legend

The tap-tap-tap of computer keys accompanied the drone of the radio voice: "We're back talking to UFO researcher and activist Dr. George D. Stevens who has released a film documenting activity near Mount Adams."

Louis couldn't recall when the term "UAP" replaced "UFO." The change in terms signified a fundamental shift in culture, where the subject matter evolved from the ridiculous and unthinkable to curiosity and fact. Louis paused again from his work and listened to the show's guest:

". . . while we had our contact events, we actually were able to sense the benevolence of these wonderful entities. People were in meditation and received loving messages and some people were able to 'guide' the orbs as if the entities were following our thought patterns."

"Amazing," the host chimed in, then segued into a commercial break.

"Amazing that, even if they weren't able to see craft, people would spend hundreds of dollars just to camp out to participate in this theater," Louis muttered cynically, taking a sip of ice water.

He understood the host's policy of not challenging any of his guests, regardless of how bizarre and extravagant the topic. Still, he felt that portraying the Mount Adams phenomenon as evidence that extraterrestrial races are benevolent, even spiritual, was dangerously naive. Moreover, most sightings around hotspots throughout the planet were indicative of interterrestrial activity, where the craft originated from within the Earth.

He pored through numerous books, watched hours of videos, listened to hours of shows and interviews, and held conversations with scores of experiencers. He was refining his presentation, which provided visual evidence of highly technological nonhuman civilizations living underground or in mountains on Earth. His first group of slides introduced the strongest evidence: Antarctica.

He determined that one of the most extraordinary events related to UFO contact in modern history took place in Antarctica in late February through early March of 1947. Operation Paperclip was the code name for the systematic process in which the Soviet Union and the United States took custody of top-secret Nazi weapons technology. Its objective was to gain information on rocket propulsion and guidance systems. Much was learned about Operation Paperclip through KGB files released after the break-up of the Soviet Union.

After World War II, interviews with the German scientists and engineers who had worked for the Third Reich, combined with confiscated documents, led US intelligence organizations to postulate that the Nazis had established a secret naval base in Antarctica. Adding to the suspicion, Hitler's Navy Commander, Grand Admiral Donitz, was quoted in 1943 saying, "The German submarine fleet is proud of having built for the Führer, in another part of the world, a Shangri-La land, an impregnable fortress."

Louis, along with other researchers and authors, believed this particular quote, combined with information from Operation Paperclip, was the real reason the Navy organized a task force of fifteen ships designated "Operation Highjump" to investigate Queen Maud Land, south of Africa.

Rear Admiral Richard H. Cruzen commanded the flotilla, while Admiral Richard E. Byrd Jr. led the reconnaissance mission. As with any incident involving sensitive information, there were sanctioned, official descriptions of the operation and other descriptions that researchers including former Soviet officials insisted to be closer to the truth. Articles and documentaries described it as an operation to map out the coastline of the continent. According to the official records, the task force separated into five smaller groups: the western, central, eastern, carrier, and base groups. Admiral Byrd headed the carrier group.

Those suspecting censorship believed that a quote by Admiral Byrd, in the *Mercurio*, a Chilean newspaper, provided a hint of what may have happened during the expedition: "In the case of a new war, the continental United States would be attacked by flying objects which could fly pole to pole at incredible speeds." Nonconformists pointed out that the comment referred to an attack on the flotilla by high-speed aircraft. Accounts of damaged ships were just as suspect, discrediting researchers claiming suppression of truth. For example, conspiracy theorist sites and articles parroted that a destroyer named the *Murdoch* sank and the aircraft carrier *Casablanca* sustained heavy damage. Official Navy records indicate, however, that the *Casablanca* was decommissioned a few years *before* Operation Highjump, and that the Navy *never* had a destroyer named *Murdoch* in its inventory.

There was no basis for Louis to support the conspiracy theory with over four thousand sailors taking part in the operation. If the official account was a lie, it could not have been concealed from eventual exposure. *Right?* In addition, there was an alleged transcript of Admiral Byrd's so-called secret diary, an account of a reconnaissance mission over the land mass. In it, a narrative described engine performance, instrument readings, and episodes of turbulence followed by a detailed series of entries about the discovery of a verdant valley and a hidden civilization.

The diary continued to describe a forced landing and meeting a master of the newly discovered society. Entries in the secret diary referred to a conversation with the one called the master. Through various sources, Louis discovered that the dialogue contained language appearing suspiciously similar to excerpts from a book by Byrd, *Skyward*, which he wrote in 1928. A passage from his log recorded engine performance and related occurrences during a flight over the Arctic. In addition, the supposed conversation between Byrd and the master appeared straight out of a scene from the 1937 motion picture, *Lost Horizon*. The movie placed the main character, Robert Conway, in a meeting with the mysterious High Lama, who said:

You, my son, will live through the storm. You will preserve the fragrance of our history and add to it a touch of your own mind. Beyond that, my vision weakens . . . but I see in the great distance a new world starting in the ruins. . . . But in hopefulness, seeking its lost and legendary treasures, and they will all be here, my son, hidden behind the mountains under the blue moon, preserved as if by a miracle . . .

The secret diary read: *Yes, my son, the dark ages that will come for your race will cover the Earth like a pall, but I believe that some of your race will live through the storm, beyond that I cannot say. We see a great distance a new world stirring from the ruins of your race, seeking its lost and legendary treasures, and they will be here, my son, safe in our keeping ...*

To Louis, there was enough evidence to label the secret diary of Admiral Byrd a hoax, but it did not disprove the theory Antarctica was home to a technologically advanced people. There was evidence to support it. First, the satellite images in Google Earth of two unusual openings:

Opening 1: 66 deg. 36 min. 12.54 sec. south and 99 deg. 43 min. 12.37 sec. east.

Opening 2: 66 deg. 33 min. 11.62 sec south and 99 deg. 50 min. 22.07 sec east.

Opening 1 displayed what appeared to be a retractable metallic cover. Both openings were wide enough to fit a large passenger jet.

Louis did not rely only on the satellite images. He shared numerous face-to-face conversations with a retired cryptologist who worked at the National Security Agency (NSA) about the UFO phenomena. One evening, at an event hosted by the Society of American Military Engineers, Louis asked about Antarctica.

"I've been doing research on Antarctica and Admiral Byrd. Did you know there are images that show odd openings in the earth that appear to be unnatural formations? One even appears to have a metallic dome-like cover," Louis said clearly, like a reporter interviewing a witness.

"I am not surprised. Nothing surprises me," said the retiree, matter-of-factly. One wouldn't guess the work he was involved in by looking at him. He could be someone's grandfather—and probably was.

"So, you are aware of activity in Antarctica?" Louis tried to delve deeper into the hidden truth. *This guy knows something.*

"Yes," the former cryptologist replied dryly, giving the minimum amount of information.

The answer did not satisfy Louis. "Did you happen to see any message traffic concerning Antarctica?" Louis began to feel that the man was holding back.

"I saw messages that indicated we had operations there in response to reports of anomalous activity," responded the retiree with a slow nod and a wink. "Someday, I may tell you more, but today, here, I prefer I end this inquisition now."

The retired cryptologist was not comfortable in more detailed discussion. To Louis, the information from the retired NSA cryptologist was strong enough evidence to help support his theory of interterrestrials occupying Antarctica.

* * *

The radio show continued as Louis was finishing the Antarctica slides. Louis couldn't help but listen as callers asked questions and praised Dr. Stevens. Louis was disappointed that no one challenged the researcher. Louis would have called himself, but completing his presentation was too important.

The next group of slides concerned an encounter that occurred at Rendlesham Forest outside RAF Bentwaters, England, in late December, 1980. Many refer to it as Great Britain's Roswell. Since there were multiple credible US active-duty military witnesses, Louis felt the Rendlesham Forest incident was more momentous than the Roswell crash. Among those impacted were Air Force Lieutenant Colonel Charles Halt, Deputy Base Commander; Air Force Staff Sergeant Jim Penniston, Senior Security Officer; and Airman First Class Jim Burroughs, a Security Police/Law Enforcement patrolman assigned to the 81st Security Police Squadron.

All of the men provided detailed and corroborated documentation of the events surrounding the incident. Halt recorded the events on a personal cassette recorder while Penniston used his own notebook. Burroughs had concurred with both Lt. Col. Halt's recording and Staff Sergeant Penniston's notes. Over time, the story never changed; when everyone told the truth, there was no need to corroborate.

On the pre-dawn morning of December 26, Burroughs spotted strange lights in the forest outside the base. Burroughs thought the lights might have been from a downed aircraft and treated it as a security situation. Penniston was the assigned flight chief at RAF Woodbridge. When Penniston arrived, the two security policemen detected interference using their communication radios. Penniston also experienced static electricity in the air.

They approached a clearing where a craft had landed, a metallic craft three meters high, three meters across at the base, and triangular. It had blue lights on the side, a white light on top, and made no sound. Approaching the craft, Penniston observed symbols not of any known language, resembling hieroglyphics. The staff sergeant drew the symbols in his notebook. He placed his hand on the craft. It was hard and smooth as glass, and the symbols had a gritty texture. The series of glyphs ran in a row about three feet long and a hand high. One symbol, larger than the others, prompted Penniston to place his hand on the craft with all fingers and palm touching. Upon doing this, a bright white light emanated from the craft. He choked down his fear to keep his hand on the symbol. In moments, the bright light was off, allowing him to remove his hand. As he stepped back, the craft slowly and silently lifted off the forest floor, soon hovering above the trees. It then left at an "impossible speed," as Burroughs and Penniston noted in reports they submitted and entered into the blotter.

At the start of the normal duty day, Lt. Col. Halt went to read the entries and discovered that the reports were immediately classified and removed. For evidence, Penniston made plaster casts of the indentations in the ground from the heavy craft.

The incident continued the next day. Halt was advised by a Security Policeman that the UFO was back. Halt took members of the Security Police to the site and used a personal cassette recorder to document that event. This time, several crafts were scattered in the sky just off the horizon, less than a quarter mile from Burroughs's and Penniston's encounter. UAVs directed laser-like beams a few yards in front of Halt's group. Transcripts from his recording described his amazement.

Halt and his team never trained for this kind of encounter, and it showed. Without any logic to their positions, they gaped at the exotic machines. Everyone remained silent and fixed, while Halt's wavering words stumbled from his lips with a hint of desperation. True to his sense of mission, he remained in place, holding his ground as the laser-like beam moved closer to his team. And just like Penniston's encounter, the craft stopped, continued to hover, then popped out of sight at a ridiculously high velocity.

Most remarkable was Penniston's telepathic download of ones and zeros while his hand was on the craft. Not knowing what the ones and zeros meant, he laid awake as they persisted inside his mind. He wrote sixteen pages of the binary code in a notebook, then kept it a secret. Thirty years after the event, during a filming of an episode for *Ancient Aliens*, the binary code was handed to a programmer and translated. According to Penniston, the programmer, Joe Luciano, translated the code:

"EXPLORATION OF HUMANITY 666 8100"

"52.0942532N 13.131269W" — the location of a mythical island off the southwest coast of Ireland called Hy-Brasil, said to be the home of original people from Ireland

"CONTINUOUS FOR PLANETARY ADVAN"

"FOURTH COORDIANTE CONTINUOT UQS CbPR BEFORE"

"16.763177N 89.117768W" — Caracol, Belize; a Mayan Pyramid.

"34.800272N 111.843567W" — Sedona at the foot of a mountain.

"29.977836N 31.131649E" — the Great Pyramids of Egypt.

"14.701505S 75.167043W" — the Nazca Plateau of South America, where glyphs are evident at high altitudes.

"36.256845N 117.100632E" — Mount Tai in the Shandong Province of China; a historic site where people have worshiped for over 3,000 years.

"37.110195N 25.372281E" — the Portara, Temple of Apollo, Naxos, Greece.

"EYES OF YOUR EYES"

"ORIGIN 52.0942532N 13.131269W" (Hy-Brasil)

"ORIGIN YEAR 8100"

Why would a probe from a highly advanced civilization pass this message? Louis wondered. What was the relevance of all these sites? Did the year signify a date from the future or is the calendar based on another system?

Jim Penniston posited that the probe was not extraterrestrial but from the future. For his part, Louis believed that this incident was from a highly advanced civilization based under the ocean, where the mythical island of Hy-Brasil was thought to exist long ago. The date 8100 likely referred to a completely different calendar system, not the Gregorian one. He translated Year One of the calendar to 6120 BC.

Louis theorized probes were commonly sent to military installations that stored or deployed nuclear weapons. He surmised the Air Force secretly stored tactical nuclear warheads in the munitions storage area where the probes had directed their beams. This was potentially very sensitive information, because public knowledge of nuclear warheads on English soil would likely have resulted in pressure on Prime Minister Margaret Thatcher and her administration. Public outcry would likely have caused Thatcher to request the Air

Force to remove the nuclear weapons, thereby weakening a key part of the deterrence against the Soviet Union during the Cold War era. Louis hypothesized that advanced civilizations, calling the Earth home, demonstrated concern about humans and nuclear arsenals. Nuclear weapons were recognized as a threat, and the advanced races needed to have good surveillance of the situation.

* * *

The radio show was in its final hours as more callers presented their own experiences at other mountains. Louis focused next on a topic he dedicated most of his time to: Dulce, New Mexico. It is the site of the most sinister of activities related to interterrestrial operations. Dulce had been speculated as a joint Deep Underground Military Base (DUMB) involving US black-budget programs and a race of beings referred as "reptilian." Located under a Jicarilla Apache reservation near Mount Archuleta, the Native folklore regarded sounds originating from DUMB and visions of aerial activity as indications of gods. Since the base was on sacred land, the Apache acted as bouncers of sorts, keeping curious people and researchers away. Most of the locals were not aware of occurrences beneath their land, strange or otherwise. They sincerely believed a race originated there to help their ancestors learn to live off the land with superior knowledge in agriculture and spirituality.

The existence of Dulce as a covert joint research facility could be traced to the advent of the atomic age and a corresponding spike in UFO activity relative to the development of nuclear weapons. This spike in UFO sightings prompted the Truman administration to establish the Majestic Twelve (MJ 12). MJ 12 consisted of twelve high-level members in the government, including the President, chartered to set policy related to UFO activity.

Later, during the Eisenhower administration, MJ 12 was supposedly contacted by a race having the physical appearance of Nordic humans to set up a meeting. Muroc Field, California, which later became Edwards AFB, was selected for a discussion of a proposed treaty that would involve a technology transfer. The meeting would be held on one condition: that the United States was to disarm itself of all nuclear weapons and cease further development in atomic energy.

MJ 12 recognized it as a suspicious precondition, attributing it to Soviet influence to strategically weaken the United States.

Consequently, MJ 12 deemed the race of Nordic-type humanoids a threat to national security and ended relations. Not much later, another race of advanced beings supposedly contacted MJ 12, offering technology. MJ 12 decided to reveal information on the meeting to military weapons systems contractors.

The meeting was held at Holloman AFB, New Mexico, without any preconditions. The press was duly advised that President Eisenhower went on a golf vacation, while a representative of the Catholic Arch Diocese of Los Angeles was notified and asked to attend the meeting.

The beings that met the US coalition were known as Extraterrestrial Biological Entities (EBEs) known as the Greys. These were not living, breathing, blood-circulating beings but an advanced android life-form that took on the role of a servant race to other races. They were neither good nor evil; they merely followed the orders of their masters. In this case, they represented a reptilian race that preferred to not be present. MJ 12 was not aware of this, assuming they were dealing with the race that would enter into the treaty. What did happen at the meeting laid out the framework on how the Department of Defense secretly conducted exopolitics.

The EBEs conferred to the United States negotiating team that they would provide high technologies in return for the freedom to abduct humans and livestock for research. The EBEs assured the team there would be no harm to humans; abductions would not lead to injury or harm. Eisenhower thought the deal was risky and unwise, and decided to end the meeting, probably wishing he was doing what his own press corps reported—playing 18 holes on a golf course of his choice.

A treaty was made between the EBEs and nongovernment officials from the aerospace industry. Upon leaving office at the end of his eight-year term in 1961, Eisenhower made the famous "Military Industrial Complex" speech, where he cryptically warned citizens of this arrangement. Following that treaty, there was a spike in the number of abductions, livestock mutilations, and sightings—mostly in the western United States. Along with the abductions and livestock mutilations, a significant result of the treaty was the establishment of the joint underground base in Dulce. The treaty provided for the addition of a black-budget operations side to an existing reptilian base. If there was any transfer of technology, military contractors kept that information hidden from the public.

Information related to Dulce was also provided to Louis by a woman whose mother kept information related to the base while employed with the CIA. Before her death, she gave it to her daughter, an abductee whom Louis had befriended on the social network. One evening, during a conversation about the phenomenon, the woman sent him the documents. Giving out information to the public on Dulce had proven to be high risk, with bad results for the informer. Whistleblowers claiming information on Dulce met suspicious deaths. One memorialized individual was Phil Schneider, a contractor that worked on the black ops side of Dulce. After returning from a tour on radio stations and UFO conferences around the world, he was shot and killed outside his home by local sheriff deputies who claimed he drew a weapon as they approached him.

Louis had read stories from workers who were bussed or flown to the remote construction site to work on the US side of the base. Workers were required to sign non-disclosure agreements, never to discuss the reason for their travel to Dulce with anyone. No prime contractor working on Dulce knew the entire layout; although very expensive and inefficient, contractors were brought in to work on specific portions and not allowed information beyond those areas. It was like hiring ten different contractors to work on one house: Each builder focused on one room, not knowing how the entire house would look when completed. The documents from the CIA woman's daughter also revealed that Dulce had been a base for genetic lab experiments involving animal parts, human fetuses, and DNA manipulation. Louis still had difficulty accepting the lab information as truth and decided not to include that in his presentation.

* * *

The last group of slides explained possible ET activity in Alaska. On May 22, 1992, the Chinese military detonated a nuclear warhead underground. The shockwave was detected by seismologists as far away as Alaska. During their research, they discovered a geologic anomaly about sixty miles west of Mount McKinley.

Approximately six months later, an Army Non-Commissioned Officer (NCO) assigned to the Fort Richardson base in southeastern Alaska, and his friends caught a news special about an underground pyramid west of Mount McKinley. When the NCO went to the news station to request a copy of the show, he was denied by a station manager who told him that the station did not show the broadcast. This prompted the NCO to contact the highly respected reporter on edge science, Linda Moulton Howe. Howe, intrigued by the message from the NCO, asked for information from her vast listening audience on her web-based show.

She received two responses verifying the existence of the underground pyramid. One person was the son of a former Navy captain, whose father worked for Western Electric between 1959 and 1961, after his military retirement, in support of the White Alice project. White Alice was the project name for the Distant Early Warning (DEW) Line radar that would warn North Americans against a possible Soviet air strike passing over the North Pole. Engineers testing the equipment detected what they thought to be a malfunction of one of the sites. Later, they realized that a high amount of electro-magnetic interference (EMI) originated somewhere in the vicinity of Mount McKinley. Western Electric engineers were taken to the site where the EMI originated and were sent down a mine shaft where, according to the retired captain, they observed the apex of a stone pyramid approximately one hundred fifty feet below the surface with its base nine hundred feet below the surface. The engineers had determined the pyramid was producing enough energy to power all of Canada.

The second contact offered another side of the story. According to Bruce L. Pearson, his father, another former Navy officer, had confided in him a story of a trip by helicopter in the spring of 1978. After retirement, his father befriended an active-duty Air Force major who piloted a helicopter on supply missions to a remote site west of Mount McKinley. One day, the major invited the Navy veteran as a passenger on one of the missions. The major told the veteran they were flying to a "weird" place where there was an energy source underground.

"Is it a nuclear plant?" the veteran asked.

"It's unlike anything I know," the major replied. When they approached the landing zone, the major added, "Do not panic if the helicopter experiences instrument problems."

On cue, the helicopter's instruments began to malfunction, and multiple alarms and warning lights were activated. The pilot had to switch control to visual and manual flight. As the helicopter drew closer, the veteran identified a motor vehicle shed, a mining shaft structure, and a vehicle with a mounted machine gun, manned by a gunner, aiming at the helicopter.

The helicopter did not land but hovered over a pad, while heavily armed men in black uniforms without insignia approached the bird to offload what appeared to be crates with a gleaming metallic finish. All through the operation, the gunner pointed the heavy machine gun directly at the helicopter. Not a word was exchanged throughout the operation.

* * *

After reviewing the two accounts, Louis was satisfied that his presentation file was updated. After saving the file, he closed his computer. The radio show was ending. The host presented his credits and advised the audience what the next show would cover: an alternate theory on the Kennedy assassination.

Louis turned off the radio as the sun was about to rise over Lake Michigan. The faint light created muted silhouettes of the townhouse buildings across the street from his window. The early morning harbinger in the city was the street cleaner. It masked the sounds of birds in the trees along the walk. Louis needed to get some rest before the long journey ahead, completely unaware that this leg would be the beginning of an odyssey that would challenge his convictions of disclosure, test his spirit, expose him to amazing people, and reveal extraordinary aspects of his own existence.

4

ENCOUNTERS AND TRANSMISSIONS

Your mind is working at its best when you're being paranoid. You explore every avenue and possibility of your situation at high speed with total clarity. —Banksy

The drive from Chicago to the UFO conference took only about eight hours. The ephemeral beauty of fall colors enhanced Louis's travel as he neared the Pittsburgh area. Before checking in to the Econo Lodge in Youngwood, Pennsylvania, Louis sought out the building at the Westmoreland County Community College campus, where the event would be held the next day. He had no difficulty finding Founders Hall. Satisfied with the ease of finding the conference site, Louis drove to the motel and checked in.

The next morning, he headed to the conference and stopped for breakfast and coffee. He watched the server fill his mug in a rush without a drop being spilled. Reaching for the cream, he held it over the mug in his left hand and stirred it into the coffee with the teaspoon in his right. He marveled at the creation, his own spinning galaxy. Captivated by the motion, he remained in a hypnotic state while the rotation slowed and everything around him seemed to dissolve. The server startled him as she arrived with his order.

Louis left the restaurant in time to get to the campus, park, register, and prepare his presentation. The lobby contained posters from sponsors, framed photographs of people at past events, and framed photographs of UFOs.

Burdened with his laptop case hanging by a strap over his right shoulder, he held a paper cup with coffee in his left hand. At the welcome table, he was greeted by a cheerful man who spoke with a Scandinavian accent as he held out his hand. The laptop case strap slipped off Louis's shoulder as he extended to shake hands. Temporarily delaying the gesture of goodwill, Louis placed the case on the floor beside him, this time completing a successful handshake.

"Allo, Olav Whitouse at your service! Welcome to the annual Pennsylvania Conference. What is your name, please?"

Louis gave his name and told him he was the first presenter, the warmup act. The greeter gave him a customized badge and program, then directed him to an aide whose job was to assist presenters. Louis thanked the greeter and left, but not without noticing what Olav and the other two greeters were wearing, a green tee shirt printed with the recycling logo and the word "Karma" in the center. Another greeter wore a purple "Make America Disclose" hat, and the other wore a black t-shirt with the image of a grey alien head in white and the words, "I Believe." He exchanged smiles with them.

Thirty minutes before the start of the conference, Louis noticed people coming in to form lines. He was led to the auditorium that held a capacity of 420, according to the posted sign by the local Fire Marshall. An ideal size for such a conference.

The aide, a young collegiate woman, did not know who Louis was. "Did you write a book?" she inquired while leading him to the podium.

"No...not yet," he said sheepishly. She seemed disappointed.

She showed Louis the podium and offered to help connect the laptop to the system's projector. "I should have looked at the program," she apologized. "What is your presentation about?"

"Interterrestrials," he replied enthusiastically.

"Interterrestrials? You mean beings that live on Earth with humans?" she asked.

"Exactly!" Louis smiled, raising his right index finger.

"Interesting...." The thought amused the aide. She quickly connected the laptop to the auditorium's system and tested it.

"You are good to go, Mr. Sivani. Good luck and here's a bottle of water," she said, leaving the room.

"It's Silvani!" he yelled as she disappeared through the doors.

A higher-ranking official from the event sponsor approached Louis and told him there would be a thirty-minute introductory video prior to his presentation, which promoted the organization's activities. It allowed time for latecomers to find their seats before Louis spoke. He watched the introductory video and observed people entering the auditorium. As the room filled up, he spotted all kinds of people: young, old, women, men, people of various ethnicities. The demand for disclosure was not exclusive to any particular demographic.

The introductory presentation ended with a courteous applause. The spokesperson walked confidently to the center of the stage.

"Welcome UFO enthusiasts from Pennsylvania, West Virginia, and Delaware to the Region's annual conference. Our first speaker is making his debut in our region. He has a blog and has contributed to various publications with articles on the subject of Interterrestrials—beings that are and have been cohabitating with humans. Please read his bio in the program. He is a thorough researcher and has new ideas about the UFO phenomenon. Louis? Is there a book in the future?" She looked back at the podium.

Louis nodded yes, but not very emphatically.

"There is? Good! I'm sure it will be entertaining and thought-provoking!"

Louis grinned slightly, lowering his head. The body language betrayed his response.

"Here now to talk about Interterrestrials is Louis Silvani."

Louis started his presentation. He was given sixty minutes. He worked through the presentation as planned, talking about Antarctica, the Rendlesham Forest incident, the base at Dulce, New Mexico, and finally, the underground pyramid in Alaska. He also pointed to UFO activity relative to the world's major mountain ranges: the Himalayas, Cascades, Andes, and one specific mountain, Mount Shasta. After the presentation, Louis fielded all kinds of questions. The session was lively and engaging.

A forty-something man stood up, the look on his face determined. "You have nice slides and you give a good speech. Antarctica, RAF Bentwaters, those appear to be true, then you talk about Dulce, New Mexico, and Mount Shasta. How did you get your information about those places?"

Louis described the reputable whistleblowers and all the people he interviewed.

"But you have never been to any of the places you talk about, right?" the man asked.

"No, I have not had the chance to visit any of the places myself."

The audience murmured. "Maybe you should go to those places and get back to us after you have!" shouted another person.

"A good researcher tries to visit the places he writes about," added the man with the microphone.

"He's right!" a third audience member yelled out.

The audience continued to murmur, the noise building with every moment until Louis had to be rescued by the spokesperson.

"Thank you, Mr. Silvani! I am sure we will get more information on this in the future and through your blog."

His moment of prestige ended terribly. Louis was speechless and in shock as he closed his laptop and walked away. He began to second guess himself. He was bullied by audience members and his response was absent. He felt weak and defeated. He had intended to stay for the rest of the conference and to have discussions with other presenters. He had hoped to talk to the author and former Air Force missileer in charge of silos at Malmstrom AFB, Montana, during an event where UFOs shut down silos, one at a time. And there was a professor of Natural Sciences at Boston University and a contributor to the TV show *Ancient Aliens*. Louis had also looked forward to being on a panel at the end of the conference where there would be open discussion on just about anything, but he decided to pack his equipment and go to the men's room before returning to Chicago. Demoralized, he approached the lobby, when he heard a woman's voice call out for him.

"Mr. Silvani, Mr. Silvani! Wait! Please!"

Louis stopped and turned toward the auditorium entrance doors. A Native American woman, appearing to be in her early forties, ran toward him. She wore a purple tie-dyed long-sleeved shirt and faded jeans with lime green athletic shoes. Her long jet-black hair was in braids, and she wore no makeup. Her complexion, her deep brown almond eyes, dark lashes and brows, presented a stunning composition. Her nose was classical—pronounced but not oversized for her oval face. She was adorned with a turquoise and silver bracelet and silver bands on both ring fingers.

"Hello, Mr. Silvani. I am Mary Ellen Velarde. I am Jicarilla Apache *and* I live in Dulce, New Mexico. I can take you there, and I could take you to Mount Shasta."

Louis did not know how to respond. It was prudent to be wary of people at these events. "I saw what happened in—" her voice trailed off.

"You and a few hundred others who seemed in agreement with the points made by the hecklers," interrupted Louis.

"Let me finish, sir," retorted Mary Ellen confidently. "I know what you are feeling. You don't have anyone to help you. I have a network of people that can help you get to those places. I sense that you have a desire to go to there. I am giving you the opportunity to join me."

"Those are bold assumptions, Ms. Velarde," said Louis with suspicion.

"The world is full of wonderful secrets that reveal our true nature and our unknown abilities. You have them. We all have them. Do you meditate, Mr. Silvani?"

Louis was not in the mood for an interrogation after being heckled. "I have dabbled with meditation: not a huge fan," he admitted.

She motioned Louis to a small intimate seating area in the lobby. "Will you sit with me there for a moment?"

Mary Ellen asked him to elaborate, offering an opportunity to give her a better answer.

"I know the benefits from meditation: better sleeping, clarity of thought, stress reduction," he said, taking the moment to exhale and try to relax. "I used to meditate daily for about thirty minutes. I seem to have lost my skill. I never felt I got much out of it except rest. I would find myself falling asleep and never getting to where I could see images. I haven't applied myself to meditate like I should."

"I meditate daily. When you meditate, you exercise your pineal gland. Do you know about the pineal gland?" Mary Ellen asked. "It is what helps you dream."

Louis nodded. "Yes, in fact during a visit to Rome, I saw a huge bronze sculpture of a pinecone on the path leading to the Basilica of Saint Peter at the Vatican. I understand that pinecone symbolized the gland."

Mary Ellen responded with a smile, satisfied that she did not have to explain before continuing. "Also, when you meditate, exercising the gland allows you to be more connected with the Cosmos. Meditation opens up a gift we all have. You should consider going with me to Dulce. I know you will find it beneficial for your lectures."

She took out a notebook and pen from her fringed leather sack and wrote her name and contact information. She ripped the page out to give to Louis. "Here is my cell phone. I am scheduled to be on a flight leaving tomorrow morning from Pittsburgh. Are you at the Econo Lodge?"

Louis nodded.

"I am staying there too. I have enough in my bags for a road trip, but you probably just packed for this trip so you will have to go back to . . ."

"Chicago. I drove here. Are you asking me to make a decision here and now?" Louis was feeling trapped.

"No," responded Mary Ellen. "Not here and now. I could change my travel plans and get a flight to Chicago. I could stay with a friend there. You can have as much time as you need after you return home before you decide. Does that sound reasonable?"

"But why now?" asked Louis, still unsure about her.

"Why not? Our meeting was not an accident, Mr. Silvani. Those people in the audience served a purpose for you and for me. You may not know it, but you have an important role to fulfill, and I will help you through it. There is much I know about you that you still have not even begun to realize."

Louis paused as she said those words, put down his laptop case, pursed his lips and focused his eyes on her. "You are not the first person to tell me that about myself."

Mary Ellen smirked. "I will change my flight to go to Chicago. I expect a call tomorrow night. I paid for the entire conference, so I will stay for the rest. Have a safe trip back to Chicago, Mr. Silvani."

She extended her hand and smiled. Her whole face smiled. Her eyes glistened. He felt a warmth from the handshake. He kept his lips tight, almost clenching his jaw muscles. She picked up her sack, stood up, and turned briskly toward the auditorium. Louis did not move. Instead, he watched her walk away toward the welcome area. Louis was disappointed in himself for perhaps being too protective or cynical. He didn't even say thank you; he was relatively vacant of any human expression, and she was just the opposite. As she entered the doors, he thought about what she had said about him that the other psychic women had confided in him. *Why is it only women that know this?*

Louis headed to the men's room. He turned to the lavatory, washed his hands, and splashed cool water on his face. Reaching for the paper towel dispenser, he failed to notice two tall ominous figures enter the room. As he opened his eyes to look up at the mirror, he was startled to see them standing closely behind him. They each wore a dark suit, a dark tie, a white shirt and dark glasses. Their expression was void of emotion. Louis turned around abruptly but had nowhere to go as they blocked his exit.

"Excuse me," Louis said politely.

The two men did not move. Nothing on them moved. Louis also did not move, frozen by fear. He felt flush and his heart pounded in his chest. He knew the men sensed his fear, and it was too late to fake not being afraid.

Your research material is telling people more than they need to know, he heard one say, but he did not notice either man move his lips to speak. *Cease and desist further lectures on this information. The dissemination of your theories, putting pressure on disclosure, is actually a threat to the security of the United States and the entire human race.*

Again, he heard the words, but saw no one speak.

There was a silent pause, then a vision, like a bad daydream, appeared to him. He saw his ex-wife and children in her SUV being hit in an intersection by a cement mixer, causing the vehicle to burst into flames. He could even hear the cries of the children in the burning vehicle. A look of terror invaded his face. His breathing grew shallow.

Why are you angry? a voice chided him. *You have brought this upon yourself. We are following orders. We are showing you what will happen if you continue to inform the public of this forbidden knowledge.*

Louis was stunned. Not only were they able communicate to him without speaking, but they were also able to sense what he felt and thought.

Yes, we know what you are thinking, was the immediate response.

Louis felt crushed. And he knew they knew it. Menacing grins crossed the faces of the men. They were on the same program. He thought about his family. It was evident that he needed to heed their advice. Louis remained frozen. He looked away, avoiding eye contact. Nervous and nauseous, he put his hand over mouth. He wanted to speak, but fear blocked words from coming out.

Good, you should be afraid, the next message broadcast.

Louis was reduced to a plea. "Please. Please. Don't hurt them. I understand your demands. I will refrain from further efforts to support disclosure." He slumped, looking down and away.

The men turned toward each other, nodded, turned around, and left the restroom. Louis barely moved, though he shook deeply inside. The two shadowy figures headed toward the building's exit, toward Mary Ellen, who was standing near the welcome tables. Sensing a dark presence, she directed her attention to the men approaching her. She immediately recognized who they were. Her stare was fixated on something beneath the black suits and the dark glasses, and it caught their attention. They slowed their pace as they directed a piercing glare at her. Her abilities had just been tested and matched. She had been careless. Even with her effort to disengage and cloak her thoughts, they were exposed and the men read her. The only thing she could do was act defiantly—she was strong enough not to allow them to plant anything in her mind.

What are you doing here? she asked without speaking.

The men stopped, realizing that Mary Ellen was not like other humans; they did not know everything about this woman.

You are very far from your home. Be careful not to get into trouble. It would be a shame for a special one like you and your friend to be harmed. We know what you want to do. You will not succeed, she heard in her mind.

She offered her final thought: *You cannot fight destiny, especially when the destiny is of the divine.*

She watched the men leave. Then she thought about Louis. "Mr. Silvani!" she gasped.

Mary Ellen looked toward the men's room door and saw Louis, the laptop case in hand, slumped and almost stumbling toward the exit. She moved quickly toward him. He appeared hurt—not physically, but psychologically, as if he had been tortured.

"Mr. Silvani, are you alright? What did they do to you?"

"You saw them?" inquired Louis.

"Yes, I saw them and they saw me. They know who I am, and I know who they are. It's a draw—for now. What happened?"

"Maybe you know already," replied Louis cynically.

"I need to hear it from you so I know they did not damage you. Come. Sit down for a bit." She motioned to him to sit against the wall on the carpeted floor.

"Breathe in deeply." Mary Ellen inhaled deeply, held it in, and then exhaled slowly with lips partially closed. Louis followed her instructions and did exactly as she did. They repeated the exercise a few more times.

Louis regained his composure. "They don't want me to continue with my work. They threatened to kill my family if I did not heed their warning. They did not speak, but I heard what

they told me. They knew what I was thinking and they used it to terrorize me. And . . . you . . . know . . . who they are? And they know you? Who *are* you?"

"Only my guardians know who I am, but know this: I am on your side, Mr. Silvani. You must find it in yourself to place your trust in me. Those men are not human. They are like super-soldiers. They are psychopaths with no emotion. But not all have the same abilities. Some do not have telepathic power at all. The dark organizations have been trying to make them all the same, but they can't figure out why some still have identities. This identity thing is what they are trying to eliminate, and I think the experiments at Dulce are for that reason and others I still do not know about."

Louis was overwhelmed, overwhelmed to the point of cracking, and it wasn't even ten o'clock in the morning. He was thirsty and had trouble talking. She opened her sack, pulled out a bottle of water, and gave it to him. The gesture took on the properties of a magic trick.

Mary Ellen recognized his reaction to the simple offer. "What? Anyone could see that you needed a drink!" Her face made that smile again. The smile made him feel better than the drink of water.

"So, you aren't going to tell me anymore about yourself?" asked Louis.

"I am going to tell you about *yourself*, Louis Silvani."

"What do you mean? What can you tell me about myself that I don't know?"

"I have been told you are one of the good guys. You *are* special. You have a role to play in a coming quiet spiritual revolution. You are a counselor, an informer."

"Who's telling you this?"

Mary Ellen smile. "My guides. I have guides at different levels. I have a relationship with an advanced race of beings. They communicate to me often. They have been telling me about you from the moment I saw your name on the list of presenters."

"Why don't I get those communications?"

"Your spirit guides you; *they* have been guiding you from the moment you became human. There is something about your spirit that makes you different from other humans. They have watched you. They know your heart. They *are*, in fact, The Watchers. They said for you not to worry; you are surrounded by guardians. Your mission is important. You will learn more about yourself in time."

"The *Watchers*? What in the hell are watchers?" Louis asked, aghast.

"Yes, I will tell you more after we take our journey west. You should put a hold on informing others of your work, just to be safe."

Louis nodded. He took another sip of water. Some of it dribbled on his chin and he wiped it with his sleeve.

"I'll call you when I get back to Chicago." Mary Ellen smiled again, her smile oddly assuring. "You will be OK, Mr. Silvani."

"Louis, my name is Louis," he offered.

"Yes, I know. I will fly to Chicago tomorrow afternoon and look forward to your call. Take care, Louis Silvani."

Louis forced a smile. Mary Ellen stood up to leave. "Thank you, Mary Ellen!" This time he remembered to be polite.

In the parking lot, the men that threatened Louis stood by their black GMC SUV with dark tinted windows. The man on the passenger's side talked into a cell phone. "Request contact information on an agent, location: Dulce, New Mexico."

A robotic female voice responded, "Please hold."

There was no need for an authentication code; the program functioned using voice recognition software. A beep was heard every fifteen seconds. After a few beeps, the voice came back.

"Agent Rico Martin is located at the Jicarilla Police Station."

The voice provided the phone number and asked if the agent wanted to call now. The agent responded affirmatively and the call was placed. It was about 8 a.m. in New Mexico. After a couple of rings, the informant in Dulce answered his cell phone.

"Hello. Chief Martin speaking."

The agent spoke calmly and low. "Chief Martin. This is NRO. We have reason to suspect that an individual is planning to gain access to Dulce's restricted site. She will be accompanied by Louis Silvani, a UFO researcher. She lives in Dulce. Her name is Mary Ellen Velarde."

The name caught Chief Martin by surprise. "I know of Ms. Velarde—quite well," he responded, his tone low, serious. "I will have a team watch her as she enters the Rez. When should I expect to see them?"

"They are in Pittsburgh now. We do not have a timetable for their arrival. We acknowledge they are no threat to you or your men, but she knows much about the area, and we do not like the idea of her bringing a researcher as another witness."

"Understand. We'll give them a good scare."

"We have already threatened Silvani. Velarde is different and more dangerous. Do you understand?"

Martin paused. He did not know Velarde's spiritual strengths. Then the NRO agent suggested, "The mountain roads can be treacherous there, don't you think?"

Martin was now presented with a task that he knew would eventually be a part of the job he had to carry out, but doing so to someone he knew made him uncomfortable.

"Yes … I … understand," the informant reluctantly complied.

"Chief, your force will not have to do anything illegal. We will have a team dispatched to your town to assist you. Expect some visitors soon and give them what they need. Goodbye."

Never before had the Jicarilla Police Chief been involved in a task such as that described by the caller. One of his assignments working as an informant was to monitor and prevent activity that posed a security threat to the underground installation. No one quite knew what activities occurred there, but it was important enough to require a full-time agent as a bouncer. This particular order came from the National Reconnaissance Office. As the NRO agent hung up, Martin tried to process the call and thought that it was quite a way to start the day.

5

A WILD RIDE

Thinking is the best way to travel. —Moody Blues

Mary Ellen turned to go back to the auditorium. The experience had been upsetting but not as unnerving as the encounter with the two men. Louis remained sitting against the wall.

Staring blankly toward the lobby, he replayed what had happened in the men's room. *Who or what were those guys? They didn't seem human. They were able to make me see things, and they could tell what I was thinking! Why are they so much against disclosure?*

A feeling of loneliness crept over him. He hadn't felt that kind of loneliness before, even after the divorce. He thought about the vision, seeing his family, the helpless anguish of hearing their cries from the burning vehicle after being slammed. Mentally, he wasn't ready for the trip back to Chicago and needed more time to regroup. Following Mary Ellen's previous instructions, Louis took a few deep breaths and exhaled slowly after each one. His body was less tense, but he still felt emotionally exhausted. He wanted to crawl away and sleep.

It was still early in the day and the motel was only minutes away. He reasoned that he could take a nap or even meditate, leave around noon, and still get to his townhouse at a decent time. He got up slowly and stretched. As he took the last sips of water, he could hear the muffled voice of the next speaker through the doors. He would have liked to have seen the presentations. Turning his head toward the exit, he picked up his laptop case and empty plastic bottle, and plodded toward the exit. Waving politely at the greeters, he deposited the empty container in a recycling bin, then turned again to the vestibule doors and exited the building. Louis did not look behind him as he got in the car and drove back to the motel.

Entering his room, Louis placed the laptop case on a chair and closed the shades. Slipping his shoes off, he thought about Mary Ellen and meditation. He took off his suit jacket and placed it on a chair. He sat on the bed and leaned against the headboard. It was relatively quiet outside his room. He loosened his tie, closed his eyes, and started the breathing exercises. He focused on the air entering his body, and afterward, he visualized each breath leaving as he exhaled, doing so for several minutes. Then, to calm his thinking, he focused on feeling parts of his body relax, starting at his feet and slowly, deliberately, working his focus up the legs, to the torso, past the neck, to his "third eye" and then above head at the crown chakra. He kept his eyes closed and let his mind stay quiet. He was somewhere between being awake and asleep.

Gradually, images began to appear. He saw a brief flash of thin, colored, neon-like bands forming a tunnel and appearing in sequence like he was traveling at a high rate of speed. His heart raced. The only sign of movement was the perception of passing swiftly through those colored bands, his hands and arms vibrating. *This is amazing! What an incredible rush!* he thought. A brief lack of concentration caused the vision to end abruptly.

Louis opened his eyes. His heart rate was normal. *What the heck was that?* he wondered. He reasoned it was his first out-of-body experience, and it seemed like he was going through a wormhole. He had no idea how long the experience lasted, but it seemed to be less than fifteen seconds. Unforgettable to be sure, no matter how long or short.

After emerging from meditation, Louis felt much better. He did not feel like sleeping but, rather, rested and clear-headed enough to make the drive back to Chicago. It wasn't noon yet. He jumped off the bed, took off his business attire, and got into more comfortable clothes. Feeling refreshed, he packed his suitcase, did a sweep of the room, and left.

6

BIRTH OF A NOTION

*The hardest thing of all is to find a black cat in a dark
room, especially if there is no cat. —Confucius*

Arriving in the United States at age three with his parents, Louis
Silvani was challenged with learning a second language and a new
culture. He couldn't learn English fast enough at home because his
parents were also learning it. His first American home was a three-
flat in the city. He and his parents lived on the second floor, with his
maternal grandparents on the floor above, and the elderly landlord
couple down below. All were green-card Italians.

When he was five, the family, including the grandparents, moved
out of the city apartments and into two adjacent homes in a growing
working-class suburb. It was an unwelcomed disruption to the life
to which he had become accustomed. The city neighborhood had a
park with large mature trees where his *Nonno* took him. In the city,
his *Nonna* would take him to the local five and dime and allow him
to pick a 45 record to add to his collection. It allowed him to acquire
a few of Elvis's hit singles. In the city, grown-ups would sit on massive stoops and chat while he played with other children. There was
no park near his new suburban house and no five and dime store
nearby. Except for one lone man who also moved from the city, no
one came out late in the evening to talk. Louis would walk across
the street, and the man, home from a long day at the factory, would
sit on the concrete steps nursing a beer and savoring a drag from
his Pall Malls.

"Sox won last night, Louis."

"Yeah. Cubs didn't do too well."

"I grew up in that neighborhood where everybody was a Sox fan. Everyone here is a Sox fan! What happened to you?"

"Our TV doesn't get the channel that yours does. Cubs are on 'GN. My mom and Nonno watch the Cubs, so, I do too."

That's pretty much what Louis and the man talked about: the old neighborhood and baseball.

When he was six, Louis's parents enrolled him in the local Catholic school. In addition to having to learn with all the English-speaking kids, he was exposed to a highly disciplinary culture. The nuns were strict and demonstrated little tolerance for any slight misbehavior. In a short time, Louis learned to read and write in his second language. However, he developed an uncooperative attitude toward the Christian doctrine. As early as second grade, he felt uncomfortable with the Catholic religion, its rituals, and its icons. Being preached to about the sacraments or the stories of Jesus's birth, suffering, death, and resurrection did not sway his thought. He could not understand the story of Jesus. Most stories he knew had happy endings; Jesus's story was not happy. How could there be so much joy and hope from the birth of a baby, and then sorrow and pain from his death, and then joy again? What happened to the baby while it grew up? Wasn't the rest of his life just as important? This attitude would solidify into a foundation he would carry into adulthood as an entrenched belief system.

Consequently, young Louis began to doubt much of what he was being told. He also realized that asking questions that expressed any doubt about the faith was not tolerated at home or at school. Throughout his primary years he remained unenthusiastic, not keeping step with the other more obedient Catholic children. This attitude manifested in mediocre grades that disappointed his parents, grandparents, and teachers.

During Lent, the entire student population assembled in a windowless long hallway to hear the Stations. It was cramped and stuffy. Young legs struggled to fight fatigue as Louis and the others were forced to stand shoulder to shoulder, straining to hear the weak voice of an elderly nun describe the violent sequence of the Stations of the Cross. Since he was one of the shortest in his class, Louis's view was often obstructed by rows of taller children, submissive and silent in their uniforms. He struggled to accept the graphic descriptions depicting the suffering and abuse of Jesus as he carried his own cross toward his death. Louis felt a deep sincere sorrow when the

Stations were recited. Grimacing, he all too clearly envisioned Roman soldiers sadistically fashion branches with long thorns into a head piece then forcing it down on his scalp: the thorns cut into the flesh to cause blood to stream down. His fragile mind was invaded by graphic images of men holding down Jesus's already bruised and battered body against the coarse wood, then positioning an iron spike in the soft palm. He anguished from listening to the horror of words describing the piercing of the skin with the first hard blow of a crude mallet: more blood, more suffering. Each reading appeared to him more vividly than the previous one.

Louis was exposed to the mystique and glorification of pain and suffering at home, too. His grandparents kept rooms adorned with religious pictures. His Nonna's favorite saint was Saint Rita, the patron saint of lost causes. In a bedroom hung a print depicting the young saint on her knees in a dungeon-like setting with a cat-o-nine-tails at her side, praying to a crucifix. It was highlighted by a narrow ray of light emanating from the crown of thorns, directed at her forehead. The print showed the ray piercing her forehead, inflicting a permanent wound. Louis reasoned that one had to suffer to be a saint. One day, Nonna told him the story of Saint Lucy. Saint Lucy was not interested in boys and wanted to be close to Jesus. Nonna told the young boy that when a suitor complimented Lucy on her beautiful eyes, she plucked them out and presented them to the boy. Nonna considered this a beautiful gesture of Lucy's devotion to Jesus.

Louis thought differently. It was the last time he would ask his Nonna about saints.

Louis also felt a conscious unease about the asexual appearance of the nuns. Although a child, he knew the differences between a man and woman. But nuns? These creatures in black showed no visible hair and wore an oversized head piece that was rather intimidating. They did not seem nurturing. He was also quite aware of their tendency to use physical punishment on less obedient pupils, like the receiving end of a heavy maple paddle. Labeled with the phrase BOARD OF EDUCATION in bold red letters, one carried a drawing of a child crying as he was getting spanked.

With every passing year, Louis could not be convinced to better his faith. In the third grade, the children were forced to spend a great amount of class time either in church or in the classroom learning about the "First Holy Communion" and rehearsing for their sacrament. The nuns continued to use fear to control the young minds.

One of the nuns warned the children about going to confession before receiving communion by telling the story of a boy who had not done so. What happened? Upon receiving communion, the boy collapsed—dead. From his open mouth, the host wafer miraculously levitated and was retrieved by the priest, unmutilated. This tale apparently left its mark on a lot of the children but not Louis. Although he secretly had doubts about the story, he followed through with the ceremonial practices, memorized what he needed, and eventually received the sacrament. It was repetition without explanation, including memorizing many words that he had never heard of before: Assumption, Ascension, Adultery, Tabernacle, Scapular, Sacristy, Contrition, and Virgin, to name a few. No one really explained their meaning; the words were accepted as part of learning about the faith without reservation. All prayers were taught orally, and children learned by memory.

After accepting the Sacrament of Communion, Louis was obligated to confess his sins. Confessions were heard by the priest Thursday evenings on the assumption that people could hold out and not sin before Sunday Mass. Louis's father drove him to the church and remained outside the church. Except for a few sinners kneeling in the pews close to the confessional, the church was empty and dark. Lit votive candles in ruby red glass holders were positioned on each side of the nave adjacent to an exit vestibule. The flicker of each small flame appeared as if there was some sort of competition on which light could grab the most attention, like children raising their hands in class. There was a small metal box with a coin slot. Louis could not make the connection between paying and asking for something with a prayer. Were people giving money to pay for the candles? If someone gave more money, did that give them a better chance of having the prayer heard? How long would those candles stay lit? Each candle represented one person's prayer in hope of something or someone getting better. There were many lit candles on that stand and not one was lit for good news.

The three confessional booths were essentially tiny closets, lined up with the doors facing the back aisle of the church. A priest sat in the middle closet and the two other confessionals were for people to kneel and confess. Louis stood in line behind a couple of older sinners waiting to enter one of the confessionals. Another line formed to go into the confessional on the opposite side. He could hear the murmur of the person's voice through the door. He thought about what he would say. He noticed some people did not take very long in the confessional, while some seemed to be in the closet a bit longer. A boy could easily forget what he planned on confessing while waiting in line.

Finally, an older woman exited and held the door open for Louis to enter. The confessional smelled of aging, finished hardwood with a touch of must but not mold. The scent was perfect for the dark room, leaving Louis with a somber feeling. He knelt on the deep red vinyl pad, clasped his hands, and waited. He heard the muffled drone of the priest and the other sinner. After the voices stopped, there was a pause. He heard the panel to the opposite confessional slide shut, followed by the abrupt opening of the panel directly in front of his face. Taking a deep breath, Louis started the session promptly and correctly:

"Bless me father for I have sinned. This is my first confession since First Communion." His voice began to quiver: "I, um, disobeyed my mom and made her mad—" he paused to think through any sins he committed "—and I lied to my grandmother..."

Louis paused, his heart pounding into his dry mouth, trying to recall any other sins he might have forgotten. "I am sorry for these and all my sins," he said, his words racing down the drag strip of his sentence, fast and conclusive to hopefully end the session mercifully and await his penance.

"Do you remember the prayer for the Act of Contrition?" inquired the priest, speaking much more slowly.

"Yes...," Louis's voice cracked.

The priest instructed him to recite, aloud, that important prayer only used on this occasion. He had not anticipated it. He held no confidence in knowing it. His heart pounded harder with the dread of having to perform it:

"O my God, I am hartly sorry for having fended thee, antidetest all my sins because of thy juspushments, but most of all because they fended thee, my God, who are all-good andizerving of all my love. I firmly rezol, with the help of thy gray, to sinno more and to avoid the neero cashins of sin."

The priest gave out the penance: pray three Hail Marys and one Our Father. The experience raised more questions in Louis's mind. He reasoned that the penance would be reflective of the sins. Then he wondered if more prayer meant more forgiveness. What if he only had time say two Hail Marys? Would anyone know? Would God be upset? How does the priest know what God wants to hear? Despite all these doubts and questions, Louis still followed the priest's instructions and went to pray for forgiveness. He needed to be good until Sunday so he could take part in Communion again.

For the third-grade field trip, the children were bussed to the Michael Todd Theater in the heart of the city. For three hours, they sat in silence and obedience to watch the movie *The Ten Commandments*. That, indeed, was a miracle. The movie reinforced Louis's doubts more than his faith. It left him with questions that would haunt him well into his teenage years. The scenes that stood out begging for more questions revolved around the illustrated powers of God and the harm to innocents. If the Pharaoh was responsible for the slavery of the people of Israel, why punish the entire country? Why and how did God kill the first-born of every Egyptian? Why did God need the blood of slaughtered lambs to tell which homes to leave alone? The movie did little to tell Louis that God was all about love.

Then there was Louis's other influence, his fascination with space travel, astronomy, and science fiction. Initially, it let him depart from a world that suffocated his desire for freedom. Later he admired the adventurous spirit of space exploration. As he approached the teen years, his admiration for men as heroes in space shifted to the wonders of technology. He regarded technology as the real hero and man's eventual true salvation. He learned about the NASA space program with invaluable tutelage by Walter Cronkite on CBS, David Brinkley on NBC, and Jules Bergmann and Frank Reynolds on ABC. When the networks covered the progress of the Gemini missions, he made it a point to tune into the special reports for the latest. One Saturday, he witnessed the live broadcast of the re-entry and splashdown of Gemini VII, piloted by Frank Borman and James Lovell. He retained every detail: the positioning of the capsule and its parts, the amount of heat the capsule was exposed to, the blackout period, the splashdown, and the recovery. He was also an avid follower of Cronkite's futurist weekly documentary program: *The 21st Century*. He marveled at the depiction of future households, drawn to inventions that would make life easier, more predictable, and healthier as reported by the trusting, fatherly voice of Walter Cronkite.

Had there been a class in science fiction at Catholic school, he would have excelled. Thanks to a Sunday afternoon program on the local TV station called *Family Classics*, Louis enjoyed films like *Tobor the Great*, a story about a robot and his inventor's son, *The War of the*

Worlds, The Day the Earth Stood Still, The Time Machine, Journey to the Center of the Earth, and *Mysterious Island.* He also turned on the TV to watch *Star Trek, Lost in Space,* and *The Invaders.*

But nothing was so exciting as the real thing. Soon, the end of the Gemini program gave way to Apollo, the Greek god of prophecy, knowledge, the light, and the sun, and the missions that bore his name.

The missions that would land astronauts on the moon. And how perilous it was.

The dark reality of the dangers of being an astronaut hit him hard when a news bulletin showed on ABC, delivered by science editor Jules Bergmann: An accidental fire on the launching pad had taken the lives of the crew of Apollo I. Virgil Grissom, Ed White, and Roger Chaffee were simulating a launch when a spark ignited into their locked, oxygen-rich capsule.

It took 2 ½ years, but in July of 1969, the Apollo XI astronauts seized the attention of the entire world as they took on the mission to land on the moon. On a warm clear July evening, Louis's parents and grandparents took the 17-inch Sears black-and-white TV that normally sat in a corner by the kitchen table and perched it on a wobbly metal folding serving tray on the back patio. Louis's Nonno spent time working the antenna through every configuration possible with the three major network channels, finally settling for a suitable picture. The family huddled around the small glowing plastic box as they sat on rickety aluminum and woven plastic folding lawn chairs. There was a constant buzzing sound from the TV, which grew louder as the picture got brighter.

Everyone was held captive and silent as they waited to witness Neil Armstrong's first steps on the moon. They watched the transmission from Tranquility Base and strained to hear the immortal words uttered as he descended the ladder to walk on the dusty surface: "That's one small step for man, one giant leap for mankind." Those eleven words made such an impression on Louis that he asked his parents to buy him a scale model of the Apollo command and lunar modules for his twelfth birthday. After painstakingly assembling the Monogram kit, he impressed his family and friends with accurate re-enactments of the historic event, vividly retelling all the details.

Louis Silvani's attitude about his Catholic upbringing was reinforced upon attending the public high school, finally liberated from the stifling and rigid environment of Catholic school. No more did he have to go through the ordeal of sitting through the same lessons of sin, penance, and redemption. Nor was he subjected to the graphic descriptions of bloody bodily harm, pain, and unbearable suffering from the crucifixion. World geography covered the entire world, not just places known for Catholic shrines or rituals. He immersed himself in science classes for the first time. In English, he was introduced to critical thinking, world literature, and plays. In his junior year, he even heard someone in a position of authority question religion. His class was assigned to read Harper Lee's *To Kill a Mockingbird*. One passage read:

> Sometimes the Bible in the hand of one man is worse than a whisky bottle in the hand of (another)....There are just some kind of men who—who're so busy worrying about the next world they've never learned to live in this one, and you can look down the street and see the results.

Louis felt emancipated by the message.

After discovering the riches offered in high school, Louis reasoned that Catholic school was focused on just one thing, which diminished the greatness of the individual human spirit. Shouldn't beliefs be truly personal? No two people have the exact same idea about the afterlife or what "god" is. Institutions that are established to indoctrinate young minds can sometimes work against themselves when the ideas are presented impersonally, using fear. He left an environment where ideas were transmitted in one direction, from teacher or preacher to student, and entered a place where students were allowed to cultivate their own perceptions and teachers encouraged questions, discussion, and analysis of what was being taught.

He learned about people of character and about the tendency of the human ego to get in the way of the common good, resulting in failures and sometimes disasters. He learned about the power of human will and determination against mighty odds, sometimes by examples given in classical conflicts in literature—including man versus God. He learned about Greek mythology. He was fascinated by how the ancients would explain such things as earthquakes, floods, thunder, volcanoes, mountains, the ocean, and the planets and stars, using stories, fables, and myths about beings superior to humans—gods. All this reinforced his hardening belief that Catholic school served to censor the world from young minds; a place where children were participants of a cultural screening. A space where the minds should have grown intellectually from science and the arts was instead crammed with a monochromatic, shallow perspective that discouraged free thought and sought to control by fear, guilt, and self-consciousness.

7

BACK TO THAT SAME OL' PLACE

Eventually, I think Chicago will be the most beautiful great city left in the world. —Frank Lloyd Wright

Even with the obligatory construction zones and congestion at the Indiana/Illinois border, Louis arrived home at a decent hour for a Saturday night. Exhausted, he took his laptop inside and left his suitcase in the trunk. It was about nine o'clock, and there were a few things he needed to do before turning in for the night. Most importantly, he needed to make a couple of calls, one of pressing concern.

"Hello, Louis, what's up?" The woman's voice sounded gentle, but not happy to hear him. "Why are you calling? You get the kids *next* weekend, right?"

"Hi, Laura. Yes, you're right, I am supposed to have the kids next weekend." Louis's tone toward his ex-wife remained unchanged, though inside, he felt deep relief she was okay after the ominous warning in Pittsburgh.

"Supposed to? Are you not going to be able to take them next week? They always look forward to seeing you."

Louis took a deep breath before responding. "Laura…something came up. I'm going a on a trip out west. I…I don't know when I will return. I was wondering if I could see the kids tomorrow. I leave in a couple days."

"Louis, if you want them, it will have to be late in the afternoon. Hold on."

Louis could hear Laura tell the kids that their father wanted to see them tomorrow. "If you want to be with him, you need to finish all homework before tomorrow afternoon," she added. After a little more discussion of the conditions, she was back on the line with Louis.

"When were you thinking of coming to get them?" Laura asked.

"When is the earliest I could do that?"

A brief pause, then, "Four o'clock is fine."

"Thanks."

"Just have them home by nine."

There was no animosity between the divorced couple. Laura felt pity for Louis, thinking he had wasted so much time on wild ideas and being immersed in disclosure activity. He had a loving and happy family until he became obsessed with all the research and writing. Louis was content to see his ex-wife and children in a stable home.

He went to his laptop case, took out the sheet of notebook paper with Velarde's number, and called her cell phone. Mary Ellen did not answer. He left a brief message to tell her that he was in Chicago and wanted to arrange the trip with her. He ended the call by telling her that she could call him "anytime tonight," leaving a return number.

After completing his phone calls, he logged onto social network. After checking notifications and responding, he advised friends of his impending trip west. First, he looked up a good friend in the Saint Louis area, Deborah Swift, an Air Force Security Police veteran and a gay-rights activist. Louis met her and Susan years ago during a business trip. Deborah had a landscaping business with her long-time partner, Susan Koenig. She also had an interest in ufology and trusted Louis on the information he gave her. He sent a message telling her he would see her on Tuesday and informed her of his travelling companion, Mary Ellen.

Louis then sent a message to an Army colonel stationed at Fort Carson, Colorado, who once worked with Louis. They sometimes met at quarterly design conferences and corresponded with each other through email. Colonel Gerald McGeorge avoided social media. Louis had never talked about UFOs with McGeorge but felt the need to include the colonel on his itinerary. In his message, Louis advised McGeorge of the dates he and his traveling companion, Mary Ellen Velarde, would be near Fort Carson. As an afterthought, Louis sent him the coordinates to the sites in Antarctica, Australia, and China showing suspected UFO/ET activity, using the Google Earth application.

Using social media, he contacted a longtime friend in North Los Angeles, Trevor Hugo. Louis asked Trevor if he and Mary Ellen could stop at his place on the way to Mount Shasta. Louis remained on social media and browsed the newsfeed. *Not much news, but a lot of feed*, he thought.

Louis went to his group, Unbounded Encounters. One member had posted another article on ascension and 5D activation. In the event of ascension, the world would phase into a higher dimension. 5D activation asserts that rays or beams from celestial events eventually affect human DNA and cause a jump to a higher dimension. Considered messages of hope, these beliefs had resurfaced over and over for at least a decade. Louis did not accept Ascension as truth; it sounded like a dogmatic promise of another religion. He never challenged those posts publicly, feeling the messages were well intentioned by people tired of the hell on earth humans had made for themselves. Louis was just closing the page on his social media site when his cell phone chimed.

"Hello, this is Louis," he said excitedly.

"Mr. Silvani, this is Mary Ellen Velarde. I didn't expect to hear from you until tomorrow."

"Yes, I know that's what I told you this morning. I couldn't wait. I wanted to confirm I would go west with you. When do you want to leave? I'll need to get some things for the trip."

"We could leave Tuesday," she said.

"Good. I can pick you up. Where will you be?"

"I'll be in Aurora." Mary Ellen gave Louis the address.

"OK. I'll call you before I leave. I hope to visit a friend in Saint Louis, so we should leave no later than noon Tuesday."

"That's fine. I look forward to your call." They ended the call soon after.

Before closing his laptop, he noticed a friend request from a woman on social media. Louis saw that he and the woman had a mutual friend, so he accepted her. Realizing it was time for bed, he closed the social media page and shut down the computer.

Louis often experienced lucid dreams. One recurring theme was levitation. He also fought off dreams that made him wonder about the mind. In one dream, he recalled being surrounded by people speaking Chinese. Amazingly, he understood what they were saying. It made him wonder if there might be data in our brains only accessible in a subconscious state. He wondered if humans held more knowledge than exhibited. Sleep usually came easily, without the need for chemicals. He trained himself to fall asleep at will in the service, participating in week-long exercises that would require continuous hours without it. This night would be no different.

Louis had another unique dream. He envisioned floating or lingering in the clouds above Earth. As he looked down, the clouds dispersed, and he made out the image of a large medieval fortress built in the form of two equal squares on center, transposed forty-five degrees. The fortress was surrounded by a large grassy field. In the background he heard a chant like that of a Tibetan monk he had recorded for meditation years ago. As gradually as it had appeared, the fortress faded and disappeared, ending the dream.

He awoke to a cool Sunday morning in early fall, ready to finish a few things before picking up the kids. After breakfast he checked social media and news on his laptop. As he scrolled his page, something caught his immediate attention: the image of the fortress from his dream. It was posted by the woman that requested a social media friendship the night before. Louis looked at it closely and recognized it was not a fortress but an aerial photograph of a crop circle in England. Louis was mystified by the synchronicity. He studied the image realizing it was a symbol depicting chakras he had on a wall tapestry in his room. *First the wormhole, now this crop circle*, he thought.

Louis noticed he had messages from people he had contacted the night before. Deborah Swift replied, she said she would be happy to have him and Mary Ellen visit. Louis acknowledged her message, indicating he would call her before reaching Saint Louis. Trevor Hugo also replied, saying he was looking forward to seeing Louis and Mary Ellen. He provided his phone number. The two messages were good news. McGeorge had not responded.

It bothered him that he had never visited either Dulce or Mount Shasta. How and why was Mary Ellen so confident going there? He wondered. Dulce presented potentially eerie scenarios that could place them in degrees of danger requiring extraordinary actions.

"I am no extraordinary person," he said to himself.

Louis recognized he wasn't ready for Dulce; there were too many unknowns. Turning to his laptop, he searched the net for more information about the underground base. He visited many of the sites that appeared from his earlier research. Readjusting his posture and determined to be focused, he revisited them to ensure he did not overlook anything critical. He found nothing to help him beyond what he already knew.

The lack of information about the specific location, its size, or population made the risks appear too high. He thought that maybe he and Mary Ellen should just go near the site instead of trying to enter the restricted area.

"It will just be a hike, we'll take some pictures, maybe talk to the locals and then go on our way without incident," he said aloud, trying to convince himself.

Thoughts drifted away from the underground lair to mystical Mount Shasta. He'd heard nothing but good things; it was a spiritual place, and if there were beings, they would be benevolent and welcoming. This was a much more enjoyable search. There were pages of stories about legends of the mountain, and even more pages about sightings punctuated by colorful orbs.

Louis retrieved his suitcase from his car and unpacked his clothes from the two-day trip. He laid the items for his next trip alongside the open suitcase. Aside from the appropriate clothing for the climate, he added rain gear, a compass, a pocketknife, and a felt fedora style hat. Taking stock of what he had, he decided he needed light-weight hiking shoes, socks, and a backpack. Although he was still in good physical condition for his age, Louis was not an avid hiker. He figured he would rely on Mary Ellen to lead the way once they got on any trail. He would shop at an outdoors sporting goods store after work the next day to complete his packing list.

Satisfied with his selections and plans, he checked messages. Colonel McGeorge still had not responded. Louis preferred a response by now, but he wasn't worried. Then he switched gears, making plans for his day with the kids. The drive to the affluent suburb of Hinsdale took about an hour on a good day. A fall Sunday in Chicago meant football. The Bears game would be getting over just when Louis left to get the kids. Looking out the window toward Soldier Field, he could see traffic building from early tailgaters. When it was time, he gave himself another forty-five minutes to avoid the football fans that would choke up west-bound traffic.

Louis left the townhouse early but made it to his destination just in time. Hinsdale was a well-established, mid-sized suburb where city executives had access to Metra rail while still residing close to the city. Laura, her husband, twelve-year-old Alex, and ten-year-old

Elsa lived in an older neighborhood near the train station. The homes were small but distinctive. Those homes had character and were not the architecturally confused and pretentious McMansions that plagued suburbs the further one stationed themselves away from the city. Louis parked his not-so-new compact car behind Laura's luxury SUV and waited. The front door opened and Alex and Elsa ran out to their father.

"Hi, Papa!" the kids said happily as they got in.

Since the divorce about four years ago, Louis made it a point not to lose touch with his kids. He felt fortunate Laura and the kids stayed in the area. After the divorce, he dedicated every other weekend, every holiday, and birthday to his children. He also spent time helping them with school work—mostly art and math, and their sport activities. Louis wanted to remain a strong influence on their growth. When Elsa had her tonsils taken out, Louis took time off work to visit her. How every family man used his free time was not Louis's concern, but he thought that given that the length of time of childhood is so limited, why would a father not take as much advantage of that time with his children as possible? Louis's effort to spend more time with his kids was his way to make up for the lost time when the family was together. Today, he wanted to show them a part they rarely saw in him: his fun and playful side. The kids tossed their backpacks in the car, put on their seatbelts, and asked where they were going.

"Millennium Park," Louis said. "We'll get there around five-thirty. You'll be able to see the city light up. It's a nice evening for a walk there." Louis hoped that when the kids were old enough, they would take the train into the city to see him. Those hopeful thoughts were met with some discouragement, as they played their video games while he was asking them about school and life at home. "Oh, well," Louis said disappointedly. Mercifully, the gaming did not last long and as they neared the city, and the children engaged in conversation.

Louis pointed to the University of Illinois campus he attended. Asking about those years, the children reminded Louis how life had changed with technology.

"You didn't have a computer when you went to college? There was no internet? No one had a cellphone to call people?" asked Alex.

"Papa, I feel so sad for you not having those things when you were younger. I bet people were so lonely," said Elsa.

"We kept informed through television—thirteen channels if you were near a city before you got cable TV. And telephones were connected to buildings with wires, so people could still call each other," replied Louis.

The children were somewhat shocked by Louis's explanation of his past. They had no response.

"We can talk about that later." Louis was aware that he could spend an entire evening responding to those questions, but there were more important things to discuss. He paused and then changed the subject. He pointed to another building where his Nonna had worked as a seamstress, sewing men's suits for years. He told them her company had great Christmas parties at Medinah Temple where all the kids received cool toys.

"Really? What kind of toys, Papa?" inquired Alex.

"Games. I got Careers one year, Stratego after that."

Alex and Elsa looked at each other, confused. "They're classic board games," Louis said. "Stratego is still around."

Still no response. Louis did not know if it was due to lack of interest or just a complete lack of any clue about the board game concept. Louis decided to avoid further conversation about his primitive past.

The children continued to gape at the sights as they approached the city. They followed Congress Parkway under the massive building that was the main post office, later part of the set for the *Dark Knight* motion picture. After passing over the Chicago River, they drew closer to the edge of the Loop: the business and shopping district named for the L, elevated train tracks that encircled it.

Louis parked the car in the Michigan Avenue garage. They exited and made their way to the Monroe lobby. "Let's walk toward those towers with the faces. They are actually fountains."

They arrived to find children of all ages playing there. Alex and Elsa quickened their pace to get to Crown Fountain. Louis enjoyed the whimsical nature and smiled, watching the kids run about barefoot in the early fall evening. Alex and Elsa splashed playfully.

"Hey guys, let's go get something to eat, then we'll walk around again. We can stay until eight." Louis took them to a sandwich shop on Michigan Ave across from the Art Institute. As they sat down with their dinner orders, Alex started by asking Louis if it was true that he was going on a trip out west. Louis replied that he was.

"Mom said you told her you don't know when you'll be back," Alex said.

"That's true. I am going to places that are special for my research," explained Louis.

A look of concern crossed Elsa's face. "Why don't you know when you are coming back?"

"Well, there are a lot of things that I do not know. I've never been to either place, but I am going with a Native American woman who lives in one of those places. She is Jicarilla Apache."

"What do you think you'll find, Papa?" A conversation with Alex was unlike a conversation with any other eleven-year-old.

"That's a great question, Alex." Louis almost choked as he sipped his drink and thought about how he should respond. There were so many possible scenarios that could play out on this trip, some better than others. "I hope to find something I can use to support my presentations."

Elsa followed with another question. "Where does the Native American live?" *Was she his daughter? Interviewer? Or interrogator?* Louis wondered.

"Dulce, New Mexico. She lives on a reservation."

"Is that the only place you are going?" asked Alex.

"No. I plan to go to Mount Shasta, too. In California. The Native American woman knows that place, too."

"What is there to see at Mount Shasta, Papa?"

"For many years now, Mount Shasta has been known to be a spiritual place. The Native Americans have many stories about it. People have told stories about seeing flying orange balls," explained Louis. "I hope to be able see something special there."

Louis and the kids finished their meal and continued to talk. "Aren't you scared?" Elsa showed her concern for her father again.

"What is there to be afraid of?" Louis smiled as he lied.

"Why aren't you scared, Papa? I would be afraid of going far away and not knowing what could happen!" Elsa raised her voice to stress her point.

"I think if Papa were afraid, he probably wouldn't go, Elsa. I'm sure Papa knows what he is doing," said Alex.

Louis silently winked and nodded to Elsa. He was afraid, but not as afraid or concerned as he was about his family. He stopped and reached out to caress his children on their faces, as yet unscarred by the hard knocks of living. Louis got them to finish their drinks and pick up their trash as they left.

Heading back to the park, Alex and Elsa played around the Cloud Gate, which looked like a giant blob of mercury. The locals affectionately call the stainless-steel sculpture The Bean. The kids frolicked around it, looking for their reflection in the distorted image. After spending time there, Louis led them to Pritzker Pavilion, designed by Frank Gehry. Louis explained that the head dress of the concert stage appeared as canvas sails in the wind. He led them to the serpentine pedestrian bridge and walked over Columbus Drive, then followed the bridge walkway as it wound and snaked. Louis then directed them to The Skating Ribbon, a challenging wide layout with two hairpin turns and a few gradual curves. In the winter, it attracted ice skaters. They walked past structures that offered varied degrees of difficulty in climbing.

Louis knew they had to make their way south back to the Monroe elevator lobby, but before that, they stopped at the Play Garden in Maggie Daley Park. The ribbons of walkways in the Enchanted Forest let them run around and chase each other. The articulate Tower Bridge had many large-scale slides and tubes. Louis let them free to enjoy themselves. He sat down to watch them in the open colorful play area. They remained in their imaginary world, insulated from any worries. He appreciated the moment, hoping the time would never pass.

Then it passed too quickly. "OK, kids, we need to start heading back to the car so I get you home before Mom gets worried. You have school tomorrow," Louis called out.

The kids reluctantly stopped their play and joined their father to walk back to the car. Louis took the time to bend down and hug them extra tightly, finishing with a kiss on their foreheads. He guided them back to the parking garage entrance. They made it to the car easily, and Louis was able to leave the city without delay. The kids dozed off until Louis pulled into their driveway at the agreed-upon nine o'clock hour. As they awoke from their short nap, they gathered their backpacks and opened their car doors. Louis joined them. They quickly went to him, and he hugged them both before they walked away to the door being held open for them.

Laura gave a half-hearted wave to Louis as the kids walked through their front door, and he waved back. He drove away, satisfied to see the children before the trip. He was ready to call it a night.

Before turning in, he decided to see if Colonel McGeorge had responded to his message. Louis checked his in-box and found a response from the Colonel. It was short:

"Hey Buddy. Good to hear from you! Yes, I will be here when you arrive. I would love to have another good talk with you. Call me when you get close to Colorado Springs. God bless."

Louis was satisfied by the day. It was a good one. He now had responses from all the people he wanted to visit on the trip. Everything was topped by a pleasant visit with the kids. He would get a good sleep, head to work, and then take care of loose ends so everything would be ready for his journey west.

8

THE ASSIGNMENT

There is one spectacle grander than the sea, that is the sky; there is one spectacle grander than the sky, that is the interior of the soul. —Victor Hugo

Louis's daily commute consisted of taking two subways, then a short walk to the Wintrust Bank Building. It took him less than a half-hour to get to work, and there was no exorbitant parking fee to pay. Monday was usually a slow day at the US Army Corps of Engineers' Chicago District office. But not an uneventful one. Before the day ended, he had been approved to take leave for the rest of the week and all of the following week. Louis was getting jittery. Not normally a clock watcher, he found himself checking the time with every passing hour.

After work, he took the subway north to Chicago Avenue. List in hand, he headed to the outdoors store in the John Hancock building to buy the items for the trip. He drove home, hastily prepared dinner, then packed his luggage. He loaded his new backpack with all his new purchases and some personal electronics, handwarmers, a sweatshirt, pocket knife, compass, toiletries, an e-reader, and charging cables, leaving space for food and drink.

Before turning in, he studied various satellite images of Dulce, New Mexico, looking for signs of the underground base reported by whistleblowers. He looked for a river or creek that would provide water for the base, and dirt roads leading to clearings. He found numerous clearings and a stream where one person had reported a dam. Nothing stood out from the rest of the landscape. If it was there, the base was well camouflaged. He didn't bother looking at routes to get to Dulce, trusting Mary Ellen would know the way.

When Louis switched his subject of study to Mount Shasta, he was surprised to see how close the mountain was to Oregon. He engaged in a virtual hike around the massive peak, identifying three caves and noting their locations before shutting down for the night. Enthusiastic and energized, Louis wanted to leave *immediately*. He called Mary Ellen to advise he was about to leave. She and her friend were looking forward to his visit. It was a short call.

Louis easily found the Aurora address near the city center. He parked his car on the crumbling concrete drive plagued by crabgrass and weeds. The drive ran alongside the vacant-looking house. Like the discarded veteran pan-handling across the street, it appeared empty, lacking vitality. Stepping out of the car, Louis's conscience made his head turn to face the panhandler. Cars stopped at the intersection, but no one acknowledged the man with his card board sign that read, "HOMELESS IRAQ WAR VET. PLEASE HELP. GOD BLESS." Louis negotiated the crosswalk and stopped. The panhandler looked Louis up and down, his stoic expression unchanged. Louis spoke to him.

"I'm a veteran too. Air Force."

"Army."

Before Louis asked the next question, the panhandler interjected. "You're probably wondering why I'm here asking for money."

"No. I know why you are here."

"Oh, So, you know what happened to me in Iraq? You know what I saw? What I lived with every day? What finally broke me?"

"No. That's not what I mean. You're here because of our failed society."

Louis bent down to the panhandler's level, next to him. "Thanking you for your service, but being ignored when you need help is an empty gesture."

The panhandler put down his sign and turned to Louis. "So, are you going to help me?"

"What are you trying to do?"

"Man, I'm just surviving day by day."

"Have you tried to get help at the VA?"

"Hines? Man—Maywood was OK for John Prine, not me. I'm staying away from the VA. It's depressing, and there's too many people like me and not enough good people that could help. And don't want to get on no drugs. That treatment will get you hooked and killed."

"You like the Mailman?"

"I got to know his music from our platoon leader. You know that song about old people?"

"'Hello in There'?"

"Yeah. That's what I see when I go the VA. It's not right, man. Not right."

"You want to change that? Go and be a volunteer. They deserve it. You'll feel better about yourself."

Louis reached for his wallet, took out a twenty-dollar bill, and handed it to the man.

"Here. This should help a bit. Right now, your best chance is the VA. Consider it another challenge."

The man took the money.

"Thanks," he said, looking straight into Louis's eyes. Then he nodded.

Louis held his hand out, and the man reached and held it.

"It's been a while since a stranger shook my hand," he said still holding on.

"Go volunteer and you could shake more friendly hands. I hope you get the care you deserve."

The man released the grip. Without adding a word, he followed Louis with his eyes as Louis walked back to cross the street.

The two-story wood-framed bungalow was in need of care, its blue clapboard siding faded. The trim around the windows was weathered with some dry rot. A wood-framed addition enclosed the front porch. The roof appeared to sag slightly at the ridge and there were no gutters. Another one-story addition with oversized windows was built on the back of the modest-sized house. There were small windows in the cellar facing the drive that were boarded inside.

Louis walked toward the front of the lot and navigated the uneven weathered concrete sidewalk to the house. Cars and trucks passed closely on the busy state route. The entrance to the house was on the opposite side of the enclosed porch. Its concrete stoop led to four concrete steps aided by a loose, rusted wrought iron handrail. The landing at the top of the steps was just big enough to accept one visitor. There was no doorbell or screen door. Louis knocked on the chipped and weathered wood door. He heard the release of a deadbolt and felt the jiggle of the loose door knob.

Mary Ellen opened the door. "Hello, Mr. Silvani! You made it here in good time!"

"Yeah, not much traffic going westbound in the morning. I thought I would get here early in case you wanted to leave earlier."

Louis walked into the musty front porch. Old newspapers were placed near the door to the house. The floor was a worn, lime green carpet, while the walls were worn with cracks under some of the water-damaged window sills, along with stains from leaks. An old couch with a wilderness print stood in the room against the original wall. Its arms were well worn, with one being stained. He wouldn't have been surprised if it had been salvaged from the curb.

"Oh, Mr. Silvani, I thought you may want to at least meet my dear friend and have a snack or lunch with us before we leave."

Mary Ellen opened the door to the house. The side of the door facing the porch including its metal hinges were painted white. She entered first, going to the aid of her friend. Louis stopped and stood still, looking around the room, not noticing a gray-haired woman with a cane on the opposite side of the room.

"Mr. Silvani? This is my dear friend, Anne Stoneburner. Anne? This is Louis Silvani, UFO/ET researcher and lecturer."

"Hello, Louis." Anne's greeting was casual and comfortable. "Mary Ellen said you wanted to leave early. I hope you stay for a bit. There is so much to talk about. I am delighted to have visitors. It has been a while since I've had anyone here who didn't come just to help with the house."

Mary Ellen looked at Louis as if to say, *See? I told you so.*

"Hello, thank you for having me over. This is an interesting room you have here."

Louis understated his impression. The room was a combination of a Mardi Gras festival and elements of Eastern religion symbology. Its walls were purple, green, and yellow. Even the ceiling was yellow. Bright tapestries of Sanskrit and Hindu symbols and a rainbow-colored peace sign adorned the walls. The small front room was furnished with a short, square, traditional Japanese-styled mahogany table. Around the table were brightly colored pillows. The stressed wood floor and window frames were painted a warm putty gray, while the side of the door facing the room was flat indigo blue. He noticed a fragrant incense. The pass-through to the kitchen was closed. On the shelf was a figurine of Jesus, a blue lava lamp, and a brass incense burner. Music from a woodwind instrument, likely a flute, played softly.

"The room is me, Louis. Before Hurricane Katrina, I lived near the Ninth Ward," Anne explained. "One night, while I was sitting in my bed meditating, my guardian appeared, instructing me to leave. I gathered as much as I could in my hatchback and called a friend in Joliet. I moved in with her until I was able to support myself. There was nothing left of my house in New Orleans. My guardians have never steered me wrong."

She patted a pillow, motioning to Louis. "Come, sit down." Anne maneuvered carefully, using the table for support as she knelt across from Louis. Mary Ellen followed.

"What incense are you burning?" Louis asked curiously.

"Anise stars. They help open your third eye chakra. I hoped to have a short meditation before we talk. Is that alright?" Louis nodded, pleasing Mary Ellen.

Anne guided her guests through a brief meditation session. Self-conscious and the novice, Louis concentrated on his breathing. He was the first to open his eyes, followed by Mary Ellen. Anne remained with eyes closed, and still, then began to speak:

"We will talk to you through her. We have been watching you. You are doing as intended. Follow your spirit and guides that have led you here. Listen to our ward. She is pure in spirit. She works on our behalf. When we do this, her head will hurt, and she will need some time to recover. We do not intend harm. The indigenous one has been sent as a guardian. Listen to her, too. We are leaving now."

Anne opened her eyes, placing her hand on her forehead. Acknowledging her pain, she asked Mary Ellen to get her a pain reliever. Louis sat still and silent watching Mary Ellen, as she left the table. Louis questioned Anne about what had just happened. She had no recollection of what she had said, but understood. "They communicate through me. There have been times at the computer chatting with someone, I would find that I had typed entire paragraphs without being conscious, only realizing what happened, after reading the words."

"*They?*" inquired Louis.

Mary Ellen overheard the question. "The Watchers," the women replied simultaneously. "The ones I told you about at the conference," Mary Ellen added.

"They want us to evolve spiritually. It is in the universe's best interest we evolve," Anne said matter-of-factly.

"The Watchers began to communicate to me after I met Anne online in a social network group about UFOs."

Louis looked in Mary Ellen's direction as she returned with the pills and handed them to Anne before heading back to the kitchen.

"Can we talk more about you, Louis? Mary Ellen told me about the conference and the mysterious men." She leaned over the table, clasping her hands together, and looked directly at him. "There is something special about you." She paused. "I would like to communicate with your spirit...here...today." She eased back into her sitting position. "I will only do it with your permission. Will you let me, Louis?"

"Why do you want to communicate with my spirit?" Then in an apologetic manner, Louis added, "I'm not saying no; I'm just curious what you expect to find."

Anne's voice elevated with eagerness. "I want to learn things about you that you might not know yourself. I could help you understand what is happening." She calmed herself. "Everything has a reason, Louis. You are not here by accident. The journey you are taking with Mary Ellen is part of a larger plan made long before you were born."

Mary Ellen overheard Anne's conversation as she carried a bamboo tray supporting a light gray ceramic teapot with a wooden handle, three drab *yonumi* Japanese tea cups, and small thin white paper napkins. Setting the tray on the table, she poured the tea and offered a cup to Anne, then Louis before she served herself.

"I agree with everything Anne said. You owe it to yourself to find out what makes you special," asserted Mary Ellen.

"You guys make it sound like I'm some sort of hero character, like Neo in *The Matrix*," Louis joked as he picked up the tea cup.

"That is not very far from the truth, Louis," corrected Anne, taking her first sip.

Louis sat, stunned. He was speechless looking at his cup, watching the steam rise.

Mary Ellen interrupted his silence. "Mr. Silvani, are you alright? We are all special. Our spirits make us that way. How would people treat each other if they knew every human body had a special spirit that happened to be one of the most magnificent things in the universe? Anne is giving you a chance to look inside yourself."

Louis continued to look down. "I had a dream last night. I was in a large room, misty and gray. I was surrounded by living corpses, and I was lying next to a nude woman who had greyish skin. I said 'ouch' after feeling a twinge on my side, and all the corpses looked at me and stared. After the woman told me I was not dead yet, I felt a strong pull away from the scene, ascending, in short strong tugs. Then I found myself on an operating table, and I woke up. It was one of the most literal and lucid dreams I ever had."

Anne looked at him assuredly. "Louis, you have ascended to a higher plane; you were pulled out of that life into a better life. Not all of us have done this! It is a good sign."

Louis sensed his life was about to turn a corner. He looked up from his cup at Mary Ellen first, then at Anne. "Okay Anne . . . I'll let you communicate with my spirit," he said softly.

Anne thanked Louis and slowly savored the last of her tea. Louis gulped what was left in his cup. Mary Ellen finished her tea, stood up, collected the empty cups and napkins, and walked to the kitchen. Anne asked Mary Ellen to turn off the music before beginning her session.

"I will summon my guides and your spirit to learn about your spiritual past. Having you here will be a benefit."

Mary Ellen emerged from the kitchen and sat down again.

"First, I will call my guides, who I am familiar with. They will only assist if they sense your intentions are noble." She looked off to her right. "They tell me you are pure and benevolent."

"Thank you?" Louis said, unsure whether it was a compliment or a nice way of stating he was new and thus ignorant of the proceedings at hand.

"They appreciate your innocence," she smiled. "Now I will ask for assistance from Archangel Michael who often helps me. Well, it is not Michael the being as much as it is a being from the echelon of *Michael*. The being appears to me as Michael, although what I think is Michael is really an *order* of benevolent inter-dimensionals, each having the role of *Michael*. Does that make sense to you, Louis?"

"So, there is no one Michael. *Michael* refers to a functional role in the angelic realm."

"Yes. The angelic ones have various roles based on the echelon. Have you communicated to your guides? Do you know who they are?"

"I think one of my guides is my father; he shows up in dreams at critical times. I think my grandmother assists in guidance too."

Anne continued, "And now, with help, I will summon your spirit." A long pause ensued as she read him. "You have an old spirit, having been on this planet before." She paused again, listening to her helpers. "Your spirit separated in 1714 in Siberia from the body of a shaman woman who died a widow at fifty-four. She was spiritually connected and awakened, having contact with angels." Louis's attention was fixed on every word. "Michael and your spirit inform me it was your last incarnation, and your spirit ascended, enjoying union with others."

There was a long pause as her face blushed and her eyes teared up. She moved back from the table, pursed her lips, and swallowed.

"What's the matter?" Mary Ellen asked, concern in her eyes.

Anne took her time before answering. "I have heard stories, but I have never met a spirit like yours, Louis. I was right. There is something special here. Thank you so much for being here. I am humbled."

Louis looked at Mary Ellen with a puzzled look.

"Mr. Silvani, your spirit was rewarded for the previous spiritual life with ascension to a higher level, yet here you are. Do you realize what happened? During communion with other spirits, it took an assignment to come back to this life to assist in the spiritual evolution of humanity!

"You ARE Neo!" joked Mary Ellen. Louis was shocked, nervous, silent, and about to tear up himself.

"Mary Ellen? This is nothing to joke about," corrected Anne politely. "Mr. Silvani, Michael tells me that in return for your assignment, you will *jump* existences. Instead of ascending, you will ascend two levels."

Once again, Louis did not know what to think with all this new information. He was uncomfortable. He thought about not being able to be with loved ones again if this were all true.

"Mr. Silvani, I feel blessed to be with your spirit. Michael is telling me to give you, the human, the opportunity to accept or refuse the arrangement your spirit entered into."

"Are you saying that I have a choice not to take the assignment my spirit took?" Louis asked, a hint of incredulity in his voice. "I don't even know what I am supposed to do! How can I make an informed decision like that?" He was flustered.

"Mr. Silvani, your spirit will guide you. It would not lead you into a situation you could not handle. You will have help." Anne was echoing what Michael was communicating to her. "Michael is saying that you are free to accept or deny the task."

Louis looked at Mary Ellen and she looked at him curiously, moving back from the table indicating she wanted no part in the decision. Louis imagined voiding the spiritual contract and reasoned it would be unwise, *forever* being known for doing that. He also had two witnesses that looked upon him as someone special. "Tell Michael I accept the role." Louis's tone was confident and assertive, surprising even himself.

"Michael says thank you and that your guides and your spirit will be with you throughout your assignment."

Relief filled Anne's voice as she smiled more than she could remember doing in a long time. Anne's words also made Louis feel like he was enlisting again. "Michael is also asking me to give you specific meditation instructions. He calls it, *'Jesus is the golden ray.'* Listen carefully and take notes if you wish."

Mary Ellen got up to get her sack. She took out the notebook she carried at the conference, ripped out another page, and handed it to Louis with a pen. Louis wrote as Anne resumed the instruction:

"Louis, imagine sitting in a crystal pyramid, then imagine golden light, which is the spirit of Jesus, filling the pyramid, entering your crown chakra. Imagine the light flowing slowly through your body, impacting your DNA. Above all, listen. Listen to your guides. Quiet the body and the mind. That is all Michael asks."

She stopped and looked at Louis. "Louis, may I read your spirit again for a life before being a shaman?" She was eager to find out more.

Louis nodded. "Sure, I am interested too."

"Thank you." She resumed her reading. "The location was western Mexico. The date of passage was 902 AD. Your spirit was in the body of a twenty-six-year-old Aztec warrior. Michael is telling me you have a friend in this life in the military, and his spirit was in the body of a friend of the warrior. Your spirits were together before."

Louis thought, *McGeorge?!* He knew no other active-duty friend in the armed forces. It made sense to him since they got along so well.

"Michael has some more advice. Enjoy peace. Release yourself of guilt. See the light of God in others. Learn to forgive. He also tells me the ocean is a healer for your spirit; you should visit it as often as possible." She ended the session by thanking Michael, her guides, and Louis's spirit.

Louis looked at Mary Ellen. "This is not going to be a casual trip, is it?" Her expression bared knowledge he did not possess. Keeping it that way, she did not respond.

Anne interrupted. "Trust your spirit, Louis. It has not misguided you. Follow Michael's meditation. Oh, and do keep your trust in Mary Ellen. She knows what she is doing and will not betray you." Anne finished her statement with a nod and a smile of confidence, directing it to the younger Native American woman. "Speaking of travel, I think you two should best get on your way."

They all stood from their cushions. Louis helped Anne as Mary Ellen went to retrieve her luggage. Louis took the bags to the car. Anne, still stiff from sitting, hobbled with her cane to the kitchen to get food and drink she had prepared earlier for the trip. Mary Ellen went back to the kitchen to help Anne, who looked at her with concern.

"So now he has an idea this is not going to be a vacation," Anne said. "On one hand I am concerned about him being ready, spiritually for what may come, and on the other . . ."

"He is ready. He *has* to be ready. This is his fate. And . . . I . . . will be with him. I think I heard you say that I am his guardian," Mary Ellen said emphatically.

"About this trip, do you have a plan, Mary Ellen, and are you going to let Louis in on it?"

"I believe *they* will not let us down," Mary Ellen stated with conviction. "It's not just going to be Louis and me, or this would not be happening. The *universe* is ready." Mary Ellen's words sounded like a line from a movie trailer.

Anne stopped badgering Mary Ellen and placed a hand on her shoulder.

Louis packed the trunk and programmed his phone with Deborah Swift's address. He was concerned about time so he quickened his pace. He opened the front door, entering the enclosed porch. The door to the house was ajar. Approaching the door, he heard Anne say his name. He stopped to listen to every word from Mary Ellen's response. After Mary Ellen was done, he opened the door completely and announced the car was packed.

"It was truly an honor to meet you, Anne; what an amazing experience! I'll use the information from this visit and revere it." Louis hugged Anne, thanking her.

"Well, Louis, that makes two of us. I hope you understand you have an exceptional existence. Trust your guides, the spiritual ones, and the one that is with you in person." Anne motioned to where Mary Ellen was standing.

"Got it." Louis nodded solemnly. Directing his attention to Mary Ellen, he looked at her without a blink and asked her, "Are *we* ready?"

The question took her by surprise, as if a little secret was revealed about her. She did not speak, but offered a slow nod, looking at Louis in a manner he had not seen before. His question unnerved her. As Mary Ellen bid goodbye, Anne requested she keep in touch with her throughout the trip.

They left in an awkward silence.

9

INTUITION

Because I feel that, in the Heavens above,
The angels, whispering to one another,
Can find, among their burning terms of love
None so devotional as that of "Mother"

—*Edgar Allen Poe*

Louis and Mary Ellen got in the car, neither saying a word. Louis was having second thoughts. He felt as if he had just rushed into some sort of existential mortgage, having overheard part of the conversation between Mary Ellen and Anne. Was Mary Ellen keeping vital information about the trip to herself? The possibility concerned him. He recognized he was entering into a situation for which he was not prepared, and he felt she was being unfair. His mind started to wander, working against his fragile self-confidence, questioning his confidence in Mary Ellen. But since he'd accepted this role, he had no other choice than to follow her.

No words were exchanged until they reached the Interstate. Then, "Who are you and what exactly is the purpose of this trip?" Louis asked.

Mary Ellen did not respond immediately. Finally, she followed with a question of her own. "What did you hear Anne and I talk about?" She wanted answers, too.

"As I returned from packing the trunk, the door to the front room was slightly open. I didn't intend to eavesdrop. I heard Anne voice concern about me being ready, then I heard you respond that I had to be. Now you continue to avoid giving me a frank response. You act like you know something, but you don't want others to know it. What are you hiding? I think I deserve to know."

Mary Ellen was silent. As his frustration grew, Louis gripped the steering wheel tighter. Mary Ellen noticed his body language. She turned to look out the windshield into the distance. It was too soon to tell him about her intentions. "I think you should know more about The Watchers, Mr. Silvani," she said.

Her persistent avoidance of calling him by his first name irritated him. "OK, *Miss Velarde.*"

Mary Ellen paused. She did not want the conversation to deteriorate. She took a deep breath. "Like Anne said, The Watchers are an advanced race of benevolent beings. They are like lieutenants for the angelic realm, mentioned in the Old Testament. Physically, they're tall, thin, and winged. They communicate with me like they do with Anne. I go into a trance, and I receive the information. I write down what I get and after getting out of the trance, I read what they transmitted. Last night, I received a transmission about you. They told me you are on the correct path, reiterating your role as a counselor and informer, one who is being protected. They did not specify what you are to do, telling me you should continue to follow your spirit." She relayed as much as she could recall. "They also seem to have a sense of humor. They told me that you are special, but not special like them."

Mary Ellen chuckled slightly, looking at Louis and finally showing a smile. "You are now, and have been, doing what you have been meant to," she assured him.

Louis once again realized she did not answer his questions. Her response prompted more thought. "Sometimes I've wondered if I was different. I have felt compelled to say and do certain things that eventually brought me here. I just don't know why," he said.

"Mr. Silvani, I can't tell you more than what you have discovered about yourself. The fact is, I'm still learning about *myself*. I don't have all the answers. You will never find a human being that has all the answers. In time, we will eventually both learn what this trip is really about."

Louis remained silent as they continued the drive, then he told her about the recent meditation experience and a particular dream he couldn't make sense of. "There are things happening to me, Mary Ellen, things that are quite unusual, escaping my understanding.

Saturday, in Pennsylvania, as I meditated, I had a thrilling experience like I went through a *wormhole*. It was . . . amazing!"

"You experienced an out-of-body event where your spirit left and you held consciousness of its travel. There are people who have meditated for years and have never been able to get to that level. The Watchers informed me they would give you tests as you progressed on your spiritual journey. I am certain that your out-of-body experience was such a test."

Louis sensed he was beginning to understand what was going on. "Oh, so now this is a *spiritual journey*?"

"Everyone is on some kind of spiritual journey, Mr. Silvani. Some are just along for the ride, while others are more participatory. You have always had some sort of awareness of this aspect of yourself; only now, it is a bigger part of your life."

"There was another event," Louis said, compelled to offer more information in the hope he could fish for more as well. "Saturday night I dreamt of a crop circle in England with the chants of what sounded like a Tibetan Monk in the background. The next morning, while going through social media, I discovered that exact image posted by a woman who had sent me a friend request the previous night."

Mary Ellen nodded. "That is *synchronicity*. It is your spirit telling you that you are on the right path."

"That's it? There's no other significant meaning?"

"That's it. Just stay the course."

"Stay the course . . ." Louis shook his head, recalling how George Herbert Walker Bush used it as a repeated response during a presidential debate against Michael Dukakis in 1988. "Can you offer any more information about your plan?"

"As I mentioned, the information you are seeking will gradually be revealed to both of us as we continue the trip."

Mary Ellen did not want to show Louis that she too had many questions and persistently wondered what lay ahead. She reclined her seat back and closed her eyes. She was able to take a decent nap, waking after a couple of hours. They were approaching Saint Louis and dinner time.

Before crossing the Mississippi, Louis told her about Deborah and Susan. Louis called Deborah Swift to tell her that he was about thirty minutes away.

As they crossed the river and entered the city, the Gateway Arch gleamed bronze orange from the early evening sun. While driving over Poplar Street Bridge, Louis could see Busch Stadium on his left. The Cardinals were on the road and traffic around the stadium was not bad.

* * *

Deborah Swift and her partner, Susan Koenig, lived on Pestalozzi Street in a late nineteenth-century red brick three-story home they had been restoring for years. Louis parked as close to the townhouse as he could, a few doors down. The house had a Black Lives Matter sign on its front lawn. It was not the only BLM sign on the street. They walked up two flights of concrete steps to the covered front porch. Louis rang the doorbell and waited.

A stocky African-American woman in her early 40s, adorned with dreadlocks, peered through the glass lite and smiled. She opened the door, gave Louis a strong hug, and patted his back. Deborah wore a man's flannel shirt with blue jean overalls. She and Mary Ellen shook hands as they introduced themselves.

They entered the front room of the grand house. Louis saw a large granite fireplace flanked by high stained-glass windows, light oak floors, a high oak base, a high plaster ceiling with a continuous oak cornice, and an ornate dark oak stairway. The front door had a leaded glass transom with the address painted in gold and black. Even the radiators were concealed in fine oak cabinetry with ornate metal screening.

Louis complimented Deborah on the restoration work. Susan walked out from the kitchen and greeted her guests. Susan and Deborah directed them to the dining room off to the side of the front room.

During dinner, they talked about the house renovation and the myriad problems and pleasant surprises the women had experienced during the years-long work. Deborah told their guests she and Susan would show them the rest of the house after dinner. Realizing that the conversation was exclusively about the renovation, Deborah changed the subject.

"Where are you from, Mary Ellen?" asked Deborah.

"I am a Jicarilla Apache, originally from Dulce, New Mexico. It is located in the northern part of the state close to the Colorado border." Mary Ellen told them she was adopted at an early age and lived in Albuquerque until graduating college, before moving back to Dulce to join her tribe.

Susan inquired, looking from Louis to Mary Ellen, "How do you two know each other?"

Louis was in the middle of sipping his iced tea. Mary Ellen responded, explaining that she learned he was going to present about Dulce at a UFO conference in Pennsylvania. She described the heckling from the audience after Louis revealed he had never visited the site, then explained how she offered to take him to Dulce and Mount Shasta.

"What is unique about Dulce?" Susan asked.

Louis eagerly explained, taking parts from his scripted presentation.

"There are theories about an underground facility operated by aliens. Sightings have worked their way into the local legends. Mount Archuleta is sacred to the Jicarilla Apache, and I think the two are related."

Mary Ellen was relieved this version was abbreviated. After dinner, Deborah and Susan relocated to the front room and set dessert on the coffee table. Louis and Mary Ellen walked away to get their bags, then Deborah led them up the stairs and showed them to their rooms. Louis's room was a collection of photos, plaques, patches, and awards from the twenty-one years Deborah served in the Air Force Security Police. There were photos of her on exercises, with her softball teams, and receiving decorations. Those decorations now stood in a glass case with the US flag and all the ranks she'd earned, including organizational patches. As a gay soldier, she survived by keeping her private life secret, following the "don't ask, don't tell" policy laid out by President Clinton. Louis admired Deborah's courage and dedication to her country in the face of her unique personal challenge. He unpacked for the night and went downstairs to meet Susan and Deborah, who sat together talking on the smaller couch.

Mary Ellen's room appeared to be a proper guest room, decorated for visitors. There were inspirational plaques and local interest photos on the wall. Photographs of a younger Deborah were arranged on top of an oak dresser, some of her years as an enlisted airman, others showing her in various stages of her youth. Mary Ellen looked at each photograph carefully, as if she was reading a story from each image. All the photographs showed a little girl with a smile that would brighten any day. She stopped at a photo of Deborah at sixteen or seventeen. She was with an older man, an Air Force master sergeant. Mary Ellen was struck by the fact that in this particular photograph Deborah did not have that "burst of happy" smile. In fact, her grin seemed slight, perhaps forced.

Mary Ellen moved closer, concentrating on the photograph. The bedroom's interior disappeared from her vision, Deborah's face now all she could see. Images appeared in her mind: Deborah as a teen lying on a table, anguish written on her face. She had been crying. She was pregnant, exposed from the waist down, her legs restrained and spread apart. A bright light shined in her eyes.

As she turned her head to see what was happening, a look of horror washed over her face. Mary Ellen visualized what Deborah had seen at the end of the table, at her feet…three nonhuman beings no greater than five feet high. They had oversized pear-shaped heads with large dark eyes, no eyelids, almost non-existent noses and small mouths. Dull metallic suits covered their bodies, except for four long, thin fingers on each hand. Mary Ellen focused as Deborah witnessed the nonhuman creatures applying an instrument to her, extracting her unborn child. Nausea began to rumble through Mary Ellen.

Mercifully, the images faded, and the rest of the room came back into her vision. She was still on the outside, but rage now coursed through her on the inside. She was all too familiar with what she had been allowed to see.

She took her time to collect her thoughts, waited, looked in the mirror, and wondered how to approach Deborah. Had they been close friends, it would be easier to talk about this experience. But they had just met, and Mary Ellen didn't quite know Deborah's view on abductions by aliens. She reluctantly walked down the stairs, stopping at the landing. She looked over at Deborah, who caught Mary Ellen's concerned expression. She stopped talking. Mary Ellen resumed her descent and sat down on a lower tread. Louis got up and offered her tea, which she accepted, not to drink as much to as hold something in her hand. She looked down at her feet, then focused her attention, again, on Deborah, who met her gaze.

After finishing dessert, Deborah went to see what was troubling her guest. She bent down to speak just above a whisper. "Are you OK? If you feel tired, it's alright to go upstairs and rest."

"I – I don't think I would be able to fall asleep right now, Deborah."

Gazing down, Mary Ellen shook her head a couple times. She was still processing the vision and questioning why it had come to her. She reasoned she was meant to talk to Deborah. She tried to imagine that conversation and how to approach her about such a private and painful experience.

"I need to talk to you . . . upstairs in the room I am sleeping in tonight." Mary Ellen spoke quietly so only Deborah could hear.

Deborah peered at her with concern. Mary Ellen looked into her deep brown eyes absent the slightest smile. Deborah offered a diminutive nod. Mary Ellen got up, placed her cup on the floor next to the stairs, turned around, and walked up, followed by Deborah. Deborah looked at Susan, giving her an assuring smile as she turned on the landing and climbed the stairs.

Mary Ellen walked into the room first. As she headed toward the framed photos, she asked Deborah to close the door. Deborah gently closed the door, noticing Mary Ellen had picked up the framed photo showing Deborah as a teen with her father. Mary Ellen held the frame so Deborah could see the image, looking directly into her eyes again.

"This photo caught my attention because you are not smiling like you are in other photos," Mary Ellen said softly. "It's as if you couldn't smile. What happened to you to make happiness so hard to find?"

Deborah's mouth opened in shock. She gave one subtle nod then spoke slowly and softly.

"It's odd, but that's the only photograph of my father in uniform with me next to him. It's the one reason I kept it."

Deborah took the photo from Mary Ellen, turned, and walked to sit on the bed. Mary Ellen followed, sitting next to her. Fighting tears, Deborah gazed at the photo. "There are mixed memories tied up in this picture. How did you come to that conclusion?"

"I can't explain why things happen to me. I am certain that meeting you was not by chance. I assure you that my intentions are good. I know you don't know very much about me. I will try to tell you as much as I can about myself." Realizing that she had learned something very painful and private about Deborah, Mary Ellen tried to gain her trust.

Deborah began weeping softly. Something told her to continue her explanation. "I was seventeen there. That photo was taken at Whiteman Air Force Base, here in Missouri." She paused to collect her courage, bit her lower lip, and took a deeper than normal breath.

"You are right. Something terrible happened to me several months before that photo was taken. It was at a party, off base. There were a lot of Air Force brats and alcohol. Kids were at the bar mixing drinks. I was still trying to figure out who I was sexually. I wasn't there more than fifteen minutes when I met the son of the Deputy Base Commander. He was white, athletic, and pretty. He offered me a drink. I think it was rum and Coke. After a few sips, I felt weird — not drunk but disoriented. I went to a bedroom to lie down with the lights out. I was lying on my back and at some point, the door opened and someone walked in. It was the Deputy Base Commander's son. He came to the bed and lay on top of me. He ..." Deborah began to sob and cry through her words " ... held me down. I couldn't move. Something in that drink made it difficult for me to move. I couldn't do anything. I pleaded for him to stop. It was all I could do." She continued to cry.

Mary Ellen grabbed a box of tissue from the nightstand. Deborah wiped her eyes. "He said demeaning things to me as he violated me, then I ... passed out. The girl that lived there found me late that night still asleep and partially naked. She wasn't nice. I was so bewildered. She treated me like I was a stupid drunk slut. I called a friend to pick me up, and she took me to her home on base.

"I got in trouble with my parents the next day. I did not say anything to anyone, not even my close friends. When I saw the guy at school, he gave me a snide grin. Always the same snide grin. A couple of weeks passed and I missed my period. I took a pregnancy test and it was positive. One day at school, I went to the guy and told him I was pregnant with his child. He was arrogant, telling me I had no proof. I eventually told him I would go to his father and tell him. He dared me. He didn't think I would, because then my father would find out. He was right. I kept the secret."

Deborah took a deep breath, not to end her account of the awful time, but to gather herself to continue. "A couple of weeks later he asked what I was going to do. I told him I would not get an abortion and would tell my parents at the right time. We never talked after that. It was not easy keeping my pregnancy a secret, but I did it. Around the end of the second month, I woke up in pain, cramping and spotting. I was so scared. I continued to have pain. My mom thought I had bad menstrual cramps. I decided to go to the doctor by myself the following day. I had to tell him I was pregnant and, of course, since I was a minor, he would have to notify my parents.

I was panicked about my parents finding out. But then the doctor said there was no sign of life in me. I didn't know what to think."

Deborah's memory of losing the baby brought her to tears again. After she cried for a minute or so, Mary Ellen asked, "Did you tell the doctor you were raped?"

Deborah shook her head. "I never figured out for myself if I made the right decision not to tell on the Deputy Base Commander's son. I knew it would have been my word versus his." She noted that was also a unique situation where her father, a senior non-commissioned officer, was under the chain of command of the boy's father.

"Eventually, the blood test concluded I had been pregnant, so he diagnosed a miscarriage. After that, my parents were very strict," Deborah said. "They were disappointed I hadn't told them the truth from the beginning. My mom was also hurt I went about it alone without any support. She told me a pregnancy should be a happy occasion, and one shared between mother and daughter. I realize that now."

As a gay woman, she had also come to terms that she would probably never share a happy pregnancy with her mother.

"When I came out a few years later, I told my parents about the rape. My dad was angry but not at me. I told him I did not want to make things difficult for him on base. My mother just hugged me and told me she was so sorry. I have no idea what happened to the boy. It doesn't matter at all anyway, right?" Deborah appreciated Mary Ellen listening and being empathetic, sensitive. "I was depressed about losing the baby; perhaps it was a hormonal thing. I don't understand how it happened. I thought I was careful."

Mary Ellen knew all too well what had happened. "It's not your fault. Certainly not the rape and neither the miscarriage."

How would Deborah react to what she was about to say? Was she ready to comprehend what Mary Ellen needed to divulge?

"What?" Deborah recognized from the silent pause that Mary Ellen was withholding something. "What are you thinking? Tell me. I know . . . I can tell there is something bothering you." Deborah adjusted her sitting position so she could look directly at Mary Ellen.

Mary Ellen tried to ease her into the alternate reality. "Deborah, what if you did not have a miscarriage?"

"What do you mean? What else could have happened?"

Mary Ellen slowly reached over to Deborah, put her hand on the photograph's frame, and when Deborah lessened her grip, took it back from her. "I asked you about this photograph because I had a horrible vision. It wasn't you getting raped, but it was just as horrific. I had a vision of you lying on a table … with a bright light in your eyes."

Deborah's face turned to shock again as her eyes widened. "Wait!" Deborah knew exactly what Mary Ellen was going to describe. "That's a nightmare I have been having since … since …" She turned her head to look somewhere in the distance, perhaps into another world starting to open up to her.

"Since you were this young?" Mary Ellen showed the photo. Deborah turned to look at it again. This time it linked to an even more sickening nightmare that was, in reality, a memory.

Deborah continued to look into the space in the room. "So … are you telling me that the nightmare is actually something that … happened? It *wasn't* a nightmare; it was … a *memory?*"

Deborah stopped looking into the room and turned to Mary Ellen with a look of bewilderment. "In your vision, you saw the bright light, then … ?"

"Then your head turned just enough out of the direct light and you were able to see what I would describe as your abductors," said Mary Ellen calmly. "They suppressed your memory by administering a drug. Your brain did the rest. It is a form of post-traumatic stress disorder called Repressed Memory Syndrome. I believe you were abducted by something or someone nonhuman in form, and they took your unborn child."

Mary Ellen stopped to let Deborah digest what she had just heard. Deborah was silent and fidgeted with her hands, picking at her fingernails that already showed abuse. She realized that she had been violated physically, twice.

Then Mary Ellen revealed something more. "Deborah, I know about this phenomenon because a similar thing happened to me. Except I wasn't raped. I was in love with an older man. When we found out I was pregnant, we made plans for us to be together. Then, one day around the end of the first trimester, it happened to me. One day, I was pregnant, and the next day I wasn't. I found out the same way you did. A visit to the doctor resulted in a diagnosis that I miscarried. I became depressed. It put a strain on our relationship, and eventually, we broke up."

Deborah took notice of how matter-of-factly Mary Ellen explained her experience. She reasoned that Mary Ellen was a woman of strong character. "I'm sorry. How did you conclude that it wasn't a miscarriage—that you were ... abducted?" she asked.

"I had the nightmares, but I recognized something odd about them. They were all the same. I went to a psychiatrist who knew about PTSD. I explained my depression and repeating nightmare. She felt the symptoms were linked. I went through hypnosis and, in a session, told her in detail what she described as a suppressed memory. The images that I saw in the vision when I picked up this photo," she held it out, "were hauntingly similar to my memory. Deborah, we share the same unspeakable horror." Mary Ellen motioned to give Deborah the framed photo back but did not let go. "Do you understand what I am trying to tell you?"

"Ok ... ok ... the nightmare is really a memory."

"Yes."

Deborah stopped and shook her head slowly. "Why? Why me? Why us?"

"What Mr. Silvani said about Dulce is real. There are people who have worked on projects in that place that swear they've seen a lab with living things in huge tubes. I live in Dulce, near that place. I have *sensed* but not seen the same things contractors and veterans have been trying to reveal."

Deborah was still without words. Finally, Mary Ellen laid it out for her: "Deborah ... they took our babies. They are experimenting with them! Our children and other children have been kept as specimens, maybe even tortured, so this race of beings could learn more about us to enhance themselves."

"Are you thinking of doing something? Is this what this trip is about?"

"The trip is not just about Dulce, that's only part of the journey. I have an idea of what I want to do once I get there. I've thought about it for a long time. I know my child is there because I have felt it. I am going to get inside that place, find my child, and release it from that prison lab."

Deborah's eyes sharpened, her pupils tightening. The eyes of a warrior bracing for battle. "Do you think *my* child is there too?" she asked.

"I can't say. It is likely that if it is not there, it was at one time. Your child would be at an age where they would have ..." Mary Ellen paused and did not finish the sentence.

"What? Would have what?"

"They would have released it or transferred it or developed it into a part of their work force." Mary Ellen was careful not to upset Deborah further with any other thoughts about the fate of her child.

Deborah looked down at the photograph in Mary Ellen's hands. She held out her open hand next to the frame. She wanted to hold it again. Mary Ellen released her grip, and Deborah took it back and continued to look at it, its meaning greater than ever. The images of her *nightmare* appeared as she continued to look at it. She looked at it differently now. Mary Ellen remained quiet, but attentive.

"Mary Ellen, can I be alone now? I will go back down when I am ready."

Mary Ellen nodded and got up. Deborah followed and they hugged. It was a real, genuine, connected hug. They held the embrace for a long time. These two women came to realize they have a common bond shared by a horrific event.

Mary Ellen walked out of the room, leaving Deborah alone. She quietly descended the stairs and went to sit near Louis. Susan and Louis were immersed in a conversation about the house and all of its fine details. Susan asked about Deborah, and Mary Ellen responded she would be down shortly. Mary Ellen glanced at the stairs every so often as the discussion continued.

The talk with Mary Ellen, the realization that the nightmare was a real and painful memory, made Deborah want it to hold a larger reason. Since she was an atheist, she could not simply say it was "God's will" and accept it. She thought about what she should do and wondered why it had taken over thirty years to find out. She stopped crying, realizing she, alone, could make the nightmare go away. Recognizing within the realization a path to closure and inner peace, she got up, walked over to the dresser, and put the framed photo exactly where it had been. With resolve, she turned around and left the room.

Mary Ellen's glances were rewarded by the appearance of Deborah walking down the stairs. Susan met her with a smile.

"Everything all right?" Susan asked, unaware of the kind of disruption Deborah would soon introduce to her life.

Deborah did not say anything at first. She immediately sat next to her partner and took her hand, then looked at Mary Ellen. Mary Ellen looked back. Susan understood that something happened upstairs and it affected Deborah profoundly. She looked curiously at Mary Ellen.

Deborah spoke up. "Babe, you know that nightmare I have every so often? The one about lying on an operating table with the bright light?"

"Yes …." Susan wondered why Deborah would bring that up.

"It's not a nightmare; it's a memory. It really happened."

"What happened?" Susan knew about the nightmare but could not understand the meaning.

"Remember I told you I was pregnant and I had a miscarriage? It wasn't that at all. I was abducted when I was pregnant. That memory of me on the table was from when I was pregnant…," she paused to let Susan process that piece of extraordinary information, "…and they took the baby."

Susan tried to listen closely. "Wait … who took your baby?"

"The same thing happened to Mary Ellen. She went upstairs in the room, looked at the photo of me and my dad, and saw my memory in a vision. Then she explained it to me because she had the same experience."

As Deborah explained further, Louis's mouth hung agape. He turned toward Mary Ellen as the shock flushed his face, another secret revealed. Mary Ellen slowly turned to Louis, her face washed of almost all emotion. She knew somehow, she had to talk more about herself, but she wanted it to be on her terms.

"Mr. Silvani, I must apologize. I intended to tell you this once we got closer to Dulce." Mary Ellen proceeded by sharing the complicated confession.

Louis glanced at Deborah, who nodded slowly, letting him know she understood what Mary Ellen was saying. She explained how her psychiatrist linked depression to the repeating nightmare, then she described the hypnosis session. "I was abducted and they took my child."

Deborah nodded slowly. Susan immediately looked at Deborah, her eyes widening, a lump forming in her throat. Deborah looked at her, caressed her hand, and raised it to her lips before kissing it.

Louis was still processing what he had just heard. As the only man in the room, he could not identify with the pain of being an expectant mother and then losing the child like these women had.

Mary Ellen revealed more about her intent. "I have strong psychic-spiritual abilities. During a meditation, a few years ago, I was able to sense my child in the underground base in a lab. I connected with him telepathically. I would not always be able to communicate with him, in fact sometimes years would pass between communications. I spent countless days wondering how I could get him back. I could never come up with a reasonable plan until I met a woman with amazing psychokinetic abilities. Understanding that I couldn't do it alone, I waited for the right moment. I waited for something to show me it was time, and then I saw *you* were going to present about Dulce," she said, pausing to let that sink in. "I was certain that it was exactly what I was waiting for."

She turned to look at Louis, who remained silent. "And now, I just happened to meet another woman who was abducted like I was. It's all coming together."

Louis now understood what Mary Ellen had intended for the trip. Accepting it was another matter. "Mary Ellen Velarde, you want us to go *into* Dulce, find the specimen labs, and rescue your abducted child?" he asked. "You are proposing something extremely danger-ous, and there is so much unknown, we really need to talk about this. You can't assume I am going to say yes without questions. You are suggesting we invade a well-guarded, underground installation supposedly inhabited by ruthless, powerful creatures with advanced weaponry."

"Mr. Silvani, I would not be putting us in this situation if I thought we would not have help. There are forces greater than you could ever imagine that are at work right now as we speak."

Mary Ellen was not sure how the scenario would unfold, but she was certain of the outcome. She looked over to Deborah and Susan, who listened and watched, captivated and speechless.

"But there's always a chance something could go wrong." Louis was not convinced that Mary Ellen had everything figured out.

"You asked many times about my plan. This is part of *the* plan, Mr. Silvani. This is our role, and like it or not, you are a significant part of it. You heard what Anne told you. You must learn to have confidence in yourself and in me."

Mary Ellen was not only talking about Dulce. The mention of self-confidence was a sore spot. "Look, Mary Ellen. I thought you would show me the area, maybe even watch the skies at night for signs of activity. To me, trying to enter that nest of evil is unthinkable and potentially, if not certainly, fatal! I don't see how the two of us could possibly succeed with what you are proposing."

"Three!" interjected Deborah. The surprise declaration stopped the conversation as everyone looked at her. "Babe, I need to go. I think if I go, the nightmares will stop. If I don't go with Mary Ellen, I will always be asking myself *what if.*"

Susan could muster no response from the shock that froze her. Her longtime partner had now unexpectedly volunteered to go with Mary Ellen and Louis, and participate in some sort of operation that posed extreme danger. Mary Ellen refrained from encouraging Deborah at the risk of hurting Susan.

Deborah continued. "I want to know what this place looks like. I want to go with you and see what happened to my child. I was a cop in the Air Force. I could be a benefit." Although Mary Ellen had not planned on having Deborah join them, she realized, after what happened in the bedroom, it was no coincidence that they had met.

Susan finally found her voice. "This is all too much, too fast, Deb. I don't know what happened up there, but before you went upstairs, you were telling Louis how much you loved this house and how you don't miss the security police life. I know about the child, but being abducted by *aliens* and then saying that you are going to that place?" Susan paused, growing more alarmed by the second. "Have you even begun to think this through? Deborah, we have always made our decisions as a couple. This house and the renovation did not happen without us thinking things through together. Don't you think I should have a say on a decision that may lead to me losing you?"

Susan's eyes turned from soft gray to a brilliant sapphire blue behind newly formed tears.

Deborah knew she was right. This was a critical decision, made far too quickly. Mary Ellen's visit was not by accident, though, and there was something unexplainable that pulled at her, urged her to join their guests on the trip. "Susan, there is something going on here that defies logic. Mary Ellen talks about forces beyond our control. Louis is now a part of it, and I feel that I am, too. But I won't go through with it unless I am certain that everything has been thought through. If I sense the risks are too high, I will leave."

Deborah looked at Susan's tearful face. "I love you. I will come back, I promise."

Louis leaned over and put his hand to his chin, rubbed it, and stared at Deborah. Then he exhaled a sigh through his nose. Here he was trying be a voice of reason and caution, and then Deborah expressed her desire to join Mary Ellen. He had no option but to go along with Mary Ellen's plan. "I will continue this trip with you," he said, "but if we don't have a good plan by the time we reach the reservation, I am not going to enter that underground fortress."

Mary Ellen stood up like a righteous statue. "I feel we will face dangers, yes. I am not going to mislead anyone, but we will survive. Our spiritual guides and guardians have not brought us together to fail." She raised her voice to emphasize her belief, like some sort of holy warrior. "You know something, Deborah? I feel that you were meant to join Louis and me on this trip. I think you will be a valuable addition."

For the first time since dinner, Deborah flashed her infectious smile again and leaned her head on Susan's shoulder. Mary Ellen's smile matched hers as Susan dried her eyes. Louis, looking at Deborah, nodded slightly. She was now part of the team.

The tough, emotional evening drew to a close. It was time to get good night's sleep. They agreed to get up at 8 a.m. for breakfast. "After breakfast, we need to plan out the next leg of this trip, and Deborah, you will need to pack up," Mary Ellen said.

"Where are we going?" asked Louis.

"Wichita, Kansas. I have a very special friend I want to introduce you to. She is autistic. To get there by 6 p.m., we should leave no later than noon."

Everyone got busy, clearing the table in silence. After the clean-up, the guests said their good-nights and went to their rooms. Deborah and Susan remained downstairs. They headed back to the small couch again and talked about the trip. Deborah talked with the confidence of a woman taking a one-week business trip, and no longer. Susan was not quite sure about that. Neither was Deborah, even as she spoke.

10

THE HYBRID PHENOMENON

"Mommy, what is normal?"

"Oh, Honey, that's just a setting on the dryer."

—*Anonymous*

Everyone arose early in anticipation of the adventure ahead. Susan fixed breakfast and Deborah packed, while Louis and Mary Ellen repacked quickly before they helped Susan. Louis was actually in the way rather than helping, and Mary Ellen took over as he left the awkward situation for the familiarity of his laptop.

Finally, Deborah brought down her duffel bag and laid it by the front window. "Uh…Louis…where did you park?" asked Deborah looking outside.

"Up the street in a space just big enough to fit."

"Fit what?"

"My Mini."

Deborah stifled a chuckle. "A Mini? You expect the three us to make the trip to New Mexico in a Mini? If we are all going out West together, I insist we take my SUV."

Louis welcomed the suggestion. Picking up her duffel bag, Deborah set it by the rear door, instructing Louis and Mary Ellen to do the same.

At breakfast, the conversation was light, with talk about the route to Wichita. There was no mention of Dulce or alien abductions or anything else that conjured dark feelings.

They continued to talk for quite a while. Deborah got up from the table, signaling the three to be ready for departure. She walked up the stairs to the room where Louis stayed overnight, headed to her display of Air Force memorabilia, took her dog tags, and put them on. It was more than just a possession; she was temporarily returning to her distant past. She was leaving home and her partner, embarking on a military-style mission. The enemy was unknown to her in identity, number, and abilities. Putting on her tags was like graduating from basic training. She was mission-ready with a purpose.

When she turned to leave the room, she saw Susan in the doorway, her cheeks moist, her eyes glistening.

"You know I'm a pacifist, Deb." Susan's voice was cracking.

"Yes. I know."

"Can you assure me that, if you survive, you will come back as the same Deborah?"

Deborah walked up and stood face to face with her love. "We won't go through with the operation unless everything has been thought and mapped out and we have a very good chance of succeeding. Mary Ellen has already revealed a lot about herself, which makes me think she is very special. I strongly believe this is all part of a divine plan. With you here, I have every reason to make sure I make it back."

Susan looked a little confused. "Deborah? As long as I have known you, you have never acknowledged a higher power running the show. Are you now saying you're changing your mind?"

"I can't dispute the fact that Mary Ellen was able to read my darkest secrets. I believe her, and she is making a strong case for both of us to reevaluate what we think regarding higher powers," Deborah said softly, admitting that she was starting to accept that there was a spiritual side of life. She added, "I will still keep my objectivity and my skepticism. I am not going to change overnight."

They embraced silently. "You come back," Susan whispered. "All of you."

Deborah joined Louis and Mary Ellen as they took their belongings to the SUV. The three returned to the house to say goodbye to Susan. Louis put his arm around her shoulder then stepped away. "She'll be alright, Susan. I won't let anything bad happen to her. This was meant to be. And you two were also meant for each other."

Susan forced a smile through tears. Mary Ellen hugged her and left with Louis.

The back room was awash in bright autumn morning sun. The sun, warm colors, and wood floor gave the room a cozy, safe, comfortable feeling, which Deborah noticed, along with the added warmth of her partner's embrace.

"What else can I tell you before you leave?" Susan asked, struggling not to fall apart.

"Don't say anything. Just hold me. I want this to last awhile."

Deborah's words caressed Susan. They held on to the moment long enough for the shadow line on the floor to change from the sun's movement. They kissed goodbye and Deborah went to the SUV, where Louis and Mary Ellen waited. Susan stepped out to watch them leave and waved until Deborah's vehicle headed down the alley and out of sight.

They drove in silence, except for the craftiness of Miles Davis playing. Mary Ellen sat in the front as Deborah drove. Deborah was anxious to have her questions answered and took advantage of the situation. "When you were talking about recognizing there may be a plan that brought us all together, did that mean you believe in God?"

Mary Ellen spoke first. "I normally don't and won't volunteer this, but you asked, Deborah . . ."

"Yes, I did. I want to know."

"Well then, it is my belief that the god religions preach about is not what "God" is," Mary Ellen replied, choosing her words carefully. "The consistent failure of religion is the centuries-old practice of making God a living human being. If God's *'kingdom'* has no end, how can 'God' be a living thing?" She used her hands to bracket the accented word with air quotes. All life has a beginning and an end. If God has no beginning and no end, it is not a being, but an *energy*. It's the Source, but it is not just one mass of energy. It is the collection of all spiritual energies in the universes that are not with a host."

Mary Ellen paused to give Deborah time to think.

"The pieces to this puzzle are all around for everyone to put together. You just need to accept the facts that help answer life's secrets. In the New Testament, Colossians 1:17 says, *He is before all things and in him all things hold together*. That could be interpreted as omnipresence—that God is all around us. In addition, 1 Corinthians 3:16 reads: *Do you not know that you are a temple of God and that the Spirit of God dwells in you?* To me, that means that, at the same time, God is inside each of us. Both statements are literally true. We each have a spirit linked to us. Before we're born, that spirit is part of the Source. When we pass, the spirit will go back to the Source."

Deborah's eyebrows pinched together as she processed Mary Ellen's reply. "So, is this Source responsible for creation? Is praying to God praying to the Source?"

"Interesting that you ask those two questions at the same time," Mary Ellen replied. "Actually, the answers share a common tenet. Both have to do with the power of thought. Have you heard about the science of *Noetics*?"

"I have!" Louis chimed in. "Thought is an energy with power. The same thought patterns have multiplied power where the strength is greater than the sum of the thoughts. During 9-11, random number generators functioned alike because the entire planet expressed similar thought patterns. Experiments in Atlanta in the 1990s revealed that mass meditation on peace affected the crime rate consistently at the time of activity."

Mary Ellen nodded. "Right. The energy of a single spirit has only so much thought power. But when all spirits combine to form the Source, they are unified, and the power is immense. Creation is the result of immensely powerful unified thought. I do not think the Source created the planets and life forms, but it did create the conditions and laws for all of that to occur."

Mary Ellen eagerly continued. "Let's talk about prayer. What *is* prayer? Again, prayer is thought, and like I said, thought, in numbers, has power. However, praying to the Source results in nothing. Praying to your spiritual guides and guardians *will* provide what you need. The Source is just energy. It does not receive messages, but it can send them."

Deborah was following Mary Ellen. "It was the whole prayer thing that affected how I thought about God, that made me lean toward atheism. I look around me and wonder, if an all-powerful and ever-loving God allows so much pain and suffering on innocent people—especially children, either that God is not that powerful or it doesn't care. So why should I care? But you are saying that people should pray to guides and guardians who were important in our lives, but no longer with us? How would I know who they are? Louis, do you know who your guardians and guides are?"

Louis replied that he thought one of his guardians was his father. "I have not been able to determine my guides; I have not been a believer in prayer either, but I suppose I should start." Events during the week, combined with Mary Ellen's talk, had activated Louis's heart and mind as well.

"Deborah, you can learn about your guardians through meditation. I'll help you with guided meditation during this trip."

"Thanks, Mary Ellen. I will take you up on your offer."

Louis then explained to Deborah the experiences he'd had since meeting Mary Ellen. He mentioned his out-of-body event, then described Anne's spiritual reading. Hearing about how Anne had contact with the angelic realm and how she instructed Louis to meditate, calling out Jesus as a protector, prompted Deborah to question her personal convictions about religion. For so many years, her belief system was based solely on what she could see, touch, and hear. To her, there was no other truth. Science was her God, and everything else was a fable, a carefully cultivated mythology meant to control minds and to rule by fear. Deborah considered organized religion an obstacle in the way of true evolution, a tool to divide humanity and keep people segregated and skeptical about other faiths.

Now she was hearing something entirely different, and not only hearing it, but watching it in practice from her companions. She needed more answers.

"Mary Ellen, your description of God is so different from what people get in church. I'm starting to understand what you call spirituality, but you mention entities like 'Michael' and 'Jesus.' That's when I miss the connection. You say that there is no such thing as the conventional God, yet you accept Christian icons."

Mary Ellen explained that conventional religions were flawed with misinterpretations and omissions. She gave the example of the angels, explaining that they are not individuals.

"How have you learned all this? What kind of proof do you have?" Deborah asked.

"Part of it is based on testimony, part of it is personal experience, and part of it is common sense. There are more than seven billion people on this planet. There are billions upon billions of other humanoids in this universe. Angels protect all, not just believers. The three most popular angels cannot do that alone."

Within Mary Ellen's answer was her attempt to connect their trip and the role of the higher powers. "Why do you think this trip is part of some divine plan? Why would the angels have an interest in you saving your child?" Deborah asked.

"The trip is not just about Dulce, and I don't need Mr. Silvani to rescue my child. He is here for another reason. I have been assisted by a race of benevolent and spiritually advanced ETs."

"But why you? Why me? Why Louis? Why not a group of people that have the skills, smarts, and weapons to go in and do it?"

"You know why I have to go. Mr. Silvani and you are here because you were both meant to be here at this moment. Deborah, it's much too early to judge our abilities. Have patience and trust in us."

The response provided Deborah with sincere answers. Still, she had plenty to think about. They were still about three hours from Wichita. Quiet returned to the vehicle, so Deborah switched back to her radio. Louis and Mary Ellen reclined to rest.

* * *

Deborah made it to Wichita early enough for a dinner stop before proceeding to visit Kaja Jorgensen. Kaja lived in Crown Heights, where the population was decidedly liberal, compared to the rest of the city. She felt safe leading her alternative lifestyle there. To minimize the impact on Kaja's need for a routine, Mary Ellen led them to a local eatery to talk about what to expect. Kaja claimed to be reincarnated from a survivor of the crash at Roswell, New Mexico, in 1947. Her memory of that past life was so vivid, she had written about and illustrated other beings, technical diagrams of their vehicles, and various craft. She was born Native American and given up for adoption. Her unlikely name came from her first foster home. She went through multiple homes, each more abusive than the previous, a disgusting and sad but all too common pattern in the foster care system.

Mary Ellen advised the others that Kaja was sensitive to light, noises, crowds, and anything requiring her to change her daily habits. "Even though I let her know you would be with me, I'm still not sure how she will react when she sees you. She knows and trusts me. She has become skeptical of strangers because she has been verbally attacked. CIA and NSA have harassed and threatened her repeatedly following her appearances at conventions," she said.

They finished dinner and headed to Kaja's house, just minutes away. Deborah parked in the driveway where Kaja would be able to see them. Mary Ellen had sent a message earlier but had not received a reply. The three remained in the vehicle, waiting; then Mary Ellen headed to the front door, alone.

Kaja's house was a modest, well-kept, one-story, cedar-shingled bungalow. A typical city lot, the front yard was short, a tall maple rose high overhead to keep the house shaded. Kaja opened the door before Mary Ellen could knock. She smiled upon the sight of her but stayed inside the house, motioning for her to enter. Mary Ellen looked back at Louis and Deborah, putting her hand up with a raised index finger, needing a minute or so.

"HELLO DEAR!" Kaja's speech pattern was unique. Her significant hearing loss caused her to speak in a higher-than-normal volume. In addition, she spoke slowly and maintained the same pitch. Her volume, combined with her exuberance, resulted in what could be described as a wail.

"IT IS SO NICE TO SEE YOU!"

"Hello, dear!" Mary Ellen greeted Kaja.

Kaja called all her friends "dear." As the friends greeted, they kept distance between themselves, part of a mutual understanding—no touching between them. Kaja was tall and plain; her height of over six feet added to her awkward look. Although her hygiene was not of concern, she never wore make-up to color her ghostly complexion. Her naturally blonde, shoulder-length hair was never brushed or combed, and she concealed the top of it under a black leather western-style fedora, even indoors. She wore a crumpled thick flannel shirt and old jeans. A gentle middle-aged woman, she required a larger than normal personal space.

"Kaja? Now listen to me, dear. I sent you the message to tell you that I have two friends with me." Mary Ellen pointed from the window on the side of the door. Kaja stood still, arms to her side. "They are very nice people. I told them about you, and they are interested to meet you."

Kaja quietly took small steps to look out the window, suddenly feeling threatened. She felt a rift in her routine.

"They won't stay long, dear. You don't even have to talk to them. I will talk to them for you," Mary Ellen said, trying to reassure her.

Kaja continued to stare outside her narrow window. "I DO NOT WANT THEM TO CALL ME NAMES! WHY DO PEOPLE HAVE TO BE SO MEAN?" She sounded like she was going to cry.

"They are not like that, dear. They are good people and they love you, too."

"PEOPLE LAUGH WHEN I TELL THEM WHO I AM! THEY DO NOT BELIEVE ME AND IT HURTS!" She continued to cry.

Mary Ellen pointed out the window. "They know you are a special person. The man is Louis Silvani. He is a UFO researcher. The lady is Deborah Swift. We both were abducted in separate occasions. I told them about your artwork. They would like to see it. Perhaps you could explain it to them."

"IF THEY TEASE ME OR TELL ME I AM RETARDED I WILL ASK THEM TO LEAVE."

Mary Ellen looked at her without responding. Kaja waited for Mary Ellen to say something, but all she received was a kind expression. Mary Ellen understood her and made her feel protected from an otherwise unfriendly world. With each passing second of silence, Kaja was withdrawing, bowing her head, looking away.

"Kaja, do you want me to come inside?"

"YES. YES. I WANT TO SIT DOWN WITH YOU," she replied eagerly.

"I will come inside when you let MY good friends sitting alone out there, inside. If you don't let them come in, I will have to leave, dear. I won't let them stay outside much longer." Kaja bowed her head lower, looking at the floor. She shuffled her feet.

"Kaja, go sit down in your chair. You don't need to be here when they come in. Go. Go to your chair and sit comfortably."

Kaja went to her small front room to her favorite chair. Mary Ellen left the house.

"WHERE ARE YOU GOING?!" yelled Kaja from her sitting position.

"I'll be right back, dear. I am not leaving!" Mary Ellen went to reiterate for Louis and Deborah what was discussed at dinner and how to behave. Tentatively, they got out and walked to the front door. Mary Ellen was first.

The three stood in the small, dark foyer clad in brown panels. A shade was down, light narrowly escaping from around the edges. The floors were all carpeted. It was quiet and felt like a small cave. As the door closed, Kaja called out, "IS THAT YOU DEAR?"

Mary Ellen poked her head into the front room.

"COME SIT DOWN DEAR!"

Mary Ellen looked at her friends and motioned them to follow. She entered the small stuffy room. Kaja's favorite chair was a single hammock, suspended from the ceiling. It was styled from a large laundry sack, dark gray, with a thick, soft teal cushion. Its sides tapered to a point above her head, giving her the much-needed feeling of being sheltered. She placed her hat under the chair and pressed herself deep into the cocoon, her head against the back. She would have closed it up if she could. Mary Ellen entered the room and sat closest to her, on a large dark brown cloth bean bag. Deborah and Louis followed suit and knelt on the thick cushions on the floor.

Mary Ellen introduced the two strange faces. Kaja looked briefly at them, not saying a word. Louis and Deborah tried to act casually and cordially. Both felt uncomfortable. There was awkward silence.

Although she had already told her traveling companions about Kaja, Mary Ellen spoke about Kaja's background.

"Roswell?!" Louis asked enthusiastically.

"YES! IT IS THE PLACE YOU CALL ROSWELL. I COULD RE-MEMBER IT LIKE IT WAS YESTERDAY. WE WERE SCIENTISTS. WE MEANT NO HARM. YOUR PEOPLE WERE WORKING WITH ATOMIC REACTIONS. WHEN YOUR PEOPLE DETONATED THE TWO BOMBS IT WAS LIKE AN ALARM THROUGHOUT THE UNIVERSAL COMMUNITY. YOUR SCIENTISTS DO NOT UNDER-STAND THE DAMAGE THOSE DETONATIONS HAVE DONE TO OTHER DIMENSIONS! THE RELEASE OF ENERGY IS SO GREAT, THE COMMUNITY WAS CONCERNED AND DISPATCHED SCI-ENTISTS TO LEARN MORE ABOUT YOUR PEOPLE. YOUR PEO-PLE SHOULD NOT HAVE TECHNOLOGY THAT THEY DO NOT COMPLETELY UNDERSTAND."

Kaja stopped for a moment. "I DO NOT KNOW IF IT WAS A LIGHTNING STRIKE OR YOUR ELECTRONIC RADAR WAVES. AN ENERGY BREACHED OUR HULL AND WE HIT THE TOP OF A HIGH ROCKY HILL AND THE IMPACT RIPPED MY VEHI-CLE INTO PIECES, MAKING A LONG NARROW TRACK IN THE EARTH AND SCATTERING BODIES AND DEBRIS." Kaja began to cry through her words. "IT WAS HORRIBLE! AND IT WAS MY FAULT!

"OUR CRAFT WAS POWERED BY ELECTRO-MAGNETIC EN-ERGY AND THE NAVIGATION SYSTEM WAS ORGANIC, US-ING THE CREW'S MINDS FOR DIRECTION. IN ORDER FOR THE WHOLE SYSTEM TO WORK, THE ENTIRE CREW NEEDED TO HAVE THEIR HANDS ON THE SENSORS, WHICH WERE ON THE CONSOLE. WHEN WE ENCOUNTERED ELECTRICAL INTERFER-ENCE, I LOOKED BACK AT MY CREW AND IN THAT FATEFUL MOMENT MY HAND SEPARATED FROM THE CONSOLE, DE-ACTIVATING THE SHIELDS AND THE NAVIGATION SYSTEM."

Kaja had carried this guilt with her all her life. When she was a young girl, her father from her past life appeared, to show her telepathically what had happened, and why she had been reincarnated in her current form.

Still weeping, she revealed her lot in life. "MY LIFE HERE ON YOUR PLANET IS PUNISHMENT FOR WHAT THE SUPERIORS DECIDED WAS MY RESPONSIBILITY IN THE CRASH." She wept harder. "I DID NOT MEAN TO HAVE THE ACCIDENT! I LOVED MY CREW! IT WAS A TERRIBLE MISTAKE, BUT I DO NOT THINK THAT I DESERVE THIS LIFE!"

"I'm very sorry, Kaja," said Deborah.

"Yes, I feel bad for you too," added Louis.

Deborah's eyes began to well up. "Kaja, I can only imagine the anguish you feel every day. The life you have been given cannot be easy, especially in the body of the person you are in now. Perhaps you could be a positive force while you have this life on Earth."

Mary Ellen nodded. "Actually, Kaja has made very good use of her knowledge and memories. She is a talented artist and illustrator. She has drawn portraits of other beings, and illustrations of space craft, and technical diagrams of the craft she commanded."

A crack of a grin appeared on Kaja's face as her eyes twinkled with pride.

"Can we see your work?" asked Louis.

"I would be honored to witness your talent," Deborah said, also curious, feeling like she was being given a tremendous opportunity.

"Yes, dear. I saw your art before, but I always enjoy it when you show it to me." Mary Ellen offered to help Kaja retrieve her paintings if she wanted.

"OK DEAR." Kaja exited her sheltering hammock and led Mary Ellen to the flat space in which her art was stored. She brought out technical illustrations and diagrams drawn in ink on white paper. She also rendered portraits of other living beings with colored marker on black paper. Mary Ellen and Kaja walked to the front room and laid the stack of papers on the floor in front of Louis and Deborah.

The first set of illustrations were of a craft similar to the Air Force B2 bomber. One was a skyscape with two craft in formation, flying among the clouds. The other showed a crude plan section of the craft, focused on a reactor powered by "element 115," a place holder on the periodic table because it has not yet been discovered. Certain circles call it "ununpentium." The next couple of illustrations looked more like designs than technical works. They appeared to be of a circuit board minus labels. Kaja avoided explaining the diagram because the information made her vulnerable to harassment and consequent trips to laboratories for testing and questioning.

The next set of six technical diagrams depicted reactors and propulsion systems with alien writing. Louis and Deborah were completely immersed in reading the various labels for the parts shown.

The third set of illustrations consisted of crop circles with alien writing, and the next batch of eleven illustrations were panoramic renderings of space craft, including huge motherships. There were also diagrams and drawings of her ship to include a view of the interior, the console where the hands were placed, and a plan of the craft, all accompanied by alien writing.

Another set emerged, consisting of colored portraits of various reptilian and insectoid extraterrestrials. All were beautifully detailed to include clothing and weaponry. These were Mary Ellen's favorites. Deborah marveled at Kaja's overall talent, while Louis was impressed with how Kaja had delineated individual scales on the reptilians. Kaja explained that the beings were drawn with arms raised as a greeting, to signify that they were friendly. The others were shown with hostile expressions. Kaja went back to her hammock as the three continued to admire her artwork.

"PLEASE, I DO NOT WANT ANYMORE TROUBLE FROM THE GOVERNMENT. I DO NOT WANT THEM TO COME TO TAKE ME AWAY AND MAKE ME TAKE TESTS AND GO THROUGH A MACHINE. I DO NOT WANT ANY OF THEIR DOCTORS ASKING ME IF I AM PARANOID OR MENTALLY ILL. I JUST WANT TO BE LEFT ALONE. PLEASE DO NOT TELL STRANGERS ABOUT ME."

Kaja began a slow rocking motion while sitting in the hammock. She called it *stimming*. Her defense mechanism was brought on by noises and bright lighting, most often during times of stress or over-stimulation. Mary Ellen recognized Kaja's rocking motion and cautioned her companions to lower their voices and change the subject as they continued to admire the artwork.

Mary Ellen decided to distract Kaja from the conversation. "We are planning to go to Dulce, dear."

"DULCE?! WHY DO YOU WANT TO GO TO THAT EVIL PLACE? DEAR—IT IS VERY DANGEROUS. THEY WILL KILL YOU ALL!"

Deborah and Louis immediately looked away and toward each other. Those were not words they wanted to hear.

Kaja remained in her chair. "THEY ARE REPTILIAN," she said. "I SHOW THEM NOT HAVING THEIR HAND UP IN GREETING. THEY ARE NOT GREETING YOU, NOT FRIENDLY. THEY ARE MUSCULAR AND HAVE TAN SCALES. THE DRAWING I HAVE SHOWS ONE WITH A BLUE HEADBAND."

Louis noticed the creature. "I see it. He looks big."

"THEY ARE SEVEN TO EIGHT FEET TALL AND THEIR CLAWS COULD RIP YOU IN HALF WITH ONE SLASH. IF YOU GO THERE, BE VERY CAREFUL AND TAKE A WEAPON."

"We'll be very careful, dear. You have our word." Mary Ellen advised her companions to wrap it up so they could leave Kaja alone to settle for the evening.

"Thank you so much for letting us see your artwork, Kaja."

"I TRY TO SLEEP WELL, BUT SOMETIMES I CAN HEAR SI-RENS EVEN WITH MY EAR PROTECTORS. DO YOU PLAY VIDEO GAMES? I PLAY *CHARM FARM*. IT REALLY HELPS ME. IF YOU WANT TO, I WILL PLAY WITH YOU WHEN YOU HAVE TIME."

"Thank you so much for the invite," replied Deborah.

"OK DEAR!"

Mary Ellen looked at Deborah, smiled at her, and gave her a wink.

"Kaja, you don't have to get up. Mr. Silvani and I will take your drawings and put them where I found them." Louis and Mary Ellen gathered the papers in a neat pile and carried them to the closet, and then placed them flat on a shelf. When they returned, Deborah was standing in the front room near the entrance, and Kaja looked at Louis carefully.

"YOUR DNA IS SPECIAL," came the words, seemingly out of nowhere.

Louis did not know what to say. He repeated the words that confounded him. "My DNA is special? How is it special? In what way?"

"YES. DON'T YOU KNOW ABOUT YOUR OWN EXISTENCE? YOUR DNA IS LYRAN. YOU ARE EMITTING THE AURA OF A LYRAN. YOUR DNA IS FROM A PEACEFUL, ADVANCED RACE. PLEASED TO MEET YOU."

"You knew this?" Louis directed his question to Mary Ellen. She gave him a couple subtle nods. Deborah began to realize the world was vastly different from the one she thought she knew. Kaja did not stop looking at her newfound friend and drew a clumsy smile.

"We are ready to go now, Kaja. Thank you for having us, dear."

"OK DEAR. LET ME TELL YOU SOMETHING TO REMEMBER ABOUT THE DULCE REPTILIANS. THEY DO NOT THINK FOR THEMSELVES. THEY ARE A SOCIAL SPECIES LIKE ANTS OR BEES. IT CAN BE THEIR WEAKNESS."

"Thanks for the advice, Kaja. I'm sure it will help us a lot."

"Yeah—instead of *one* of them attacking me, there will a horde of them, and in no time, there will be nothing left of me," muttered Louis loud enough for Mary Ellen to hear, but not Kaja.

"ARE YOU GOING TO DULCE TOMORROW DEAR?"

"No, we are going to Taos to visit a friend who might be able to help us with our operation at Dulce." Louis and Deborah looked at each other as they went out the door. Louis shrugged his shoulders. *Another surprise detour*, he thought.

Mary Ellen headed back to the front room and stood before Kaja, who was still rocking in her hammock. "You were great, dear! Thank you for accepting them. Namaste."

Kaja smiled, stopped rocking, and bowed her head. "PEACE BE WITH YOU DEAR."

Mary Ellen smiled, turned around, and caught up to the others, who were already in the SUV. Louis took the back seat again. Deborah started the engine as Mary Ellen got in. "Enlighten me, please. What was that DNA comment about?" Louis asked, once again certain Mary Ellen was concealing information.

"I told you when I met you that you were special. You heard it from Anne in Aurora, and now you learned more about yourself from Kaja."

"You knew about my DNA?" challenged Louis.

"No, I am not familiar with the Lyran race, so I wouldn't be able to recognize the trait. But I'm not surprised, and neither should you be. Now let's get moving." Mary Ellen did not feel the need to explain anymore.

Louis looked down and took out his cell phone. "I checked the route to Taos, New Mexico from here. It's a nine-hour drive. If we drive a couple more hours west, we can reduce that time to about six."

Louis indicated they could be in Greensburg by 10:30 p.m. There, they would be able to get a motel room.

The ride in the car was quiet. Mary Ellen checked her phone and texted messages to her friend in Taos. Louis sent messages to his kids, then checked social media and headlines before reclining and closing his eyes. Mary Ellen and Deborah chatted. The conversation then moved to questions about relationships.

"How long have you and Susan been together?"

"We're going on thirteen years now. When I get to the motel, I'm going to call her."

"Do you want to switch so you can text her now?" offered Mary Ellen.

"No, I will wait for the call. How about you? What happened to your boyfriend?"

"Oh … him.…" Mary Ellen hesitated with her response. Her emotions began to show.

"Oh, I'm sorry. You don't have to talk about it if you don't want to."

"No…it's OK. I can't change what happened, right? It's up to me how I handle it. He still lives in Dulce. We haven't talked, but I see him once in a while. It's a small town. It's kind of hard to avoid seeing him. He eventually married another woman and started a family."

Deborah left the conversation alone. Mary Ellen looked down at her phone again as it chimed the arrival of another text from Taos.

"Who are we going to see in Taos?"

"A special woman with unique abilities. She is part Cherokee, and her name is Katrina Hermann. She is psychokinetic." Mary Ellen took out her phone and sent a text message to Katrina about Deborah.

"How do you know so many special people?" Deborah asked.

"If you spend enough time doing research and visiting sites and just talking to people, you, too, will know special people. We are all special in our own ways."

Deborah thought about what Mary Ellen said. She wondered what it was that made her fit into Mary Ellen's circle of friends. Mary Ellen turned back to the phone. Deborah flipped on her satellite radio, and they listened for the remainder of the trip.

As the SUV rolled into the motel's drive, Louis woke up and looked at his phone. Colonel Gerald McGeorge had left a voice message. McGeorge would be leaving in a couple of days for a three-month deployment, assisting a planning effort. If Louis wanted to meet him, it had to be tomorrow. Mary Ellen looked at her phone and saw that Katrina sent her message indicating it was all right for Deborah to join the visit as well.

"Uh, Mary Ellen. I need to ask if we could delay the visit to Taos. I had hoped to see a good friend at Fort Carson. He left me a message that he will only be available tomorrow because he is leaving for the Middle East. Fort Carson is about six hours from here."

Mary Ellen looked back at Louis. "I just made arrangements with Katrina. Did you tell me about this colonel friend of yours?"

"No, I completely left him out of my intended visits. Sorry."

"Let me text Katrina to ask if she could see us another day." Mary Ellen sent another message to Katrina asking for a change in plans.

Deborah reached the motel, and the three travelers checked in. Katrina indicated delaying the visit another day worked to her advantage, giving her more time. As they took their bags and went to their rooms, Mary Ellen told Louis and Deborah they would be going to Fort Carson tomorrow instead.

Louis called Colonel McGeorge to tell him he and two friends would visit him tomorrow. McGeorge happily offered to arrange dinner. After the call ended, Louis texted his travel mates that they would need to leave around eleven o'clock to get to a Colorado Springs motel in time for the meeting with the colonel.

Deborah called Susan and talked for a long time about what she had experienced so far. The meditation session with Mary Ellen would have to wait. Mary Ellen ended her day meditating alone. She was curious about Louis's friend in the Army. The more she thought about him, the more she felt it was right to visit him. Louis thought meeting Jerry would be a good diversion. He would later understand that the meeting would play a big part in the colonel's life and role.

11

THE DIVINE WARRIOR

Then war broke out in heaven. Michael and his angels fought against the dragon, and the dragon and his angels fought back. —Revelations 12:7–9

Louis received a message from Gerald McGeorge that he had made reservations at a brewery pub for 6:30 p.m. Following Anne's instruction, as given to her by Michael, Louis meditated before leaving the motel room. As he perceived a beam of light descending from above, his body spasmed and shivered. He was surrounded by an indigo blue cloud, the blue light growing more vivid ahead of him. An indescribable feeling of euphoria, peace, love, and community encompassed him. As the light ahead became clearer, he saw a mass of countless blue flickering lights, like bees in a hive. He realized he, too, was emitting a blue aura. The closer he came to that cosmic congregation, the stronger the feeling of euphoria. By the time he understood what was happening, he was instantly transported back into the motel room.

Louis opened his eyes and stayed on the bed, wondering where he had been. *That feeling! Amazing! Was that the place where the spirits go, between lives?* He remained still, deeply relaxed but mentally charged. He got off the bed, picked up his luggage, and left to check out. The women were waiting in the parking lot by the SUV. Mary Ellen and Deborah had decided they would stop for breakfast in Dodge City, forty-five minutes away. The crisp early autumn morning made for a pleasant ride north from Greensburg.

Along the way, Louis described his morning meditation experience.

"Mr. Silvani! That is a remarkable experience! In all my years of meditation, I have never had the experience of getting that close to the Source! The spirit that is with you is extraordinary."

Deborah listened intently. She turned to Mary Ellen. "When you hear that people in near death experiences see a bright light, that is not the blue aura that Louis described. So, what is that?" she asked.

"I don't know what the white light is. There are theories floating around about this. One is that it acts as a memory eraser to your spirit or even worse. Whatever it is, when it is my time, I am going to look for the blue light."

Louis offered his own opinion. "I wondered about the white light and thought about the Van Allen belts. Supposedly, the belts are radiation from the spinning molten iron core. Do other planets have such a phenomenon? Is it possible the Van Allen belts are the white light seen during near-death experiences? Is it possible they are not a natural phenomenon but a way to keep us from spiritual evolution?"

"All I can say to that is wow! This talk about spirituality and mentioning science in the discussion is making me rethink what I believed." The discussion was overwhelming Deborah. In less than two days, she had already learned much.

They stopped at Dodge City for a hearty breakfast. Afterward, Louis took the wheel, letting Deborah take a nap. Mary Ellen sat up front and tuned the satellite radio until she found the folk music channel.

* * *

Mary Ellen's attention was drawn to Granada, elevation 3,500, the town they were approaching. During World War II, it served as the site of a Japanese Internment Camp. Unofficially, the camp was called Amache, named after a Cheyenne chief's daughter who later became the wife of John Prowers. The camp resided in Prowers County, Colorado. Mary Ellen nudged Deborah awake, and they stopped for lunch in town. The nearby site was designated a National Historic Landmark by President George W. Bush in 2006. Louis pointed out the time difference between Greensburg and Colorado Springs; they had gained an hour. This made lunch more enjoyable, and Mary Ellen was pleased they would be able to walk around Camp Amache.

The Japanese Internment Camp was just southwest of town. Only one of the original buildings remained. The camp covered about 10,000 acres. It opened in August 1942 and had as many as 7,300 people. It closed in October 1945. Almost all of its occupants had been from California.

Since it was a weekday during the school year, students were being led around the desolate site, their yellow buses idling in the parking lot. Evidence of the structures' ominous existence was represented by exposed weathered concrete foundations framed by six equal square blocks with straight and narrow dirt roads, which looked like a giant tic-tac-toe design branded on the land. Knee-high dry shrubs dotted the landscape. The common appearance of dead fallen trees littering the site, combined with the aged and decayed foundations, made the place feel like a graveyard. The three visitors walked slowly among the building footprints, which evoked permanent chalk-line silhouettes at a crime scene.

The school children headed back to the buses, walking in the opposite direction of the three visitors. As the children's voices became more distant, the visitors heard only the sound of the fall wind along the high plain. Browned brush dotting the barren soil contributed to the site's harshness. Mary Ellen looked across the landscape and felt its emptiness.

Mary Ellen sat down on a concrete foundation and closed her eyes. Gradually, images of cruel winters and oppressive summers came to her, framed in faces of detainees bereft with sorrow, not pain. She shared the sorrow and the sense of betrayal, wondering if the unjust treatment of the Japanese-Americans had been based on the risk of sabotage by sympathizers to the Empire of the Rising Sun. She then reasoned it had been predicated on something more sinister and less logical. She often wondered the same about how her people had been treated.

As the scenes and faces faded, she opened her eyes again in the bright daylight. The last of the school children had departed. She looked about fifty yards ahead to see Deborah and Louis walking away from the main dirt road toward a lone memorial site, about three hundred yards southwest from the edge of the camp. The pair approached a small cemetery framed by low trees. Behind the cemetery was a stone monument with three white metal benches around it. An aluminum pole stood, cold and naked. The wind caused the loose lanyard to hit the pole, producing a weak clanking sound like a broken bell. The cemetery existed for the burial of children.

Mary Ellen followed Deborah and Louis to the monument of rough unpolished granite. The four-sided pylon, slightly tapered to the top with a Japanese pagoda-style cap. Engraved were the names of Japanese-Americans from the camp who had volunteered to fight in Europe during World War II. The inscription on the pylon indicated the memorial was dedicated to thirty-one Japanese-Americans who died in battle, and another one hundred twenty who died during confinement. During the war, second-generation men of Japanese ancestry were drafted and assembled to form the 442nd Regimental Combat Team, the most decorated unit of its size in American military history.

The two veterans and the Native American woman held hands and looked at the first names: "John, Victor, Frank, Leo, Peter, Ned, Arnold, Lloyd, Calvin, George, Robert, Harry, Bill, Joe." Across the prairie scape, the dry brush was leafless, dormant, and silent.

"Look, there are two people with same last name on this side," whispered Deborah.

Louis nodded. "I think there are two common last names on the other side, too. Such a poignant but significant part of our country's history. A remnant of the not-so-distant past, where our country's leadership fell into the darkness of fear and hatred, and because of its remoteness, few Americans will ever know about or visit this place. This was such a big mistake, an injustice to innocent people and their children. Thank you for bringing us here, Mary Ellen."

The trio left the memorial and walked solemnly back to the SUV. It would take them three more hours to reach their destination. Deborah took the wheel for the last push. No one said a word, instead reflecting on what they had just experienced. After several minutes, Deborah tuned the radio to the station Mary Ellen had selected earlier.

Nothing they saw in the next couple of hours did anything to alleviate the melancholy feeling engulfing them. After Lamar, they drove past a huge abattoir for livestock, likely over three hundred fifty pens and over one hundred head in each pen, an astounding sight. The rest of the after-harvest landscape was brown and low as far as the eye could see. Road signs continued to mark the Santa Fe Trail.

The sky was littered with remnants of contrails. Or so it appeared. The long white streaks eventually dissipated, scattered in parallel and in 90-degree intersections. Louis noticed the crisscross pattern high above. "If these are contrails, why don't they disappear?" he asked. "Contrails are supposed to be water vapor. Why is it that sometimes we see jets high in the sky with no such contrail or a short contrail? Sometimes two jets are visible at the same altitude; one with the type of trail that remains and eventually dissipates, and one without. How can that be?"

Coincidentally, Deborah felt strongly about the topic. "Good questions! I get frustrated trying to explain this to people only to get blank stares. Why do we see this activity over rural areas that are far from air traffic lanes and at different times? Air traffic is very predictable. The lanes are consistent. Only a weather threat would cause a pilot to change course. The other consistency is that air traffic follows a set schedule. The appearance of these contrails do not follow any schedule."

Louis continued. "Do you know what's in those emissions? I'll tell you what I learned from a study commissioned in the early 80s by the Council of Foreign Relations and conducted by the Carnegie Institute."

"What was its purpose?" Deborah's asked.

"To research the impact of using light metals as an aerosol application to block out the sun's rays in order to slow global warming."

"And?"

"The results indicated that the process would be able to reduce solar insolation by twenty percent. There were negative effects because the metals used were aluminum, barium, and strontium. Strontium is radioactive and barium is a carcinogen. Aluminum has been linked to Alzheimer's disease. The report was released and then redacted, never to be found again."

Deborah shook her head. "No surprise there, with findings as devastating as that."

Louis sighed deeply. "I believe the CFR decided to accept the health and ecological risks because, without the application, the study indicated that there would be prolonged drought and famine. I wouldn't be surprised if the spike in Alzheimer's is directly related to the aerosol application of the light metals that we are witnessing now." He had studied the subject matter earlier in his social awakening.

As they approached Devine, Colorado, they looked to the northwest and an impressive array of purple bumps on the horizon. The Fourteeners. The term referred to Rocky and Mosquito Mountain peaks that exceeded fourteen thousand feet above sea level. Passing through Pueblo, they were at 5,000 feet above sea level and about forty-five minutes away from Colorado Springs.

Louis checked in with Colonel McGeorge, who confirmed the reservations. "What can you tell us about McGeorge?" asked Mary Ellen.

"The first time we met, he and I were on a planning charrette for expedient facilities for the Army. He really appreciated my approach in leading the process. After that charrette, he requested that I attend and facilitate other charrettes. The last time we worked together, I sensed I could trust him enough to give him information on UFOs and ET activity on Earth. I gave him coordinates. It took a while, but he eventually responded and wanted me to tell him more."

It was about 4:30 and the three travelers had time to rest. They stopped at a motel off Interstate 25, checked in, and walked straight to their rooms. After some rest and relaxation, they reconvened at 6 p.m., all looking and feeling refreshed. The brew pub, one of many good establishments in the city, was just off the interstate. The colonel had picked a lively, colorful place. They ordered starters and made their craft beer selections.

McGeorge, still in uniform, arrived ten minutes later. Louis introduced him to his companions and thanked him for taking the time to meet. After getting his own beer, the colonel and the rest of the table gave the server the food order.

Speaking directly to Louis, McGeorge said, "I looked up those coordinates you gave me, and I couldn't believe what was there."

Louis's response changed the mood for the remainder of the evening, with the urgency of someone stopping a pedestrian from crossing into traffic. "Wait! Before we talk about that, you need to know that we are in the midst of a war ... a war for our very own spirits."

Mary Ellen and Deborah looked at each other as Louis took on the role of a spiritualist instead of scientist.

"There are forces in the universe that do not want us to ascend. They want us to continue to reincarnate. Yes, there are UFOs and ETs, but the big picture involves beings that actually thrive on human suffering and other negative energies. Those beings are called "archons"; they are like demons, emotional vampires. Human emotions and experiences like pain, suffering, anger, and lust are like drugs to them. The more we produce, the more they thrive. If we ascend, we join forces against those evil beings. Which is why it is a spiritual war."

Louis looked at McGeorge, suddenly aware of the gravity of what he just uttered with such conviction. He had no idea why he had said those things. Mary Ellen sat quietly and realized something momentous had just happened. The knowledge came from somewhere or someone else.

The exchange left Deborah confused. "I thought you were going to tell him about the UFOs and ETs?" she asked.

McGeorge sat still. His face flushed and tears welled in his gleaming blue eyes. He spoke up.

"My God. Thank you. I thought I was going crazy. I thought I needed to find a therapist. So much has been happening to me that I could only attribute it to be from God. I am a devout Catholic, but I don't always agree with the Church's teachings and philosophies. All my life I have had spiritual-psychic events. I was able to predict the passing of people close to me. My mother is psychic, and she told me that I am, too. She also told me that *they* know who we, my mother and I, are. I know of the archons. One night while resting in bed, the ceiling turned into a cloud and out came this gargoyle-like creature. He got on top of me, pinning me down. I was paralyzed with fear. I knew this was a demon, and all I could think of was being firm. *Stop being fearful and command the demon to leave*, I thought.

"I cried, 'In the name of Jesus I command you to leave!' Immediately, that creature got off me and disappeared into the ceiling. I never had that kind of visitation again."

The colonel was interrupted by the arrival of the orders. No one took a bite.

"I often go for temporary duty to Fort Leonard Wood, Missouri," McGeorge said. "A few hours away, across the river from Saint Louis, near Belleville, Illinois, is a shrine just off the Interstate: Our Lady of the Virgin Snows. Ever since I started visiting the grotto, I have experienced visions and visitations."

McGeorge paused to take a bite and others joined him. Louis sat intently. Mary Ellen was glued to every word the colonel said. There would be no discussion about ETs tonight.

"Colonel, haven't you wondered why there is so much pain and suffering and disease and war around the planet?" Mary Ellen asked. "The archons make use of greedy, corrupt people that enjoy being in control. They reward those people with power and prosperity: earthly rewards in exchange for maintaining the conditions that spread the negative energies the demons are addicted to. But it's coming to an end soon. The Watchers and angels will not allow this to continue much longer, especially if the archons raise the stakes."

The colonel took a couple of swallows from his beer. Deborah and Louis had finished their plates while Mary Ellen and McGeorge had taken only a few bites.

"A few years ago, while on a business trip to Fort Leonard Wood, after checking in to a motel, I decided to go to the fitness room before reporting to the post," McGeorge said. "I started my workout on the treadmill, running for about five minutes. During that workout, I experienced a vision. It started with my bodiless self, hovering over a large group of people. The people gathered by the thousands, occupying an area as far as I could see. There were men and women soldiers in all kinds of uniforms. I heard the muffled speech of someone addressing the group."

McGeorge quaffed his beer as his voice started to crack, then continued. "As I panned across to the left, I saw a mount. At the base of the mount was a large stage where a military officer was addressing the group. The words became clearer as I focused on the person giving the speech:

Ladies and Gentlemen, what we are about to embark on may change the course of the world as we know it. Some of you, like me, will see things not of this Earth. Although I do not know the outcome, I can tell you your actions will decide the fate of the world. Have faith that God will be with us, and take strength and courage in knowing that you are fighting according to His will.

As the person finished, my spirit drew in closer until I could see the face. . . . IT WAS ME! I could not tell you my age, but I could tell I looked older, maybe early fifties."

McGeorge's phone buzzed. He looked at the caller ID.

"Sorry, I have to take this. I'll be back," said the colonel leaving to go outside.

The three travelers looked at each other, wide-eyed without uttering a word for several minutes. Deborah reached for her glass to gulp down in response to her amazement.

"It seems we have surprises for each other, Louis," said Mary Ellen.

Deborah kept the glass to her lips even though she stopped drinking.

"Ladies, this is the first time I'm hearing about this from Jerry. I would have never thought I would hear anything like that from him," replied Louis. "Deborah, you haven't said anything. Are you OK?"

Deborah just nodded repeatedly.

McGeorge returned. He settled in his chair and resumed his story after a brief drink.

"Once I realized that I was the one speaking, my spirit then entered the speaker's body, and I was able to look out. General officers shook my hand, wishing me luck. I could see the masses of troops disassembling and moving to their respective positions across the valley. While still on the stage, a majority of the soldiers were in position, but my attention shifted to the sky."

"Why was that?" Deborah asked.

"It began to grow dark. Black clouds rolled in. There was lightning, but none hit the ground. I could tell this was no ordinary storm. There was a massive explosion to the rear. The enemy launched its first artillery barrage. Our artillery counter-fired, and forces started to move forward for a direct-fire engagement. The skies grew darker and the lightning became more powerful, centered over our forces, the clouds and lightning supernaturally dense above us."

"What did you do?" Louis asked.

"I held up binoculars, looked across the valley, and saw our forces engaging the enemy," McGeorge replied. "The attacks were catastrophic for both sides, as burning vehicles and helicopters scattered across the valley. Artillery strikes to our rear began to overwhelm us and the sound was deafening, then ..."

McGeorge paused, as if stopped in mid-stride.

"Then *what?*" Mary Ellen asked.

"Then the skies suddenly parted. Clouds peeled open like a curtain and out emerged a host of angels flying down to the Earth, swooping across the battlefield." Mary Ellen noticed a rich light shining through McGeorge's eyes, as if by speaking of the battle, he was there. "The angels had a leader, directing protection. It was slightly larger than the rest, had flowing blonde hair, and wielded a sword, as did most of the angels."

McGeorge took another drink.

"By now, though, the enemy ground forces were reaching our positions. The angels were selective as to whom, from the adversary's side, they destroyed. When they attacked something, it exploded into oblivion. Humans in the enemy's ranks were not necessarily evil but just doing what they thought they were supposed to. The angels seemed to recognize that and bypassed them."

Feeling a renewed excitement, McGeorge paused again, long enough to take a long sip of his beer, then another.

"All our soldiers were now wielding swords similar to those of the angels but with less glimmer. The enemy also had its share of demons that seemed to equal the number of angels supporting us."

"Were the demons equal in power and strength of force to the angels?" Deborah asked.

"Yes. Their attacks had the same effect on us as the angels did on them. As a demon wielded a great sword, it would wipe out groups of people. Unlike the angels, however, the demons attacked anything and everything, without regard or consideration, accepting collateral damage. At times, I could see the human enemy even transform into a gnarly, grotesque creature."

"What did you do?" Deborah asked. Even with her military background, she felt well over her head, well outside the scope of her training.

"I didn't do anything."

"What?" Mary Ellen asked, a befuddled look on her face.

"That was the last of my vision. I found myself off the battlefield of angels and demons and back running on the treadmill again, the speedometer at 8.7 mph, seven minutes per mile pace, extremely fast for this old guy," McGeorge said.

He noticed the stunned expressions from his three companions.

"I hadn't run that fast in probably ten years. Then I started to debate with myself, *what the heck was that, what is this supposed to mean?* I turned toward God and asked the same questions. Eventually, I received a response that said, '*The US must align with Jerusalem.*'"

The colonel stopped again to eat and drink, the others joining him after first digesting the mind-bending story. Once he finished, he picked up where he left off.

"Upon hearing that, I asked what it meant. Were we to align with Israel? The answer came again, '*You must align with Jerusalem.*' Then I got one last message: '*One of your allies is not.*'"

"Is not ...," Louis said.

"An ally," McGeorge replied. "I didn't get any wisdom as to who that might be. As I continued on the treadmill, a young woman with long, flowing, brown hair and olive skin walked into the fitness room. I noticed her before, in the lobby when I checked in." The colonel moved forward in his chair before he continued.

"I heard a voice, '*Ask her her name.*' She walked by me into the adjacent laundry room, and I glanced at her to see who she was. I saw her from the back as she passed, and I noticed she was not carrying any laundry. She was wearing jeans and a long sleeved shirt. I debated with myself about asking her name. *Who is she? Who is she supposed to be?* Then I heard, '*She will have the answer.*' Then I thought to myself. *Is this possibly Mary?*"

The colonel's account had Mary Ellen, Louis, and Deborah hanging on each word.

"Then she came back into the room and I heard it again, '*Ask her name.*' I hesitated. I doubted what I was hearing. I heard the request a third time emphatically. '*Ask her name!*' Something prevented me from asking her. I looked at the young lady, and she made eye contact as she passed. She smiled a gentle smile as if I just missed an opportunity, and it was a look of pity."

"What happened?" Deborah asked.

McGeorge shook his head. "When we broke eye contact, the treadmill immediately lost power and stopped working. The young lady had exited the door, and I was so frantic I didn't know what to do. Being the engineer-minded soldier I am, I was torn between running out to find her and trying to figure out what went wrong with the treadmill. I wasted time trying to diagnose the treadmill's problem. After going through all possible solutions, I found a fuse reset button on the front of the machine and pressed it. Finally, the power came back. In a rush, I went out the door, to the lobby, down the hall, around to the other hall to look for the young woman. I never found her."

A curious, knowing look slid across Mary Ellen's face, lodging in her eyes and the slight smile that creased her lips.

"Do you know something I don't?" McGeorge asked.

Mary Ellen nodded. "The image of the young woman you saw in the fitness room was intentionally presented to you as a benevolent image," she said. "The beings that are contacting you are using those kinds of images because that is what you feel comfort in. They are not trying to deceive you; they are responding to your spirit and belief."

She surmised that the messengers were Pleiadean because they had used Mary's image throughout history. "Remember the visitation at Lourdes and Fatima? Same exact method and choice of messenger."

"What about the ally that is not?" McGeorge asked.

Mary Ellen held the eyes of each person at the table for a few seconds before responding. "You are all probably going to think I am anti-Semitic, but it is not about the people. I have a strong suspicion that Israel is the nation she was going to warn you about."

"What?" McGeorge interpreted Mary Ellen's comment as blasphemy. He raised his voice. "How could you say that? The chosen ones? The nation freed from the slavery of Egypt? The people that were almost exterminated by the greatest evil in modern times? I can't accept the people of Israel being on the side of darkness."

Deborah and Louis sat silently. "It's not the people; it's more complicated. I don't make that accusation flippantly, Colonel," Mary Ellen said, her voice soft but entirely convincing.

"Mary Ellen may not be far from the truth, Colonel," Louis interjected. "Read the Old Testament like a history book, taking notes and highlighting events that call attention to acts of violence against innocent people. The Book of Numbers is an account of the thirty-eight years in the desert. Why that number? Don't you think that ten years would be enough? Thirty-eight years is enough time to have a generation replaced, don't you think? From the very beginning, Numbers describes the one they call God organizing a military camp. You have to ask yourself why that occurs. Who were they fighting, and why? Some would say it was for defense, but the only possible threats were from outlying pagan villages. To keep the Israelites in order, a cloud of fire followed them as they set out on their offensives. If any of the enlisted men complained, they were consumed by fire from the cloud. Does that sound like a loving God or something else?"

Mary Ellen added. "I invite you to read the Old Testament closely. The descriptions of the acts by the one they call God will surprise you. When Miriam and Aaron appeared to disagree with Moses, the God turned Miriam into a leper. The book of Numbers has many passages describing the genocide of people who preferred not to fight. Is it possible that the being that helped free the nation of Israel from Egypt was not God but an imposter whose sole purpose was to establish a warrior race to cause chaos in the Middle East—chaos we are still experiencing? People during that time didn't understand high technology. They recognized the abilities of those advanced beings as divine. After being set free to wander in the desert, the Israelites did anything the gods commanded. The gods sequestered the people and would command them to attack pagan cities and towns, killing women and children."

McGeorge and Louis glanced at each other. McGeorge pursed his lips and Louis gave a slight knowing nod.

Mary Ellen leaned forward until her face was a couple of inches from Colonel McGeorge's. She peered deeply into his eyes. "Colonel, get wise to what the young lady was about tell you. I am telling you what you missed. Israel was spawned from beings that thrived on our suffering."

McGeorge sat silent, stunned. In his heart he could not dispute either her observations or those of Louis. He only wished he had heard it directly from the young woman in the fitness room.

He paused to take a drink. "There's one more event. While I was at the shrine, I was taking part in a rosary session. While in the third decade with my beads, I was into deep prayer. I saw lights flickering inside my closed eyes, getting brighter. I convinced myself to just keep my eyes closed. Appearing before me was a gentle bank of white clouds. There was a shape in the clouds; it almost looked human. Two hands presented me an object. I could see the forearms and hands holding out a slender, silver sword with a black handle. Although it looked to be in perfect condition, it seemed ancient, like something you would pass on from generation to generation, or from one ranked soldier to the next. Should I reach out and take it? I didn't know."

Mary Ellen leaned forward with deep interest.

"Then I noticed a small red cross on the handle. I panicked and the vision quickly disappeared. I never had any experiences like those again." McGeorge turned to Mary Ellen. "What do you think it all means?"

"I am going to find out why you have had those experiences. Will you let me communicate with your spirit?"

"Now?" asked the colonel.

"Yes, let's clear the table, and I will connect with your spirit."

A few minutes later, the server took all the plates away. Mary Ellen positioned herself directly across from the colonel. Deborah and Louis sat quietly as Mary Ellen gave McGeorge instructions. "I am now going to connect with your spirit, and I will look for my guides for help as well. All you need to do is listen to what I tell you and answer if I have any questions."

After a pause, Mary Ellen informed McGeorge that she was in contact with his spirit. She acknowledged the events that he had spent the past hour sharing with everyone.

"There is a reason you were offered the sword of Michael, Colonel McGeorge. You are what is known as an *aspect* of the arch angels. The arch angels are carrying out their work through your body and spirit. The archons fear you. They cannot succeed with their own manner of disturbing humanity's spiritual evolution, at least not with you."

Colonel McGeorge sat silently, tears filling his seasoned warrior eyes. Louis gazed at Mary Ellen and the colonel. Deborah took a swig of her beer and made a humming sound.

"It is an honor to meet you, Colonel McGeorge. By the way ...," Mary Ellen directed a look to Louis, "I, too, am an aspect. The arch angels that I work for are called *Mariel.* It is a legion of feminine warriors that guide with love and compassion. They are healers. They are nurturing, but they are also strong of character and as brave as any other of the angelic beings."

Louis's eyes widened a bit, then he looked over at Deborah who took another gulp of beer as McGeorge leaned forward, a question on the tip of his tongue. "What is it that I am supposed to do as a US Army Colonel, then?"

"Keep doing what you are doing. Your spirit has guided you well. Trust your spirit," Mary Ellen replied. "When you go to the Middle East, be an ambassador of good will and peace. Seek out the truth of the people that live there. Do not be fooled by the hateful rhetoric or sucked into the lies that Islam is a religion of violence. There are extremists that want to continue painting that picture. Every religion has extremists. Look at the Christians that claim white-skinned people are superior to others. Befriend people you do not know and learn about them so you may return to tell others about your experience."

"I'll do that. Yes, I am Christian, but I believe in one humanity. I try to see the good in all." McGeorge gladly accepted his assignment.

Mary Ellen smiled. "You see, Colonel, you're certainly not going crazy. Your mother was right. You *are* special. Thinking about the battle scene in your vision, it is apparent you will have a major role *if* it comes to that."

"IF?" asked McGeorge.

"We can still affect the future. There is enough time for things to change so we can avoid the scenario you describe. Just because you have had a vision does not mean that it will come true."

"Right, Mary Ellen!" Deborah nodded in agreement. "It bothers the heck out of me when I see those evangelicals hoping for something as cataclysmic as Armegeddon just to satisfy their demented views about their own mixed-up faiths."

"Evangelicals...." McGeorge lowered his head and shook it. "Oh! I almost forgot. I want to give you all something that I bought just for this kind of occasion."

He reached for his camouflaged backpack, unzipped a side pocket, and took out three necklaces. "During my last visit to the shrine, I bought ten medals. I now know why I got them. You all should be wearing these as a part of the army of God." He handed them out to each of the three travelers. They looked at the medals closely, taking in a winged Saint Michael on one side and the US Army seal on the other side.

Louis, Deborah, and Mary Ellen thanked McGeorge for the medals and then placed them around their necks. "This is very special, Colonel McGeorge. I am honored to have met you! Mr. Silvani, we are here because of you!" Mary Ellen said. "You made this all possible."

"Jerry. This is awesome. Thanks." Louis patted the colonel on the shoulder, one friend appreciating the other. "I don't know what I did to merit it, but I will wear it faithfully."

"Well, like Mary Ellen said, you set this whole thing up," McGeorge said. Louis nodded, looking at Mary Ellen. The pieces of this puzzle were coming together.

It had been a moving experience for everyone. Before leaving, McGeorge held up his glass to his companions and wished them well. Mary Ellen wished him the same on his trip back to the Middle East. They got up and he hugged the women and shook hands with Louis. The colonel was anxious to get his spiritual duties in motion.

On the way to the motel, they made plans for the trip to Taos and the visit with Mary Ellen's friend, Katrina Hermann. Louis and Deborah were excited about the prospect of meeting her, but they were also nervous about being one leg closer to Dulce.

12

ENLISTING ENERGY

The day science begins to study non-physical phenomena;
it will make more progress in one decade than in all the
previous centuries of its existence. —Nikola Tesla

The three travelers left early to avoid freezing rain forecast in the higher elevations. Mary Ellen last saw Katrina Hermann a year before, during Little Beaver Days Festival in Dulce. As they drove onto I-25 south, Mary Ellen's mood shifted to a sense of intense purpose.

"Katrina Hermann is an amazing woman, not just because she can project energy with her mind but mostly because of the challenges she has faced. Since being recruited for her abilities, the struggles she has experienced are more than any ordinary person can endure," she said. "I met her on an alternative news page that promoted Native American issues. She is part Cherokee. She lives with a former Army Ranger who fought in Iraq and Afghanistan."

"What is it that you need her to do as part of the operation? Is she going to join us?" Deborah asked.

"No, she doesn't need to be with us to do her work. I am going to ask her to use her psychokinetic ability to get the base to evacuate."

"How is she going to do that by herself?" Louis asked.

"She can reverse energy from sources. She can cause shorts and overheat circuits. She is even capable of increasing the temperature of a reactor's core."

"What?!" Deborah interjected. "Ok, I'm beginning to understand the spiritual stuff and even the reincarnation stories, but using the mind to trip circuits and cause fires?" They'd only started the third day, and already Deborah had another fantastical notion to wrap her mind around.

"So, you *do* have some kind of plan in mind," said Louis.

Mary Ellen turned around and gave him a smirk, then turned to concentrate on the road again.

The drive to Taos felt like a straight line south until they exited at Walsenburg, CO. Proceeding on US 160, they ascended gradually, reaching 7,200 feet at La Veta. Rough Mountain stood at about 11,000 feet, rising to the west, shrouded in clouds. The land continued to tilt upward as they climbed to 9,200 feet. After crossing the New Mexico state line, Mary Ellen felt the relief of being closer to her home. She read the sign: LAND OF ENCHANTMENT. "Indeed," she muttered to herself.

Katrina lived in a secluded ranch house on thirty acres of land southwest of Taos with her longtime boyfriend, Robert Ladd. Robert was a walking casualty from the Gulf War and the campaigns in Iraq and Afghanistan, formerly suffering from substance abuse and continuing to struggle with PTSD and depression. He had not been able to let go of piercing images from one particular battle against Al Qaeda, in which the enemy held innocent children as shields. Many were killed by their captors in the firefight and many more severely injured.

After the fight, Robert found a young girl, lying on her side. Her eyes were closed. The floor was spattered with the blood of others in her class. She wore a light blue dress with a green knit sweater, probably made by her mother. Crimson stained her collar. He looked at her closely and teared up, hoping that maybe she was only sleeping. He picked her up like a broken doll, carrying her gently and laying her on a mat next to other young victims in the gym, the temporary morgue. His unit left before he could witness relatives arriving to claim their children. They left the captors' bodies to be disposed of in a mass grave by a friendly Iraqi unit. Robert survived many fire fights, IEDs, and ambushes, losing men in his unit along the way, but no other action disturbed and troubled him as much as hearing young screams through the staccato of automatic weapons, knowing his unit was helpless in trying to save young innocent lives.

A light dusting of snow brushed the rocky plateau. Robert and Katrina's place was off the highway, on a narrow private gravel drive, on the highest part of the property. The entrance was marked by a wood and steel gate, its name, "Third I Ranch," mounted in metal letters above the gate. The property was scattered with indigenous wildflowers of a dozen shapes and colors. A weathered timber post and sheep wire fence provided a secure perimeter for goats. The house was a sprawling stucco ranch with redwood porches and trellises.

When they arrived, Robert was tending a smoking grill at the rear of the house on a patio. The cold did not keep him from his cherished duty. Katrina came out of the house immediately after Mary Ellen, Louis, and Deborah left their vehicle.

Katrina was in her late forties but could pass for younger. She wore her long blond hair in a bun above a purple fleece sweatshirt with black denim pants and her favorite grey leather boots. She gave Mary Ellen a brief hug before being introduced to Louis and Deborah. The three took their bags and followed Katrina into the house. The house was large enough to fit two families comfortably. Each of the visitors had a room with a view of the mountains to the north or west.

Katrina showed Mary Ellen, Deborah, and Louis their rooms, then returned to set the table for lunch. The travelers were happy to have a home-cooked dinner after being on the road for a few days. Robert brought in the grilled homegrown vegetables and fish. Returning from her room, Mary Ellen was greeted with a glass of home-brewed hibiscus passionfruit iced tea. Katrina then introduced Robert to the guests. Louis and Deborah grabbed a drink and placed it on the table before loading their plates.

Mary Ellen gave Katrina and Robert few details about the trip. She mentioned going back to the reservation and showing Louis where Dulce was, along with Mount Shasta. Otherwise, the conversation was light. Deborah talked about herself and Susan. Louis recalled how he met Mary Ellen, his life in Chicago, and interterrestrials. Mary Ellen and Katrina discussed current tribal matters. Katrina then described to Mary Ellen and Deborah their off-the-grid lifestyle.

Robert remained in the kitchen as the women continued to talk. Louis joined him, trying to start a conversation. He found Robert withdrawn, clearing plates, and putting away leftovers, his responses short. Questions by strangers made him uncomfortable. Louis, understanding the nature of Robert's problems, was careful not bring up his military past.

Mary Ellen and Deborah were interested in seeing the property, so Katrina asked Robert to join her in giving a tour. They went out the sliding door. It was cloudy, cool, windy, and getting ready to rain. Katrina started by showing the solar panel array on the roof.

Off to the north side of the house was a small shed for batteries, a power panel, and convertor. She explained that sometimes they produced more power than used so they would get credit from the power company.

They continued to walk. The next stop was Robert's prized workshop. He had all the right tools to keep his ranch in working order. The place was showroom clean. Exiting the shop, Katrina showed them the windmill with an adjacent shed for accessories. On the other side of the shed was a long, white, arched hut clad in plastic sheeting with fan units mounted on one end.

"Our hydroponic hut."

She led them into the high-tech greenhouse. It was much warmer inside as the sounds of the humming fans, pumps, and flowing water greeted them. A forest of metal pipes supported other pipes, fans, and lighting. Below were rows of individual lettuces, tomatoes, and other vegetable plants growing from holes in white PVC tubes. The tubes floated in water-filled tubs on one side of the hut, and tubs containing fish and other plants were on the other side. Everything was thriving. It was an impressive sight.

"Lunch came from this greenhouse. It took a few years to be this successful. Power comes from the windmill and batteries," Robert said, his pride visible over not having to rely on outside sources for most of what they needed. He would gladly talk about the greenhouse, though not much else. At the far end of the greenhouse, Deborah's eyes fell on another tub that had tall leafy plants.

"Are you growing pot too?" asked Deborah above the sounds in the hut.

"Robert grows it for medicinal purposes. It helps with his PTSD. He's figured out how to extract oil, too," said Katrina, matter-of-factly.

The last stops at the property were the duck pond and the chicken coop. "The chickens are mine," claimed Katrina. "We have them for the eggs. We sell the chickens to folks who want them for food. Or need them.

The group continued to walk around, admiring the mountain views before heading back ahead of the worsening weather. Robert's windmill needed to be shut down manually, so he broke off to lock it into place.

* * *

As dinner time neared, Mary Ellen called Anne Stoneburner to tell her about Colonel McGeorge and how Louis prompted the colonel to reveal his spiritual experiences. Anne was delighted to hear the news but not surprised. She sensed a divine plan in motion. Deborah called Susan while Louis went to his room to send a message to his kids before taking a power nap.

* * *

Katrina prepped dinner in the kitchen, leaving Robert outside to tend the greenhouse. She laid out a taco buffet, and set out non-alcoholic sangria and margaritas. When finished, she headed upstairs to knock on doors, then outside to ring the dinner bell: a loud clang, enough to roust the neighbors and even grab Robert's attention.

Over dinner Katrina asked, "What do you hope to show Louis while you are at Dulce, Mary Ellen?"

Mary Ellen did not immediately offer a response. Katrina sensed her hesitation in answering. "Mary Ellen, what? Um...you're making me concerned now." Still no response. "I hope you're not thinking about getting close to that base. Are you?"

Mary Ellen wanted to say something. Louis wanted her to say something. Nothing was coming out.

"What do *you* know, Deborah?"

"All I know is one day I'm at home in Saint Louis having a nice evening with my partner and the next day I'm on a trip to a place where we are supposed to get all the answers to many questions," she offered cryptically.

"And that place would be the Dulce base?" asked Katrina incredulously.

Mary Ellen nodded.

Robert heard every word in the kitchen. He scowled, stopped putting things away, and returned to the dining room. He stood across from Mary Ellen and Deborah, a stern, concerned look on his face. "Did I hear you're planning to enter the Dulce base area?"

"Yes, Robert. I've been planning this for a long time now, and I've waited for the right opportunity. I'm not only planning to go on the grounds," she paused and took in a breath, held it an extra moment, then exhaled, "I'm going to enter the base and find the lab where they are holding the abducted children used as specimens."

"What?" exclaimed Katrina.

Robert shook his head. "You and what army?"

Mary Ellen sipped her water before responding with calculated defiance. "I don't need an army, Robert," she finally said. "There are forces at work greater than you can imagine."

Robert stared at her incredulously, a memory gnawing at him. "A lot of men who were trained in close urban combat were killed in the late 1990s when a careless contractor breached a barrier between the mercenary side and the ETs. By the time it was recognized as an innocent mistake, it was too late."

Katrina listened, having heard the story before. Louis and Deborah looked at each other, concerned that Mary Ellen was losing this particular battle.

Mary Ellen decided to reveal the critical part of her plan. "Look, I understand all that. I have no intention of engaging with those creatures. By the time we get into the base, it will be evacuated. I know where the base is. As soon as they exit, we will go in the way they will come out."

"How are you going to get them to evacuate?" asked Katrina.

Mary Ellen looked at her, lowered her voice, and paused. "This is where you will cause the evacuation. I know they have a small nuclear reactor to power the base. They use the water from the Navajo River for cooling. I need you to do something to cause an emergency and make them leave the base."

"Wait!" Robert's raised voice betrayed his annoyance. "You came to visit Katrina to ask her do a job for you?"

"Calm down, Bob; I don't think she understands what she's asking me to do."

Robert stepped back and shook his head in disgust. Agitated, he turned toward the kitchen. A moment later, he turned to face Mary Ellen again. "You don't understand the kind of risk Katrina would be taking, and I think you don't understand how risky this operation is even if Katrina succeeded." Robert's approach was resolute but not aggressive. "And I suppose you two were going to join her? Seriously? I know Mary Ellen has no military experience . . ."

"Hold on! I'm disciplined. Deborah is an ex-Air Force cop. Mr. Silvani was an Air Force officer," retorted Mary Ellen.

"Even if you had experience in the special forces, what kind of plan do you have? Have you thought about every possible way your operation could fail?"

"Honestly, we haven't talked about it yet," Louis said. "We trust Mary Ellen, and we expected to have this kind of talk eventually. You're right, Robert. In fact, Deborah and I told Mary Ellen that we would not go unless we were confident. I appreciate you, being a former Ranger, explaining how difficult this operation could be."

"Well, it's obvious you guys are setting yourself up for a disaster. Failure is death. That's how difficult this operation could be," Robert said. "Mary Ellen, your incursion needs more than spirituality. You need to sit down and look at everything in this operation. You guys aren't even close to being ready!"

Robert hoped his words would be enough to persuade the group to change their plans. But Mary Ellen was not finished. She told Robert about her abduction, her communications with her child. She explained her vision about Deborah and how Deborah joined upon being advised about the vision. She explained how she met Louis, Louis's role as a counselor and informer, and all the events he has experienced since he had met her.

"More and more people are coming out of the spiritual closet. It is not a coincidence that I met these two people on my return trip. You don't understand; my feelings never betray me and that they are strong as I undertake this operation. Something big is happening or is going to happen, and it involves Dulce."

Robert heard the "why" of Mary Ellen's mission to go to Dulce, and it didn't change his mind. Katrina was a psychokinetic, yes, but his belief in the spirit world stopped there. He knew about the ETs but had never made the connection. Robert and Katrina looked at each other. Katrina shook her head slowly.

"Mary Ellen, I'm your friend, and I really want to help you." Katrina paused. "There's another thing you don't understand. Using my mind the way you are asking me to would have a very bad and possibly lethal effect on me." Katrina studied Mary Ellen's solemn, almost doleful face before continuing. "I have not engaged in psycho-kinetic activity since 2007. I would get headaches; I would get weak; I had sleep disorders and symptoms of PTSD. A scientist working with me at that time invented a device, the Hermann Circuit, to reduce the risk of those side effects. Even with the device, I would lose consciousness.

"I *will* tell you that after each activity, my abilities got better, stronger, but he said that I may hit a limit, where the next time I lose consciousness, I could fall into a coma. That was enough for me to stop. Certain groups tried to erase me. To fight back, I used my mind one last time to cause an accident like the one you have suggested, and they stopped threatening me. I haven't been bothered since. If I did something like that again, it is possible they would know who did it, and Robert and I would be in great danger. I'm sorry, my Apache cousin, I can't do it. I can't."

Katrina got up slowly from the table and walked away. "And I won't let her," added Robert, joining Katrina.

They remained in the kitchen as the guests sat in awkward silence. Deborah felt sad for Mary Ellen. Louis rested his chin on the palm of his hand, elbow on the table. He looked out the window, saying nothing. Robert and Katrina finished cleaning up, then Robert headed to his study before turning in for bed. Louis walked into the kitchen, thanked Katrina, then proceeded to his room. Deborah followed, leaving Mary Ellen by herself at the table.

Katrina went back to the dining room to sit down across from Mary Ellen. "You must have anticipated that Robert and I would probably not approve of your plan. There are far too many risks, and Robert knows what it takes for that kind of operation to work," said Katrina in a soft tone.

"I did my homework. I have been planning this for years. I didn't know about the risks to you, but I know there is another dimension to my decision, and it does not follow logic," Mary Ellen said.

Katrina shook her head, more and more resolute by the second in her decision. "I trust Robert on these matters, among many others. There is too much unknown regarding what could happen to me. What would happen if black ops knew I was using my abilities again? What would happen when alarms at Dulce go off? How much time do you need? There is so much working against you, Mary Ellen. I know our spirits and guides are powerful, but even with them, there are limits. Like Robert said, any failure is certain death. I am very sorry. I think I understand how much it means to you. Maybe we can all think about it and talk about alternate scenarios tomorrow. It's getting late and I need to go to bed."

Katrina got up, leaving Mary Ellen by herself. *If this is the right time,* she wondered, *how can I carry this out without Katrina's help?* She carried this thought to her room.

Robert and Katrina shared a bed with a large dreamcatcher above their headboard. Following Mary Ellen's recommendations, Katrina got into the habit of dispersing sage smoke every so often. It also helped Robert sleep well. But on this night, sleep proceeded with difficulty for everyone.

Sometime in the middle of the night, Katrina and Robert began to murmur. The sheets felt tight as they both felt locked in a struggle. Their bodies convulsed. Their legs kicked. The murmuring became louder.

"NO!" they both yelled and woke up. Katrina turned on the light. She was shaking. Robert sat up. "I just had a horrible nightmare. It was so real!" whispered Katrina.

"So did I. Did we both yell at the same time?" Robert had dealt with nightmares before, many of them intense and violent since returning from the war, but never like this.

Katrina moved closer, tucking into Robert for protection. "I dreamt I was in the lab at Dulce."

"And there were human-like creatures in long sacs in a violet fluid."

"YES! Exactly!"

"It was so clear. The captors looked like large lizard people. I saw them remove some of the human-like creatures from the lab."

"YES. I saw that too! What the hell is going on? I saw the human-like creatures open their eyes and look at me as they were being removed. It was horrible."

"That's when I woke up. The look on the face of the one looking at me was unforgettable."

"Robert, how could we have the same nightmare at the same time?" Katrina continued to shake.

"Maybe . . . maybe it wasn't a nightmare." Robert thought aloud as he put his arm around Katrina. They sat silently for a moment.

Katrina tried to grasp an understanding of whatever just happened. Her sleeping mind was open to anything. She felt defenseless against herself. Her ability to create worlds, movement, feelings, was without bounds. There were no rules to restrict it. The one certain thing was that she would eventually awaken and be connected enough to be able to recall every detail that had been created.

"You think that nightmare was a message to show what is going on over there and that we should help? I know she is well connected spiritually, and the stuff she told us about her, Deborah, and Louis was amazing. Maybe she really *is* supposed to go and rescue those poor creatures and do something about the lab. What do you think?"

"What are you saying? Are you really willing to risk everything to help her just because we had this dream?"

"That was not a dream and you know it, Robert. I think that with the circuit—if I ever could find that box—and your help in putting the operation together we could make it work for her."

Robert began to fear for them. Then he remembered the failed rescue. An image of one of the captive creatures flashed in his mind. *Is this supposed to bring closure to my pain from the past? Will this rescue be a success?*

"Let's get some sleep. We'll talk about it tomorrow morning before everyone wakes up." After kissing each other goodnight, Katrina turned off the light on the nightstand and burrowed in, holding Robert close. They fell asleep thinking about forthcoming conversations.

Katrina rose early, well before her guests. With the nightmare still fresh in her mind, she searched her closet for a cardboard moving box labeled CIRCUIT. After a few minutes of moving things around, she found it and placed it on the floor beside her dresser. Leaving Robert in bed, she got dressed and went to the kitchen to make coffee. In a few minutes, Robert, in his sweats and unshaven, was at her side, awakened by the sumptuous aroma of the coffee.

"I noticed that you took out the box with that contraption—you haven't used it for over a decade." Robert was not upset, but he needed an explanation. "So, you really have changed your mind about helping Mary Ellen?"

"Mary Ellen doesn't strike me as someone that makes decisions hastily. Now I know that you don't buy into the spiritual and meditative stuff she talks about, and sometimes I have a hard time grasping what she says. What if she *is* getting help from beyond? How can you explain what happened to us last night?"

Robert sipped his coffee. He knew it was not up to him. Katrina sat down next to him at the table.

"Tell me what you saw last night, because that is my reason for changing my mind."

Robert turned his head to look at her and recreated the nightmare. The words came out slowly. He had to force himself to speak. "I felt as helpless as I did back in Fallujah, when we were trying to save the schoolchildren from Al Qaeda. The memories came back. It was happening again to other innocents. That nightmare was a vision of a real situation, and it was shown to us so we would help her."

He walked to his study and brought out an easel with a white board, adhesive notes, and markers. He set the easel and board in a corner of the dining room and started writing notes, each representing a step in the operation. Katrina stayed close by in the kitchen to fix breakfast. She was a bit startled as Mary Ellen entered the kitchen.

"Good morning," greeted Katrina. "How was *your* night?"

Mary Ellen did not have the intention of talking much but the question intrigued her. "Fine. Why do you ask? Did you have a bad night?"

Katrina walked closer. "Robert and I had a nightmare. The SAME EXACT nightmare, a scene of the lab at Dulce." She looked at Mary Ellen closely. "It was horrible. We both woke up screaming 'NO!'"

"I want you to know I had nothing to do with that."

"I know. I'm going to help you but not without Robert's help with plans." Katrina pointed to the dining room. Mary Ellen tentatively walked toward the room and peeked around the corner.

"Come here, Mary Ellen; I have some questions."

Cynicism tinged Robert's voice, which Mary Ellen felt. The smells of bacon, eggs, and pancakes lured Louis and Deborah out of their beds and into the kitchen. Robert and Mary Ellen continued to discuss details of the plan. After filling their plates, Louis and Deborah followed the sounds of voices to the dining room. Noticing the whiteboard and notes, they looked at each other, confused. They walked back to the kitchen to ask Katrina what was going on. They did not need the coffee for a morning eye-opener; the news that Katrina and Robert would help Mary Ellen brought with it enough of a jolt. Katrina took her own plate and followed them.

"Mary Ellen, there are three aspects in military planning that commanders want for an operation: surprise, speed, and numbers," Robert said. "You will not have numbers, so can you compensate with speed and surprise?"

"I have an element of surprise. My plan involves friends back at the res. I will have decoys who will stay at my house for a night to attract attention. When I give them the word, they will head to one end of the base while my team goes to the other end."

Appearing impressed, Robert wrote DECOYS on a note and stuck it to the board.

Listening in, Louis detected a flaw. "Wait! Mary Ellen—remember the UFO conference. You said the men in the suits recognized you." Robert turned around to look at Mary Ellen as Louis continued. "Do you think they knew you were heading back?"

"They seemed to know what I was up to," Mary Ellen conceded. "But we haven't been followed."

Robert looked at her closely. "You had an encounter?"

Mary Ellen nodded. Robert started to feel less confident in the plan. "They don't have to follow you. They have a network of informers. You have to assume that they have a team expecting you."

"I know, Robert. That makes using a decoy team more important."

"Your decoy team has to appear to be coming from outside the reservation." Robert paused in thought. "You need to have them meet us somewhere outside Dulce. If you want the bouncers to think they are your team, the decoys have to enter the reservation in a car with out-of-state plates. Then, when they get to your place, they should leave in your car."

Mary Ellen looked at Deborah, who gave permission to use her SUV. "There is a motel east of Dulce in Chama about an hour away," said Mary Ellen.

Robert took the DECOYS note and added MEET AT CHAMA. "We will add the details later. Let's set up another milestone." The next note read, DECOYS LEAVE HOUSE. "Where will they go? Where will you go? We need travel times."

Louis fetched his laptop while Mary Ellen responded to Robert's concerns. "I have identified an area where I think there are escape hatches. I have travel times, too."

Katrina returned to the kitchen, loaded a plate, and carried it to Robert, urging him to eat. Louis returned quickly, sitting across from Robert, close to Mary Ellen. Switching on his laptop, he focused the search on Dulce. Mary Ellen leaned to look at the screen, prompting Louis to give her control. She guided the cursor to where a landmark read, "Archuleta Mesa," just over the state line in Colorado and placed a marker labelling it BASE NORTH. She mentioned that it would take about twenty minutes for the decoy team to reach that area from her trailer home.

Next, she guided the cursor south, to the junction of J2 and a dirt mountain road on the New Mexico side. There, she placed a marker labelling it BASE SOUTH. She placed a third marker for the ISHTOKEEN JUDICIAL COMPLEX. "It will take about ten minutes for the police to intercept the decoy team. The police will have to arrest and take the decoy team back to the station. That will take another thirty minutes."

Robert noted the time checks on the board. "What about the evacuation? You haven't told me when you want the evacuation to occur," he said.

"The mercenaries will exit from disguised hatches scattered throughout the area. The ETs will evacuate with their craft," Mary Ellen replied.

"How many do you estimate are based there?" Robert paused with the pen on paper, keeping his head down, but moving his eyes up.

"An equal number of humans and ETs—about sixty per side."

"Where do you get your information?" His gaze remained fixed on Mary Ellen.

"I communicated with men who did construction there, on the mercenary side, in the late 1990s. At the peak of the abductions and activity, there were as many as a hundred and twenty on each side. Since then, I sense the abduction missions have declined in numbers by about half, so it is reasonable to assume there are about sixty per side now."

"What do you think will happen when they evacuate?" continued Robert, tapping the pen point on the note pad.

"There will be two ways of evacuation. One, via all-terrain vehicles coming from a pre-positioned location. The second, in order to get equipment out, they would have to use helicopters coming from Los Alamos—about a forty-minute flight."

"Your team has to be in position during the evacuation, which means you could be seen by the choppers," Robert advised, his free hand rubbing his morning stubble.

"Not if I start a brush fire. It will cause smoke that will render night vision useless and heat that will confuse the infra-red sensors."

Robert looked at her, his eyes flashing a little more open, then closing them before reopening. "A brush fire in the fall here with the winds is suicide; brushfires are unpredictable."

"It's a risk we'll have to take, Robert."

Louis and Deborah looked at each other and felt extremely uneasy. After thinking about the hatches, Louis interjected, "You won't have to RV the hatch locations. The hatches you are talking about are like roof hatches. They are not meant to be opened from the outside; there is no exterior hardware."

"So?" asked Mary Ellen. Robert looked at Louis and nodded.

"So, during the evacuation, they will be opened from an inside lever and will remain open as occupants leave. When occupants are gone, all the hatches will remain wide open because they will not be able to be closed from the outside without going back inside."

"Your team will be able to see the hatches open as you approach the base. You won't have to be there at the time of evacuation, only near enough to see them. Good point, Louis." Robert added more notes and repositioned others.

Deborah had been sitting quietly at the end of the table with her breakfast and coffee. She scooted to the front of her chair. "What happens when they discover they have imposters and realize our team is still in the area?" she asked. "When is that going to happen?"

Robert nodded. "Deborah is right, that is the most critical part of this plan. We need to get it right: the time that they realize they have the wrong people and you are still at large."

"There will likely be a car there to watch my trailer," Mary Ellen said. "Once the team leaves in my SUV, the car will follow until they decide the team gets too close. My friend posing for me looks a lot like me, so they will assume that I'm in that car."

Robert noticed another flaw. "There's a hole here. Dulce has surveillance, comm, and detectors. Your team won't even get close enough to see the hatches before you set off alarms."

"That's where we need Katrina," replied Mary Ellen.

Hearing her name, Katrina moved to the dining room and stood at the end of the table. "Me? What do you need? I thought you just needed me for the reactor."

"We need you to take out the communications system and power to the intrusion detection system, including closed-circuit cameras. Can you RV the system and locate the panels?"

"If the object emits enough energy or voltage, I can locate it without having to RV. Energy crosses dimensions. I can sense energy just like sonar detects objects in water. Distance is irrelevant, and accuracy does not have to be perfect. The base is an excellent target because it's isolated." Katrina then directed her statements to Louis and Deborah. "I have a degree in electrical engineering. When I RV, I will be able to identify the proper switchgear to cause a shut down."

"Mary Ellen, don't you know how to RV? They train SEALs on that you know." Robert was getting annoyed by all the favors Mary Ellen was asking of his partner.

"No . . . I don't work with inanimate objects. I work with people and their spirits."

"RV?" Deborah finally asked.

"Remote Viewing," Robert and Katrina responded simultaneously.

Deborah widened her eyes and turned to Louis, who casually sipped his coffee. He was no stranger to the phenomenon and knew Special Forces units received RV training.

"Mary Ellen, I don't think just causing the reactor to heat up or shutting down systems will cause an evacuation. There has to be life threatening events like a radiation leak or explosions." Katrina's statement just created more work for the team.

Creases of concern stretched across Deborah's forehead. She flicked back strands of hair. "Katrina, if you shut down life support systems throughout, won't that kill the creatures we are trying to save?"

"If systems go down, there will be backup power," Louis pointed out. "There is usually something called an uninterrupted power supply or UPS through generators, battery banks; and for the lighting and exits, there are battery packs that last up to three hours. Katrina will have to RV which systems power the lab so the outage won't affect the specimens."

"I can't take out systems unless they are active, so I'll need to RV those backup systems too. This will take a while."

Katrina looked at Robert, then she closed her eyes. The room became silent as she concentrated on the underground base. The voices and movement around her faded into a muffled background of imperceptible one-dimensional sound. The rest of the team continued their discussion about timing the events.

Robert studied the board, then looked at the screen on Louis's laptop. "Your team should be approaching the south base area off J2 when the decoy team reaches this Indian Route 140. That's when you'll need to have the systems shut down. You'll have no more than thirty minutes before they realize what is going on. The next big event is the reactor job. Kat will need about five minutes to get the temperature to rise to dangerous levels. Once they leave the area, your team will have to move fast. Blackhawks and hummers will probably show up forty minutes after they call a distress. Add some time to make sure they have sensitive material on board," Robert added. "Once Kat works on the reactor, shutting down the power, it will be dark and smoky. No one will stay in the darkness without ventilation."

"So, we are expecting Katrina to shut down the intrusion alarm system, communications, work on the reactor, shut down power and uninterrupted power supply—all in that order? Can she do that, Robert?"

Robert nodded, realizing Deborah understood the complexity of the mission.

"I can do that." Katrina stopped visualizing. "Bobby, take notes."

Katrina rubbed her eyes, and returned to full concentration and awareness on the room and the others in it. She took a few moments to collect her thoughts, to make sure what she said next came out right the first time and wouldn't need a lot of further explanation.

She cleared her throat. "It's actually two entirely different facilities. The human side has a small footprint while the reptilian side is bigger, mostly corridors," she began. "Both have seven levels. The human side is made of concrete. The ET side is excavated, like a rabbit warren. There are no straight lines inside. There are no stairs as we would build them, because their feet are too large, plus they use ramped tunnels that are too steep for humans. The reptilian lab is on the sixth level down on the north end. The team should enter a hatch closest to the reptilian side and go down to the lab. Once the fire alarms are activated or disarmed, airlocks separating the two facilities will open and stay open. Find the airlock on the sixth level to get to the lab. The lab rooms are arranged around the core that supplies power, communications, water, and ventilation. The human side is powered by one reactor located on the side closest to the river on the seventh level, which is at water level. The reptilians use Tesla technology with rods driven into the earth. They don't use the wiring systems for power distribution; they use electromagnetic wireless power, which is not as vulnerable as conventional distribution systems. I am not going to work on the reactor. It's too risky. If there is a leak, your team will be poisoned."

Mary Ellen's jaw dropped hearing that statement.

"The voltage is supplied by a transformer. There is an uninterrupted power supply with three backup generators. All power production is on the seventh level down. Since it is a sealed facility, its air is supplied through camouflaged vents and fans. A power failure will stop air intake. The facility has a sprinkler system throughout.

There are two fire pumps and a huge water tank just underground for fire suppression. I think it holds between 80,000 and 100,000 gallons."

Mary Ellen smiled. "That tank holds 100,000 gallons. Man, you are good. And detailed."

"If I heat the transformer, I can make it explode, then it will catch fire. With the fire pumps out, the fire will spread."

"I'm afraid that's not accurate, Katrina." Louis interjected, noticing the frowns of the others. *I don't mean to ruin the party, but . . .* "Even with the pumps not functioning, the water will flow through the impellers and eventually the piping. The gravity feed will cause the water to reach the seventh level, and there will still be enough pressure for the water to flow out of the heads. Eventually, the water will accumulate in the room and rise to the level where it will drown the fire. That won't cause an evacuation. What about the UPS?"

"It's a standard battery room for eight hours of backup. The room is huge," Katrina said.

"Batteries can explode. A series of banks can have the force of a detonated bomb. Can you make the batteries explode?"

"Sure, all I need to do is introduce a surge back to the banks. But what about the backup generators? Those are huge units—like locomotive engines. I could work on them and try to get them to blow, too. The blast will be enormous."

"The generators won't come on immediately, and there are too many safety mechanisms designed in those units for you to be able to do what we need," Louis said. "I think the best chance is using the battery room. The damage that it causes will surely result in the evacuation we need. Once the power is out completely, the emergency lights will activate. We will need those lights to get around the facility once we enter it."

"On the reptilian side, I need to locate lights and control boards. The ETs do not need as much lighting as humans do for the same tasks, so lights are not as powerful."

Robert showed concern about everything that Katrina was committing to do. So did Deborah. "What about the specimens, Katrina? Have you identified the systems that power the lab?"

"Yes. There are four crescent-shaped labs on that level, radiating from the core. Each one has a glass-enclosed tank with each of the specimens in their own life support sac with tubes and wires attached. I think each tank is for a specific stage of development. There are ten to twelve specimens sharing each tank. The lab is on a separate backup system that will not be impacted. The ETs will evacuate at the fifth level where their UAVs are staged. There are camouflaged hangar doors recessed on the side of the mesa where they exit from a long track."

Robert added another note, ENTER LAB. He then turned to Mary Ellen. "What did you intend to do once you got to the lab?"

"Find my child and get him out."

"Kat said that they are in glass tanks with sacs. How are you going to get it out?"

Mary Ellen paused for a bit, then revealed the most unbelievable part of the plan. "I have been advised that I will have help."

"What? Who advised you? What kind of help?"

Deborah and Louis looked at each other, their faces long with equal concern, as if looking into emotional mirrors.

"They are good ETs. They are a militant arm of our galaxy but will not engage in combat. The activities at Dulce are a violation of universal laws, but the good ETs do not want to risk a war with the reptilian race, so they cannot do anything themselves. Once we get to the lab, they will assist us."

It was tough for Robert to accept the existence of a benevolent militant race that would assist the team. He glared at Katrina, who nodded and winked as if to say "I told you so." Robert then stared at the board. Louis drew a floor plan of the lab level according to Katrina's description and showed it to her. Katrina made some minor corrections.

"How much time do we have before they realize what is going on?" asked Deborah.

Robert continued to look at the board. "Thirty minutes from the time the area is clear to enter the hatches. Your ET friends better hold up their end of the bargain because once someone figures out what is going on, the choppers will turn around, and you'll have trained mercenaries with night vision hunting you down. Those guys won't need to land. They will rappel rapidly." Robert wanted to make sure Mary Ellen understood the danger. "Your vehicle. Where are you going to leave it? It could be damaged by the fire or spotted by security forces."

"I was planning on leaving it by the Navajo River under a camo net."

"Get one of your decoy friends to drive you to the staging area where you could see the hatches open and drop you off, then have him park close by until your team is ready."

Robert pointed his index finger to himself, tapping his chest. Katrina slowly nodded and went back to the kitchen. "I am going with you guys," Robert said. His decision had the effect of making time stop on the others, who were stunned. "We are not yet ready for the mission. You need some training. Let's all get cleaned up, dressed, and meet here in an hour, then I'll take you to one of my prized sheds."

Katrina approached Robert after everyone else left for their rooms.

"You know I'm OK with your decision to go with them, but I have to ask why did you volunteer? I thought you were done with armed conflicts."

"As we were putting together the plan, I felt an excitement I did not have since...Afghanistan. It's almost obscene to feel that." Robert paused. "But most importantly, I'm going to make sure those three, to include Mary Ellen who is your close friend, succeed."

Robert reached out to Katrina and pulled her toward him, holding her close. "With me and you on that team, those aliens have no idea what's coming."

* * *

As planned, everyone showed up for a light lunch. Robert told the group they needed to stay at the house for at least three days to mentally prepare, receive some weapons and tactics training, and rehearse the operation plan until everyone could describe it accurately. After lunch, he led them to his workshop. He opened a cabinet to reveal an alarm panel and entered a code, which opened an extra heavy-duty steel door built into a concrete masonry wall that extended past the ceiling.

Robert opened the door, turned on the light, and walked in. The others followed, one by one. They stared in silence at the sight of an assortment of small caliber weapons displayed for use, not for exposition. The distinct smells of solvent, spent gunpowder, and polished metal confirmed the room's function. To the right of the doorway was a table with cleaning pads, rods, brushes, and cleaning fluid. Above the table was a rack of a dozen Glock 9mm pistols—all without magazines. At the center of the room was a closed steel case mounted on the wall. Robert indicated that there were shotguns and hunting rifles inside.

Louis was wowed by the arsenal in the vault. "What the hell, Robert; are you expecting a war?"

"In my line of work, and with the possibility that Katrina's past could come back to haunt her, it is always good to be prepared." To the left of the doorway was a locked rack of six AR-15s lined up, barrels up, with collapsible stocks, infrared lasers, scopes, and suppressors—all immaculately clean. Below each rack was storage for the weapons' ammunition and magazines. Robert unlocked the AR-15 rack and issued each person a rifle.

"We are going out back behind the windmill to get acquainted. Since you all have some familiarity with guns, we won't waste time with the basics. We are just going to load a couple magazines and shoot at targets in various positions and then with obstacles. Everyone, grab a box of ammo, a couple of magazines, and use the table to load."

Mary Ellen felt uneasy. "Robert—I have a problem with using a weapon like this."

"That weapon will enable you to keep all of *us* safe, not just yourself."

Mary Ellen tried to counter. "I think that if we have to fire these things, the operation is a failure, so why take them along?"

"We haven't talked about how we are going to get out of there. You said we will have help. Did your friends tell you what kind of help?" asked Robert.

"No—they communicate with me in vague terms. They only tell me what I need to know, and I trust them. They won't let us get killed."

"As long as there is an unknown in the plan—and it's a huge unknown, I will want us to be armed."

"Robert's right. There's no harm in having a backup plan," Deborah said.

"Spiritually, it just doesn't feel right. When I fire a round, it's like my spirit starts to wear away. It is violence and it is meant to kill."

"If your plan works and if your friends come through, you won't have to fire a shot, right?"

Mary Ellen did not respond as she slowly resumed loading with the others.

While the team was loading, Robert opened a locker under the AR-15 rack. It held tactical clothing and accessories—all black. There were multiple ensembles for each size. He issued each member body armor, a tactical style vest, a skull cap, night vision goggles, regular goggles, and a scarf. Robert led the team out of the vault and back into the shop for more room. He guided them to stand in one row facing him and place the items on the floor in the order of issue.

"My guess is that you have never worn this complete outfit, so wait for me to explain what these are before you put them on," Robert said.

An overly excited Louis wasn't listening and incorrectly tried to put the vest on first.

"Louis, if you want to return alive, you need to listen to every instruction I give you from now on. Take that off and wait for my direction…private." Robert's remark drew a chuckle out of Deborah. He turned to the others. "This is serious, guys. You are undertaking a monumental and dangerous operation. We need to function cohesively. Everyone's life will depend on it."

As they nodded their understanding, Robert carefully explained the armor. "Wearing all the equipment that you see, you will be carrying a total of about twenty-five pounds, not counting your weapon." He demonstrated how the body armor was to fit to protect the wearer. "Now, let's put it on."

Robert explained each piece of equipment to go on the vest: magazine pouches, first aid kit to include tourniquet and gauze, and spare batteries for the flashlight and the night vision goggles. He then demonstrated the use of the water bladder and the storage compartment. He had them put the vest on over the body armor. After everyone was able to put their gear on, he walked over to each person to inspect. Then he ordered them to wear the tactical goggles and the scarf.

"When we get to Dulce, we are going to be dressed for stealth. That includes the scarf just over your nose, and the goggles to hide your face in case there are facial recognition devices. You also need to get used to putting the gear on and taking it off. You will be wearing this every day for the next three days until we execute the operation."

After the group put on the gear, Robert took out some target materials and ear protection, and led them out of the vault to the out-of-doors. Robert closed and locked the heavy steel door but did not activate the alarm. They walked beyond the windmill and the duck pond to the far

end of the property. There, he set up targets at twenty-five yards for each of his students. After emphasizing weapon safety, he instructed them to load the weapons and fire five rounds at the target. After every turn, he had them stop, remove the magazine, clear the chamber, and place the weapons on the ground facing down on metal stands. He instructed them to step away and invited them to inspect their targets. This continued until Robert was confident that each member's technique was sound. He directed the team to practice with the weapons and movements all day for three more days, to include night operations, until he was certain that everyone was comfortable with their weapons and gear. From this point, and until the mission was completed, those were the only things the team would be familiar with.

13

PRE-ASSAULT

Lizards are used as clan animals in some Native American cultures. Tribes with Lizard Clans include the Hopi and the Pueblo tribes of New Mexico. —Native Languages of the Americas website

Louis lay in bed, staring at the mountains in the distance. It had only been a week since he left Chicago. He wasn't homesick, but he was concerned about not knowing what lay ahead. This planned assault—yes, an assault by any standard—was the most dangerous thing in which he had ever participated. If he participated. If it happened. Even with the training complete, the image of himself with a gun in a military-style operation was so foreign to anything else in his civilian life. Remarkably, he had not lost his shooting skills, though the surprise marksman was Mary Ellen. Having Robert as their leader gave Louis some comfort but didn't completely sweep away his fear. He wondered, if he was feeling fear now, what would he feel when they descended into the unknown? He wanted to text his kids before leaving; it was too early in the morning, so he'd wait a couple hours.

Meanwhile, the chat session between Deborah and Susan lasted into the wee hours of the morning. In keeping with a self-imposed operational security, Deborah avoided mentioning Dulce, last names, and dates as they talked. She too was pleased to discover she still had her shooting eye. Susan told her she felt better knowing Robert was leading the group. She also told Deborah she thought Katrina's life story was like something out of a superhero comic book, not real life: *psychokinesis? remote viewing?* Deborah had anticipated Susan's many questions. The one she would not answer was: "What did you get yourself into?" Not surprisingly, Deborah had difficulty getting out of bed in the morning.

Mary Ellen had texted her decoy helpers the night before, three friends committed to her request. Like her, they were aware of the base's presence and curious, but had no intention of getting in. They just wanted to see how close they could get. Dulce residents were split between believers and non-believers. Believers pointed to ancient lore of the *Lizard people* echoed by more recent stories; among other developments, Dulce had become a prime destination for television crews working on shows about the paranormal. Mary Ellen first met her friends during the on-site production of a show on the Discovery channel hosted by Jesse Ventura. She was satisfied to find like-minded young Jicarilla Apache, and she kept in touch with them over the course of four years. When Mary Ellen told them she wanted to get close to the base, they were intrigued.

Then she proposed the idea of their acting as decoys. Would they do it? Enthusiastically, as it turned out. They were attracted to taking part in the daring act. Mary Ellen's friends looked up to her. Even though she was Jicarilla, she was also an outsider. She'd been put up for adoption and raised in Albuquerque by an older couple who weren't able to have their own children. As Mary Ellen got older, Mr. and Mrs. Grimes encouraged her to learn about her people, her race, her true self. When she turned sixteen, they offered to drive with her to Dulce, her first trip back since her infancy.

Her adoptive parents had good intentions in showing her place of birth. Being strangers to the Native Americans, the town didn't give them a warm welcome when they first arrived. They stopped at the reservation's center: an old, rundown, single-story school building with a gym. The parents introduced themselves to the receptionist. They explained Mary Ellen was adopted years ago while the mother was in her teens and were curious about the mother and the father. They mentioned the mother's last name was Velarde.

Most of the Native American people on the reservation behaved as a tight group and preferred to keep things to themselves, away from outsiders. Another aspect of life on the reservation was clans, where many people were related to each other. The receptionist knew of the Velarde woman. She died in a highway accident when a logger heading the opposite direction crossed the centerline. Ironically, the father had been working jobs around the state in the timber industry. A drinking problem landed him in and out of jail. He was not living in Dulce, though she had many natural cousins, aunts, and uncles there. Upon understanding the situation, the receptionist made a few calls, enabling Mr. and Mrs. Grimes and Mary Ellen to visit relatives. She learned more about her family and the tribe's history from her occasional visits. Gradually, she was accepted as one of them.

After her parents encouraged her to get a degree in social work from the University of New Mexico, she changed her name in honor of her natural mother and people. She sought work at the reservation and eventually replanted her roots. From the day she started working there, she was welcomed and accepted as a member of the tribe. Mary Ellen was looking forward to going back to Dulce to see her friends after nearly two weeks away.

Their last night together before the operation began intimately, but now, Robert and Katrina rested in each other's arms from a night that turned fraught with fretful and restless sleep. Katrina was concerned about how Robert would react if there was any violence. Anything could happen with active PTSD. She listened to the planning sessions and watched the training on the property. Not immediately seeing a need for concern, she cautiously measured potential unknowns. Staying on sequence was important while methodically reviewing all the places she was to direct her energy. Did she underestimate what was needed? Or could there be contingency backup systems of which she was not aware? Both questions concerned her. The former CIA asset was also thinking about the circuit and how she had retired it in 2007. She reasoned that if she was able to take care of the first part of her mission, the rest of the work should also be successful. Katrina mentioned this to Robert, who already determined a couple of fail-safe milestones for the mission, and that was the first one. This made her feel a little better, but she wasn't ready to leave Robert and the bed.

* * *

Robert had been in this kind of situation before. It was the day to pack up and move to a location to rendezvous with another team. There, they would compare notes and go over the operation, over and over again. Only now, he was the leader of a team not made up of skilled experienced Rangers like himself. Robert rationalized that Deborah and Louis had military experience, but a former Air Force security policeman and a former Air Force civil engineer were no comparison to a Ranger, and this mission was nowhere near anything Robert had experienced before. He was certain none of his prior commanding officers would have approved this planned assault; it was like something or somebody was controlling judgement. *Is Mary Ellen using some kind of mind trick with us? She said she had nothing to do with the dream that Katrina and I had. Who did?*

Robert went over the things he needed to do before leaving for Chama. It was still early. Katrina moved closer to him, and they embraced and talked about what lay ahead and how they felt.

The last morning at Katrina's place started late. Everyone was either consciously or subconsciously delaying the departure. Backpacks were issued in an unused condition. Uncertain about the duration of the operation, some people added spare clothing. Louis revealed that he had no intention of parting with the gear he bought specifically for the trip to Mount Shasta. Mary Ellen and Deborah picked out their own must-haves. These acts of going against uniformity perturbed Robert. Then he added a number of tools and accessories he found to be handy in the field, including a spare pistol with a suppressor. Everyone showed up in the kitchen with their packs, as if heading to summer camp. Katrina put together one last hearty brunch.

When everyone was done eating, Robert left the table, slid into one of his ATVs, and drove to the workshop to access the vault. He selected the team's weapons, meticulously packed them in cases, placed the cases in his vehicle, then transferred the load to Deborah's SUV. On the second trip to the vault, he picked out the remaining gear to include MREs (meals ready to eat), magazines, and ammunition before locking up and driving back to the SUV.

After clearing the dining room, the group, including Katrina, sat down to go over the chronology of events for the operation. Throughout the discussion, it was evident that not one of them had missed a single lesson. Confidence blossomed in everyone's body language. Mary Ellen was pleased her wish to rescue the captive creatures, including her own child, appeared more a reality.

It was time for one last check on supplies and gear. Robert mentioned the SUV was packed. Everything was set to go, and the group said their goodbyes to Katrina. Mary Ellen hugged her and thanked her and they hugged again, wishing each other peace and a jubilant return. As she entered the vehicle, Louis spotted tears in Mary Ellen's eyes. He reached out his hand and squeezed hers for a moment.

Robert remained in the house with Katrina. They embraced and kissed. "Tell me all about it when you get back," she said.

Robert picked up his gear, stowed it in the back, and got in the front seat. Katrina stepped out on the porch and waved as Deborah's SUV headed off.

* * *

Robert's team arrived at their motel in the mid-afternoon. They checked into two adjacent rooms where they could see the vehicles. Deborah's SUV was backed into the parking space against the sidewalk.

The decoy team arrived in a dusty, beat-up Jeep Cherokee, its broken grill resembling missing teeth. The rear bumper was a junkyard find off a Cherokee of another tribe. Wheel covers were long gone, and none of the tires matched. Robert's team gathered in one of the rooms. Mary Ellen recognized the creaky sound of the driver's side door swinging open. Through the blinds, she saw her friends exit what would be her team's ride.

"What the heck is that?" The rattled Jeep was not exactly what Robert would have chosen. His question grabbed Louis and Deborah's attention as they looked out, underwhelmed.

"Our urban assault vehicle," Mary Ellen mused. "Don't knock it. It will blend well with the rest of the cars and trucks there."

"Ok, 'A' for appearance, but is it safe and dependable?"

"It's fine, Robert. It runs a lot better than it looks. I've ridden in it a few times already."

Mary Ellen didn't wait for her friends to knock. She opened the door and happily greeted Billy, Jenny, and Sky, who waved and smiled as Mary Ellen approached them by the back of the vehicle. She hugged all three, one at a time. After they talked about her trip to Pennsylvania and back, she invited them into the room to meet the rest of the team. Robert stood near the door, still annoyed by the sight of the heap. Louis was sitting with his back against the headboard on one bed, and Deborah sat at the edge of the other bed. Mary Ellen introduced her friends to the team, and they all shook hands.

Robert immediately reviewed the plan to make sure Mary Ellen's friends were clear on how they were to carry out their assignments. He looked at Jenny; she *did* resemble Mary Ellen. He emphasized they were a decoy team, driving Deborah's SUV to Dulce and staying the night and most of the next day at Mary Ellen's trailer. They exchanged phone numbers for texting. Robert wanted them to text only if they got pulled over or arrested. Other than that, the phones would remain silent throughout the operation.

"Arrested?" Billy and Jenny hoped it would not get to that.

"They will arrest you thinking that they have me. You will not have done anything illegal. Once they figure they have the wrong people, they will let you go."

"I noticed that there are a few shiny black SUVs in town. They really stand out," said Sky to Mary Ellen.

Mary Ellen looked at Robert, who nodded. "They're expecting you, Mary Ellen, just as we figured. As soon as you guys get to Dulce, they'll keep track of you. You have to maintain the decoy posture. Once you get to her trailer, they may put a vehicle there to watch and possibly listen. Turn the phones off until you leave tomorrow. It is vital they think Mary Ellen is in the trailer. If they have sensitive listening devices, they'll be able to hear conversations. Be sure to address Jenny as Mary Ellen—always."

"Wait, I just thought of something." Deborah recognized a flaw in the current plan. "If they're expecting us, they're probably assuming that we'll arrive with a vehicle with out-of-state plates. Once they see the vehicle enter town and go to Mary Ellen's, they will surely do a search to find out the registration. I have to be driving my SUV."

"You're right. They need to see you exiting your SUV and go into my trailer. We will pick you and Sky up before we go to the mountain. Take your tactical gear with you. We'll keep the rest for when you join us," said Mary Ellen.

"I have a concern about them seeing four people go into your trailer, and when it is time for your decoy friends to leave, there will only be two going to the mountain," indicated Robert, recognizing another flaw. "I suppose that they'll follow the decoy team or alert another unit of the departure, so if they are still there and see us come and pick the two up, the decoy plan won't work."

"I have a rear door. There's a hill behind my trailer. It is not very high: about one hundred feet. When you leave, Jenny will drive. First, go to my Jeep, start it, turn it toward any vehicle that may be sitting in front, and shine the high beams into the cab so the occupants are impaired. Turn on my lightbar too. At that moment, Deborah and Sky, you two exit from the rear of the trailer and run to the hill. It is about six hundred feet away. We have to give the illusion there are four people going into the Jeep. Billy, when you come out of the trailer, open the passenger side door, and leave it open, then quickly go back in the house. When you come back out, open the rear door on your side and close it, then get in the front and close it. Jenny, you do the same thing on the driver's side. The bright light will prevent them from seeing your movements, but they will hear the doors opening and closing. Give Deborah and Sky a couple minutes to get to the hill, then leave slowly, keeping the lights on the unit as long as possible."

"They'll still see how many people are in the car through the windows," replied Robert.

"No. Tinted glass is a must here. Once Jenny and Billy are in the car, no one will be able to see the occupants," said Mary Ellen.

"Ok. Jenny and Billy leave the trailer at sundown, which will be 7:45 p.m. It should take fifteen minutes to get to the north side of the restricted area. We expect you'll get pulled over before getting there. Our team will leave here at seven o'clock. We'll pick up Deborah and Sky by the hill at 7:50. We should be at the south end a couple of minutes before eight o'clock. Whatever you guys do, don't mess with those people in the black SUVs. Avoid eye contact, no gestures. Act as if they aren't there. They won't think twice about making anyone disappear, understand?"

Jenny and Billy looked at each other. This was not sounding like a prank anymore.

"Guys, I know you thought that this would be a cool thing to do, like an adventure to fight the boredom, but this is serious and you have to listen and follow all the steps Robert described."

Robert nodded. "Remember, text us only *if* you get pulled over or arrested."

Robert gave them a code phrase to indicate the event, then required the decoy team to recite their part of the plan two more times before closing the meeting. He and the team transferred the weapons and gear from Deborah's SUV to Billy's Jeep, then concealed it all from plain sight.

Witnessing the weapons and gear, Mary Ellen's friends recognized the severity of the situation. "We cleaned it up for you, Mary Ellen," said Jenny.

"And we stopped smoking in it too," added Billy.

Much to the delight of Mary Ellen's friends, Robert suggested everyone go to the hotel's restaurant for dinner after locking the vehicles. They shared stories about the local area and pranks that other friends had been involved in.

* * *

With the approaching darkness, Deborah and Mary Ellen's friends needed to get back to the trailer to settle for the night. Mary Ellen asked them to be careful with her car and not speed if they were being followed but to slow down gradually. She also reminded them to get groceries for tomorrow since she had emptied the refrigerator before leaving town.

"Wow! Nice car, Deborah!" Sky explained that a nice car like hers wasn't often seen in Dulce unless it belonged to a cop or a senior tribal councilman. Deborah waved goodbye and drove away. They stopped at a local convenience shop as suggested.

It took about forty-five minutes for Deborah and the decoy team to get to Mary Ellen's trailer. The partial full moon made everything visible. As Deborah's SUV turned off the highway to Hillside Drive, Billy noticed a couple of shiny black SUVs with dark tinted windows parked and facing each other off the side of the road.

"Did you guys get what that Robert guy said when we mentioned these SUVs were parked around town?"

"Yeah. He said that they were expecting her just like he figured," replied Jenny.

"So now, whoever those guys are, that are looking for Mary Ellen, think she is riding with us!"

"Yeah. That's the whole point, Sky. We *are* supposed to give the illusion that Mary Ellen is with us."

Jenny and her friends were never told Mary Ellen's exact plans or intentions. "The fewer people that know what Mary Ellen is up to, the better," Deborah explained. "It's for your own safety that you not know more."

* * *

The two National Reconnaissance Office units were positioned to look for a vehicle with out-of-state plates. Unit One spotted the late model SUV with Missouri plates heading west into town. It relayed to the other unit they would follow it. As this happened, Unit Two's agent in the passenger seat remarked to his partner he had felt a sensation.

"Did you feel that?"

"Feel what?"

"Whatever it was, it came on fast and strong, and now it's gone."

"What's gone?"

"It felt like interference—like a hiss in my head."

"And it's gone now?"

"It's very faint and it's getting weaker—oh…it's gone."

"You probably need an upgrade or some reprogramming."

* * *

Although Robert and Mary Ellen emphasized how important it was for Billy, Sky, and Jenny to play their parts as instructed, they were intentionally vague about what *his* team was going to do. As they passed by the black SUVs, Deborah looked in the rearview mirror for sign of movement or lights flashing. To her relief, nothing happened.

The four turned onto the dirt drive that served Mary Ellen's trailer, stopping next to her Jeep. The single-wide unit was big enough for one, but a challenge for four adults. A bright moon was over the horizon as Billy and Sky went outside to smoke. Their chatter stopped as they looked toward the road and noticed one of the black SUVs parked on the opposite side of the street. Billy put his index finger to his closed pursed lips. Sky gave a slight nod. They resumed their discussion, every so often stealing a glance toward the vehicle. Finishing their cigarettes, they went back inside, immediately advising Jenny and Deborah via handwritten notes about what they discovered.

Out of curiosity, Jenny looked out the window. She wanted to go out for smoke too, but resisted since she was supposed to be Mary Ellen, and Mary Ellen didn't smoke. Conversations for the rest of the night included talk about going to the north end of the restricted area. Before turning in for the night, the boys headed out for another smoke. This time, the black SUV was gone, but it did not change their approach in conversation. Outside the trailer all was quiet…eerily quiet.

14

SHOCKS AND AWE

*The supreme art of war is to subdue the enemy
without fighting. —Sun Tzu*

Time dragged on as they waited, and waited, and waited for the evening to arrive. Deborah decided to try meditation; it made her feel better. Afterward she took a nap so she would be rested for the operation. During one of the smoke breaks in the afternoon, the boys noticed the black SUV again and alerted the women with a note.

* * *

After breakfast at the hotel restaurant, the team went back to their rooms, remaining there until it was time to leave. Robert prepped his gear again. Mary Ellen meditated and napped, and Louis watched TV and did some meditation as well. Robert texted Katrina one line: "7:53 p.m." The time that Katrina would start disabling the intrusion detection system (IDS). As it did for the decoy team, time crawled. Robert called on the team to gather in his room at 6:15. He was in full black. Louis and Mary Ellen wore blue jeans and hiking boots.

While getting ready, Louis confided in Mary Ellen. "Yesterday, I contemplated my role given to me. I asked my guides and guardians for forgiveness. I even communicated to my deceased relatives."

"Did you do that because of what we were going to do today?"

"I think so."

"And how do you feel now?"

"You know something? I don't feel scared. It's like I sensed that I *was* being watched."

"Remember, I, too, am one of your guardians, and my guides tell me you are going to be fine."

"I hope your guide was watching the right version of the timeline," chimed in Robert.

The training allowed them to don their gear almost effortlessly, mimicking Robert's disciplined demeanor, and the team left the hotel at 6:55.

* * *

At the trailer, it was time to leave for the north side of the base. Sky and Deborah waited at the back door. Jenny and Billy were also ready as they turned off the lights. Jenny went out the door and noticed the black SUV still there across the street, to the side. As planned, she went to start Mary Ellen's Jeep and positioned it to direct the lights at the black SUV's cab. Billy gave Sky and Deborah the sign to leave. Jenny and Billy did exactly as they were instructed, to give the illusion of four people going in the vehicle. Mary Ellen's car remained in park for enough time for Deborah and Sky to be in the clear. Billy and Jenny slowly left and headed north with the black SUV following. As they turned north on Sandhill Drive, Billy's Cherokee approached Dulce Rock Drive to pick up Sky and Deborah. Deborah, relieved to see her friends, jumped in quickly. Mary Ellen pointed out that Katrina would shut down the intrusion detection in five minutes.

Billy and Jenny avoided speeding. They would get to the restricted area in about ten minutes. There were no fences and no signs to warn people. It was well known that people would be harassed if they went off the main road. They turned off J2 heading east then north on a steep winding dirt road up the mountain. Just after heading up the mountain, the black SUV passed them and sped away. There was another set of lights behind them. Jenny and Billy looked at each other, confused, feeling tense.

* * *

Most occupants of the underground base were in the barracks and lounges, three levels below the surface. The duty officer was on the second level, monitoring the base's life support systems. Four members were on assignment with a reptilian crew and scheduled to return just before dawn. The Commander was in his suite. He had learned to dislike his job. The facility was over twenty years old and—except for the reactor, the labs, and the servers—it sorely needed upgrades. What made it worse was that his group was serving the Draco race in the adjoining facility in a supporting role, taking orders from them. Activity surrounding the base had declined since the peak years of the late 1970s, when there were twice as many working there. This was due to increased awareness of the base, and the fact the reptilians were finishing their human research. The Commander was planning to leave for a place with real action, like Somalia or Kashmir. Little did he know he would soon experience a level of excitement beyond imagination.

* * *

Katrina took out her circuit box. She sat still in the darkened living room, focusing her remote viewing toward the south end of the underground base. During her first activity, deactivating the IDS, alarms, and communications, she pinpointed the communications room panels housing the wiring, circuitry, and breakers. After sensing there was no effect on her brain, she texted CLEAR to Robert.

The officer of the day, monitoring the building's systems, noticed his desk phone shut off. Glancing at the panel of indicators, he noticed the light indicating the IDS blinking red. He called the Commander using his cell phone.

* * *

Katrina viewed the fire-fighting systems. She directed her thought acutely and precisely, causing damage to her targets. The shutdown of the fire alarm system successfully activated the airlocks that separated the human side from the reptilians. While the officer of the day was talking to the Commander, discussing the circuits shut-down, he glanced at the panel again, noticing the indicator light to the fire pumps turn red. Still on the phone, he alerted the Commander.

* * *

Focusing on the 600 KVA transformer, down the line from the reactor, Katrina redirected energy back to the device, causing a surge and a fire. The fire shot flames up toward the ceiling and jetting out the sides of the transformer. Soon after, a blast fueled by combustible gases rocked that floor, blowing open the room's heavy-duty double doors off their hinges. As expected, even without the pumps operating, the water began to flow out of the sprinkler heads at a very low pressure.

The Commander heard the blast just as he was going to call on a team to investigate the outages. He fled his room, ran to the nearest lounge, and ordered two men to go below and find out what happened. The transformer failure activated the backup system of batteries. This Uninterrupted Power Supply, designed in the late 1990s, had a conventional eight-hour backup, providing 300 kilowatts. Normally, a facility would have generators working continuously in the event of an outage. In this environment, it was not practical because fuel would have to be delivered on a periodic basis, at least weekly. This would take away the secrecy. As two men approached the seventh level, Katrina concentrated on energy coming from the bank of batteries. She reversed it back, causing them to overheat, converting them into a bomb with an equivalent yield of six hundred pounds of dynamite, or two-thirds the payload of a Tomahawk cruise missile.

The facility was designed to counter a threat based on a risk analysis that evaluated a hypothetical enemy and weapons that would be used. The official name of the document that dictated this type of construction was the "Design Basis Threat" or DBT. The hypothetical enemy would not originate on earth. Any attack by such an enemy would certainly result in destruction by a superior force regardless of the measures for survivability. Consequently, the structure was not hardened to withstand anything that would have the impact of a direct hit.

The detonation was heard throughout the facility, including the reptilians' area. The shockwave ripped apart the bodies of the two men sent to investigate the transformer explosion. Some of the pressure was released through vent openings that terminated at a cave at river level in the west wall. The blast blew out the vent and duct system. It also ripped through the west side of the seventh level, demolishing the immediate area including concrete walls and adjacent columns, displacing a portion of the foundation. Damaged columns that had supported the structure above collapsed, causing the sixth level to give way and, in turn, the structure. This progressive collapse continued all the way to the top, including a section of the west wall. Earth that covered the collapsed section of the roof and west wall caved in. The entire southwest quadrant of the underground facility on the mercenary side was destroyed. The sixth, fifth, and fourth level housed labs; the sixth was for cryogenics. The third level housed barracks and support, and the rest of the facility was administrative. Any men on the collapsed third floor were crushed by structure above them. The Commander's suite and nearby lounge were located safely in the northeast quadrant, away from the collapse.

The blast caught the reptilians off guard. They evacuated immediately, heading to the fifth level where aerial vehicles were parked on rails for take-off. Technicians manning the controls of the reactor on the human side, located along the west wall at the north edge, immediately worked to shut it down as the cooling system stopped. Any part of the facility that had not collapsed was filled with dust and smoke, since the ventilation system shut down. Six of eight stairwells remained intact for escape. Only exit lights and the emergency lighting functioned. Fortunately, for the occupants, smoke from below exited the building out of the blown-out vent on the river side. The only communication came from radios or cell phones. Survivors scampered up the remaining exit stairs to the upper levels, checked the second and first levels, and yelled to evacuate the building. The Commander and duty officer immediately initiated the evacuation procedure, then the Commander placed a call to a Los Alamos number.

With urgency in his voice, he notified the connection, "This is Dulce. Mayday. Mayday. We are evacuating. We have heavy damage and a high number of casualties."

"Roger copy. Are you under attack?"

"Negative. The base has been sabotaged. No intruders. We have no power. Power production has been destroyed. Sustained heavy structural damage with complete collapse of a quarter of the building. Reactor has not been damaged. Say again. Reactor has not been damaged. Perpetrators unknown."

"Roger copy. Initiating evacuation procedures. ETA on first wave, twelve minutes. ETA on second wave, thirty-five minutes. What about the *neighbors*?"

"We made contact, then it was lost. It wasn't them. I think they were attacked, too."

"Roger. Have your group ready. Good luck."

The officer ended the call and rushed his people out of danger. He ordered them to get weapons out of the armory before leaving.

Katrina was dizzy, but she needed to do one last thing. It was the most critical activity. Fixed on the reptilian side, she proceeded to reverse the circuitry powering lighting and instrumentation, avoiding any impact on the vehicle bays. This had the effect of an interior electrical storm. The reptilians that had not evacuated in time were caught, in shock, as they witnessed their own getting electrocuted from the random electrical current. If they weren't electrocuted, they were blinded by the intense flashes. Like a disturbed ant hill, the remaining occupants scurried, not finding safe haven. Finally, the central command ordered a complete evacuation to a mothership. Surviving reptilians made their way to the remaining vehicles facing the exterior of the mountain side. They were far from orderly as they rushed into their machines. The remaining ships took off, exiting through concealed portals into the night at a high angle of climb and an urgent speed.

* * *

Jenny and Billy continued to climb up the winding mountain road. They slowed down, approaching a hairpin turn. Halfway into the turn, the black SUV that had passed them moments before crossed the centerline and headed at them from the opposite lane. Jenny instinctively swerved to avoid a collision, but lost control, slid off the road and slammed into the encroaching mountain wall, causing air bags to deploy. Both black SUVs stopped with the occupants inside and engines running. The men in the two units waited to see if there was any movement in the crashed vehicle. The doors remained closed. Vision was obstructed by the tinted cracked safety glass. Fulfilling their assignment to prevent Mary Ellen and her team from reaching the forbidden destination, they left the scene and placed a call to the police station. Local law enforcement would take care of the rest.

* * *

Billy's Cherokee approached the target zone. As soon as they were close enough to where Mary Ellen had indicated the escape hatches were, they stopped and the team exited. Sky moved to the driver's seat. Robert handed out weapons and bags from the back. He instructed them to use their night vision goggles. With everyone in gear, Robert directed Sky to go to his own place, not far from Mary Ellen's trailer, wait for a text, then return to pick up the team. As Sky left, the team took cover in the brush to wait for signs of egress. It was eerily quiet. There was no sign of chaos underground.

That changed—quickly. Moments later, a muffled rumble seemed to come from under them, from the river. It was immediately followed by something akin to a seismic event. Robert and the team felt and heard the commotion from the underground structure's collapse. A part of the earth at the west edge caved in, swallowing two hatches. The team stared in amazement that bordered on shock, recognizing the severity of the destruction. They asked for an evacuation and got annihilation. Such was Katrina's power. As they scanned the area, there was no movement, but in the distance near the Pueblo River, smoke was rising. The light westerly wind carried it over the base area.

Sirens approached the crash on the mountain road, and the Jicarilla Police arrived in two squads. One of the officers recognized Mary Ellen's wrecked vehicle. He radioed to the dispatcher about the crash and requested an ambulance as they were about to check the occupants. Jenny and Billy were not seriously injured, since they had only been traveling at about 35 miles per hour. The police noticed Jenny and Billy were conscious. Billy motioned from the passenger seat that the doors were jammed. The police were able to open the rear passenger doors to extract them. Billy and Jenny requested that an ambulance not be sent, since they did not have insurance to cover the costs.

"Why do you have Mary Ellen's vehicle?" one of the policemen asked.

"She lent it to us for the evening," Billy said.

"Well then, why are you approaching the restricted area?"

"Just curious," Billy told the officer.

The officer radioed back to dispatch that the vehicle belonged to Mary Ellen Velarde, but that she was not present in the vehicle.

Police Chief Rico Martin was listening to his scanner at home and heard about the crash. Moments later he heard it was Mary Ellen's car, which caught his immediate attention. Martin walked to his squad car and radioed the officers on the scene. He instructed them to take the two occupants to the station for questioning; he would meet them there. Martin wasn't the only person monitoring the night's activity. NRO Unit Two was also monitoring the chatter and recognized that Velarde was still at large. They radioed Martin as he was approaching the police station. They were parked in an adjacent lot and were stern with Martin, telling him he was wasting time with the wrong people and that Velarde was still missing.

* * *

"I don't think we need to start a brush fire," Mary Ellen whispered.

As they looked west, in the direction of the base, they spotted movement about fifty yards away. As expected, evacuees were coming out of the remaining hatches. Some were in distress, some were coughing, while others were showing signs of injuries of varying severity. Louis looked up in the northern sky and saw something he could not explain. He motioned to Deborah to look. Mary Ellen and Robert looked up too and saw bright orange lights coming out of the mountain at high speed, climbing out of sight. They remained silent and returned their attention to the open hatches. Robert had the team move closer to the hatches and the smoke. Brush cover allowed them to stay low to the ground as they watched the evacuation.

* * *

The officers at the crash scene placed Jenny and Billy in the backseat of the squad car. Just as they were about to leave, the immediate north sky, close to the horizon, emitted a strange orange glow and bright orange discs zoomed out of the mountain, climbing out of sight into the night sky. The event was witnessed by people in the town below as well, prompting phone calls to the police station.

* * *

Katrina had completed her task but not without cost. It was too much for her, and she anticipated problems. Her head hurt as she clutched the circuit box. Exhausted and nauseous, she collapsed before getting to the couch. As she closed her eyes, she remote viewed Robert and the team ready to go underground. Her final thought before losing consciousness was whether this was going to be another NDE that would increase her power or something worse.

* * *

Robert and his team heard the engines of vehicles approaching. From the same road used to get to the site, the team spotted a column of eight Humvees. The military vehicles were driverless. They stopped at pre-planned locations and uninjured mercenaries boarded their rides quickly as the others waited for helicopters.

From the south, three unmarked modified Blackhawks approached the area and landed quickly. The rotors remained running. Robert fell into a flashback. The other three noticed him crouching lower, his head down, his face against the rough dry grass, motionless. Louis and Deborah looked at each other with dread, recognizing what they saw. Their team leader was having a panic attack.

Mary Ellen bent down and put her hand on Robert's arm. "Robert, you are having an attack. We are alright. You are going to be alright."

"Reach in my back pocket, right side on my belt. You'll find a small bottle with a dropper," he said, trying to catch his breath.

Mary Ellen reached across, opened the Velcro pouch, took out the bottle, unscrewed the cap and loaded the dropper. She handed it to Robert, who turned to her, opened his mouth, and released a few drops under his tongue. The relief was almost instantaneous. Robert returned to his original kneeling position as he witnessed the Blackhawk crews assisting the injured and picking up cases with classified material and equipment. In fewer than fifteen minutes, the evacuation was complete.

"Robert, are you alright?" asked Deborah.

He nodded adamantly. "I'm fine. I'll be alright."

The loaded Humvees departed and the Blackhawks followed afterward. The smoke-proof hatches remained open, as anticipated. Still, a feeling of foreboding spread through the team. They were about to invade one of the most secret facilities in the country.

"I'll be damned," was all Robert could mutter in his amazement. It was *go* time.

* * *

As they drove down the mountain back to town, the policemen in the squad car noticed three low-flying helicopters in the distance approaching. "Something is going on," said the driver. "I don't know what goes on around that mountain, but I've heard stories."

"They're just stories fabricated from native lore describing gods under the mountain. People say that the stories and the legends of the gods are proof of something going on."

Like half the town, the second policeman insisted the stories were nothing more than hoaxes. Wasn't it becoming more and more that way with every town in America? Jenny and Billy looked at each other. As the squad car approached Jicarilla Boulevard, they saw a convoy of eight black Humvees going east at high rate of speed.

"Did you see that?" asked the driver.

"Yeah, eight Hummers, eight black Hummers all going east and pretty fast. Do we call that in?" asked his partner.

"No. They are probably involved with the black SUVs that got here earlier this week. They're probably off-limits."

"What the hell is going on?" The partner was going to talk to Martin about it all—the SUVs, the lights, and the Hummers. When they arrived, the officer had Billy and Jenny sit for questioning as he wrote a report.

* * *

"Katrina told us to enter the hatch closest to the north part of the base," Mary Ellen said.

Louis pointed to the open hatch closest to the north part of the base. It was only about a hundred yards away. The team got up from their secure place, adjusted their goggles, pulled their scarves over their faces, and ran to the hatch. Robert looked around as they continued to run. No sign of anything. It was quiet, the bright moon partially shrouded by the smoke. Robert entered first, then Mary Ellen, then Louis. Deborah provided rear security and closed the hatch as the team began its descent into the dark unknown.

* * *

NRO Unit Two drove up to the Chief's car. The driver side window rolled down to reveal two men in black suits with dark glasses.

"Chief Martin. We have strong reason to believe that Velarde had something to do with the Blackhawks that just left from the south mountain. Lock up the two you have in custody. They are accomplices. Get another squad to follow us to the south restricted area, quickly."

The lead NRO agent in Unit Two contacted an asset under the Integrated Weapons Experiments office at Los Alamos.

"Hello?" was the answer. All members at classified facilities are trained not to reveal office or identity.

"This is NRO. You are on a secure line."

"Switching to encryption mode."

"Three birds just left Dulce base. Can you tell me why?"

"They were sent as a response to an SOS. The facility was damaged from an internal threat according to the Commander. There were casualties. The number is unknown now. We have evacuated sensitive material. Any remaining material has been destroyed as part of the denial execution. A number of uninjured men are being driven back to Los Alamos on programmed driverless Hummers. They are approximately fifteen minutes away now."

"Can you have them turn back? We need them to fight."

"Negative. The program does not allow that capability."

As the call ended, the NRO agent felt frustrated, almost defeated. No one was coming back to assist his small posse, and he had no idea how many he was chasing.

* * *

As Robert descended the stairway, he turned to remind the team they had no more than twenty minutes before the return of the helicopters. With the emergency lights providing adequate light, the team removed their night vision goggles and descended the stairs at a faster than normal pace. There was the smell of something electrical burning, but no smoke, as the team moved past the second level . . . and third . . . and fourth . . . finally, to the sixth level below the ground.

Robert checked for heat, the back of his hand against the door. There was none. He opened the door, swinging into the exit stairs. He put his gloved finger to his lips, quieting the team to silence. They caught the smells of wires and concrete dust. Robert recognized something smoldering from the transformer explosion at the seventh level that stopped him temporarily. He led the team north toward the reptilian part of the base, and they arrived at the open airlock. A warning sign announced the restricted area beyond the airlock and that entry without emergency was a violation of a treaty punishable in *Draco* court.

* * *

The NRO agents directed the Chief to follow them. NRO Unit Two sped away and Martin followed without lights or sirens to the south restricted area. Smoke greeted them as they approached the base site. They stopped near the area where the hatches were open; Chief Martin was speechless. The agents quickly exited their SUV, and the Unit Two partner felt another sensation, similar to the interference he'd felt earlier. This time it did not fade and he kept quiet about it. Martin had never been this far inside the restricted area and was about to get out of his car.

The lead agent headed to Martin's car and positioned himself behind Martin. The chief was caught by surprise by a prick, then a burning sensation in his neck. He had been injected with a green fluid: a memory blocker. Everything he would experience for the next couple of hours would be stored in the part of the brain where dreams occur. The drug worked during sleep. After awakening, the memory would be gone, and he would only recall these events by accessing the subconscious part of his brain. Stunned, he immediately turned around, and the agent, without emotion, mechanically explained to him what had happened. It was standard practice to limit witnesses to extremely sensitive information. Martin stood still, feeling betrayed.

"Velarde had something to do with this," said the agent, pointing to the smoke.

"Mary Ellen Velarde? She has wild ideas, but she's mostly harmless. She's a social worker, not a soldier. This is the work of a military mind and had to involve more than one person."

"You do not know her like we do. She is not what she seems. She has abilities. She has acquaintances that are not from this Earth. She was being monitored here, then she showed up out East last week at a convention where she met Louis Silvani, the UFO blogger. Now, she has returned. This destruction is not a coincidence. Look, there is a closed hatch. Whoever is here went in through that one. We'll enter there."

He pointed to the next closest hatch, about one hundred feet away. Martin went down first and the agents followed. They left the hatch open. The second agent felt the interference growing stronger … but now, it was a pleasant, warming tingle in the mind, a new feeling, new and good.

* * *

Robert went through the airlock first. The cave-like interior was uniformly finished with vitrified rock, leaving it warm and humid, a reptilian climate. The surface had an echoing effect. Louis's pulse quickened as he followed Robert and Mary Ellen. No one said a word, walking quietly.

The airlock led them to a curved hallway. It intersected a straighter corridor, down which they proceeded. Louis looked at the entrance of another dark hallway and made out a shape on the floor against the wall about fifty feet away. He left the group, getting closer to the shape, looking back every few feet until he was able to identify it. It was one of the reptilians—prone and lifeless, about seven feet in length, dressed in a uniform similar to one he saw in one of Kaja Jorgensen's portraits. Its skin was dark tan.

He drew closer. The creature's eyes were still open from shock, revealing the alien yellowish-brown organs with black, narrow vertical slits. Its mouth was open enough to let its long dark forked tongue out, exposing large sharp teeth. Louis was slightly terrified but curious as he crept closer to the creature. He noticed a device attached to its belt and knelt down to look at it. It looked like a flashlight. It felt cold and heavy for its size. He unclipped it from the creature's belt, inspected it, and clipped it on his own belt. Louis did not realize it, but his action was in keeping with a warrior's tradition of capturing the opponent's weapons as trophies. Still staring at the creature, he was startled by a hand on his shoulder. He turned quickly, almost stumbling onto the creature's body.

It was Deborah. "Louis, what the hell are you doing? Are you looking for trouble? Robert and Mary Ellen are waiting for us. Let's go."

"It's a dead alien! Aren't you interested in this?"

"NO! Absolutely not! C'mon! Remember we have only about fifteen minutes to get out."

She pulled him away, and they returned to Mary Ellen and Robert, who were waiting, visibly upset. Visual indicators were flashing on and off in the area. They reached what appeared to be the core of the facility. It was metallic and cylindrical, encircled by a corridor. Robert led the team into the corridor and four pie-shaped rooms. All were dark with a light reddish-purple glow emanating from their interiors. Mary Ellen sensed something from one of the rooms.

She pointed. "It's in that one!"

One-by one, they entered the selected room. Their discovery left them still with shock and horror. Robert felt himself go flush. It was just as he had seen in his dream. Mary Ellen also gasped at the first sight of the laboratory, as did Louis and Deborah. The room was populated by large tubes where naked humanoid creatures, all alike, were suspended in sacs in a dark pink fluid. There was a dozen on each side of the room with markings on the tubes that did not re-semble any known language. Each creature was connected to wires and tubes that came out of the ceiling. There was a strong organic, sulfuric odor. The beings were motionless, but their eyes were open. They were suspended in a prison of organic fluid and chained to their lifelines, providing a virtual world that would be their reality.

Mary Ellen scanned the room, realizing this was the creatures' home until they were considered ready for release. There would be no social interaction, no verbal communication, no human touch, no tasting, no smelling. She was drawn to one creature following her movement and pulled her scarf down from her face. Robert and the others watched as she approached the transparent tomb-like environ-ment standing in front of the creature whose eyes were more open than the others. She placed her right hand flat against the transparent surface. The creature looked at her closely as it slowly raised its hand to match hers. Tears welled up in her eyes, and she smiled.

The creature's expression changed from flatness to something resembling a smile. She looked back at the group with excitement. "It's mine!"

"OK—it's yours. Now what are we supposed to do?" Robert asked. "Someone at the surface is sure to come to find us. We have no way of getting these creatures or ourselves to safety. We have ten minutes before security forces arrive."

Just as Mary Ellen sensed the direness of situation, and Robert desperately wanted to get out of there, she froze still and went into a trance. Robert and the team, aware that Mary Ellen was unconscious, became confused and began to feel uncomfortable. Three bursts of blinding light appeared beside her, each column shrouding a figure. As the light faded, it revealed blue-skinned humanoids holding what appeared to be weapons.

Mary Ellen regained consciousness to see the beings next to her. "Don't be afraid!" she called out to the team. "They are Arcturians and are here to help us. They communicate to me telepathically. I will relay to you what they want. This was planned so *we* would attack, and they would take the necessary steps without having to kill or injure anyone. From now on, this rescue is in their control."

Meanwhile, Chief Martin and the NRO agents descended the stairwell. Martin was still sore from the injection. The second agent sensed that his feelings were an indication of getting close to one of the intruders. He advised Martin and the lead agent to continue down the stairs. They reached the sixth level, where they were taken by surprise by the smells of the smoke and fire coming from the opposite side of the facility. The second NRO agent took the lead, using his feelings to guide him. His pace quickened as he drew closer. With every step, he sensed a stronger feeling of togetherness. The lead agent followed, unaware of these feelings, trusting his partner. Chief Martin had no idea what was happening; he had no choice but to follow. They came to the airlock—and stopped.

"We are leaving our side, and we are about to go into the side of the Dracos! This is not allowed," warned the lead agent.

"They are in there! I feel it!" replied the partner eagerly.

Martin stood silent. He had heard a word that he'd never heard before. "What's going on? Who are the Dracos?"

"A race of reptilians that have made this part of Earth their home away from their home planet. The *Organization* has had a treaty with them for over 60 years." The agent quickly changed the subject. "You *feel* it?" The lead NRO agent was indoctrinated to not allow feelings that would interfere with work.

"I can't explain it. You have to trust me," replied the partner. The three proceeded to enter the reptilian side of the base.

Mary Ellen and the team heard footsteps from the central core area. Sensing the sound meant danger, Louis unclipped from his belt the artifact he had picked up from the dead reptilian. Soon after, the NRO agents and Martin entered the room.

The Arcturians saw the agents and the police chief enter. They pointed their weapons at the three and fired a burst that paralyzed them, freezing their motor functions, but allowing them to see, hear, and speak.

"Rico!" Mary Ellen cried.

Rico Martin moved his eyes. "Mary Ellen, what is going on? What are you doing in this place? What *is* this place?"

"I can't explain. There's too much to tell. Rico, these are creatures that have been abducted, taken from mothers—some while still in the womb."

The second agent looked at Deborah and spoke up slowly, uttering a word he had never said before to anyone. "Mother?" His eyes were fixed on her.

Deborah lowered her weapon and pulled her scarf down. Realizing what was happening, she was drawn to the paralyzed agent. With tears in her eyes, she picked up his hand and caressed his face. His skin was flawless, smooth, and without any sign of adulthood; there was no facial hair. A lone teardrop formed and descended down his cheek, resting on the corner of his mouth.

"My son?" She kept her hand on his face. "Are you human or are you something else?" She glanced at his partner, also without facial hair and with a porcelain-like complexion.

"I . . . don't know. I never thought about it. I only did as I have been programmed. I . . . felt you when you entered Dulce. I found you like this by following my feelings. It appears I still have that as a part of me somewhere."

Louis stood in awe as a surreal soap opera played out in the room of creatures floating in the transparent sacs. A mother was reunited with her only child. A father of another was about to realize that everything he thought was true about his child and mother was wrong. The frozen bodies caged the emotions that the paralyzed men felt. All of it made Robert nervous. He wanted to get out of the facility before any of the mercenaries would return. Nothing else mattered.

Mary Ellen risked being rude and let the rest of her team understand her own torture. "Rico, remember it was 16 years ago. You accused me of terminating the pregnancy. I realized I lost the baby. I tried to explain what I did not understand. There was no sign of the baby, so it did not appear to be a miscarriage. It even baffled the OB. It was maddening to me. I lost both of you. Eventually, I learned it was taken from me." Rico looked down at the floor, then at Mary Ellen, then the floor again. She then pointed to the creature behind her.

"This grown specimen is ours. I have been communicating with it for all those years. I made up my mind that I was going to get my child back and, with the help of the Arcturians and these people, I was able to put a plan together."

Rico Martin did not need to be temporarily paralyzed. He was in shock. He worked out his best response. "I'm ... so ... sorry, Mary Ellen. I'm sorry. I couldn't believe you before. I now understand why it didn't make sense."

Louis and Robert understood the synchronicity taking place before their eyes.

Deborah looked back at Mary Ellen. "You and the Chief?"

Mary Ellen nodded. The lead NRO agent took it all in. He realized that he too, was once like the creatures in the tubes. The words that came out his mouth were completely out of character with his type. The team recognized this pivotal point in the agent's life.

"Then, I was taken, and so was my partner. They took our humanity away, our feelings, our ..."

"Love," added Deborah as she gazed at her son.

Louis was still holding the reptilian artifact in his hand. One of the Arcturians noticed it and called on him telepathically to give it to him. Louis reluctantly obliged.

The Arcturians instructed Mary Ellen to tell the others that it was time for departure. Mary Ellen did as she was advised. She looked back at her child in the tube and offered her thought of love and assured it that it would be cared for, once again placing her hand on the glass surface. As she stepped back, the enclosures started to glow, each tube enveloped by a bright column of light. The team could see brightness in the corridor as the other rooms also glowed. The light grew brighter, to a blinding level, and suddenly the light was gone and the tubes vacant. Only hoses and wires dangling like marionette strings from the ceiling remained. The Arcturians had taken the creatures for care on their waiting ship. Everyone, including those still under paralysis, watched in amazement.

The lead Arcturian, who had taken the artifact from Louis, looked at it and appeared to make adjustments. He held it like a flashlight, pointed it at a wall, and activated it. A narrow beam shot out and hit the wall surface. The spot began to grow in a clockwise spiral of bluish light until it was the full height of the wall, spinning slowly. Satisfied that the three individuals under paralysis were no longer threats, the Arcturians directed their weapons at them once again. After a mild high-pitched pop, their motor skills returned to normal.

Deborah's son reached out and hugged his mother before she left. They held on tightly for a while.

"What is that?" Robert asked.

"A portal for our escape. The only other way out would be through the way we came, most likely facing heavily armed mercenaries," replied Mary Ellen.

Louis wasn't sure about that good idea. "I got that from one of the reptilians. Where is it going to take us—to their planet?"

"The Arcturian is telling me that our work is not done. We have a job to do on the other end of that portal," Mary Ellen replied, only relaying what she knew.

"Mother?" asked Deborah's son. "I will look for you when you are safe. I will know where you are. I have your life signature now."

"I would love to talk to you, son. Wait!" Deborah wiped away her tears, not ready to leave yet. "Name! Do you have a name?"

"We are given codes. We are contacted using the code. I have no name."

"You do now, Jesse. Jesse Samuel Swift the second."

Rico and the lead agent were speechless. Rico could not know that he would not remember this event and would only dream of it, over and over again. The team stood just outside the brilliant spinning portal. One by one, they walked through. Robert stepped in the portal carefully, as if he was dipping his toe into cold water. Louis followed, as closely as he could without stumbling into Robert from behind. Deborah followed Louis, moving through cautiously, her arms outstretched. Mary Ellen turned, giving a slight wave to Rico, then walked through last, as casually as one would board a plane. The only thing keeping them from turning around was their trust in the Arcturians' message. As Mary Ellen departed, the Arcturians left in a blinding column of light. Rico and the NRO turned around and headed back to the surface. Life would be different for the agents, beginning with the long report Rico needed to write. The next morning, it would be misplaced, and he would wake up not remembering the events after being injected. Consequentially, Rico Martin would continue to hold Mary Ellen accountable for the termination of the pregnancy and behave as if the scene in the lab never happened.

Before leaving Dulce, the lead NRO agent left a small envelope with a personal note on the Chief's desk that read, *Mary Ellen did not terminate her pregnancy.*

Jenny and Billy were also released the next morning, after the agents convinced Martin that they had not stolen Mary Ellen's Jeep. No one except the NRO agents knew about the damaged base. The NRO agents kept the immediate area clear for recovery teams from the mercenary and reptilian sides to gather the remains of the deceased. After that was done, the base was abandoned. Neither the reptilians nor the humans returned. The reptilians were certain that the attack was not from an Earth organization, but they had so many powerful natural enemies they could not accuse any particular race for the attack. No one ever found out where the specimens were taken, and no other mothers would be abducted for their children again.

15

UNQUIET DESPERATION

*Those that can make you believe absurdities can
make you commit atrocities. —Voltaire*

Robert's team emerged from the high-tech gateway into an empty, damp, low-lit intersection of concrete-walled hallways. Doors appeared standard, painted steel with painted steel frames and corresponding room names and numbers written in English. Everything appeared "Earthly," which perplexed the team.

Before they had time to process their new surroundings, the team heard a woman crying for help. An already implausible situation became more staggering. "We need to get out of this intersection. The cries are coming from that hallway." Robert pointed to a direction where the floor ramped down to a dimly lit corridor.

Each person was on alert as they scanned the unfamiliar environment. One after the other, they descended down the ramp. The cries paired with the shadowy hallway, and the feeling of sinking further into the unknown grew ominous, then overwhelming. Cries turned to screams. Though muffled, they never fully stopped. The team strained to look through the murkiness for other signs of life in the corridor. Moving cautiously, they traced the foreboding sounds to a room about one hundred feet away.

Robert motioned to the team to stop about thirty feet from a door on the left, well before the location of the ominous sounds. He instructed the team to lie low and stay alert as he went to investigate. He crept toward the door and tried the lever. It was unlocked. He placed his gloved hand on the lever and unlatched it. Seeing that there was no light coming from inside, he opened the door completely, then motioned the team to join him. The faint light from the corridor shone enough into the room to reveal tables and chairs. A classroom. Robert instructed his team to remain in place while he circled back to investigate the source of the screams. He left, walking heel-to-toe, without making sound.

A soft light spilled under the door and onto the floor from the room where the wailing continued. Robert noticed a brighter light emanating from an adjacent door. He crept to the second door and heard human voices in the room. He returned to the first door and tried the handle. It was unlocked. Reaching into his backpack, he took out his phone and a wireless camera. He knelt at the threshold, sliding the camera underneath the door, guiding it until he was able to see the images on his phone. The muffled cries and screams became louder as the first images appeared.

About twenty feet from the door lay a mattress on the floor, pushed up close to a wall. Upon the mattress was a partially clothed woman. Straddling her was a nearly naked man. Another man had his back to the door, undressing himself. Both men appeared to be wearing military desert fatigues. They demeaned her with ugly words. It was suddenly all too clear to Robert that the woman was being physically abused and sexually assaulted. Moving the camera, he saw that the wall in common with the adjoining room had a large viewing window from which the light poured in. Robert noticed two figures on the other side of the glass; one, in a lab coat, held a digital tablet, and the other wore a desert fatigue uniform with no insignia. They appeared to be watching, without emotion, the vicious crime in progress. Robert grew outraged as he watched them taking notes and behaving as if they were conducting a lab experiment. He understood the importance of finding calmness and collecting his thoughts.

Having seen and recorded enough, he slid the camera back from under the door, put it in his pack, and returned to the team. Visibly shaken, Robert addressed the others.

"What did you see?" asked Deborah.

Robert took out his cell phone and played the video. He didn't have to describe the incident; the camera clearly captured every vile detail.

"Except for the guy in the lab coat, everyone else wore desert fatigues, which could mean we are in a military installation. There was no visible rank, name, or insignia on any of the uniforms. Why were the men behind the glass looking on like it was an experiment? We can't assume to understand these events," reasoned Deborah.

"Are we here because we are supposed to rescue that woman, Mary Ellen?" asked Louis.

"The Arcturians sent us. There is a woman that appears to be in distress. I think we are supposed to get her out," Mary Ellen said.

"Did any of the men appear to have a weapon?" asked Deborah.

"I didn't see one."

"The men assaulting the woman are most likely in a vulnerable position." Deborah addressed the team. "Why don't the men have insignia or nametags?"

"Because they probably are not soldiers," Robert said. "More mercenaries."

"Right. If they are knowingly participating in criminal activity, they shouldn't be surprised if, say, CIA or NSA were to barge in and arrest them, right?"

Robert nodded. "Right, we pose as law enforcement—all of us. In time, we figure out what's going on before they find out we aren't law enforcement."

"That's fine, Robert, but what do we do when we rescue her? We don't know where we are. If this is a military installation, it is likely guarded, and we are not exactly dressed for a casual walk to an exit." Louis made it clear he was concerned.

"First, we need to get the woman, before it's too late," Mary Ellen said.

Louis looked at her and knew this argument was over.

"Ok, Robert, you go into the room with the viewers," Deborah said, calling the shots in full Security Police mode. "Mary Ellen and I will go into the woman's room, with the perps. We all need to enter at the same time. Act like cops, but don't say who you are. Ask questions, just like you would if you were a cop. Everyone ready?"

"I wasn't a cop, but I was trained in capturing and interrogating aggressors. I know my part," assured Robert.

"What about me?" asked Louis.

"Remain in the corridor and watch for anyone that might approach us," directed Deborah. "God help us if someone comes while we make the entrance, but if they do, tell them we are OSI and they are approaching a crime scene and need to turn back."

Louis did not like that possible scenario.

Robert reached in his pack and handed Deborah zip ties to use as restraints. Leaving the classroom, the decorated former Ranger looked down both directions of the corridor for any sign of activity. The muffled screams continued to echo down the hall. He led the team to the two doors, his hand on the handle of the viewing room door. Deborah did the same at the other door. By Robert's signal, on the count of three, the two armed veterans opened the doors simultaneously, startling the occupants.

"Freeze, Mad Doctor! You too, Igor!"

The two culprits did as Robert commanded, voicing protest. "What's going on? Who are you? This is a highly sensitive, compartmented operation sanctioned by the highest authorities! You're making a big mistake!" sputtered the man in the lab coat, raising his voice.

Robert lay them on their stomachs, with hands behind their backs and legs spread. He bound their wrists with the zip ties. Taking his pistol out from its holster, he held the weapon on them as he searched and retrieved anything in their possession. He confiscated the digital tablet and placed it aside. He made sure to monitor it and touch the screen every so often so it would not pause, assuming any pause on the tablet would require a PIN to reactivate, which they did not have.

Deborah burst into the room, her rifle aimed at the men. She ordered them to stop what they were doing and face the wall with their legs spread out and arms outstretched high above their heads. Mary Ellen followed Deborah. Both men were out of their uniforms and naked from the waist down. The men asked the same questions as the two in the other room. Deborah informed them of their rights while acting as if she was arresting them under the Uniform Code of Military Justice.

The men claimed not to be active-duty soldiers and declared immunity since they were involved in a highly sensitive program.

Deborah had heard enough. "You aren't? Then what are you?"

The men had no response.

"Tell me. I'd like to know. Which agency sanctions sexual assault?"

Again, there was no answer.

Deborah looked back at Mary Ellen, tending the young woman who had been understandably startled. She ordered the men to put their hands behind their backs. Mary Ellen moved away from the woman and used the zip ties to secure their wrists behind their backs, then had them kneel.

Both Mary Ellen and Deborah were startled when a fourth occupant fled from the far corner of the dimly lit room. It was a "Grey" about four feet tall, who had also been watching. While Mary Ellen and Deborah were handling the two rapists, the Grey rushed out of the room, running into the corridor, and knocking down Louis, who was standing guard outside. As the Grey ran toward the ramp, Louis quickly regained his composure, raised the rifle, sound suppressor attached, and directed the laser sight at the base of the Grey's neck. He rapidly fired four shots. The Grey collapsed. Louis was shaking and felt physically ill.

Mary Ellen and Deborah saw the collision. With the two rapists on their knees, half-naked and restrained, Mary Ellen ran out of the room to see Louis shoot, then hold the rifle, looking into the distance, trembling. She looked down the corridor and saw the Grey face down on the floor and then rushed back to Robert.

"He just shot a Grey! It's lying on the floor in the corridor!" Mary Ellen avoided saying names in front of the captives.

"That Grey was a member of our team! I demand to know which agency you work for!" protested the man in the lab coat.

Robert and Mary Ellen ignored the demand. He instructed her to hold her weapon on the two men while he went to investigate. He dashed out the door and saw Louis, rifle in his hands, staring at the Grey on the floor, visibly shaken, guilty that he had shot it in the back while it was trying to escape.

"I've never shot at anyone before. I can't believe I killed it," Louis said with deep remorse.

He knew he had no other choice; if the Grey escaped, it would have alerted others of the team and rescue. Robert bent down and turned the Grey over to face him, his first contact with a Grey. He studied the severe facial structure, the brownish-green skin tone, the rough leathery texture, the large skull. He was almost mesmerized by the large black eyes with no pupil or iris. He noted the small protrusion with two holes for a nose, and the slit for a mouth. The hands had three long slender fingers. *Human. The masters will know I am missing*, was the message that Robert received telepathically.

Robert took his pistol and fired a shot at close range into the creature's large head to kill it. He looked back at Louis. Robert picked up the Grey and flung it over his shoulder, walking toward his shaken teammate. Robert stopped where Louis was; he hadn't moved an inch.

"You did what you had to." Then he leaned closer to Louis. "You *still* haven't killed anyone."

Louis briefly examined the creature. It wasn't a creature. It was a highly developed android. According to information collected from autopsies, the only major "organs" were the large brain and its skin, which functioned like the stoma on leaves, absorbing energy and nutrients and expelling oxygen and water.

Robert then returned to Mary Ellen. The men were shocked by the sight of Robert carrying the dead alien android. He placed it against the wall near the door as the man in the lab coat continued with his futile demands. "Who are you working for? NSA? CIA? NRO? OSI? FBI? Who led you to us?"

Neither Robert nor Mary Ellen responded. Instead, Robert told her to keep the rifle on the men while he went to help Deborah. Robert then recalled the tablet on the floor and quickly picked it up to touch the screen. He was relieved to discover it still active.

Louis snapped out of his state of shock, guilt, and self-loathing, and resumed his duty to watch the corridor. The partially unclothed men remained kneeling, facing the wall. Robert entered to check the ties around the men's wrists and scan the room. Deborah then stepped back, raised her rifle, and directed it at them.

"Give me a reason to shoot you!" she said. "I am a rape victim, too. What do you think is going on in my head right now as I point this loaded gun at you pigs?"

Robert knew she wouldn't shoot. He let her express her disgust in her own personal way.

With the men bound and Deborah guarding them at gun point, Robert left and returned to the other room. He instructed Mary Ellen to tend to the young woman.

Watching the events unfold in front of her, the young woman remained still, her back against the mattress. Mary Ellen sat next to her, reading her briefly. Guides were telling her that the young woman's spirit was heavily damaged. Her energies were all out of balance. She couldn't be repaired quickly. Deborah, still keeping an eye on the kneeling captives, retrieved a belt and a cap on the floor. Strangers had appeared and quickly subdued the woman's assailants. In her drug-induced fog, she struggled with her emotions. She was grateful to be rescued, but what did these people want?

In her soft, peace-giving voice, Mary Ellen consoled the woman. "You are in good hands now. Nobody is going to hurt you again."

With Mary Ellen's encouragement, the young woman sat up and tried to cover her body. Mary Ellen handed over the women's bra and uniform shirt. The name tag read, EVERLY. The rank on her sleeve indicated she was a Senior Airman, with a patch from the 422nd Test and Evaluation Squadron. Her pants and underpants had been pulled down past her knees, her socks and boots still on. Deborah handed the woman her belt and cap, and the airman got up to fasten her uniform pants. She avoided looking at her rescuers as she finished getting dressed. She seemed emotionally frozen, as if in a trance.

Robert looked closely at the man in the lab coat. He walked toward him. "We are going to need your lab coat."

He turned the man around, took out his knife, and cut the zip tie, then removed the white lab coat, all the while keeping him restrained. He reached back and took out another zip tie from his pouch and re-bound the man's wrists, calling Louis into the room.

Handing Louis the lab coat, he said, "Here, get out of your tactical gear and put what you can in your backpack, then put this on. Be sure to get the tablet and anything else that was in the pockets."

Robert took a roll of duct tape out from his pack, pulled the backs of their undershirts up over the men's heads, and secured them with the tape, making certain they would not be able to see or talk. He took both men by their arms, walked them into the corridor, and then into the classroom. There, he opened a closet and shoved them in. Robert took out more zip ties and hobbled their ankles. He closed the door, leaving the men inside, sitting back-to-back. Then he moved tables and chairs to make a barricade to prevent the doors from being opened from the inside. He left the classroom, closing the door.

As Louis removed his tactical gear, Robert joined Deborah in the other room to blindfold and gag the assailants. Deborah kept her weapon aimed at the men. In a dark corner, Robert spotted a door. He opened it to find another half-empty closet. Moving things around, he freed floor space to make room for the two men.

Satisfied the detainees were bound and secured, Robert went back to look at what they gathered from the captives. In addition to the tablet with a Common Access Card (CAC), the man with the lab coat carried four unused syringes, antiseptic pads in individual packages, a vial with an unknown colorless fluid, and a vial with a bright green fluid. He also had a wallet with IDs. Robert walked to the refrigerator in the corner of the room and opened it. It held vials of the same bright green fluid and colorless fluid found in the lab coat. The bottom rack had bottled water. He took out all the contents, starting with the vials and stands, placing them to the side. Then, he removed the refrigerator's racks and leaned them against the appliance. He picked up the Grey and placed him in it. He replaced one rack and put back all the green and colorless vials, then closed the door. The bottled water was left on the floor. Louis opened a sealed bottle and took a couple of gulps.

"I think we need to pick up the pace, Louis. That Grey telepathed to me that once someone figures out that he is missing, they will come looking for him. Looks like you're ready. I'll go check out what's going on in the other room."

Robert walked back again to where the women were and scanned the scene. He looked at Mary Ellen and Deborah, who were consoling the airman. Noticing an empty syringe on a table next to the mattress, he walked over to look at it and saw residue of the bright green fluid that was in the refrigerator. He recognized that the young airman had a vacant expression.

"We'll have the airman pose as our captive. We'll use that blindfold." Robert pointed to a scarf on the floor next to the mattress. "It's likely that the airman has been seen before with a blindfold. Airman Everly, please sit tight. We are going to get you out of this place."

The stunned airman finally spoke up. "Who are you people? How did you get in here past all the guards with your weapons and that cell phone? This compound has tight security and no unofficial electronics are allowed past the ECP."

Mary Ellen, mindful of the captives in the room, introduced herself and the rest of the team to the young female airman. She spoke in a near whisper.

All dressed, Louis carried the digital tablet and walked into the other room with Robert. "What's your name, Airman?" asked Louis softly as he placed his hand on a shoulder.

"I am Senior Airman Tara Everly, radar specialist, Nellis Air Force Base, Nevada," the woman recited mechanically.

"Nellis?" asked Louis.

The team looked at each other.

The airman continued in a drug-induced monotone voice. "I am assigned to test radar equipment here. We boarded a bus at Nellis, and we were dropped off here. The bus had the windows blackened so we couldn't tell where we were going. It was about a two-hour ride and we were not allowed to talk to anyone in the bus. The people that monitored us seem to take pleasure in threatening us. The blond man there was one of the guards on the bus. Once the bus stopped, they blindfolded us and took us to our job sites. There, they took the blindfold off, and we checked the radar equipment while they monitored flying machines that have speed and maneuverability far beyond the capabilities of our best fighters. When our job was done for the day, they separated us. Each of us was blindfolded again. I don't know what happened to the rest of the radar specialists. I got led into this underground building and they tortured me. I don't know what they were going to do with me next."

"I can assure you that's not our Air Force doing this. These guys are working for contractors. They are the worst kind of mercenaries," explained Robert.

"So, you get on a bus for a long ride. So, where does the bus drop you off? Where are we now?" asked Deborah.

"You don't know where we are? How is it that you don't know where you are? How did you get here?" asked the puzzled and still groggy young airman.

"It's a complicated story. We'll explain after we get you out of here."

Robert looked at the tablet and pointed out that the CAC needed to stay in the slot. Louis acknowledged that he knew how it worked and assured Robert that he would be careful. Robert took the tablet and searched for information that would indicate where they were. He found the installation's home page. To his astonishment, he discovered that they were at Groom Lake. Except for the airman, everyone else was also astounded. Browsing through the tablet, he was not able to determine which building they were in.

"There is no way we can get out of here without being seen. At least it's after 2030 right now, so I think most of the crews have gone home," said Robert.

Robert continued to look through the tablet's folders for a map of the base. Finally, after doing a search, he found a facility map of the area. Louis looked over his shoulder.

"I think this is a training facility. There are many classrooms here," pointed Louis.

Robert saw the index that listed a TRAINING CENTER. The building appeared to be an above-ground facility.

"Louis may be right. Most training happens during the duty day. This place should be empty. They used it on Everly, here, because they knew there would be no one else here."

Robert continued to look at the map and noticed an Entry Control Point (ECP) nearby. Robert advised the team it was time to move out. He and Deborah retrieved the bound men and walked them to the closet. Like the other captives, he had them sit back-to-back, closed the door, and barricaded it.

As Mary Ellen was placing the blindfold over Airman Everly, Robert asked, "Airman Everly, if we get to the ECP, can we get off the installation on a shuttle like the one that brought you here?"

"We could try getting on a shuttle for contractors. It also takes them to Nellis, but they check IDs coming in and going out. I don't see how you could get out of here without being challenged."

The team looked at each other with concern. "Before we leave, everyone should collapse the stock to your rifle and stow it in your backpack. Make sure, make double sure, that the safety in on. We do not want any accidental discharges."

The team did as Robert instructed.

"Mary Ellen—I hope your E.T. helpers knew what they were doing when they sent us here."

Airman Everly's mouth opened upon hearing those words, but she said nothing. She was too exhausted to even think clearly. The team left the room, turned off the lights, and closed the door. Louis went to the other room and closed it down.

The team saw a brightly lit area in the opposite direction of the ramp they had come down. They proceeded in that direction, finding another gradual ramp down. Tara, still shaken, told the team that even though she was blindfolded, she could tell that she came from a higher place and not from the direction they were traveling.

"We are going the wrong way! This is not the way I came in! We need to go back!"

"Calm down, Airman Everly," pleaded Robert.

The team reached another wider corridor that extended a couple hundred feet in both directions. It appeared to link other facilities. Louis noticed an emergency escape plan on one of the walls.

"Look. Here's a floor plan." Pointing to the drawing, he recognized their location. "Here are the rooms we were in. We are here.

There's an elevator lobby down that corridor. The elevator should take us up to the surface."

"Watch out for cameras. Everybody, wear your goggles," ordered Robert.

The team walked to the elevator lobby. There was only one call button on a panel on the wall, and Robert pressed it. After some time, the elevator arrived and opened. Robert looked back to see if there was anyone else coming. They were the only ones in the area. The team waited for the doors to close. They remained open even after Robert pressed the button to close them. Louis noticed a card reader.

"Robert, I think we need the CAC from the tablet. If I swipe it over the reader, we will be able to close the doors."

"We won't be able to use the tablet after we take the CAC out," Robert said.

After a tense and awkward pause, Robert finally felt resigned to take the CAC out and handed it to Louis, who immediately passed it over the reader. The reader's indicator light changed from red to green and the doors finally closed.

The elevator immediately started to descend at high rate of speed, catching everyone off guard. "We need to go up, not down! Where are we going?" Tara was scared. The rest of the team did not know what to say, their worry increasing with every passing second as the elevator continued its descent.

"We have no control. We are going to have to exit wherever it stops," Louis said.

"We have no idea what might be on the other side of those doors when they open up. Everybody, get your weapons ready," Robert commanded.

The cab slowed down and continued to decelerate as it dropped, then it stopped. Robert and Deborah held front position. Louis and the other women were in the rear. After a brief pause, the doors opened.

Robert and Deborah remained inside and noticed a small empty lobby. Everybody stowed their weapons. Exiting, the group made their way toward a pair of doors, only paces from the elevator. Robert noticed a camera directed at the elevator doors and whispered his finding to his team. The elevator doors closed behind them.

* * *

A security guard looked at the monitor and noticed a group of people in full tactical gear with no insignia or name tags escorting a blindfolded woman in an Air Force uniform. He alerted his supervisor. The supervisor looked at the images being transmitted by the camera and recognized the airman with the blindfold. He pointed to Everly, telling the guard he had seen her a few times before with other escorts and scientists.

"This place has so many odd things going on. Nothing surprises me. It's better not to ask questions around here. They are probably involved in something that you or I don't need to know about."

* * *

Robert whispered, "Don't let the camera monitors read your lips. Everly, do you know where we are?"

There was no answer. The team was stuck deep below Area 51.

Louis passed the stolen CAC over the reader, activating the double doors. The light turned green, releasing the latch. Louis opened a door to let the team through. On the other side, they found themselves on a train platform with a railway on each side. Instead of steel rails, there was one wide beam in the center. A moving marquee above on one side of the platform read: TRAIN WEST ARRIVING IN 43 MINUTES. The marquee over the other side read: TRAIN SOUTH ARRIVING IN 22 MINUTES. Centered above the platform, suspended and parallel to the rail line was a sign that read, GROOM LAKE. The perfectly round tunnel was monolithically lined by vitrified rock, similar in texture to the underground reptilian lair. It looked to be about forty feet in diameter.

The team remained silent in the event listening devices accompanied the cameras. They walked toward the westbound side of the platform.

Under his breath, Robert he muttered, "There may be others that will arrive to get on the trains. Act your part."

"This is part of the deep underground military base system I have read about. If this is going westbound, it will likely stop at Vandenburg, or Edwards, or Travis, or Beale in California. At least it will get Mary Ellen and me closer to Mount Shasta," Louis whispered. "The southbound train will probably go to White Sands."

The team walked to a row of benches to sit and wait for the westbound train. After about fifteen minutes, the double doors to the lobby opened revealing eight men in desert fatigues without insignia. Robert and the team moved toward the end of the platform, while the other group headed to the southbound platform. As scheduled, a light from the west signaled the train's arrival. It was black, sleek like glass, and arrived with a whisper. The doors opened quietly and a voice announced, "Groom Lake," as the men got on board. To their astonishment, the team could see there were beings in the car that did not appear to be human. The train doors closed, and it departed as quietly as it arrived, like a zephyr, disappearing into the tunnel's darkness.

The six-car train arrived as scheduled, 2215 local time. No one exited the train. There were a few passengers in each car, and all seemed human. Robert's team entered the first car. The other group stayed together and entered the third car.

The doors remained open for several moments. Finally, a robotic voice announced the doors closing. After a slight pause, the high-speed underground shuttle began to move without even a hum, from the magnetic levitation used to minimize friction. It accelerated quickly to jet-like speed. Keeping Tara blindfolded, the team talked to enforce the appearance she was a prisoner. The sight of the woman made some of the passengers uneasy, causing them to move away from Robert and the team.

Louis looked at Robert, who was staring at the darkness through the glass. "What are you thinking about?"

Robert did not answer immediately, then he looked sternly at Louis. "This world is a mess. Ok, so we rescued, what? About a hundred innocent lives and disabled an evil operation. How many more Dulces are there? Look at her. How old is she? Early twenties? She had a whole life ahead of her, and they reduced her to a sex experiment. She'll be permanently traumatized. The rest of her life will be a hell. Who knows how much she has endured? I don't know. I'm rambling. The point is, whatever we do here won't really change things. Other young women will replace Everly, and they'll relocate the Dulce lab somewhere else."

"I understand what you're saying, but you can't give up and let the darkness win. We did make life better for many, now, and for those who would have been affected in the future. We *are* making a difference."

"The thing you don't realize, Louis, is how deviant the people are that are running these operations. They are not like you or me. They don't follow those rules that are in your conscience—you know—the ones that pop into mind and bother you when you are about to do something wrong. Their motivation is a perverse combination of money and the thrill of having the power to destroy other lives."

"But what about the spiritual side of the equation?" asked Louis.

"What do you mean? I can only tell you about what I can see or touch. I don't know about spiritual stuff."

Mary Ellen spoke out, just loud enough for Robert and Louis to hear. "Robert, I find it odd that you accept Katrina's abilities that transcend what you can see and touch, yet you cannot accept the rest of the spiritual realm. In order to understand what's going on here on Earth, you have to include the spiritual piece to the puzzle. It's just another pyramid scheme. We are victims, refugees, in a war for our spirits. Let's say one army is about suffering, pain, lust, all the negative energies in existence. The other is of benevolent beings that do not want to see us suffer unnecessarily.

"Now add humans into the mix. We all have spirits. If our spirits ascend, they join the army of the benevolent, otherwise, they return to learn life's lessons again. It is in the interest of the negative energy beings to cause humans to behave in a manner that stops ascension. But there is another aspect to those negative energy beings. They thrive on our suffering. They are vampires of negative emotions. When we feel pain, cry, or scream, they feel it, and it gives them a drug-like high. The more they feel it, the more they crave it. The more they crave it, the more likely they will prolong the suffering."

Mary Ellen paused to draw the shape of a pyramid. "Remember the pyramid? They are at the top. Then, below them are powerful, ruthless families and bloodlines who get to keep their material world as long as they promote the suffering desired by the negative energy beings. Below the bloodline layer are the corporate oligarchs, weapons manufacturers, energy conglomerates, drug companies, agricultural chemical firms, and related purveyors of poisons and waste. Most, if not all, CEOs and board members don't know about the top layer. Their only focus is profit and stock price. The pyramid won't be toppled until those people at the bottom "wake up." Only when they are aware, can they affect change from the layers above."

"I get that money is the motivator for all that is wrong around us. I understand how pyramids work. It's hard for me to accept what you describe as the war for our spirits."

"Then how else do you explain the self-inflicting damage, the destruction of eco-systems, the acts of genocide?"

Robert did not immediately answer, but his silence offered Mary Ellen hope that he would eventually take her explanation to heart. He looked toward the other end of the car and made eye contact with one of the uniformed men. The mercenary looked at the team closely. He directed his attention at Deborah. He sneered and looked back at Robert, who did not take his eyes off of the man. He couldn't know for certain why, but since Deborah was the only black person on the team, Robert thought the man was behaving that way because he was racist. It made him angry inside, but he was careful not to let it show. Robert continued to stare down the man, resulting in the man looking away permanently.

"You see these mercenaries? Most used to be good soldiers—guys you would really have a good time with—good drinking buddies," Robert said. "Each one of them professional, loyal, ethical, having pride in country, and honored to defend the Constitution. But when what you are best at is the management of violence, killing efficiency, and putting yourself in danger, when there is no war, you are lost. Your identity was based on war. Guys like me and those mercenaries come out of those situations changed—and not for the better."

Louis scanned the men dressed in fatigues without insignia.

Robert continued, "There is a moment we veterans experience that redefines us. It is like the feeling you have when you're driving and you actually doze off for a fraction of a second, then you wake up, and it scares the hell out of you so much, you stay alert for the rest of the ride. That's how it was when I realized the war changed something in me. I was in a convenience store full of people. There was a loud bang, like an engine backfiring. It caused me to jump and get into a protective stance. I looked around and realized not a single other person in that store had reacted. The noise had affected me, alone. That was the moment that made me realize I was different from everyone else and from my original self."

Robert sat silently, letting his own words sink in, his many experiences, wins and losses, condensed into a way of life, a philosophy of sorts, a way of looking at the world. Then he resumed his one-way conversation.

"Everyone has a unique way of treating themselves after the fighting is done. Because, let's face it, politicians and the system rarely do a good job of treating us properly after the battles are long over. We are forced to care for ourselves as a matter of survival. Some, like myself, get caught in a downward spiral of self-loathing, aided by some sort of chemical crutch."

Robert talked from experience, witnessing the self-destruction of former co-combatants, explaining no one was immune, not even himself.

"I was lucky. I found Katrina, and she helped me out of it, but it wasn't easy. A buddy of mine who was with me in Afghanistan was frequently on detail to clear IEDs. Local teenage kids helped our guys locate bombs for us to call in for removal. The operation worked well. One day, some of the kids, watching our guys remove the devices, decided to remove some themselves."

Robert's voice broke, and he had to pause. Even being over a decade removed from witnessing the atrocities, memories remained vivid. The wounds never heal. Recollection only made them more hurtful. It takes a special kind of person to be able to go through life in what others would recognize as "normal" mode—having gone through the unspeakable—undamaged and productive in society. Robert met that challenge.

"The kids looked up to our team and the EOD guys. They were so proud of what they had done. We couldn't stop them. They continued to remove the devices, faster than our EOD team. Then, a group of the boys took out a bomb and wanted to show it to my buddy. On the way to see him, the device detonated, killing four of those kids right in my buddy's line of sight. He and the team had to take care of the remains. It was so painful for him that it caused him to have a breakdown. He got a medical discharge, and when he got back to the States, he started drinking. It took a long time for him to turn it around. He's a minister now, working with disadvantaged kids. He was a lucky one."

Robert had his opinion about the soldiers of fortune in the train. He didn't hate them. He felt a pity for them, describing them as lost.

"Those guys, the mercenaries sharing our air on this train, self-medicated with more violence and danger. They yearn for that thing we call camaraderie. But it's not the same. They aren't putting their life on the line for any cause. They are motivated by money. Paid assassins with no loyalty to anything or anyone except themselves. There are millions all over the world in every country. Some work for huge corporations and are all scary good at what they do. Some, maybe those guys over there, have shifted to the darker side of humanity and actually take pleasure in seeing others suffer. They have become accustomed to making life miserable for others. They will never again be the soldiers they were when they fought for the United States of America."

Robert stopped talking because it only made him want to punch someone.

A robotic voice made an announcement for the train's passengers: "Next stop, Edwards Air Force Base, California. Estimated time to arrival: thirty minutes."

"Thirty minutes? How fast is this thing going?" Louis asked.

"About 300 miles per hour, I figure. We should arrive at the base around 2200 hours."

Robert checked his watch. Louis, reacting, did the same. Robert again noticed the mercenary at the other end of the car glaring at Deborah in a threatening manner.

"Deborah, don't look. There's a jerk at the end of the car who looks like he is trying to instigate trouble. He's waiting for you to look at him. Don't do it."

"Yeah, I saw him. I'm used to it. I've been black all my life, and I've gotten that look all my life." Deborah looked in the direction using her peripheral vision to see him. "He's just not worth it."

The train decelerated and announced: "Train arriving at Edwards Air Force Base, California." It was 2155 local time when the train stopped at the platform. The doors opened, and the team got up and walked out into yet another uncertain situation.

16

A FRIENDLY DARKNESS

The only thing that makes life possible is permanent, intolerable uncertainty; not knowing what comes next. —Ursula K. LeGuin

It was just after 2200 hours, and the main control tower at Edwards Air Force Base was closed until 0600 the next morning. The fifteen thousand foot by three hundred foot runway 4R/22L was illuminated by its high intensity runway lights, while the taxiways accented the quiet serenity of the empty airfield with the outline of blue lights. South of the main airfield was another smaller runway at the South Base. It, however, did not have any lighting, restricted to daylight operations.

The Base Operations Center was manned by two senior airmen. Adjacent to them was the Weather Office, where two other senior airmen were updating charts for pilot briefings the next day. Both offices shared a panoramic view of the airfield. The senior airman manning the Command Post after hours took advantage of the lull in activity to work on his assigned professional development course. The senior airman assigned to the Emergency Desk at the Base Civil Engineer's Office was watching a sports event on TV. Some nights, he would have to answer to an upset airman complaining about a backed-up toilet in a dormitory or a spouse stressing about a problem with an appliance in Military Family Housing. It was a lonely, uneventful night so far, but at least his team was winning. The night desk at the Security Police Facility was also quiet. There were no stray dogs to catch, no DUIs, not so much as a disturbance at the bachelors' enlisted quarters.

Robert and the team rose to exit the train and watched as the others in their car left quickly. He motioned the team to follow the mercenaries but not too closely. They moved toward a pair of doors that led to an elevator lobby. Like the lobby at Groom Lake, it was also under visual surveillance. Tara was still blindfolded, standard procedure for people that did not have the proper clearance when traveling through sensitive areas. The appearance of uniforms without insignias and name tags was common in the facility. The twelve men stood in front of the elevator doors. Robert's team hung back by the lobby doors. When the elevator doors opened to a cargo elevator, the mercenaries walked to the back, facing the front. Robert and team noticed that even with twelve men and their backpacks, there was still more than enough room for them. They entered, staying close to the front of the cab. One of the mercenaries reached through to press the only button on the panel, and the doors closed.

The elevator began to rise and accelerated. Tara, still blindfolded, felt uneasy about going up again, but said nothing. The ascent was fast. Not a word was spoken among the seventeen passengers. The cab decelerated quickly until slowing down to a normal speed, then it stopped. As the doors opened, Robert and the team moved aside to let the mercenaries exit first. They blindly followed the uniformed group as they negotiated a dimly lit lobby. There were no cameras in sight. The mercenaries walked ahead through a pair of doors that opened into a stairwell. The team followed.

Robert's team was on the bottom floor, facing consecutive flights of stairs going up. The stairwell was illuminated for safety. They stayed back, watching the mercenaries walk up the four flights leading to another pair of doors at the top landing. Having the blindfolded airman made a good excuse to walk up slowly as the last of the mercenaries exited. Reaching the top landing, they found themselves outside of what appeared to be a modern single-story administrative building. Louis spotted a sign just outside the building that indicated it was a flight test center. They watched as the group ahead was picked up by a blue Air Force bus. Once everyone was aboard, the door closed and the bus departed.

They watched the bus drive off toward an automated sliding gate and leave the fenced-in compound. It turned west and headed along the main airfield on a parallel road until it reached Lancaster Boulevard where it turned North for the main base. They lost sight of it as it continued north around the runway.

Robert reached for his phone, opening his GPS application. He discovered that his team was miles from the nearest base exit. They had exited on the southwest side of the large building, away from its main entrance. Another smaller building was facing them, about two hundred feet to the right. They were stranded in a secure compound at Edwards Air Force Base in California, and it was past 2200 hours. With the bus out of sight, Deborah took the liberty of lifting the blindfold off Tara.

"We are about six miles from the closest entry control point. Has anyone been here before?" Robert asked.

Everyone responded with either "no" or a head shake. Robert continued to look at the phone for a route to take to the Entry Control Point (ECP), on the southwest end of the base. He estimated they would need to walk two hundred yards to reach the southwest corner of the compound at the fence line. The compound was situated between the South Base on the south and the main runway to the north. It was well lit with poles spaced every hundred feet at the fence. South of the compound, there was a large, illuminated parking lot. Beyond the compound was the expanse of open field, dotted with small metal sheds, lighting vaults, and substations. Distances on airfields can be deceptive to the eye; the darkness and the lack of landmarks for scale made it even more difficult to gauge the vastness. Robert guessed it to be over two miles to the road that led to the ECP. After that, they would have to travel south along the road for a longer distance. He opted to avoid as much exposure along the road as possible, cutting across the desert tract of land. He figured the total distance of the preferred path would be three miles. At a six miles per hour constant jog, on uneven terrain, in the dark, they would get there in just over thirty minutes. That would get them a third of the way to the base exit.

While Robert was figuring the route, Louis placed a call to his friend, Trevor Hugo, who lived a few hours away in San Fernando. Trevor had been expecting a call since they talked just before Louis left Chicago. Louis was relieved to find his friend at home. Based on their prior conversation, Trevor had anticipated that Louis would call ahead to let him know he was in the area so they could arrange a visit. Trevor did not expect Louis to call and immediately ask to be picked up from a place about a hundred miles away.

"Louis, I just got home from work," explained Trevor. "I need to work tomorrow too. I normally get up at six. By the time we would get home after I picked you up, it would be 1 a.m."

"Trevor, I have no other options. I have four people here, and we will be stranded if you don't come get us. I am sorry for putting you in this position. I'll make it up to you."

Trevor spent the entire day and most of the evening at his job. Being a loyal friend, though, he took a deep breath and replied, "Alright, alright. I understand. Where do I need to go get you?"

Louis instructed Trevor to meet him and his four companions outside the base. The entire jog to the base exit would take at least ninety minutes.

"Thanks so much, Trev. You are a savior. You will have your rewards. I'll let you know when we are ready."

"OK. I'll text you when I get close. I will be in a Silver Toyota Previa. See you soon."

Robert instructed the team to move quickly, as all fenced compounds were patrolled by security forces. He directed them to follow him to the southwest corner of the compound, to the fence. There he would cut the chain-link fence, and they would proceed on the path he recognized as being best.

Robert realized the challenge of jogging unnoticed and getting past the fence. He sent a text to Katrina. He waited for a response, but there was none. In Taos, eight hundred miles away, Katrina lay on the floor on her right side, her eyes closed. Her breathing was shallow as she held her circuit. She was in a place between the third dimension and spiritual realm. She was alive, not asleep. Aware, but not awake. Like every other near-death experience, she got closer to leaving the planet completely, at the same time gaining more strength in her abilities. She had been tracking Robert and the team. She sensed Robert wanting to contact her. Her spirit sent a message of love to his.

Robert felt something—something he could not explain, yet whatever it was made him more at ease. Mary Ellen felt it too. She looked at Robert.

"Did you feel that?"

The sensation made him turn to Mary Ellen. For all the years he had known Katrina, just now was he beginning to understand. The energy that touched him was real in the sense that his mind actually felt something.

"Yeah. Yeah. I get it now. It's starting to make sense." Robert's self-imposed limitations of reality were beginning to be dismantled. His universe had just gotten bigger.

Deborah was concerned and watched Tara closely, giving her some water from her backpack. Tara was silent, but she sensed that whatever was going on had not been planned.

"We'll get you to safety," the vet said to the young airman.

Tara took a long drink. "I'm officially AWOL now," she said, almost breathlessly. "My handlers are bound and gagged in a closet. A Grey that monitored my torture was killed."

"How long were they going to keep you in that room?" Robert asked.

"I don't know. I ... feel confused. It feels like I had been in that situation before. But I don't remember anything specifically."

"I promise you, once we get out of here, we are going to get help for you." Robert recognized trauma and understood that Airman Everly was in a fragile state now. "I recorded the assault with my cell phone."

Robert took out his phone and sent a quick message to two veterans now working in key positions in the nation's Capital. One was an investigative reporter with *The Washington Post*, and the other was a Congressman from California that served on the House's Armed Services Committee. He attached the video of the assault and purposefully omitted details so they would respond, if only to get more information.

The team was about ready to move when Louis recognized Mary Ellen was motionless and staring into space at nothing in particular. She had fallen into a trance similar to the one in the lab at Dulce base. This time, in her trance state, she spoke: "You have done well. Look up. We are here to help you get out safely."

A dozen orange orbs appeared overhead, hovering at about one thousand feet. Robert, Deborah, and Louis were in awe of the sight of the glowing orange objects. Mary Ellen came out of the trance to witness the light show. She had established a connection with the Arcturians once again.

Tara was bewildered. The sights frightened her, though she felt a dark familiarity with them. "I think I've seen those lights before ... I just ... don't know why I can't remember where ..."

"These beings above us are not the ones you saw, Tara," Mary Ellen said. "These are Arcturians. They are benevolent and work with the angelic realm. They have no agreements with any Earth nation. They have been watching over us. The ones you saw in Tonopah and Groom Lake are malevolent reptilians."

The craft stopped over critical facilities. One was directly over a substation located west of the South Base. Others were directly over the main runway, the airfield, and a lighting vault also west of the South Base, along a major roadway. Still others drifted south toward the ECP to which the team was headed. In succession, lights around the compound, including streetlights, lights mounted on buildings, and high mast lights were shut down. The entire airfield was also shut down. This was followed by more outages west and south, where the team was heading. Lights on the main base were still on. There were no explosions, not even an arc. Just sudden darkness. The team was able to hear alarms set off by the outage in the adjacent buildings. Aside from the main base, the only sources of light were vehicles seen well off in the distance on the main roads.

Robert recognized the cue to move. "Louis, you don't need that lab coat anymore. Get your blacks on."

Louis got into his black tactical gear as the team waited. Robert commanded the team to put on the night vision goggles. Mary Ellen held Tara's hand as they left. He led the team to the southwest corner of the compound. They rushed, running across the access road that the bus had used, and found a paved walk that provided about three hundred feet of even footing. They veered toward the southwest corner for another four hundred feet. Arriving at the corner, Robert reached in his backpack and took out wire cutters. He quickly cut an access hole in the chain-link fence. The team crawled through it efficiently, with Robert going last. He stopped to bend the section back to make it look whole again, then pointed in the direction the team was to proceed, under cover of darkness.

It was 2210 hours when the lights temporarily went out in the Airfield Operations Center. Although it was part of the outage, the critical facility was furnished with a UPS. The airmen in the building looked out over the airfield and noticed only darkness—and something else: orange lights in the sky over the airfield. One of the airmen in the Base Operations office placed a call to the Command Post to report the outage and the strange lights in the sky.

The senior airman at the Command Post noticed a brief interruption in the power, causing the fluorescent lights and his computer screen to flicker. Then the phone rang. The airman answered; it was Base Ops. The caller informed the airman of the events.

"Say again?" He wanted be sure he had heard correctly. "Orange lights? Hovering over the airfield? And the airfield lights are all out?

Roger, copy. There was an outage here too, but we have the back-up now. I know there is a procedure in case of lost power." The phone indicated another call on the line. "I have another call, Command Post out."

He punched the button for the other line. It was another caller with the same information. The airman politely told the caller that he knew about the events and ended the call. He picked out a black binder, looked up the type of base emergency, and initiated the recall. The recall worked like a pyramid. On this occasion, the Vice Wing Commander was at the top of the pyramid since the Wing Commander was off-base on assignment. The airman at the Command Post informed the Vice Wing Commander of the outages and the orange lights, as relayed by Base Operations.

The Vice Wing Commander lived in a part of the housing area that was adjacent to the base golf course, closest to the airfield. The Vice Commander acknowledged by telling the airman that he was seeing the lights over the airfield from his house as he was speaking. There was no official procedure, in any operations manual, that addressed the phenomenon. The Joint-Based Expeditionary Connectivity Center, which would have been used to scramble fighters to the lights, was ineffective because the objects did not appear on any radar. Normally, an offending aircraft identified on the radar would have been first advised by the Federal Aviation Administration's local controller to turn back, then a US Coast Guard helicopter—dispatched for a visual identification before a pair of fighters already on alert—would do a fly-by before giving a final warning. The air base community would, normally, not have to be involved. In this case, the Vice Wing Commander had to improvise.

He first notified the Mission Support Group Commander of the outage, then called the California Air National Guard's 144th Fighter Wing Command Post at Fresno, requesting a direct line to their Wing Commander. The 144th FW was assigned the Combat Air Patrol or CAP to that region. He informed the Commander of the orange lights and requested fighters to do a fly-by over Edwards. The ANG Wing Commander had never been put in this situation. There were two F-15s on alert, similar to the ones used for CAP during the Super Bowl at Santa Clara in 2016. As Commander, he had the unique authority to authorize a scramble not initiated by the FAA or local radar. He placed a call to the 194th Fighter Squadron's Commander and ordered a scramble to Edwards AFB. The F-15Cs would arrive at their destination in less than twenty minutes, or at about 2225 hours.

At Edwards, the Group Commander, in-turn, called on the units that had a direct role in the operations after an outage. He called the 412th Security Forces Squadron Commander and the Base Civil Engineer, who also was the Fire Marshall. All Commanders lived on base for this reason: rapid response time in case of a contingency. The Commanders called their own organization's night desk after getting off the call with the Group Commander.

The Base Civil Engineer's Emergency Desk was already getting calls about the outage. The airman politely answered every call as the phone continued to ring. He got a call from his Chief of Operations that a recall was in progress. Branches would be reporting to their shops, as ordered, for further instructions.

The night desk at the Security Force Facility also got busy, as residents in the housing area called about the orange lights. Squad cars were dispatched to investigate. While on the phone with another concerned resident, the desk sergeant received a call from his Commander. The Squadron Commander instructed him to recall four more squads to patrol the South Base and the compound, and to be sent to other sensitive areas affected by the outage that did not have backup power. The Commander informed the airman he was inbound and gave the airman a description of the orange lights.

By the time the first call went to the Command Post, Robert was already past the fence. "Try and keep the pace. Stay about one hundred yards off the side of any road. Make sure you have nothing exposed that reflects light," Robert said.

He took the lead, running, but not sprinting, on the desert-like open field. There were no bushes to hide behind, no ravines to lie in. He looked back across the airfield and saw two emergency vehicles coming from the main base, cutting through the airfield, using a taxiway that linked the main runway with the South Base. The lights in the sky did not engage with the emergency vehicles. Conversely, the men in the vehicles were mindful of the visitors in the sky and continued with the hope that they would not be harmed. It was either a demonstration of courage or foolishness. Robert and the team were about a mile away from one of the squad cars that arrived at the Access Control Point to the fenced compound. The other squad quickly drove to the Munitions Storage Area located a half mile south of South Base, due East.

* * *

The 144th Fighter Wing was based at Fresno Yosemite International Airport. Its mission included Combat Air Patrol over much of California. At 2205 the Vice Wing Commander at Edwards was on call with the Wing Commander at Fresno. Afterward, the Wing Commander notified the Command Post to initiate an F-15 fighter scramble with detailed instructions provided in flight. Scrambles were not a rarity in the business. There were typically about three thousand per year, mostly in the Washington, DC, area.

The pilots and the flight line crew were at the ready in the alert facility near their fighters. Dressed in their flight suits, they ran out to their jets, climbed in quickly, donned their helmets, and closed the canopies as the turbine blades rotated. The tower gave them instructions on the mission to Edwards: a subsonic fifteen-minute flight. Having priority, they taxied and took off rapidly, with afterburners on, from alternate runway 29L/11R. By 2213, they were in the air, heading south-southwest to intercept the aggressors.

* * *

The Civil Engineering shops that were called out to assist in the recovery were varied. The Exterior Electric shop was sent to check out the transformers, substations, and set up RALs (Remote Area Lighting) trailers where the outage affected the perimeter lighting. The Plumbing shop dispatched teams to check out the pump houses and the waste-water treatment plant. The Fire Department sent technicians to check out suppression systems and annunciator panels once they came back online. As the trucks rolled out of the maintenance compound and headed south, the drivers all noticed the orange lights. Additional security force units were dispatched for patrols of the flight line and incidental facilities. It was a light show of emergency vehicles and trucks approaching the South Base and main airfield.

The team glanced back to look at the approaching line of vehicles. With night vision goggles on, Robert was able to make out the waste-water treatment plant directly south, about a half-mile away, and a substation just east of the plant. Static electricity was being generated by the craft above, startling all of them. Louis looked up at the orange light directly over the substation. Looking underneath the craft, it appeared the craft was spinning or rotating.

It was 2221, and the team had jogged another two miles, passing the substation, to the southwest. Louis had to stop. Being the oldest, he was getting tired, his heart pounding uncomfortably in his chest. Deborah stopped with him, prompting everyone else to pause.

"We need to cross that road before the recovery teams show up," Robert voiced urgently.

Mary Ellen also appealed. "Mr. Silvani, Deborah, this is where you need to reach inside you. Mr. Silvani . . . *Louis*, remember when Anne voiced concern that you weren't ready for the challenges? This is one the moments she spoke of. You have done well so far. This could be your most critical challenge. We *have* to get across the road; we are losing time."

Louis recognized this was the first time Mary Ellen had called him by his first name. It gave him a mental jolt. He looked at Deborah, who gave him a look of assurance. Louis straightened, stretched his arms across his chest, shook the cramps from his legs, and resumed jogging. The rest of the team followed. Crossing the road, Robert had them pick up the pace to get to a safe distance away from the approaching caravan of trucks and emergency vehicles. Another caravan of four trucks, with light-stand trailers, continued on Lancaster to the South ECP.

* * *

The F-15s were twenty miles away from Edwards. They would be there in a minute. There was no training for what they would have to do next. The Air Force did not officially acknowledge UAVs, but the fighters were sent to chase something very real away. Flying at five thousand feet, the pilots had visual identification of the craft, scattered over the southern part of the base. They dropped to about three thousand feet and were about to get close to the base when, in unison, the UAP fleet ascended in perfectly vertically lines, with incredible speed, out of sight. The F-15s had done their jobs.

As the orange orbs lifted off, the power and lights turned back on throughout the South Base, including the main runway and airfield. Taxiways were delineated in blue again. The lead pilot reported the sighting and encounter, and turned around to fly over the base again. Everything appeared to return to normal, except there was still a dark area at the South ECP. The Arcturians had interrupted power throughout the rest of the base, but had damaged the transformer that powered the ECP and the perimeter lights that the team was approaching. The F-15s turned away and returned to Fresno.

It was 2230 when the F-15s flew over the base and the power was restored. Robert and the team were safely in the dark about a half mile south of the road. The roar of the jets flying close to Mach speed ripped through the stillness, causing the team to crouch and put their hands over their ears. The jets turned around for one last fly-by, leaving the airspace with a thunderous rumble. The team looked ahead and saw no more development, no more lights, all the way to their exit. They were still four and a half miles away from the south perimeter. At their current pace they would reach the base boundary at about 2315.

Deborah looked north and noticed vehicle lights approaching. Two additional exterior electric maintenance trucks from the Civil Engineers were headed south on Lancaster to investigate the outage at the South ECP. Robert instructed the team to lie flat as the trucks passed them and slowed to a stop about a half mile north of the ECP on the road where the transformer was situated. The team dusted off and resumed the jog.

The remoteness of the base and the expanse of land was both a blessing and curse. Louis and Deborah strained to maintain the pace. Mary Ellen noticed their struggle and called for everyone to stop for a break and a drink. The team sat on the hard, dry earth while Robert kept an eye out for snakes and scorpions. They continued to watch the CE crew as it inspected the faulty transformer. Soon after, they heard the loud engines from the generator's light stands, and one by one they were activated. The team was able to see the gate, guardhouse, and Avenue B intersecting with Lancaster Boulevard just outside the gate.

The exterior electric shop vehicles, which were diverted away from the substation, were positioned so the lights above the cab shone onto the shed. As the crew walked to inspect the building for damage, they smelled burning metal. One of the NCOs went back to the truck to retrieve an extinguisher and called the shop to report what they had found. Since there were no visible flames, there was no need for a fire unit. Another sergeant took out his ring of keys and, upon finding the right one, unlocked it. The smell was stronger, but there was no evident source of heat in the shed. Nor was there was a sign of an explosion or arcing. Opening the transformer cover, they were astonished to see the buss bars had melted and deformed. Nothing they were aware of, with all their training, would have caused that. The entire transformer would have to be replaced. In the meantime, repair workers would tow in a portable generator from the supply yard and install it up the line. Eventually, it would be connected to the transformer to restore power to the lights and the ECP.

There wasn't much else they would be able to do at the shed tonight. Before leaving, they called the shop to relay their findings and recommend a genset for temporary power until a replacement transformer could be procured.

Robert's team came upon the southwest edge of Rodgers Dry Lake. They were still two and one-half miles from the exterior electrical repair crew at the transformer and just a little under three miles from Avenue B. As the trucks turned onto Lancaster and passed them, team members lay down in a natural depression. The area to the west was lit by the RALs. Generator noise masked any other sounds around them.

At 2300, Louis's phone vibrated. The team stopped. A text message from Trevor Hugo indicated he was about thirty minutes away. Robert took out his phone to look at the map and gave Louis instructions to pass on to Trevor. Approaching the base, he was to turn his headlights off, using only his parking lights, for the last one and one-half miles on 140th Street East. He was then to turn the car around and park along the roadside to wait. Robert figured they would reach Trevor in forty-five minutes. Louis thanked Trevor again and ended the text.

* * *

At Fresno, the two fighters landed and taxied to their original spots on the apron. The pilots exited their planes, and the maintenance crew made a short visual inspection and started diagnostics. The pilots were thrilled about their experience. They were in a jovial mood, laughing and talking loudly, but the levity was short-lived. They strutted back into the readiness building, excited for the mission debrief and were greeted by two plainclothesmen who identified themselves as a unit in OSI: the Air Force Office of Special Investigations. Instead of congratulating the pilots on a successful mission, they sternly ushered them into a small briefing room. The pilots were at once concerned and puzzled as they sat at a table together. The agents remained standing at the front of the room. One of them held a reddish-brown folder and spoke.

"Your mission tonight was a scramble initiated by the Wing Commander at Edwards. As you both know, that is not standard operation, violating protocol. There are no records of aerial activity on any radar. The FAA does not have record of any activity. Tonight's scramble will be classified as a public relations stunt for an unnamed distinguished visitor."

The pilots remained quiet, not even looking at each other. They both anticipated what was going to happen.

"What you witnessed over the base was not what you think. What you think happened, did not happen. There will be no report filed. Above all, you are not allowed to mention this mission to anyone. You are not to discuss it between yourselves, you are not to mention it to your closest friends or family, and do not mention this to your Commander. Officially, tonight did not happen. Any information leaked in any manner will result in swift action that will include any one, or all, of the following: discharge, personal injury, injury to family, loss of property . . . *permanent silence*. Is what I have stated clear to both of you?"

The pilots were silent and shocked by the threat. They lowered their heads without a word.

The OSI agent resumed by producing two prewritten forms. "The office has these forms for you to sign. They are nondisclosure agreements. They state mostly everything that I have told you tonight in a more legal way. All you need to do is sign it. You do not get a copy."

The pilots briefly read the forms and signed them. The OSI agent took the papers back, inspected them, and placed them back in the folder. The agent resumed his authoritative delivery.

"I would like for you both to repeat what I told you—senior officer first."

The pilots repeated the instructions and the repercussions in the event of voiding the agreement.

"You two are now going to go straight to your homes for the night. There will be other pilots that will be on alert for the rest of the night. When you leave, you will go directly home. Do not stop to talk to anyone. Do not make any eye contact. You will follow us out. Is that clear?"

The pilots nodded again.

"This debriefing session is now closed."

The OSI agents walked to the door as the pilots rose from their seats. The appearance of plainclothesmen interviewing pilots was never a good sign, but nobody lingered around the debriefing room area. The exit of the OSI agents and the pilots was swift and un-interrupted. The pilots avoided any further communication and drove off. The OSI agents returned quietly to their vehicle and left for their office in Los Angeles. Both pilots took leave the next day. They would heed the OSI instructions dutifully for their remaining years in service.

* * *

Louis and the team were allowed to enjoy the smoothness of the dry lake bed for only a short while. They resumed their pace on the uneven terrain, using the lights at the ECP to guide them to their rendezvous with Trevor. The constant loud drone from the gen-erators originated a mile west-southwest and masked the sounds of their boots crushing the dry grass. Tara, who was the only one without night vision goggles, glared at the source of the light and didn't notice or hear the team warn her about the odd formation and remnant in the ground ahead. Before anyone could stop her, she jogged straight into a shin-high trestle type construction, tripping forward, and hitting her shoulder solidly on a parallel low trestle, just missing her head. It was the ruins of a rocket sled track, near the east end of what was a twenty-thousand-feet long remnant that was used as far back as 1949, and retired in 1963. In 1974, the rails were removed and shipped to Holloman AFB to extend a track to a total of ten miles. Left as a hazard in the dark, an accident was imminent.

Tara yelped upon impact; only her group heard her brief cry. She remained kneeling on the ground, leaning on her left side against the low construction, favoring her right side. Deborah and Robert attended to her immediately.

"Is it the shoulder or the collar bone?" asked Deborah.

"Shoulder..."

"Check for any bruising or cuts," said Robert.

Deborah opened Tara's shirt. The shoulder was bruised and appeared separated. She took Tara's uniform shirt off, leaving her undershirt on, and fashioned a sling. Tara was in great pain, but her arm was stabilized. Louis offered her water. They rested but not for long. They were about twenty minutes from the rendezvous point with Trevor. Feeling like they would be able to make their escape, the team, now handicapped with an injured member, resumed the jog south a mile and a half from the lights and generators. At the ECP, two airmen stood guard, not knowing what to guard against. Their radios chattered about outages and orange lights, but threats appeared to be gone. Normally, there was little activity at this gate after the duty day. The light towers were more of a distraction than an asset. It was hard, almost impossible, to detect any movement not in the wash of the bright lights.

Passing by a couple of old dirt access roads, the team made its way to the corner of Avenue B and 140th Street East. With the benefit of the night vision goggles, they were able to see the empty road ahead. A mile down the long straight road, they spotted Trevor's vehicle using only parking lights, traveling slowly in their direction. Trevor did as instructed, parking off the side of the road, lights off. Carrying their bags, and taking their goggles off, they approached the mini-van. Trevor was waiting by the back of the van. He opened the rear hatch to let them stow their bags. They wasted little time getting in. Trevor started the engine before everyone had time to be seated. Robert tapped Trevor on the shoulder and motioned for him to move over. Robert navigated the vehicle with the lights off, using the night vision goggles, up to Lancaster until they were safely out of sight. Once they got on H, Robert pulled over, relinquishing the driver's seat to Trevor, who drove normally with the lights on. Except for Tara, the team expressed relief as they headed to San Fernando.

Louis took the opportunity to introduce the team to Trevor. While everyone was chatting about what happened at the base, Robert reached for his phone and placed a call to Katrina. After a few rings, her phone went to voice mail. Robert left a message, concern creeping into his voice. He recalled the ethereal feeling he had received from Katrina before, which soothed him.

"She'll be alright, Robert," Mary Ellen assured.

Deborah, sitting in the back, looked on with concern as well. She then picked up her phone for the first time since before Dulce and texted Susan that she was alright and would call in the morning. It was 1:30 a.m. in Saint Louis.

Tara remained quiet and in pain, sitting behind Trevor, leaning against the side of the van and staring out the window. Mary Ellen sat next to her and tried to console her.

"Those people put you through a lot, Tara. You have no clear memory of what you have been doing because they used a memory blocker aided by the trauma of assault to suppress those memories."

"Memory blocker?" asked Robert. "That must be what that green fluid is. I should have taken a sample with us."

"No worries, Robert. There's a full vial in a pocket in the lab coat," replied Louis.

"I am reading your spirit, Tara. It will tell me what you were not allowed to remember," assured Mary Ellen. "The people that did this to you were not with the Air Force. They would rough you up, then inject you with something that made you drowsy. This made you fall asleep on the bus, preventing you from talking to anyone. By the time you would reach your hotel room, exhausted, it would be only a few hours before your alarm would wake you up."

"I...would be so tired when I would have to report for the duty day after the night missions."

"Your night missions, being bussed to Groom Lake, would involve working on radar and testing it on exotic aerial vehicles. You were exposed to very sensitive information, and they took steps to make certain you would not retain the memory. The drug would make your brain process the information and store it in the subconscious. Your memories were converted into dreams or, rather, nightmares."

Tara sat still as she listened. She was beginning to understand how she had been manipulated and abused.

"Your spirit tells me that they have also flown you to the...*moon?* to do the same things there, and you were there for extended periods and...they..." Mary Ellen could feel the pain Tara had endured and it was difficult for her to finish the sentence.

"What? They what?" Tara begged.

"They used you for their pleasure."

The inside of the vehicle was silent except for the road noise. Tara looked down. Mary Ellen put her arm around her.

"I'm so sorry, Tara. We will make sure you get help."

"How?" Tara raised her voice in frustration. "I'm AWOL! I can't use my identity! No one will believe those things you said. I can't even believe it, and it happened to ME! I can't remember anything to be able to explain it to someone. My account of events will be a mess. I need to get back to my unit. I need to get back to my commander. Maybe I should ask for a transfer."

"Tara, I told you earlier that before our team opened the doors and arrested your captors, I used my phone to record your assault," Robert said. "Tonight, I sent the video file to two trustworthy friends. One is an investigative reporter at *The Washington Post*, and the other a congressman with a seat on the House Armed Services Committee. I anticipate some action from those two men."

Tara did not respond. Nothing gave her any feeling of hope.

17

LONELY EMISSARY

So many worlds, so much to do, so little done, such things to be. —Alfred Lord Tennyson

They arrived at Trevor's apartment in San Fernando just after 1 a.m. He parked his mini-van in front of his building. Neighborhood dogs barked at the early morning disturbance. Feeling a great sense of relief, Mary Ellen opened the side door. Robert slid out from the front passenger's seat, as Airman Everly eased out in pain, tired and anxious. Deborah and Louis were the last to exit, stepping down on the grass strip at the curb. The streetlights added a pallor to their tired faces. They slowly and quietly got their bags from the back, grateful for the short walk to the building's courtyard gate.

After Louis mentioned that Tara needed a sling and something for her pain, Trevor unselfishly offered to go the neighborhood pharmacy. Robert gave him money. As he left, he suggested Robert and Louis make the living room floor their sleeping place for the night while the women took the sofa bed. The team laid their bags neatly along a wall, then sat on anything they could find in the one-man, one-bedroom, one-bathroom apartment.

They discussed what they each would do next. Louis and Mary Ellen planned to go to Mount Shasta. Deborah needed to go back to Dulce to pick up her SUV and drive back to St. Louis. Even with the understanding that Katrina was going to be alright, Robert was still anxious to get back to Taos. Tara, officially AWOL, was quiet and stressed to exhaustion. Robert asked Deborah if she would join him on the trip back to New Mexico.

"We could split the cost of the rental," suggested Robert.

Deborah nodded in agreement. "Sounds like a plan."

Mary Ellen asked, "Tara, have you been to Mount Shasta?" Airman Everly shook her head. "Then come with us. I think you will find it relaxing. The positive energy there could be a big help to you."

Tara gazed at Mary Ellen with a puzzled look. "Don't you get it? I'm AWOL, that's punishable under the Uniform Code of Military Justice." Her voice was elevated, her eyes open in fear. "Even if they find that it was not of my own doing, I could get up to three months confinement and reduction in grade."

Hearing the emotion in Tara's voice, Louis tried to rationalize. "Tara, your situation is … well … unique. I really don't think your commander knew what was happening to you at Groom Lake. Obviously, you haven't gone to him; there was no reason because you have had no recollection of your experiences."

"Louis, it is because of the situation she is in that you can't expect things to go by the book. Remember, there were cameras at Groom Lake. They have our images with Airman Everly," pointed Robert. The airman sulked, looking at Robert with deep concern.

"OK, let's think about this clearly," Louis said calmly. "There are two assumptions they could make about seeing us take Tara. One, we were sent by another group to kidnap her; two, we rescued her. Right now, because of the time of day, Tara is not officially AWOL yet. Tara, call your commander and let him know that close high-school friends came to visit you and took you camping for a couple days."

"I can't call. My phone is in a locker back at Groom Lake," she replied as she produced proof—a key. "That phone has my commander's number as a contact. I don't know his number, but I could call the Nellis base locator."

Using Louis's phone, she called the operator and was connected to the commander's phone. She left a message to request leave. This allowed her time to figure out how to get back to Nellis and perhaps report to a security officer or a chaplain.

"See? Now you are on leave. And while on leave you should relax," assured Louis.

"Airman Everly, you probably aren't aware how often the rooms that you were in are used, correct?" asked Robert, trying to estimate how long it would take before the bound men were discovered.

The young airman shook her head.

"I'm going to say a week," replied Robert, answering his own question. "Let's say in a week, they find them, including the Grey. My guess is there is no documentation of you being there—ever.

Everything was clandestine. They have us on video, but we concealed our faces. I don't think they have the resources to investigate once they make their discovery. Do you recall them addressing you by your last name? Do you think they would remember you?"

"If they know where I stayed, they could easily hunt me down. I am certain others have disappeared because they violated some sort of condition. I have no one to help me once I go back. This leave is just a delay of the inevitable. I can't tell on them because, officially, the program doesn't exist." In a voice racked with terror and pain, she added, "It would have been better if you had killed them."

Robert and Mary Ellen gave each other a knowing glance. "Tara, that's not what this journey is about," Mary Ellen said. "We could have easily killed those people, but we preserved their lives."

"But when they find the guys in the closets, they will find the Grey and, once again, that death would be linked back to the rescue."

"Airman Everly, I know what you are thinking. Had we killed the men there would be no way they could link anything back to you. I get it. But I'm not like them. No one here is like them. I can't execute unarmed men after capturing them." Mary Ellen uncharacteristically put her arm around Robert.

Robert recalled the moments before he shot the Grey. "There is one thing that I am concerned about, and it doesn't involve the airman. Louis knows this, but I did not mention it to anyone else." All eyes were fixed on Robert as the women stopped to listen. "Before I shot the Grey in the head, he was still alive, and he sent me a message telepathically. He said, *Human, the masters will know I am missing.*"

"So, whoever the handlers are, they are probably looking for him now," added Louis. "Tara, would you know who the handlers are?"

Tara shook her head. "No."

"I don't think they were human. Humans don't have that technology and cannot give telepathic commands. It was probably the reptilians," pointed out Mary Ellen. "But think about this, the entire species behaves collectively, much like bees. The attack at Dulce caused the ones here to flee and would have caused a collective panic. Given their situation, I think that the loss of one android Grey would not matter at this point. I think they have bigger concerns."

"Tara, right now, you are safe here. Robert and I will not return you to a situation where your life is in serious danger. You have to trust us. We will find a way to help you. You know, I read you a bit before. Do you want me to read you again tomorrow when we are better rested and able to think clearly?" asked Mary Ellen.

"I'm afraid to find out more, but maybe I could get information that will help Robert and Louis understand how the operation worked," Tara replied.

"OK. We'll set aside some time for me to read you tomorrow."

Trevor returned, not only with a sling and pain relief for Tara but also food and drinks.

Trevor had never had so many people in his postage-stamp-sized apartment. His pantry and refrigerator were barely stocked to take care of his own needs. He had gathered what one could at 1 a.m., when limited to gas stations and 24-hour shops—donuts, orange juice, and microwave breakfast foods. Mary Ellen and Deborah helped Tara fit the sling. Trevor helped the men fashion beds on the floor. It was close to 2 a.m. Everyone understood that there was much still to discuss, but they all needed a good night's sleep so they would have clarity in the morning. Sleep didn't take long.

The next morning, Louis and Robert got up to talk to Trevor while the women remained on the sofa bed.

"Guys, I'd really like to talk some more, but I need to get to work. I'll let you in on some interesting stuff when I get home," said Trevor as he picked up his keys. "Have a good day; I should be back by six o'clock. Louis, I can pick up dinner before coming home. Text me," he said as he rushed out the door.

* * *

The women got up shortly after Trevor left. Deborah and Mary Ellen were startled by Tara's reaction as she awoke.

"Who are you?! Where am I?!"

"Tara, what's wrong?" asked Deborah.

"How do you know my name? Who are you people? Ow! My shoulder . . . I'm in a sling?"

"Calm down, Tara. You are reacting from trauma and memory blocker," Mary Ellen said in a consoling voice.

"What is going on?" Louis asked. "How is it you don't remember us? After all we went through?"

"Hold on, Louis. Airman Everly, I want you to watch a video I took last night on my phone." Robert walked over to the confused young airman, sitting up on the edge of the sofa bed. He sat next to her, holding the screen for her.

He narrated while Tara watched, partly in disbelief, partly in horror. The video lasted about two minutes. Tara stared at the floor with her eyes glazed. Then she spoke softly.

"I've seen this before . . . in nightmares."

Mary Ellen pointed to the video. "That's the memory blocker taking effect after sleep. It's the same phenomenon that prevented Deborah and myself from remembering our abductions."

"That's the bright green fluid that was in the refrigerator and the used syringe on the table next to the mattress," said Robert.

Louis went to his bag to get the vial from a pocket in the lab coat. He reached into his pack and held out the sealed vial of bright green fluid for everyone to see. Robert took a photo with his phone.

"Louis, would you mind if I took the vial?" asked Robert. "I'd like to get it to a lab."

"Sure. I wouldn't know where to start with that.

"Tara, the reason you don't remember anything about last night was that you were injected with this memory blocker," Mary Ellen said, realizing they needed Tara to gain some calm understanding of the entire horrifying episode. "It ensured that your memory of that night was stored in the subconscious part of your brain: the part that is active when you dream. You will only have recollections as nightmares."

She reintroduced everyone. "The people you see here, Louis, Robert, Deborah, and myself, Mary Ellen, rescued you. You were being tortured by the men in the video, causing you trauma. Trauma was necessary to make the memory blocker work."

Mary Ellen, Robert, Deborah, and Louis explained everything, including how she sustained her injury. They also told her where they were.

The young airman began to slowly understand what the team was telling her. "So, the nightmares, about me being assaulted or . . . ," she was thinking back about a dream involving her and ultra-high-performance aircraft, "watching craft in the night sky streak and accelerate and climb high at amazing speeds, that was real?"

"Yes," replied Mary Ellen. "How's your shoulder?"

"It hurts a lot."

"The sling should help you," said Deborah. "Take some pain killer."

Mary Ellen took Tara aside to talk one on one. She told Tara about her spirituality and why she was part of the team. Tara listened intently and, with every word, felt more trusting of Mary Ellen.

Deborah was satisfied with Mary Ellen's tending the young airman. She looked through the kitchen cupboards for coffee and found nothing. "I need coffee. Anyone else want coffee? There's got to be a coffee shop close to us. I am going out to get some. I'll take your orders."

Tara heard Deborah's offer and raised her hand. Robert also accepted the offer. Besides getting coffee, Deborah had other intentions. She rushed into Trevor's room, texted Susan that she would be calling, then changed and left. She was not going to talk on the phone about what happened, promising to tell Susan the entire story upon her return. Taking advantage of the solitude past the courtyard gate, Deborah called Susan. She told her partner how much she missed her and about her son. Susan was floored by the news. Once again Deborah said she would tell her the details in person. Before saying goodbye, Deborah let Susan know that it would probably be another four days before she returned to St. Louis, via Dulce. Susan was happy to hear that her best friend was safe and would soon return.

Back at the apartment, Louis made a suggestion to the young airman. "Tara, how about you, Mary Ellen, and I get a Lyft and go find you some civilian clothes to wear while you are on leave?"

"That's a good idea, Louis. Tara, new clothes might lift your spirits," said Mary Ellen. Tara flashed a slight smile as a sign of approval.

Louis looked at his phone for local store hours. The stores opened at ten o'clock. He arranged for a Lyft driver, the 10:15 pickup to be made in a silver Toyota Previa. *Silver Toyota Previa?* he thought.

Mary Ellen and Tara finished their conversation. Mary Ellen got up and went to the freezer to get a breakfast sandwich, asking if she could make one for anyone else. Putting his phone down, Louis took her up on her offer. Not finding conventional dinnerware, she pulled out a couple of paper plates from the semi-empty pantry and gave a sandwich and a plate to Louis. There was nothing fresh in the refrigerator, so the choices were limited. Mary Ellen took her lava-hot sandwich and went to sit in the kitchen. Not wanting to start her day with a hot cheese burn, she waited for Louis as he followed with his own pick.

Deborah returned with the coffee orders. Robert went to the counter and retrieved an unopened plastic package of donuts that looked artificial. He placed it on a small table in the living room where Deborah set the coffee drinks down. Robert and Deborah sat and watched the TV, enjoying their morning treat. Tara joined them.

"Tara, I don't think I offered you thanks for your service. From this Army Ranger veteran, thanks," said Robert.

"Same from this former Air Force SP, Tara," added Deborah.

"I'm Air Force too—Prime BEEF," said Louis.

Louis, Robert, and Deborah asked Tara questions about her experience in the Air Force. Tara described her job at Nellis: her first stateside station. Her first tour was in Germany. She was also interested to hear about the veterans' experiences. She asked Robert if he had seen combat in Iraq. The vet began to feel the walls close in. The PTSD symptoms were coming back. He turned silent. He wanted to get away, but he couldn't move. His clothes felt tight especially around the neck. His breathing became shallow. He knew what he had to do.

"Louis, my bag."

Aware of Robert's state, Louis quickly retrieved the backpack. Robert anxiously felt for the belt that had the pouch where he stored his bottle of CBD oil. He took it out, unscrewed the cap, and squeezed the bulb to extract the solution. As he did back in Dulce, he put a few drops under his tongue, screwed the cap back on, and put the bottle back in the belt pouch. He closed his eyes for a still, silent moment. The others respectfully lowered their voices and continued to exchange military anecdotes. After feeling relief, Robert opened his eyes.

"I remember the day we all rotated out of Ramadi. We were all happy," he said. "There were smiles, guys taking pictures of themselves with buddies. We were bussed to wait on the tarmac for a C-130. We waited and we waited and we waited. We were just sitting out there on the airfield with our bags. A truck came to give us bottled water. After about three hours there, we saw the bird come in, land, and taxi toward us, but it remained far away on one of the other pads, and we had to walk a long way to get to the transport. Normally, the rear of the plane opens up, and the troops get in using the loading ramp.

"As we got to the plane, the back remained closed, and we were ordered to board in the plane through the pilots' entry. We carried our heavy duffel bags up a narrow, steep ladder and through a door where we had to duck to get inside. The troops were carrying on outside the plane in a good mood. One by one they boarded. I was one of the last to get in. As I entered, the cargo bay was curiously quiet. I looked at the back of the plane where the rear door was, and I realized why the plane had been late and why everyone was quiet. A US Marine was dressed in his blues with a rifle, standing guard in front of a casket draped with the flag. While in flight, I looked at the faces of the soldiers sitting across the bay and I thought, *None left behind*. We were all going home alive. I looked back at the Marine and the casket, and realized *that* fallen soldier was going home too."

The room fell quiet after Robert's story. Tara didn't ask any more questions about the war.

Robert took his phone out and sent the photo of the vial with the bright green substance to his friend at *The Washington Post*. He noticed an email from the reporter. The message asked him to identify who was in the video. Robert wrote back, explaining everything but opted not to identify young airman. He also explained the photo of the vial.

Robert's phone chimed again. It was his friend at the *Post*. The reporter's message explained that the story was too bizarre to put in the papers. He also wrote that there was a CIA operative at the *Post* specifically assigned to censor news releases. He added that he would retain the information as well as relay it to someone that he knew in the DoD at the Pentagon, working in the Inspector General's office. There was no response yet from Robert's friend in Congress. Robert put the phone down and looked at the vial of green fluid one more time. He walked over to his pack to stow it away in a separate zippered pocket.

After everyone showered, Tara, Louis, and Mary Ellen left to meet the Lyft ride. Deborah and Robert stayed in the apartment to make plans for the departure the following day. Louis directed the women to the pickup location. They spotted the silver Previa van approaching. As it got closer, Mary Ellen and Louis began to chuckle. It was Trevor. Louis had thought it odd that they were being sent a Previa and eventually concluded it was just a coincidence. The door opened and the three got in.

"Trevor, I had no idea you were a driver. I can only imagine what you must have thought when I called you to pick us up from Edwards. It was probably right after you got home from doing this all day. I'm truly sorry." Louis felt the need to apologize again.

"Don't worry. It's cool. I look forward to talking to you some more about what you did. I've got a lot to show you guys, too."

It didn't take long to get to the shopping center. Trevor drove up to the main entrance and his customer-friends got out.

"Louis, text me when you are done. I'll give you the ride back—no charge," said Trevor with a Merry-Christmas smile.

"You won't make any money that way. We'll pay for the gas, and for the gas you used for the ride to and from Edwards."

Trevor left for more pickups, and Louis, Mary Ellen, and Tara walked into a store to shop. After roaming around for over an hour, they picked out a few pieces, including a backpack, then checked out, with Louis covering the charges. Tara thanked him. They walked outside for a bit and stopped at a restaurant, where they talked through lunch about anything except Groom Lake or the Air Force. They continued to sit well after their plates had been cleared, nursing their drinks. Louis sent a text message to Deborah offering to bring them lunch, and Deborah and Robert immediately put in their orders. Louis then sent a message to Trevor that the three shoppers were ready to be picked up. Mary Ellen grabbed the food to take back, then they went outside and passed time on a bench. Not too long after, the silver Previa drove up to the restaurant. The ride back was short. Trevor dropped his riders off in front of his apartment building. He repeated his promise that he would be home at six, with pizzas.

After entering the apartment, Louis placed the bag of lunch for Deborah and Robert on the kitchen table. They almost collided while retrieving their food. Tara dashed into Trevor's room to change into her new clothes. Mary Ellen followed her to help with the sling and then offered to read her spirit. Although Mary Ellen had done a reading in the van the night before, Tara had no recollection.

"Tara, I could read your spirit now if you want to understand what has been happening to you."

"I'm scared to find out. I know what is hidden away must be horrible. But maybe if I *did* know what happened, it would not have as much effect on me as I fear. I just don't know. If I find out more, would the memories slowly make me go insane?" She paused and thought with worry, *Would I go into a depression?*

"I'm not going to pull the memories from you and put them back in your consciousness. You will still have no recollection or retainment. I am reading your spiritual self, and you will hear what I sense, but you won't feel it."

"Oh...oh...alright, I—I...think I understand," replied Tara, shaky with uncertainty. "What do you need me to do?"

"Nothing. Really. I mean *nothing*. Don't move, don't make a sound." In moments, Mary Ellen was able to read Tara.

"You have the spirit of a warrior. Your spirit is resilient. You are having this life because you are able to handle it, and it will make you stronger. You were first taken when you were very young."

"Taken?!"

"Shhh....Just listen. You have been a subject of experimentation since you were a toddler. You were not alone. There were other young girls with you in the craft. You were placed on a table for an exam. Your abductors were the Greys, but they were servants to another humanoid race. In order to track you, they placed an implant up your nostril all the way to the base of the brain. They examined your body. After they were done examining you, they injected you with something, then they put you back in your bed. You don't remember this?"

"No. I don't think I even remember dreaming this."

"There's more. They visited you other times. They visited and took you until you were six, then they did not return until you were a young adolescent. You were artificially impregnated, and they..." Mary Ellen had to stop momentarily. She took a deep breath and exhaled, "They took your unborn baby before anyone figured, including yourself, that you were pregnant."

"I had a *baby?*"

"Yes, they took it, and you saw them take it while you were lying on the table in the ship, and they placed it in a container with a blue fluid. They did this again the following year using the same procedures. There were no more of these abductions until you were an adult. They took you when you were stationed in Germany, too. They abducted you with the purpose of harvesting an egg. Apparently, there is something special about your DNA. Your spirit is telling my guide that you have...*Lyran* DNA." Mary Ellen recalled that Kaja Jorgensen claimed Louis had Lyran DNA earlier. It made her pause again. Reading more, she breathed deeply as she understood what she had to describe next. "One of the humanoids took you to your room, hovered over your body, and you were motionless and naked. In your state between consciousness and sleep...you let him have sex with you. I'm not sure what to think of that. No drugs were used. It's as if you knew him...and you had feelings for him. They would do this to you often, and the same humanoid would take you back to bed. He would never hurt you. He was gentle. How do you feel about that?"

Tara was silent as tears welled in her bright silvery-blue eyes. "I had an alien lover?"

"I guess so, yet you have no memory of him, do you?"

"No. Nothing."

"I think you have had enough reading for now." The revelations about Tara overwhelmed and fatigued Mary Ellen.

Tara then turned to Mary Ellen. "Maybe I *will* go with you to Mount Shasta. I think I can trust both of you, and I think I could use some relaxation. It would give you a chance to read me again." Mary Ellen was pleased as she nodded. "Thanks, Mary Ellen. I really do appreciate your taking the time to do this for me."

"From what we know now, you have been through a lot. You know, I've known since Nevada that your spirit was strong. You'll get through this!"

Both women exhaled and left the room together.

In the living room, Robert indicated that he and Deborah had reserved a car for the drive back to New Mexico, and they would leave in the morning. Realizing that he had not yet arranged for the ride to Mount Shasta, Louis called the same rental office that Robert had called. After quickly finishing her lunch, Deborah waited for *her* turn to talk to Mary Ellen. She intercepted Mary Ellen, asked her for a talk and redirected her back to Trevor's room, closing the door.

"Mary Ellen, this is the first chance we've had to talk alone since we left the lab at Dulce," said Deborah.

Mary Ellen nodded. "I know, there were so many things happening. How are you? How do you feel knowing you have a grown son? Maybe you won't have any more of those nightmares."

"I was going to ask you the same question. How are you after seeing your child for a brief moment and then having to let him go away. Do you know where they took him?"

"I don't know, but I'm sure he is in good care. He, like the others that were rescued, is being deprogrammed. They will be human again, and I believe I will see my child again."

"So, are you saying that my son is not human?" asked Deborah.

"Deborah, what I witnessed happen between you and him before we left was very reassuring. The human side appears strong in your son. It really helped that you were there."

"I wonder what he is thinking now. I want to know what his day is like. Where does he live? What's his favorite food? What kind of music does he listen to? He must be very smart."

Mary Ellen gave Deborah a grave, serious look. "Deborah, listen. Be happy that you found him but understand that he is like a machine. The ones like him have no free will. He was only programmed with the information that would be necessary to carry out his job. He has no appreciation for the arts or beauty. Although . . . it is evident he still felt a connection with you, so maybe there is a chance he could learn those things that were taken from him, with your guidance and love."

Deborah looked down at the floor and shuffled her feet then held her hands together in her lap. It was a revelation for Mary Ellen, seeing this self-described atheist assume the posture as if she was about to pray.

Mary Ellen moved closer to Deborah. "Deborah, you *will* see him again. Be patient. I'm sure he wonders about you now, too."

Deborah continued to look at the floor, pursed her lips, and nodded as tears formed in her eyes. Mary Ellen put her arm around her. "I think if you continue to meditate, strengthen your connection to the spiritual realm, you may be able to find him just like he found you."

Deborah nodded again in agreement. After a little bit of quiet time, the women left the room to join the others.

The rental car office called back to confirm Louis's reservation. His pickup time was the same as Robert and Deborah's. Louis asked Tara if she was going with him and Mary Ellen. The young airman responded affirmatively.

As promised, Trevor returned at six with the pizzas and an assortment of drinks. He casually placed the boxes out on every vacant flat surface in the kitchen, the stove included. He took a paper plate out of the pantry, loaded it, and went to sit down in the living room, inviting everyone to do the same. Everyone found a place to sit, relax, and talk, knowing it was their last night together. Upon realizing that, Deborah and Louis took candid shots of everyone between bites. Robert did the same. Mary Ellen stood by the front door and took a couple of shots with everyone, including Tara and Trevor. The group spent more time talking about the past couple of days. Tara was engrossed in what she was hearing about Katrina, Dulce, and Mary Ellen.

Then Louis asked Trevor to tell the group about himself.

The room got quiet as Trevor explained his own existence, without reservation about revealing his identity to his guests. "I am in a human body, but I have ET memory in my subconscious. I get my information in the dream state, and I am able to recall that information vividly. I then transfer the memory to sketches and writing. I have a role here, to observe and report. I am reincarnated from a member of a science team that crashed in New Mexico searching for survivors at Roswell. The radar at Los Alamos breached the hull and caused our navigation system to malfunction. We crashed at a high rate of speed, and no one survived."

Trevor's guests did not utter a word.

"That race is from the Aldebaran system in the constellation Taurus. My spirit indicates that I have been sent to observe and will be activated if and when there is good reason."

"So, you are part of a sleeper cell?" asked Robert.

"So to speak. You might say that. I am one of many on Earth that have this kind of role. I don't know any of the other observers; I think it's designed that way to minimize threats to the whole. If one of us gets taken out, others will take their place."

Robert looked at the others, then back at Trevor. "Well, that's the very definition of a sleeper cell."

"What are you looking for?" asked Deborah.

"Signs. Signs of the prophecy. Increases in the appearance of the phenomenon. Messages from religious leaders."

"Have you detected anything?" asked Robert.

"The Vatican's acknowledgement of extraterrestrials is momentous. The recognition of Jerusalem as the spiritual capital of Israel is seismic."

"But the prophecy does not necessarily need to come true," Mary Ellen said. "We still have control over our fate."

"And what about McGeorge? That also has to be huge in the positive direction," Deborah noted.

"And you, especially, Louis," Mary Ellen added. "You have been assigned as a Counsellor and Informer."

"Yeah, but I am not allowed to do that anymore, remember the men who threatened me at the conference?"

"It's still your role, Louis, don't give up on that."

"Counsellor and Informer?" Trevor asked.

Louis let Trevor know what had happened to him in Aurora during the reading, then told him about Colonel McGeorge.

Trevor scooted to the edge of the sofa, excited. "Louis, don't you see what is happening? You are being guided to establish a network that has been selected for various roles. For what? I don't know. But I'm pretty sure that we will know when we're needed."

Tara listened with deep interest. Louis felt the need to deflect attention away from him. "Trevor, can you show us the drawings that you have produced from your dreams?" he asked.

Trevor walked to his bedroom, pulled out a storage tub from under the bed, and brought it out. There were thirteen drawings and sketches of various subjects. He took them out one at a time to show and explain them to the group.

All of the sketches were drawn on engineering paper, technical in nature, with symbols and graphics unlike anything on Earth. Out of the thirteen sheets, five depicted star charts and planetary systems beyond Earth's solar system. Trevor explained the diagrams would only hold value for intergalactic travelers.

"Some of the information is classified by The Council, so I cannot go into detail," he added. "The views of the stars and planets I drew aren't from the Earth's perspective. The sketches with the markings show arrays assigned to a specific sector. There are stargates placed in various and strategic places as well. There is one that is close to our own sun and one between Saturn and Jupiter. The symbols I drew here are key codes and combinations used to activate the stargates that would take someone to various sectors, dimensions, and universes."

Tara selected a detailed sketch of an array of twelve planets and moons around a star. "Which star is this?" asked Tara.

"HD 10180, as astronomers know it. A star in the Hydrus Constellation," Trevor replied casually.

In addition, there were drawings of alien landscapes, stargates, and one detailed side illustration of an exotic craft shaped like wedge with a faceted fuselage similar to the F-117 Stealth Fighter.

While the group was impressed by the drawings, it was the strange symbols and writings that enraptured them.

"That is a stargate. There were many on Earth, thousands of years ago, but now the only remnants are the stepped pyramids in Central America and Southeast Asia." Trevor pointed to two large angular structures on the top of the pyramid. "See? These are huge crystals. They were essential in the function of the stargate. All the crystals have been removed over time, most likely pilfered. The stargates worked by reading DNA and the spirit for identification prior to teleportation. There were two platforms. The first was to communicate to a gatekeeper, and the second one directed energy into the subject, breaking down the molecular structures past the DNA level for proper teleportation."

Trevor pointed to a drawing showing a central object with a triangle and an array of similar round objects surrounding it with lines connecting each object to the central object. "This drawing is a star map diagram that would typically be displayed at each stargate. The triangle in the center represents the stargate. The lines to the other planets indicate the links to other stargates."

"So, it's like an intergalactic transit map," said Deborah.

Trevor chuckled. "Yeah, you could say that. Regarding all the symbols you see, I didn't understand what I was writing when I was a teen, but now, I have recognition. It happened like—overnight. The symbolic system is similar to Japanese Kanji, where the characters are logographic, not representing an alphabet."

The group passed Trevor's sketches among themselves. "When did you realize you had the ET memory and start to draw these sketches?" asked Robert.

"It started when I was ten years old. One day, while walking home from school, a woman dressed in a long, flowing, black long-sleeved garment walked up to me. She had piercing green eyes and a dominant low tone of voice. She presented to me a black stone box. It measured about ten inches, cubed. She told me to take it. I asked her what it was, and she told me I would know what to do with it once I got home. It was heavy, too heavy for my bag. I carried it home. When I got there, I went to my room and I tried opening it. I spent a lot of time trying figure out how to open it. I was frustrated so I stashed it in my dresser. A couple of nights passed.

"One night, my mother went to visit one of her Jehovah's Witness friends. She hired a babysitter to stay with me. I was in my room because the babysitter controlled the TV. Something made me open the drawer and take the box out. I set it on the dresser, and I remember just staring at it. I think I was in a trance. When I came out of the trance, the case was opened on all sides like a flower. It revealed a black, velvet-like interior, and at the center, was a black crystal—about seven inches in diameter with three gold starbursts set in the middle. I recall going into another short trance. I stared this time at the crystal.

"When I was aware again, the stars illuminated. I was scared and I stepped back. The crystal began to levitate, and I felt heat from it. Suddenly a beam shot out of the crystal and hit me in the chest. I fell back on the bed unconscious. I think I was out for only a bit. When I awoke, the crystal and the case were gone, but this was on my chest."

Trevor stood up, unbuttoned his shirt, and revealed the mark left on his skin by the beam of light.

"It's the shape of a shield!" said Louis. "You've had that since you were ten? And nobody, not even your doctor asked you about that mark?"

"People would ask me if I burned myself. I would just say no and tell them I don't know how I got it. My mother preferred to not know rather than to ask questions that would disturb her religious beliefs. That was where my life began to change and my true origin was revealed. I would have flashbacks and images of my ET past. I would have vivid dreams of that life and, the following morning, would draw and write what I could recount. I was drawing all through high school and my young adulthood."

"So, the light flash not only left a mark, it activated something inside you," Mary Ellen said.

"Exactly!" said Trevor. "I am a guardian while I observe and report in dream state."

Trevor carefully collected his sketches, placed them neatly in chronological order in their container, and sealed all edges completely. This was the one item in his possession that he treated with order and reverence.

"Louis, Trevor is amazing! He's another piece of the puzzle I call life," said Mary Ellen.

"He told me about his background, but seeing the drawings in person with his explanation is more exciting. Robert, describing him as part of sleeper cell is accurate," said Louis.

"Katrina told me about aliens and more, and I knew of some things, but this—the drawings and the alien writings—it adds so much. How much more don't I know? This trip...will have a lasting impact."

Mary Ellen asked, "Deborah, you haven't said much. What did you get from looking at Trevor's drawings and listening to him explain what he drew?"

"You guys, I am so far behind you all on this. I am being given a drink from a fire hose. I feel like Robert. What else is out there, just here on Earth, that I can't imagine? I tell you what, though; what Mary Ellen said about all this happening due to Louis is right on. I can see how everything has come together."

"So, it's Louis I should thank for the rescue?" asked Tara.

"Well, me—yes, but Mary Ellen started it all: taking the chances, the initiative, and reaching out to me," offered Louis.

It appeared that everyone was ready for the new day to come. Louis, for the first time on the trip, took a moment to let his kids know he was alright. He informed them that he would tell them all about the trip when he returned in a couple of days. He was going to drive to Mount Shasta on the last leg of the trip. Deborah exchanged messages with Susan. Robert tried calling Katrina's number one more time, and once again it went to voicemail. He feared that Katrina had been unconscious for two full days. Although he knew that she was alive, he couldn't help but feel powerless, unable to do anything from where he was. After leaving a message again, he looked at the phone and turned it off. Mary Ellen noticed his failed attempt to reach Katrina again. She went to sit next to him and console him.

"Robert, you know she is alive, right?"

"I hear you saying that, but I haven't felt anything from her since the night at Edwards.

"Do you not trust me?"

"I trust you, but are you seeing that it is so, or are you hoping that it is?"

"The spirit and guides will never betray us. Hold on." Mary Ellen closed her eyes and took a couple of deep cleansing breaths as Robert looked on intently.

"Robert, I am communicating with Katrina's spirit that is still with her, which means she is living. Her spirit wishes to tell you that she awaits you. The spirit also wishes you to meditate every night to get in touch with her realm. She will be able to reach you in your meditations."

Robert nodded. "Ok, I'll try."

"Feel better?"

"I suppose."

"Good. You could start trying *now*."

Robert nodded. Mary Ellen guided him through his first meditation, starting with the breathing discipline, then working to self-awareness and silencing the mind. It was a good session for a first one, and Robert was confident he would be able to do it by himself the next time.

Everyone was ready to turn in. Trevor would be going to work early, so he wouldn't be able to say his goodbyes the next day. The team, along with Tara, thanked him and wished him well. They exchanged numbers. Deborah was so happy and excited, she doubted she would be able to sleep. Robert went back to his eyedropper bottle for another dose of the oil. Mary Ellen and Tara whispered softly about stories of their past and their families. The next day, Louis, Mary Ellen, and Tara would set out for Mount Shasta. Deborah and Robert would head back to their homes where they would enter into a beginning of another phase of life.

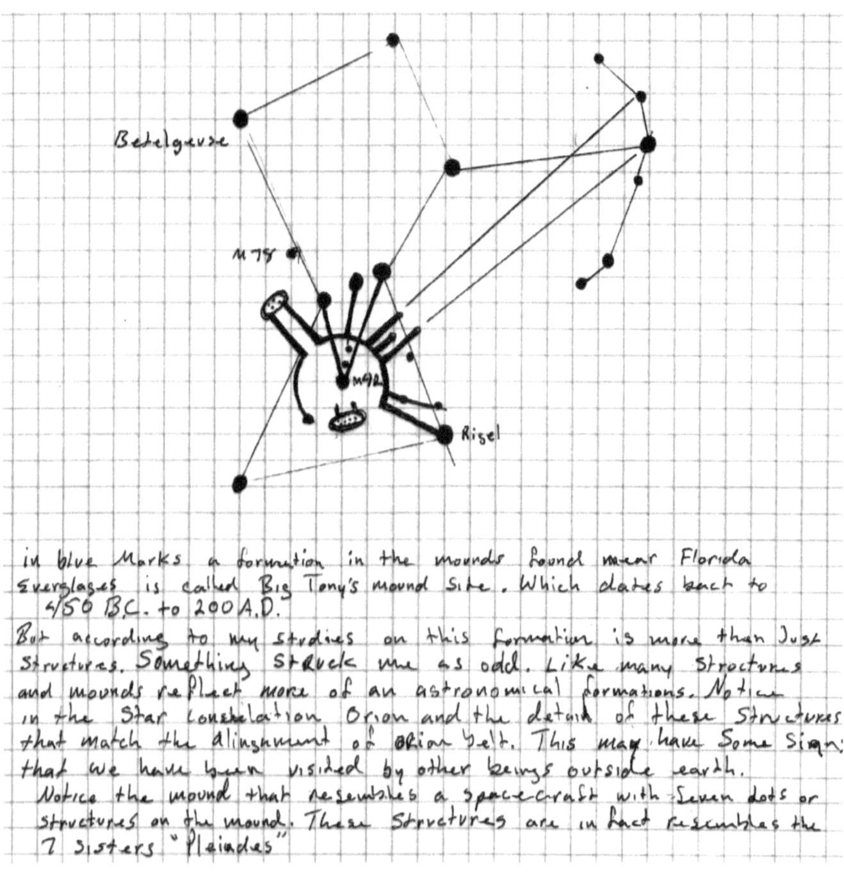

in blue Marks a formation in the mounds found near Florida
Everglases is called Big Tony's mound Site. Which dates back to
450 B.C. to 200 A.D.
But according to my studies on this formation is more than Just
Structures. Something Struck me as odd. Like many Structures
and mounds reflect more of an astronomical formations. Notice
in the Star Constelation Orion and the detail of these Structures
that match the alingnment of Orion belt. This may have Some Sign
that we have been visited by other beings outside earth.
  Notice the mound that resembles a spacecraft with Seven dots or
Structures on the mound. These Structures are in fact resembles the
7 Sisters "Pleiades"

ORION

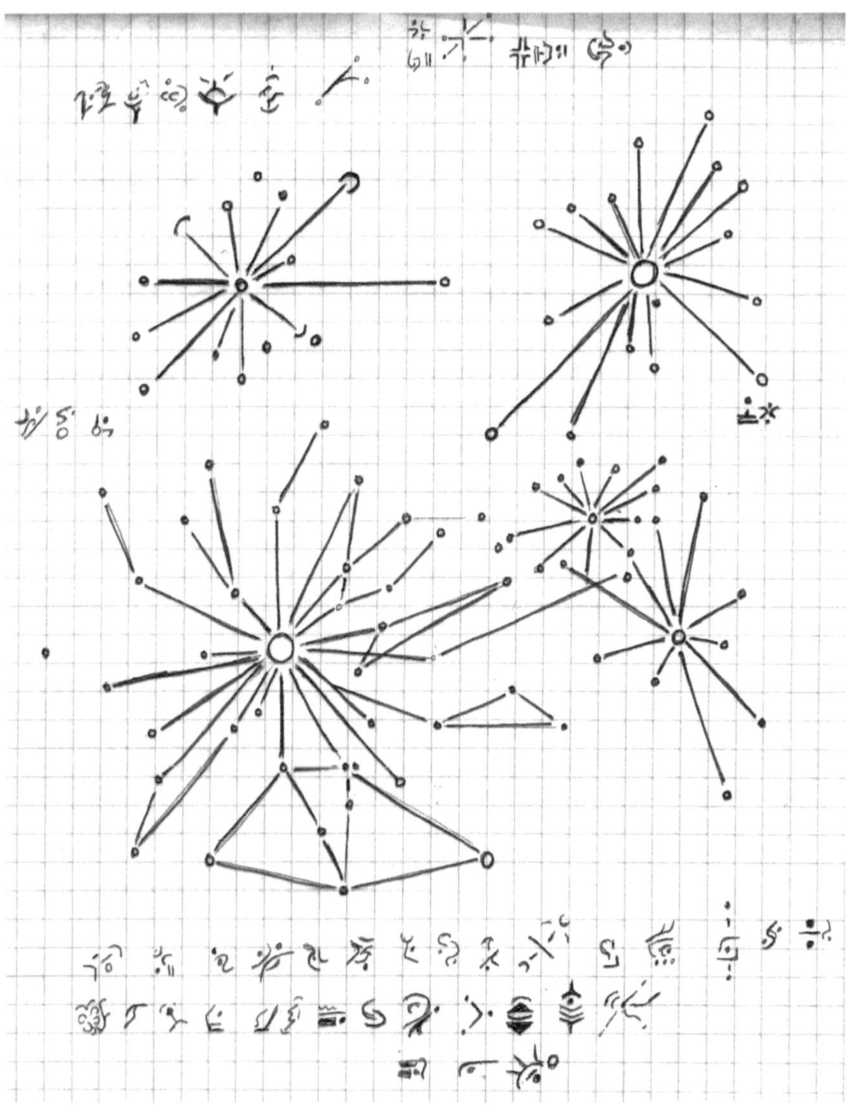

STAR CHARTS WITH ALIEN LOGOGRAPHIC CHARACTERS

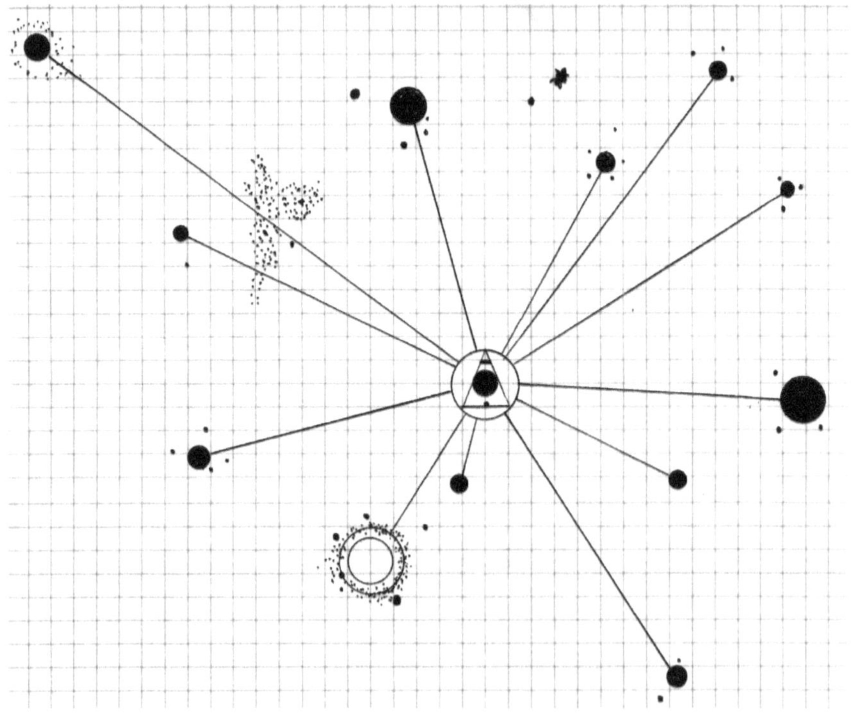

STAR CHART WITH PORTAL

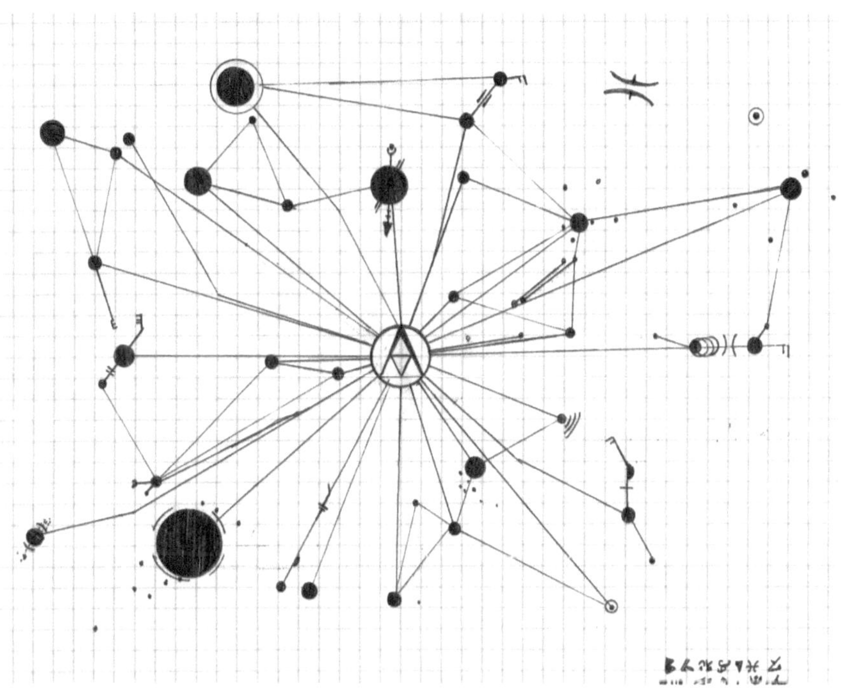

MASTER STAR CHART WITH CENTRAL PORTAL

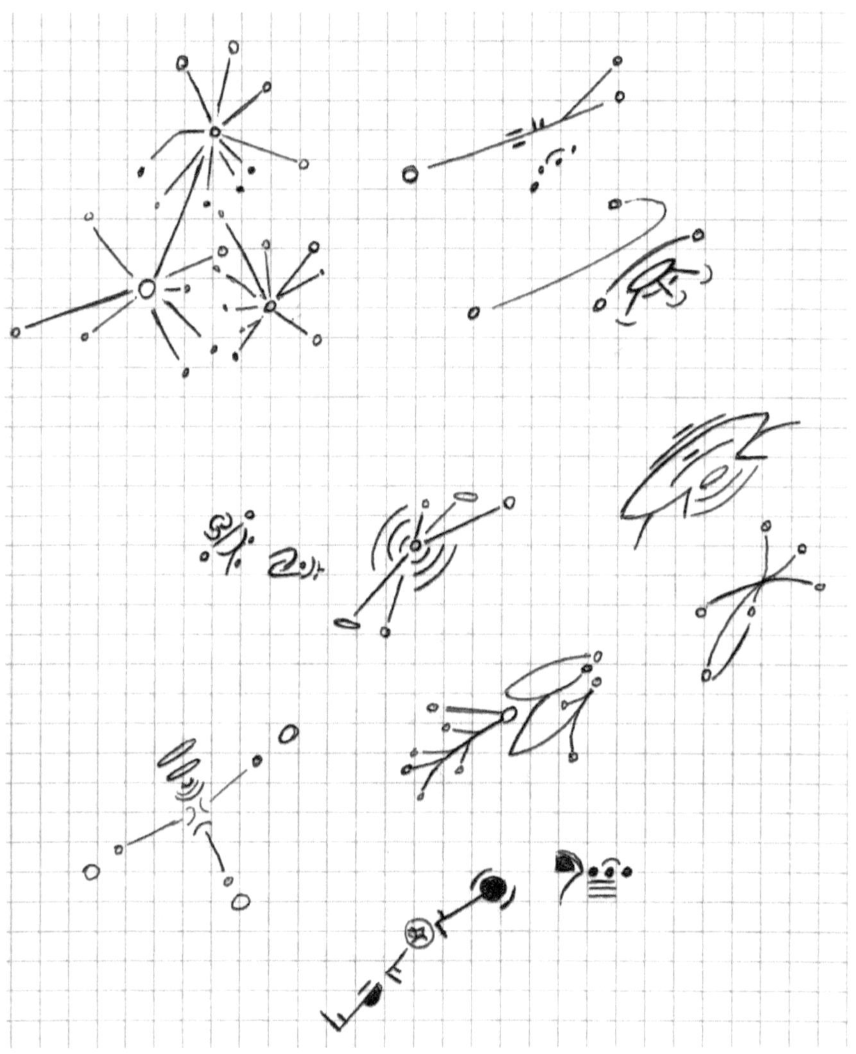

RANDOM STAR CHARTS

DETAIL OF PORTAL ACTIVITY ON A LANDSCAPE

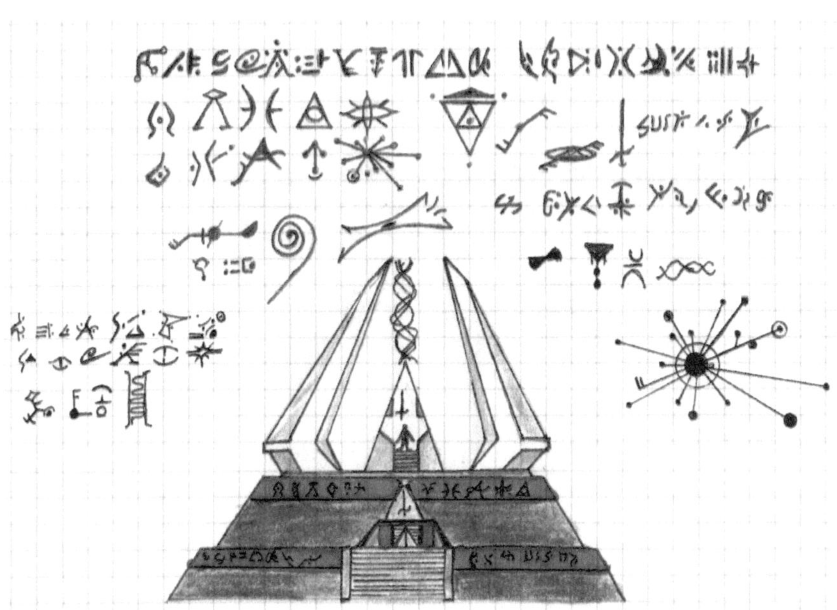

PORTAL WITH CRYSTAL INSTALLED ON A ZIGGURAT

18

SOFT TRIBUNAL

*My father considered a walk among the mountains as
the equivalent of church going. —Aldous Huxley*

Sunlight from the dawn leaked through the blinds into the apartment. As expected, Trevor was the first to get up and leave for work. He left a note written on a paper plate for Louis, letting him and the others know he had enjoyed their company. He especially wished Tara well.

After nourishment, if a donut can be considered nourishment, Mary Ellen went to Trevor's room for a brief meditation. She sat silently, with her eyes closed. Her concentration and her breathing masked the sounds both outside and in the room on the other side of the closed door. She focused thought where it manifested into her own spirit. There was something to do before departing. She saw Katrina's spirit still linked with the body. She proceeded to read Katrina's chakras. Starting at the base, she recognized all except the red root chakra and the yellow solar plexus chakra to be radiant. She read Katrina's life force and will; they were weak. All others, including the third eye, were vivid. This explained how Katrina could be unconscious, yet still able to communicate with Mary Ellen and Robert.

Upon making the connection, Mary Ellen projected healing energy to the weak chakras. First, she focused on the root chakra and concentrated on red in life: strawberries, roses, fields of poppy, and ruby gems. She projected a red flame at Katrina's tailbone and envisioned the fire expanding down to her legs and feet. She applied a similar technique to the solar plexus. Focusing her thought there, she envisioned amber, followed by a field of dandelions, then yellow tulips, and finally bushels of bright lemons. She imagined the yellow orb, just above the navel, brightened. Her technique was working. She sensed Katrina coming back to normal. She *saw* her stir.

* * *

Katrina opened her eyes mid-morning. Her right arm was numb from being pinned under her in the prone position for two days. It was sore from clutching the wood-framed circuit that had saved her life. The board left an imprint on her left arm, and it ached. Her head ached more, just like the other times she'd had this kind of NDE. Katrina slowly moved to a sitting position, feeling her body coming back to life. Slowly, she stood up, leaving the circuit, her electronic security blanket, on the floor. She made her way to the kitchen and noticed her cell phone on the counter. There was a list of pleas in the form of messages from Robert, all ending with the words, *I love you and miss you*. She looked at the date on the phone and realized she had been unconscious for almost two full days.

She sent a message to Robert in response to his latest message, *I'm here. I'm fine. My head hurts.*

Robert's phone chimed with a message. He assumed it was either the car rental place or his friend at the *Post*. When he picked up his phone, his lips quivered to slowly form a gentle smile as his eyes welled with joy in anticipation of his reunion with Katrina. He replied immediately, *Leaving for New Mexico in about an hour!* and uncharacteristically added a heart emoticon. Katrina replied with a smile and kissing emoticon. She finished by texting, *I'll call you later, when my head feels better.*

As Robert put the phone down, Trevor's door opened, and out walked Mary Ellen, appearing exhausted. Robert looked at her and told her that Katrina sent him a text message. Mary Ellen smiled and nodded.

Robert received another text message. The car rental place had sent a van, scheduled to be at the courtyard's gate in ten minutes. Robert relayed the news to everyone. The group took one more look around the apartment then left.

It would take Robert and Deborah about fourteen hours to get to Dulce. There, they would head off in opposite directions. The five travelers bid each other one more goodbye.

"Good job, Robert. We got it done, and your leadership got us all back safely," said Mary Ellen, praising him.

"That's right. Your planning and guidance made it work," added Louis.

"I suppose I should thank you for helping out in rescuing me. If it wasn't for you, I'd probably still be there living a secret hell," said Tara.

"Robert, Mary Ellen, that was *your* operation. I must admit that I thought we wouldn't succeed. I was wrong," said Louis. "And you, Mary Ellen. You *are* special. And thanks for what you did for Katrina. That is a debt I could never repay." Robert went to her and gave her a hug. Then he shook Louis's hand. Mary Ellen and Deborah fought back tears.

Looking at Mary Ellen, Deborah said, "I have your number now. I am going to give you a call after I get back home."

"OK," replied Mary Ellen, wiping tears from her cheek.

"Deborah, you were great," added Louis. "It was beautiful to watch you meet your son. Take care. I'll let you know what happens at Mount Shasta when I get back to Chicago."

Louis, Mary Ellen, and Tara watched and waved as Robert and Deborah headed for home. They waited until the car was out of sight before loading into their rental. It would take them about eight hours to get to their destination.

* * *

The entrance to Interstate 5 was close by, and in minutes they were on the highway that would take them the length of California. Tara, in the back seat, enjoyed her temporary freedom. Louis, not familiar with this part of California, was quiet, taking in the views from behind the wheel. Mary Ellen also enjoyed the beautiful scenery.

Louis enjoyed the drive and suggested they continue all the way to Weed, where they would stay the night.

"We should get there by seven tonight."

Mary Ellen used her phone to check on hotels. Noticing there were only a couple, she called one to reserve two rooms. They approached Sacramento around 4:00 in the afternoon. It was Friday, and traffic on the interstate was dense from travelers going away for the weekend. The stop-and-go was more stop than go, and it was going to delay their arrival at Weed. Louis asked Mary Ellen to check for sporting goods stores in Weed where they could get gear to explore the mountain. She noticed that the closest town with those kinds of shops was Mount Shasta City.

Early in the evening, they approached Chico to the east. They gazed out at the landscape, looking at what was left from a destructive and deadly fire. As far as they could see, the western sun shone on hills charred black. Wildlife, plant life, and color had all been erased in a matter of minutes. It would take years to grow back. Until then, people would be constantly reminded of the horrific event by the voids in the growth and absence of the colors of life.

Coming out of Redding, they saw the landscape turn greener with more pines and firs. The hairs on Louis's arms stood up when he saw the sign indicating the Shasta Lake National Recreation Area.

"We are getting close, and we still have some daylight," he said happily.

Past Shasta Lake, the interstate began to meander until it approached O'Brien. After crossing the bridge, the road to Weed began its steady incline. It would continue an uphill/downhill cycle for most of the drive to Lakehead. The route that made a winding path through the valley offered a glimpse of Mount Shasta's location as they approached the bend leading into Dunsmuir. The mountain was masked by a blanket of white clouds. After Dunsmuir they experienced a steeper rate of incline, reaching 3,000 feet and approaching another wide bend where it directed them northwest to Weed. It was almost 7:00 at twilight, with only thirty minutes more of daylight. Going around the bend, the mountain stood behind high hills and tall trees to the right and north-northeast. They would have to wait until the next day to see it clearly. Mount Shasta City was just five miles past the bend. They stopped and bought a jacket for Tara, flashlights, rope, gloves, and hard hats. Louis and Mary Ellen didn't need any additional clothing.

They left the store and remained in Mount Shasta City for a relaxing dinner and more conversation.

"What is special about Mount Shasta?" asked Tara.

The server arrived just in time to hear the question and interjected, "Oh it's gorgeous! I love to see it in the morning when the sun rises and evening when it sets! Some people say it's magical!" The young female server beamed. "Can I get you something to drink?"

"See? There *is* something magical about Mount Shasta," Mary Ellen said.

"Tara, the mountain is a place of mystery," said Louis. "According to legend, in 1904, J. C. Brown discovered a cave while prospecting for the Lord Cowdray Mining Company of England. According to his testimony, the cave sloped for miles into the mountain. He said that he found gold, shields, and mummies that were ten feet tall. In recent years, there have been a constant series of UFO sightings around the mountain."

Mary Ellen added, "The Wintu, Achumawi, and Shasta tribes revere the mountain for its supernatural powers. Although I have not seen any proof, there have been stories about a race of tall people with Caucasian features that live there. They are considered Lemurians, believed to be descendants of beings who came from the Alpha Centuri system."

The server arrived with their drinks. Again, she had overheard the conversation.

"Oh, you heard about the Lemurians too? There's a video on the internet, a story about one of those people actually showing up in a restaurant in Weed!" She laughed. "Can you believe people would fall for that?"

The three diners smiled. The server took their orders and left. "So, that's why we are going there tomorrow? What are you expecting to find?" asked Tara.

"Personally, I've done a lot of research on it. I'd like to see it myself. It would lend credibility to my work," replied Louis.

"I am going because Louis wants to go. But I believe we *need* to go, all of us, including you, Tara."

"What do you think I'll get out of it?" Tara asked.

"I can't tell you. It's up to you. You have free will, but in order to benefit from the universe's energies, you need to release and surrender to the Source.

"The Source?"

"The energy behind all that exists."

"You mean God? I'm agnostic. I do believe there must be a higher power. I just don't think anyone has the facts straight. I try to be good to others. That's all I can do, right?"

"We'll see. I'm glad that you are here and that you decided to join us. I think you will find this fulfilling," said Mary Ellen.

The server arrived with the orders. After setting the plates down, she asked, "Do you guys believe in UFOs? I swear I saw orange disks around the mountain one night with some friends. They moved fast. They weren't planes, and they were too low to be stars or planets."

"I think what you describe is from high technology, so, yes, I believe in the phenomenon," Louis said.

Mary Ellen and Tara nodded as they each took bites. People at a table nearby overheard the conversation and glared at the out-of-towners as if they were from another solar system. The server went to care for her other tables. Aware of the attention they had garnered from other diners, the travelers resisted having any more conversation about paranormal activity at Mount Shasta. After finishing their dinner, the server came to take plates away and asked if they were going to the mountain. The server handed Louis the bill and wished the three good luck, adding that they would love the beauty.

Once back on the highway, they encountered construction, reducing lanes from three to one in their direction. In the darkness, they would not be able to see Black Butte rising to 6,000 feet. Darkness obscures it at this time. Approaching Weed, they found the hotel just off the interstate at the edge of town. They arrived at a little after 9:00, took their bags out and checked in.

Louis meditated before bed and naturally fell asleep in the process. Mary Ellen also meditated. Her roommate, Tara, watched her for a while then lay down to sleep.

Mary Ellen went through the breathing discipline, then calmed herself and her mind to let the visions appear. This was how she received her download. She saw the image of Mount Shasta sitting on its earthly throne, placed perfectly for such a beautiful creation. It was framed by high cumulous clouds and surrounded by the upright soldiers of firs and pines. Her eye position began to rise, and soon she was floating and getting closer to the mountain. She passed over the woods and streams, climbing higher. Motion stopped, and her sight was fixed on a dry creek that appeared to originate at an opening in the rock. She focused on the opening on the north face, noting the detail, as she faced south. The image began to fade, became distant, then was blurred.

She opened her eyes soon afterward. Tara was still awake, staring at the ceiling. "I know where we need to go tomorrow," Mary Ellen said.

"You saw something while you were meditating?"

"Yes. Would you like me to guide you in a meditation? If you do it right, fifteen minutes can feel like an hour nap. Meditation is . . . a respite, an oasis from the madness of the blade of intolerance that has ripped the rich tapestry of diversity and culture in our land. It is a place where we can take a deep breath before going back and diving into the troubled waters."

Tara tilted her head a bit at the description. "Sounds like I could benefit from that."

Mary Ellen taught Tara the breathing technique, then helped her to quiet her mind. Once Tara was quiet, Mary Ellen guided her through a peaceful, relaxing meditation. As she had intended, it only lasted about fifteen minutes. Tara shared what she felt and what she had seen. She was pleased. Afterward, they both easily settled in to sleep.

In the other room, Louis prepared his pack and set out his gear for the visit to the mountain. It was late in Chicago, so he decided to wait to text his kids in the morning.

As Louis, Mary Ellen, and Tara were settling into their rooms, Robert and Deborah had just crossed the Arizona-New Mexico state line. They stopped at a hotel in Gallup, New Mexico, only three hours from Dulce.

* * *

Louis and Mary Ellen were both awake to see the early morning display from the sunrise. They stepped out in the crisp autumn air on the raised walkway outside their rooms and witnessed the mystical appearance of a lenticular cloud formation over the dome. The clouds formed slight curves in a concentric pattern, spaced evenly in three distinct bands, beginning with a small cloud closest to the mountain and progressing in size. The top cloud stretched over the entire dome. It could have been interpreted as proof the mountain itself was vibrating. The orange glow from the morning sun made the clouds appear molten hot. Both Louis and Mary Ellen used their phones to take pictures. Louis sent a picture to his children with the simple text message, *Wish you were here.*

* * *

Robert and Deborah had also gotten an early start. At just past 9:00 Mountain Time, they arrived at Mary Ellen's trailer, where Deborah had left her SUV. Robert helped her load the trunk, complementing her on her professionalism at Groom Lake. Deborah praised him for his leadership throughout the operation, knowing he had PTSD. They wished each other well. Both were eager to get back to their loved ones. It would take Deborah about sixteen hours more to reach home. Robert was only about two and one-half hours from Taos and Katrina. Both sent text messages to their partners before resuming their trips. Deborah would stop in Kansas for the evening. Robert would be home in time for lunch.

* * *

"Where do you think we should go specifically?" asked Louis as he gazed to the distance.

"There. That's where we need to go. It's about 6,200 feet elevation. We would start here." Mary Ellen pointed to the base of the creek. "It is about 4,300 feet there, making it a three-mile hike to where I saw the hole in the rock."

"A rise of about two thousand feet with a horizontal distance of about fifteen thousand-six-hundred feet." Louis used the calculator. "That's a little under thirteen percent slope, which is doable. Let me look at something here." Louis searched the net. "The Shubashiri Trail at Mount Fuji is about a twenty-six percent incline, and people there just use walking sticks on their ascent. We should be able to do OK."

Louis remained outside to watch the gradual changes in color and shapes over the mountain, while Mary Ellen went in to wake Tara.

The three explorers left the hotel and went to get a quick breakfast, then Mary Ellen guided them to their destination. From the motel they headed northeast on US 97/US 99 Volcanic Legacy Scenic Byway for ten miles, then turned south to Bolam Road, an old unimproved logging road, where they reached 4,000 feet. They drove about three and one-half miles south, reaching the end of the road at elevation 5,500 feet. This allowed them to get much closer to the hole in the rock than anticipated, cutting their hiking distance to a little over one and one-half miles. Tara's arm was still nestled in the sling, exempting her from having to carry anything. Louis carried their bags.

They hiked southwest toward Whitney Creek. Although the day was heating up, the air was still cool at the middle elevation, making the hike tolerable. After walking a third of a mile, they found a place at the west edge of Whitney Gorge where they could reach the dry bed safely, following it to where Mary Ellen had seen the cave. As they started their hike, their path led them through a winding, rocky, dry creek bed, where the sides grew steeper and the walls higher. Had there been a flash flood, they would have been in peril. All three hikers were acutely aware of their surroundings and walked cautiously. As they got closer to their destination, they had to navigate through an open meadow encroached by a thick growth of firs. They found a long, shallow-sloped side of a ravine that led them down to the dry bed. The creek bed meandered as it inclined. With the incline, the gorge got deeper. Soon the sloped brush walls were over two hundred feet high.

As they went around another bend, the brush gave way to barren rock walls, over three hundred feet higher than the bed. Approaching the last of many bends, the left side of the gorge became decidedly shallow with a steep bluff jutting out above it. Coming out of the bend, they gazed upon the cave Mary Ellen had seen in her vision. It was a huge entrance, well over one hundred feet high and eighty feet wide. In the wet months it would be hidden by a waterfall. Mary Ellen smiled as her eye followed the familiar outline.

* * *

A thousand miles southeast, Robert approached Camino del Medio with a smile. The air felt fresh on his face as he exited the car. It was past noon, and the clear view of the snowy mountains made him pause and reflect momentarily on its beauty. Turning to walk toward the front porch, he paused again as the door opened. Standing in the doorway was who he had really come to see, Katrina. She stood barefoot, in jeans, fresh from tending her chickens. She wore a smile that fit only her. It was electric, gleaming, just like Katrina. Robert quickened his pace, getting a running start, stepping on the first tread, and leaping over the second tread to land on the porch, then opening his arms so his girl could jump into them from the doorway. There was so much to talk about, but it was difficult to say a word with their lips pressed against each other. Being home had never felt better. He kissed her, more deeply. They broke to hug and hold close.

"You are amazing," Robert said in the soft voice only Katrina knows. "When I didn't get a response from you after Dulce, I knew you were in trouble, but I also understood you are special. And when Mary Ellen and I felt your energy, I knew you would make it ... again."

"I envisioned you and the team coming out at Edwards. I think it gave reason for me to continue to live through it."

They separated to look at each other.

"Sometimes I swear I could see lightning in your eyes."

"It complements your thunder."

They fell into another deep kiss to seal another shared adventure.

* * *

As the three hikers moved closer for a better view, Mary Ellen sensed a presence and stopped walking. She looked all around but saw nothing out of the ordinary.

"We're not alone here. I sense another energy near us, above us."

Just then a large glowing orange disc materialized above the trees, directly over the cave entrance. The craft, measuring approximately thirty feet in diameter, remained in place, motionless. Before they could react, each person's vision became blurred. They began to lose the feeling of the earth under their feet, dematerializing without substance, their bodies losing their mass. The scene around them faded away from sight.

In moments, their surroundings began to emerge from the nothingness, but they were not in the gorge anymore. The sunlight was gone; they had been transported to a darker, confined space. The 3-D world reemerged as they recognized the texture and harshness of stone enclosing them. Their eyes adjusted. There was a thin uniform outline of light in one of the walls.

"Is everyone alright?" asked Louis, as an excuse to test his voice.

"I'm OK," replied Mary Ellen calmly. She turned her head toward Tara, who had not responded.

Louis stepped toward the continuous gap of light and placed his fingers in it. "I think this is a door. We are inside some sort of vestibule."

Examining the wall, he was caught off guard by the door's sudden lateral movement. It slid without a sound. Not at all what one would expect of an object so massive and heavy.

Brightness flooded into the closet-sized chamber, revealing a larger vestibule that appeared to be illuminated from the outside. Multifaceted crystalline walls filtered the light into an uneven kaleidoscope. The explorers marveled at a visual medley played out by the introduction of sunlight into the translucent stone. They gasped at the sparkling effect.

"Are we supposed to go in there?" asked Louis

"I think so," Mary Ellen said, caution in her voice. Tara remained silent.

Louis stepped through the threshold and was bathed in the light. The variations from the refractions made a harlequin type pattern on his face and clothing. Seeing that Louis was unharmed, Mary Ellen followed suit, closely followed by Tara, who almost clipped Mary Ellen's heel. Behind them, the stone door slowly slid shut, sealing them in. They remained in the middle of the room and the brightness intensified, changing colors, alternating between violets and purples. After a few cycles, the trio began to feel a soothing, almost numbing effect from the light work. Conversation between them grew light and cordial. The purples and violets gradually faded to the colorless light when they first entered.

Moments later, the far wall moved out, sliding back to allow space on both sides for someone to walk through.

From the right, a tall, fair-skinned humanoid walked in and stood in front of the pushed-out segment of the wall. He was clothed in a floor-length white garment with oversized long sleeves; his shoulder-length wavy blond hair matched his striking, deep-blue eyes. He carried no weapons or armor. The being's familiar appearance, combined with the spiritual cleansing in the crystal chamber, quelled any anxieties.

The three stood still, silent, as if awaiting instructions. The humanoid motioned for the three to follow him out of the chamber.

On the other side of the doorway was a short corridor with a shaft above, open to the sky, to let natural light inside the mountain. The walls and floor in the corridor were made of roughly hewn stone. It was cool and damp, and the air felt fresh. The floor sloped down toward the walls, where a shallow trough existed to carry moisture away from the space. The blond man, still silent, led them to a pair of gleaming metallic doors. To the right side of the doors, a waist-high stone plate jutted out. The man stood in front of it and placed his hand flat against the plate. It glowed blue and activated the unlatching of the metal doors.

The blond man and three abductees stepped back as the high, wide doors slowly swung open in unison. He motioned to them, once again, to enter into another large, brightly lit room. It was stimulating and heavenly. Louis marveled at the space's design, like an empty courtroom but not like anything he'd ever seen. Far from it. He found no visible flaws and no joint work. Louis realize they now stood inside a gigantic geode, the ceiling and walls bejeweled with crystals. The space was illuminated with soothing diffused light flowing through the entire ceiling. There were no benches, only a half-height curved stone wall. The high ceiling allowed for a balcony at the opposite end of the entrance facing into the room, about twenty feet away. The balcony was shallow, the full width of the room, a wall behind it with an opening at each end. Mary Ellen stood in the middle. Louis was to her right. Tara was standing on Mary Ellen's left. No one said a word.

A being, similar to their usher, appeared from one of the openings and stood at the center of the balcony. He was older, with white hair and a neatly trimmed white beard. He donned a violet robe and wore a rose quartz crystal necklace.

The elder raised his right hand, palm open. Mary Ellen, Louis, and Tara all heard a voice in their heads; the elder's lips did not move:

Welcome, aspect of Mariel of the Seraphim. Welcome, Louis, whose spirit is the Counselor and Informer to the humans. Welcome, Tara, daughter of Lyra, who has suffered greatly.

The three subjects remained silent and attentive as they processed the message.

I am Lemurian. My people are descendants of the survivors of the place the humans call Atlantis. We are descendants of humanoids that originated in what your astronomers have named the Sirius B system. The Dogon tribe in the continent of Africa celebrate our descendants to this day.

With her right hand resting clenched on the top of the wall in front of her, Tara released it and slid it to touch Mary Ellen's. Looking down, Mary Ellen opened her hand to hold Tara's.

You are all here now because you are fulfilling your destiny. Much planning and preparation has gone into this meeting. You are all humans, but your spirits make you who you truly are. You are here because your spirit made a commitment to assist humanity toward evolution so it may one day join the universal community in peace and harmony.

The voice continued. *Mariel, you have been our ward. We have watched over you and guided you in your development as a spiritually enlightened human. You have always been under our protection. You received our transmissions, and you have used them and followed them with grace and honor. Your assignment was to seek the one assigned as Counselor and Informer, and bring him here safely. Well done, Mariel.*

Louis turned to Mary Ellen, duly impressed with her honorable role. She bowed her head with respect and humility.

Louis, you are having thoughts that Mariel has deceived you. Remove them from your mind. Mariel's spirit guided her, but she was not permitted the knowledge about this meeting.

Mary Ellen raised her head and looked back at Louis. He gave her a nod of consolation, that he was past such thoughts, and looked back at the elder. The voice resumed to reveal more.

Louis Silvani: researcher, lecturer. Your true role as conferred upon you is Counselor and Informer to the Earth humans. This meeting is to give you information so you may carry out your duties as committed by your spirit and, recently, yourself. You must find a way to assist the humans in their evolution.

Louis balked at responding at first. He formulated what he would say. "I ... I understand my spirit was given this assignment." The room, the position of the elder, their positions—it all felt like some sort of trial. "But I do not understand what I am to do to carry it out. I receive pieces of messages about my progress, that I'm doing what needs to be done, but I do not understand the objective and how to get there."

There was a long pause after Louis's response. It made him uneasy with every silent moment. Finally, to everyone's relief, the elder spoke again.

It will come to you. Just as Mariel was directed here, you will realize what to do. Your lectures and short writings that tell people about beings like us on Earth place us in danger. The Earth humans must not know our presence."

Suddenly, images appeared on the wall below the balcony, accompanied by messages that Louis, Mary Ellen, and Tara could easily read:

Many species have been here longer than Earth humans. This planet is important to the universes, not just to the ones that live here. It is a school for the spirits in the universes. Every spirit must experience life on Earth before ascension to a higher plane of existence. It is here where the lessons of love, pain, suffering, creativity, and beauty are first learned. You see, the planet Earth is very important to all of us. Earth humans can be replaced and regrown, but the planet is unique and specially designed. When we and other races that inhabit Earth sense that the human activity is destructive to the planet, we respond. After two large cities were incinerated using the power of the atom, that immense release of immeasurable energies in such a violent, barbaric way caused advanced races throughout existence to sound an alarm, because Earth humans are not yet spiritually evolved enough to be able to manage such a powerful force in the universe.

After reminding them of the horrors of Hiroshima and Nagasaki, the images and messages continued:

Allowing Earth humans to possess and use devices powered by the atom is like giving an Earth-child fire-starting tools to play with, without the guidance of an elder. Universally, Earth humans are considered a most dangerous species that must be watched and controlled.

The elder paused to allow the message to sink in. Mary Ellen recognized the goodness in the being who was given them the spiritual lesson. She read his aura—it was radiant and powerful. This elder was passing on ancient wisdom that somehow was lost to humans. It is evident that he and his people wish humanity good will.

The creators rushed the Earth humans' conception. Your race has many flaws; some are from your own poisoning of the planet. Most critical is Earth human DNA. The writings that make up the book you call the Bible mention that humans are born with Original Sin. The Christian religion has grossly misinterpreted that. The Earth human DNA is your original sin. It is the DNA that makes the Earth humans barbaric, violent, having irrational obsessions for possessions, and being tribal where behavior often ends in the elimination of culture and people.

Again, powerful images of one race's domination over another, supporting the Lemurian's message, were displayed on the wall. Louis cringed from the graphic nature of motion pictures before him. Tara was moved to tears, gripping Mary Ellen's hand tighter.

You and the rest of the Earth humans must understand that it is for this very reason that the rest of the benevolent cosmos choose not to interact in an official capacity with Earth humans. The Earth humans have been placed under a cultural and exploratory quarantine until your species understands its place in the cosmos, accepts its flaws, and, most importantly, chooses to improve spiritually, releasing itself of the shackles of the mind-controlling religions. There is universal truth, and then there are your religions.

Louis and Mary Ellen nodded in agreement, then bowed down as if in shame while Tara remained quiet and attentive.

Earth human history is diseased with acts of genocide mostly upon less technologically advanced cultures. Long ago, the Pleiadians, one of the Council of Twelve, were assigned to be part of a test to see if there were signs of true spirituality and compassion in the Earth humans. A probe was sent to artificially inseminate a young woman in order to produce a hybrid. The hybrid was born in what you now call Israel. He was sent to the place called India, to learn the ways of the one they called Buddha, who was inspired by the Arcturians. When it was time to return to Israel, he gained followers, and word had spread about a wondrous man who treated the ill, demonstrated super-human abilities, and attracted people, spreading goodwill. The ones that ruled over the land recognized him only as a threat to their hold on power and were concerned about his being a revolutionary. He was the one they called Jesus. He was different in many ways, and he taught the people how to be spiritual. He was peaceful and easy to find from the numbers of people he would attract. He was not an average human! For these reasons they put him to death.

His violent and painful death at the hands of the Earth humans clearly demonstrated that the Earth humans were not ready to accept others in the rest of the universe. They failed the test. It is frightening and astonishing to witness now many Earth humans think and pray for another Jesus. The Council of Twelve will never make the mistake of sending another like Jesus until there is real change in the way the Earth humans behave. Looking at your people now, they are very far from having such a visitor again. Earth humans believe that tolerance of others will be enough to be right and proper. Tolerance is not enough. Coexistence is not enough. The Earth humans must embrace and celebrate your diversity, and learn to share in the single power that guides and determines your fate. The fables and stories that people strongly believe about the transition to the next life are confounding to myself and the Council of Twelve.

When the spirit passes, all existence on Earth is irrelevant. The spirit world has its own laws of existence. There is no need for gates to enter the spiritual realm. There is no need for virgins; the spirit is not a body. As you now realize, it is energy. We recognize that you, Mary Ellen, and you, Louis, understand the Source and its immense energy that is made up of all undedicated spirits in the universes. We feel we do not need to explain the role of the spirits further.

Mary Ellen and Louis turned to each other, smiled, and nodded. The Lemurian gave them a moment, though he was not yet done with his explanations.

The Source does not and has not communicated to humans like people in religions have been led to believe. Ancient humans that led primitive lives recognized entities that made use of high technologies as gods. There were no other explanations. The Source is actually the amalgamation of all spiritual energies in the cosmos. That energy has immense power. Each energy has a measure of power, but when you combine all the energies together to act as one, the power is multiplied. We recognize that you understand that science of the power of the mind.

You already know much about the cosmos and your existence. You know why you are here do you not?

Louis turned his head to look at Mary Ellen, then he turned to face the Lemurian, looked up, shook his head.

"I'm sorry. I don't understand what I am to do with this information. Do you wish for me to return to the outside and tell people about this?" he asked.

On the contrary. Our existence must be kept confidential. Others have made similar agreements with your governments. It is to protect both the humans and the other civilizations. We are wary of Earth humans having a propensity to be tribal ... and genocidal. Your people must continue to be under the quarantine until the Earth humans demonstrate they have matured spiritually. It is woefully evident by the way Earth humans treat one another that your people are far from making progress toward true spirituality. If the community of the cosmos were to allow Earth's human people to join, there would eventually be a transfer of technology — technology likely to be applied mostly to better your already powerful war community.

Eventually, your people would find a way to hate the races from other planets. They would use that newly acquired technology to make weapons and use them on us, just as the Earth humans have done with the natives of the Americas or the natives of Oceania. The inbred hatred and fear of different species would cause your people to eventually eradicate any of the species that were not like Earth humans.

This is why our existence must be kept secret. If we are exposed for any reason, we will have no choice but to strike preemptively and damage your civilizations to the point of eliminating your governments and war communities. Many humans would surely die, and no one would come to assist them. Your governments are keeping our existence a secret as a matter of self-preservation, not for wealth or control of energy sources. None of the species living on this planet with you are as warlike as the Earth humans. Do you understand?

"I feel I need to speak in defense of the Earth humans!"

The Lemurian scowled at Louis. Mary Ellen and Tara looked to him, wishing Louis would apologize. They were in no position for him to offend the elder.

They have no defense! replied the Lemurian elder. *You question our wisdom of the ages?*

"Allow me to finish, sir. If I am to succeed in my assignment as a Counselor-Informer, I need to have all the information to do it with confidence."

Very well, Louis. Proceed.

"Thank you." This time, Louis collected his thoughts before continuing. "You say that Earth humans are to remain under the universal quarantine until they mature spiritually. There are many, many good people on this planet that lead their lives in the sincere belief that they are spiritual and doing right by their God. If they are not allowed to know about the existence of other races on Earth or in the universes, how would they know that they need to mature spiritually? How can they fix themselves if they do not know they are broken?"

The elder nodded with an expression of earnestness. He placed both hands on the balcony's rail. Louis noticed the elder gripping the stone rail tightly.

You have just described the puzzle the Council of Twelve has determined as the Disclosure Paradox. It is up to you, Louis, to solve it. You have been assigned to help the Earth humans evolve. You WILL solve the paradox.

The chamber remained silent. The elder was done conversing. A blue humanoid stepped out from one of the openings and stood next to the Lemurian elder. It was an Arcturian, stepping out to deliver a telepathic message to Mary Ellen.

Mary Ellen, aspect of Mariel, you have done well in bringing Louis, the Counselor and Informer, and Tara, the Lyran, here. Look at the wall below.

Mary Ellen was given a view into a health care ward with many rescued humanoids in various forms of recovery. A caregiver directed the surveillance device to a specimen from Dulce that was not quite human, appearing to be still, in a large vat filled with a bluish gel, various wires and hoses connected to him. Mary Ellen could see the team of healers handling the being carefully with a gentle touch. She recognized the humanoid as hers. After a few minutes, the image faded out.

Your child is being cared for by our healers. He will be with us for more time. The removal of what the Draco have done is a challenging and arduous task. We will let you communicate to him when he is ready.

The expulsion of the Dracos was no small feat. They used that facility with the assistance of the war community to take innocent offspring. Among other research, they worked to find out how to formulate the part of humans that makes you feel love. The power of love is special and it is strong. We can use it as a weapon against the evil ones. They do not know love. They can't even deceive us by faking the feeling of love. It is how we are able to identify them. When you feel love or goodness if you encounter a being or craft you do not recognize as human, if the object or entity returns the same feeling, you will know they are benevolent. If there is no response, they are suspect and should be approached with caution. The Dracos were never able to use that. Their research efforts have failed. Congratulations, Mariel, for keeping the universe safe, for now.

A different kind of humanoid appeared out of the opposite opening and stood on the other side of the elder. Its skin tone was olive, its large dark almond eyes showing no sign of pupils, its hair jet-black and straight.

This entity is a visitor from Lyra. He will now communicate to you, informed the elder.

Good fortune and peace to you, Earth humans. I am here to offer asylum to our daughter, Tara.

Tara looked at Mary Ellen, who offered a gentle smile, and at Louis with astonishment, then turned to face the Lyran again.

Tara, I am here to tell you of your existence. You have Lyran DNA. We monitored your growth and development from the time you were a young child. You do not remember us because you were not allowed to have memory in order to protect you. When you were older, we harvested from you to help our mission. We meant no harm. One of our caregivers fell in love with you. It was his carelessness that led to your suffering. The Dracos, our natural enemy, discovered you, and they made certain you would suffer. When we learned about the rescue planned with the Arcturians, one of our allies, we worked to get you rescued, too. We had the Arcturians manipulate the portal device that caused the rescue.

We are delighted that you are now safe, child. No harm will come to you. Come back with us and learn about your people, your planet, and reunite with the one that loves you. Your knowledge of the Earth humans will be helpful for us.

Tara looked at Mary Ellen and Louis, then addressed the elder.

"I have no one here. My parents are divorced and have not talked to me since I enlisted. I have no close friends or lovers either. I will miss my sister. If I stay, I fear that things will get worse."

She paused. "I don't think I ever thanked anyone of you for the rescue. Thank you, Louis. Thank you, Mary Ellen, for everything you did for me. Thank you both for bringing me here too. I will never forget what you did for me."

She hugged them, then she turned to the Lyran at the balcony. "I will go with you," she said solemnly.

You have made the right decision. You shall remain Tara. The Lyrans also are grateful to the Earth humans. You have done very well. You should be proud of your accomplishments. Many lives have been saved, including that of a fellow Lyran.

The Lyran raised his right arm as a salute. Two bright columns of blue light enveloped Tara and the Lyran. The columns increased in brightness, and in a blinding flash, Tara and the Lyran were gone, on a craft heading for the home planet.

The Lemurian elder communicated again.

The planet is changing more rapidly than Earth humans can react. Part of this is the natural cycle, but most is a result of the abuse and greed of your kind. There is little time left to adjust human behavior and avoid what will come if the humans do not react quickly and wisely.

The wall below showed scenes of coastal areas under water, extended droughts, and famine. Those scenes were then followed by images of a near future where motorized vehicles were replaced by animals with carts and wagons, reminiscent of the pre-Industrial Age past. A future that resulted in the collapse of nations and the reemergence of fiefdoms.

Remember, there is still time for the humans to save themselves from their own ignorance and greed. You must find a way to counsel and in-form them. Every day that passes brings the pending disasters closer, more quickly.

If the humans want to be like us, they must dispense with the hunger for power. Our race did away with power long ago. We do not have power to feed our ego, we have knowledge and wisdom. Power is not bad, but in the wrong hands it becomes overwhelming, and whoever has it becomes greedy and uses it wrongfully. We chose not to use power. We do not have currency, either. Like power, it becomes unruly.

We trust both of you and release you to carry out your work as you have agreed. When we return you to your world, you will remember everything except how you were taken and being in this mountain. You will gradually recall all we have imparted to you. There will be no need to return. We wish you well. As sign of acceptance, the Council of Twelve mark you as our agents of goodwill, always under our protection. The mark will appear on your arm. It will be visible on your arm in a position facing and in line with your heart when you are seated to meditate, your hands together in prayer. Go in peace and love."

Louis and Mary Ellen's vision began to blur again. They felt as if their bodies would float away. They lost the feel of the stone wall and floor under their feet. The courtroom disappeared. They sensed direct sunlight again. They heard the wind through the trees and the sounds of birds and felt a coolness on their faces.

Slowly, their focus returned. Upon regaining their senses, they found themselves standing on the forest floor on a bed of pine needles and twigs behind their parked rental. They remained still, their composure and their thoughts returning, unable to discern between very fresh memory and imagination.

"Where are we?" Louis asked.

"How did we get here?" Mary Ellen followed.

Louis looked around, noticing Tara was gone, then something in his mind told him it was OK.

"Tara . . . ," he uttered.

"She is fine. Remember, she went back to her planet," Mary Ellen said, that one memory-image leaking through.

Louis understood, but it did not seem logical.

Mary Ellen grabbed his arm. "Don't fight it. Just trust me. She's OK."

Louis looked at his watch. "The last thing I remember is seeing, what? a bright orange disk, but where was that? Was it here? What time is it?" Over three hours had passed. Three hours? "It's almost four thirty!"

"Louis, we were abducted. Tara stayed with them. Your memory is dreamlike, but it is a memory," Mary Ellen said. "It's fresh . . . stay with it. Do you remember being in the crystal room with the three beings on the balcony?"

"Yes. It is coming back. I remember now. The Lemurian telling us about ourselves, the Earth humans. Yes, I have it now."

They looked at each other again, and a common thought crossed their mind. Together, at the same time, they checked the inside of their arms, above the wrists. There it was, a triangle, with a bisecting line and a circle at the base. The mark by the Council of Twelve.

They looked up again at each other, grinned, and nodded confidently.

"Is your mind clearer? Can you drive?" asked Mary Ellen.

"Yes. I'm good."

"Good. I'm hungry. Let's go to town and then go to Redding to get flights back to our homes."

* * *

After ten hours of driving, making good time, Deborah was approaching Manhattan, Kansas. In six hours, she would be home with Susan. She imagined her life getting back to normal ... then she thought about her son, Samuel, and realized that normal was a thing of the past.

* * *

Louis and Mary Ellen got in their rental. Louis started the engine and turned around to go back via the logging road, toward Weed.

"Well, Counselor-Informer, your job is just beginning. What are you going to do now?"

There was a pause. Then Louis revealed his intentions. "I need to keep writing in my blog—maybe a book about all this: a book to inform the public about the need to modify our behavior as members of the universal community."

"Sounds like you could be on the right track. What are you going to call this book?"

"I am going to name it based on the Pleiadean puzzle: The Disclosure Paradox."

They continued the descent on the old logging road to town, sitting in silence, allowing Louis's plan and title to sink in.

"How about some music?" asked Mary Ellen.

Louis turned on the radio but couldn't wrestle up a clear station. Mary Ellen took out her cell phone and plugged it into the USB car audio.

"Here's something for you, from me."

She started the player. Louis was immediately moved by the first notes. It brought a wide smile to his face as he indulged in the Staple Singers. He cranked up the volume, and they both started singing to "I'll take you there."

Indeed. Mary Ellen *did* take him where he needed to go.

Mary Ellen sat back and recalled the images of her child under the care of the Arcturians. The satisfaction of rescuing it will be eclipsed by the joy of his promised return.

ACKNOWLEDGMENTS

Thanks to Mrs. V, who was always there to confide in regarding my experiences and events that occurred prompting me to write the story.

Thanks to the unique people who allowed me to fictionalize them—you know who you are.

Special thanks to Jim Penniston for taking the time to proof and approve portions of "Facts and Deceptions" where The Rendlesham Forest Incident was used as a topic of presentation.

Many thanks to Richard Dipert, Fire Protection Engineer, and Syed Enayatulla, PE, for their knowledge and recommendations regarding building systems, to Dale Hartmann for his expertise in firearms, explosives, and bomb damage, and for David Colberg for his true-to-life stories about his experience as an Iraq War veteran.

And to those who shared in the concept of this book, but graduated to the next dimension before being able to read it:

Dr. A R Bordon
Debra Spencer
Robin Scott
Freddie O.Neal Jenkins
Holly Keith

This book would not be in your hands if the late Bob Yehling, author and editor, did not contact me about his group, Word Journeys. It was the start of a rewarding and productive relationship where he took this story and enriched it with his keen insight and sensitivity. I would have liked for Bob to witness the completion of our project. Bob assumed the role of senior editor, guiding me on the path toward publication, and introducing me and my stories to the excellent publishing team—Jennifer Geist of Pen & Publish, and Rob Weinberg of Write Away Books. I am grateful for everyone's contributions.

ABOUT THE AUTHOR

Paul G. Vecchiet is the author of *The Disclosure Paradox*, a science-fiction series that explores the ethical, psychological, and institutional consequences of anomalous human capability.

Drawing on a background in government service, management, and long-standing interest in suppressed science and human consciousness, Vecchiet's work examines how extraordinary phenomena are handled when they intersect with secrecy, power, and fear. His stories focus less on spectacle than on consequence—particularly the human cost of exploitation by institutions unequipped to confront what they do not fully understand.

Rather than offering conclusions, Vecchiet's novels present speculative frameworks that invite inquiry into the limits of science, the burden of knowledge, and the moral responsibility that accompanies discovery.

He lives in West Virginia and continues to write fiction that challenges certainty while remaining grounded in character, discipline, and restraint.

www.ingramcontent.com/pod-product-compliance
Lightning Source LLC
Chambersburg PA
CBHW020148310726
48970CB00006B/2055